Robert Henry Forster

History of Corbridge and its Antiquities

with a concise history of Dilston Hall - description of the various places of note and

interest in the neighbourhood

Robert Henry Forster

History of Corbridge and its Antiquities
with a concise history of Dilston Hall - description of the various places of note and interest in the neighbourhood

ISBN/EAN: 9783337369330

Printed in Europe, USA, Canada, Australia, Japan

Cover: Foto ©Andreas Hilbeck / pixelio.de

More available books at **www.hansebooks.com**

HISTORY OF CORBRIDGE

AND ITS ANTIQUITIES:

WITH A CONCISE HISTORY OF

DILSTON HALL

AND ITS ASSOCIATIONS,

CONTAINING SEVERAL ITEMS OF INFORMATION NEVER BEFORE
PUBLISHED.

ALSO A SHORT DESCRIPTION OF THE VARIOUS PLACES OF NOTE
AND INTEREST IN THE NEIGHBOURHOOD.

FOR THE INFORMATION OF VISITORS AND THE PUBLIC
GENERALLY.

By ROBERT FORSTER.

NEWCASTLE-ON-TYNE :
J. BEALL, PRINTER, 32, HIGH FRIAR STREET.

1881.

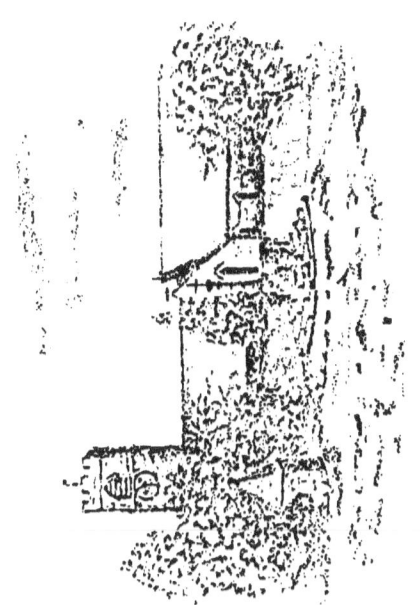

PREFACE.

CORBRIDGE being the centre of an historical and interesting neighbourhood, the writer has often been
requested to publish its history; not because he could do it
better than any other person, in fact, perhaps not so well as
some others, but simply because having lived long in the
village is thought generally to have studied its history, and to
be in possession of more information than most other persons,
he being, for many years, anxious to know as much as can be
known of the historical associations of this ancient town and
neighbourhood. The desire appears to be natural to most
people, to get acquainted with the records and incidents in
connection with their own locality, if there appears to have
been anything worth searching out; for old associations,
especially if linked to ancestorial history, have, to many
persons, a peculiar charm. Such a book as this has often
been asked for.

The History of Corbridge and neighbourhood to any considerable extent is certainly not generally known, being
scattered about in detached portions in various histories, not
easily accessible to the majority of readers. The writer
anticipates a variety of opinions as to the general nature of
the contents, but he sincerely assures his readers that his
main object (at the desire of many friends) has been, to
collect such information as could be obtained from every
available and reliable source, which might otherwise be lost,
and put the whole together into a kind of consecutive order,
commencing with the earliest period.

In presenting this work to the public, the writer makes no pretension whatever to literary attainments, being fully conscious of his defects. The reader will find much that is substantial written history (some portions not much known), a good deal derived from his own knowledge, observation, and experience; also part which is traditional, part conjectural and inferential, as is generally the case in histories of this kind, but which the writer, nevertheless, is persuaded may be correct. The book he trusts will be found both entertaining and instructive, showing the progress made from the early ages down to the present time, in the moral, social, and material condition of the people. To quote the remark of a writer in another locality, " If the reader obtains as much real pleasure in perusing these pages, as the author had in collating and producing them, he will be gratified to think that his labours have not been without fruit."

In compiling these pages, the writer respectfully acknowledges the kind and ready assistance received from the Vicar, (the Rev. G. C. Hodgson,) John Walker, Esq., Mr. Adam Harle, Mr. Wm. Greenwell, Mr. John Jemieson, and other friends.

Corbridge-on-Tyne,
Sept. 24th, 1881.

INDEX.

HISTORY OF CORBRIDGE.

CORABRIDGE, Corbrugge, and Colebruge, are some of the old names of the town of Corbridge, described by the late Mr. Fairless, of Hexham, as "hoar with age," its earliest mark being the Roman Station. There is a tradition that this was the site of a British town at the time of the occupation of this country by the Romans. There is a tradition also, supported with a considerable amount of evidence, that at the time, and long before the Roman occupation, the river from the railway tunnel for a considerable distance to the west formed one great lake, covering all the low ground on each side, caused by the ridge of the hill, called Farnley Scaur, stretching to the hill on the opposite side, thus forming a barrier of considerable height: how high, or to what extent the water was thus held back cannot now be ascertained. A correspondent of the *Hexham Courant* writing on this subject a few years ago, stated that the lake had originally extended some miles westward, be this as it may, there is evidence beyond any doubt that the soil of the Corbridge Cemetery, about one mile above the tunnel, is all alluvial soil for at least nine feet deep, not a single stone is to be found. Persons also who have a knowledge of geology state that on the hill sides opposite Farnley Scaur, as well as on the banks on the south side, are found evidences of water-marks, which it is affirmed have been the boundary of a great lake at an early period.* This barrier, therefore, may have to

* Another article on this subject, ably written, under the heading "Corbridge Notes" appeared in the *Hexham Courant*, March 20th, 1881. As the paragraph, we think, cannot fail to be generally interesting, as well as supporting the opinion we had previously written, we venture to give it entire:—"About one mile east of Corbridge the Tyne valley appears to have at one time been choked across with an enormous deposit of glacial debris. The faces of the cliffs at Thornbrough, and on the south side of the river would indicate that the whole mass had at one time been continuous. Indications of terminal moraines are apparent at the west entrance of the tunnel. If this supposition be correct it follows that a large barrier of sand stretched across the valley at

A

some extent being first removed by artificial means, which
could without much difficulty be done, probably by the
Romans when making their great highway, and afterwards
by successive floods, each flood carrying a portion away and
thus deepening and widening the bed of the river, until in
process of time the low grounds were entirely dry.* Leaving
those traditional and probable matters to be thought over by
those interested in them, we proceed to what is more
certain and definite in the history of those extraordinary
people "the mighty Romans." As the Roman period
of the occupation of Britain always forms an interesting
feature in its early history, more especially in the north
of England, and in no locality more so than Corbridge
and its neighbourhood, in fact the history of the Romans
seems so interwoven with that of Corbridge, that we
quote freely from the most reliable information within
our reach.

About one third of a mile west of Corbridge was the
Roman station, Corchester, admitted by Horsley and others
to be the Corstopitum of Antonius, mentioned in his *Itinerary
of Britain*, which is a kind of road book of the whole Roman
Empire, supposed to have been made by one of the Emperors
who bore the name of Antonius. This station is on the
famous military road called "Watling Street," and is the
second mentioned in the first route (proceeding south from
Scotland) in that celebrated book, the first being Bremenium,
or High Rochester. Corstopitum is set down as being distant
twenty Roman miles; the intermediate station Habitancum,
the modern Risingham, not being mentioned in the *Antonine
Itinerary*, has given rise to many conjectures by Roman

this point, holding back the water of the Tyne which here accumulates as a
vast lake. This inland sea would be bounded by the sand-bar on the east,
and would fill the wide basin of the Tyne valley for some miles west of
Hexham. The depth of the lake is indicated by the height of the cliffs at
Thornborough, at which point the lake water would have its outlet. Gradually
as the soft material wore away the lip of the sand barrier would be lowered,
and the level of the lake reduced till it became finally drained, and showed as
we see it to-day. The rich alluvium forming the deep black soil of the valley
here, 20 feet deep in some places, was slowly deposited at the bottom of this
still lake. The site of Hexham would at one time stand out as a promontory
of the lake, and Beaufront and Dilston would, in those dim old days, have
between them a wide waste of waters."

*Within the last fifty years the bed of the river at this part has been deepened
at least nine feet, and within the same time, on the south side, adjoining the
tunnel, but more especially below it, not less than 12 acres of valuable land has
been carried away, thus widening the river bed several hundred feet.

Historians, and has by them been accounted for in various ways which it is not necessary here to refer to. Corstopitum is thought to have been one of the stations planted by Agricola which stood, as described by Dr. Bruce "upon a gentle swelling knoll on the north bank of the Tyne." Hutchinson describes it as having stood " on the north bank of the Tyne on a tongue of land formed by the stream of the Cor at its junction with the river," and in the opinion of Roman Historians was a large station, and supposed to be the chief Roman City in Britain. We now quote from a large and exquisitely illustrated book *The Lapidarium Septentionale*, recently published by The Society of Antiquaries of Newcastle-on-Tyne. " Corchester.—To the west of the little town of Corbridge, and distant about six hundred yards from its Church are traces of an extensive Roman settlement. The situation is one which would recommend itself to a Roman engineer. It rises gently above the general surface and is defended on its southern margin by the river Tyne and its somewhat precipitous bank, and on its western by the more humble stream of the Corburn. It was probably a Roman town rather than a purely military settlement, its shape and size favour this idea." Mr. MacLaughlan after dilligently tracing out the course of its ramparts, came to the conclusion that its form was an irregular ellipse, and that it contained about twenty acres. All the camps we have hitherto had occasion to notice assume the form of parallelograms and have a much smaller area than this. Owing to the peculiar fertility of the soil the site has long been subject to the plough, and all the erections of the Roman era have been overthrown or obscured. Coins and fragments of pottery are however still occasionally displayed by the operations of the husbandman ; and when for some special purpose the ground is penetrated to a greater depth than usual, Roman masonry is often encountered. In fact the foundations of a great portion are yet untouched.[*] The Watling Street

[*] Some interesting excavations were lately made, at the instance of the late Wm. Cuthbert, Esq., of Beaufront, the owner of the ground, under the following circumstances:—Mr. Cuthbert in accordance with an agreement with the rate-payers of Corbridge a few years ago, erected at his own cost the bridge which crosses the Corburn on the Colchester Road, ordered that the stones for this purpose or as many as could be obtained, should be, from the old foundation of the station. The following particulars were given to the writer, by Mr. Davison, game watcher, who assisted on the occasion. Mr. Davison states they first endeavoured to obtain the stones from the outside

approached the town near to its south western angle, and took its departure from the North Gate. The foundations of the bridge by which the road crossed the Tyne still exist in the river's bed, and can be easily discerned when the water is low and its surface smooth. It is probable that Corchester was the site of an Ancient British town. Mr. MacLaughlan is of opinion that had the Romans not found a stronghold already existing here, they would not have brought the Watling Street so far to the west as they have done, but would have taken it across the river near to where the rail-way tunnel now is, by this means distance would have been saved and better gradients obtained.* Corchester is distant from high Rochester by the line of the Watling Street, twenty-three and a half English miles. According to the *Antonine Itinerary* Corstopitum is twenty Roman miles.—Corchester is about two and a half miles south of the wall, and is distant fifteen miles from Risingham.

wall of the station on the south east side, which was known to exist for a considerable distance, a little below the brow of the hill. The outer side of the wall was laid bare for several feet deep, but such was the nature of the building that they were unable to get any stones to advantage, some other places were tried but with the same results; however, towards the western portion of the site they were more successful, here they obtained a great quantity of stones; it was noticed that one wall was built with clay, and below this wall was discovered a large white circular stone with the end up, it appeared to have been dressed with a mason's "pick," but unfortunately the quarrymen employed split it up; several inscribed stones were found, and a small gate way was discovered, with several courses of hewn stones having niches in them as if for admitting slip rails; a great number of massive vepel or channel stones in courses were found, and what was noticed were all found dipping towards the north; when first discovered they were about one foot below the surface, they were followed and taken out until they were found too deep for further excavations. Eight of these stones are inserted in the walls of the approaches of the bridge, for the purpose of conveying the rain floods from the road into the fields; a considerable portion of the foundations still remain.

* The more probable opinion appears to be that, as they evidently could not cross the river near the tunnel owing to the breadth and depth of the water, were compelled to go as far west as to keep clear of the lake or back water, and thus make sure of a good roadway, and a safe crossing of the river for their bridge. This view appears the more probable from the names given to the fields lying between the Station Road and tunnel being called "the Eales," "Eales Flat," otherwise "the Isles" or "Islands" as the opening betwixt the hills which kept the water back widened and deepened either from natural or artificial causes, the volume of water would consequently lessen and the previously submerged land appear. Mr. MacLaughlan is in error as to gradients, as much better gradients are secured by the present line than could possibly have been obtained near the tunnel. As the Romans were an acute and strategical people, another theory is put forth, and with a good show of reason, as to why they choose this particular spot for their large station. Standing on an elevated part of their road near Whittonstall, and looking north west, a distinct view is obtained of this site as well as of the river adjoining the site, the only place where the river is seen from this stand point; and besides being elevated, such a commanding spot was not likely to escape the notice of a Roman Engineer.

As having some bearing upon the identity of Corchester with the Corstopitum of the *Itinerary*, it is of importance to settle the orthography of the modern name. Occasionally the Roman Station is called Colchester ; the present town Colbridge. In Prior Richard's *History of the Church of Hexham*, written about A.D. 1154, we have Corabridge, and in his *Acts of King Stephen*, Corabrigam. In the *Black Book of Hexham*, written about A.D. 1479, we have Corbryg and Corbrig ; Hodgson tells us that on the common seal, and in charters of this town about the year 1234, its name is written Corebrigia ; he adds, however, sometimes in public records it is written Colbrigge ; Roger de Hoveden, who flourished in the time of Henry 2nd, writes Corobridge. Camden calls the Roman settlement Colechester, the modern town Corbridge. A writer quoted in the *Appendix* to *Gordon's Itinerarium* says :—Scarce three miles eastward of Hexham, are the ruins of the Roman City now called Corchester, the circuit of the walls is still very conspicuous. Horsley says :—The place where the station has been is called Corbow and Corchester ; and according to the account I had when I was there, Corbow is a small place included in Corchester which contains several acres. — I am much of opinion that the names have been Corchester and Corbrugh. Hodgson writes Colchester. The present inhabitants of the district uniformly use the R and not the L, though they pronounce it in the Northumbrian manner which is not a little puzzling to strangers. In the *Map of the Ordinance Survey* we have the names Corbridge, Corchester, Corchester Fields, Corchester Lane, and Corburn. On the whole there is reason to suppose that the present population have not correctly apprehended the utterances of their forefathers, and that Corchester, rather than Colchester, is the name given by the immediate successors of the Romans to this place."

We now proceed to give another interesting extract on the origin of names from a paper read lately by Mr. W. H. D. Longstaff, at a meeting of The Newcastle Society of Antiquaries, on Coventina, the Goddess of Procolitia as bearing on this subject. "A curious and a fine question may occur, whether when we find the Roman Corstopitum emerging into Colebridge, (hodie Corbridge) we may not have had the ancient name of the river kept up through all revolutions.

6

The peculiarity of the spelling of the name Corbridge was not lost upon our earlier antiquaries. After mentioning the flowing of the Riddle into the North Tyne a little lower than Belindgeham "(His spelling agrees with present pronunciation,) Harrison proceeds thus—" Beneath the confluence in like sort of both the Tines standed Corbridge, a towne sometime inhabited by the Romaines, and about twelve myle from Newcastell, and hereby doth the corn run (alluding to a little stream which passes the mill west of the Roman station,) that meeteth ere long with the Tine, not far of also is a place called Colchester, whereby Leland gusseth that the name of the brook should rather be Cole than Corne, and in my judge- ment his conjecture is very lykely, for in the life of S. Oswign, otherwise a feeble authorite, the word Colbridge is alwaies used for Corbridge. It appears however, from what is printed of Leland's M.S.S., that he only thought that the pretty brook where evident tokens were still to be seen of the old bridge was called Corve, though the name was not well known, and by this brook as among the ruins of the old town is a place called Colchester, where hath been a fortress or castle." *
Before giving an account of the approaches to the Station, the Bridge, Remains, Relics &c., of the Romans, we give the beautiful and graphic description not only of the station, but of the inner life of its inhabitants ; by the author of a series of articles called " Local Sketches," which appeared from time to time in the *Hexham Courant*. " My reader must now come down from the hill, (a place above Hexham where the writer had been ' taking a sketch' the preceding week,) and if he wishes to accompany me in my rambles, follow me to the neighbourhood of Corbridge. We are now about a quarter of a mile west of the town, on a road leading to Hexham on the north side of the river. On our right you observe a very fine orchard of considerable dimensions, and on the left a good sized field of vegetable loam newly ploughed, and above, Sandoe Hall seems to look down upon us with dignified complaisance. This locality has a name, a Roman Castra, transformed into Corchester. There is nothing here of any seeming note to command our attention, yet it is surrounded with ten thousand stirring memories.—Revolu-

* From the foregoing extracts the orthography of both the Roman station and the present town seem to be satisfactorily settled.

tion is the order of creation, and change is the inexorable
logic of time. The ploughed field we are now looking upon,
and a part of the adjacent land was the site of the Roman
station, Corstopitum. In that period of the world's history a
civilisation, with all its wonderful appliances, and to which we
owe much, gave a character both to the valley and much of
the surrounding country. This station was situated upon the
line of the highway commanding the passage of the Tyne
about two miles to the south of the wall, with its great chain
of fortifications which traversed the country from sea to sea.
I can imagine how the Roman soldiers were wont to lave
their limbs in the Tyne, in company with their Barbarian
auxiliaries, when the genial warmth of our northern climate
reminded them of their own sunny lands beyond the Alps. I
can conceive too, how they had to battle with our boreal
winters, when every scene around was a wild desolation. The
country we now behold mapped into numerous divisions by
hedge-rows, and studded with shady-trees and under a high
state of cultivation, was either a barren waste or dark forests
in a state of nature, in which the wild boar, the wolf, and
the bounding stag, were wont to roam. In those days the
natives knew nothing about the arts and appliances which
result from peaceful industry, and social order. What a busy
bustling place this now quiet field must have been, when
Corstopitum was alive with soldiers and camp followers,
collected from at least three divisions of the world. I think
I can now see the imperial commissariat trains passing and
repassing along the busy line of Watling Street, with their
motley guards. Nearly the whole of the provisions for the
use of the ten thousand troops stationed along the wall,
must have been brought from the south by the three
highways, which had their starting point behind Cheapside in
London ; one of those roads passed through Newcastle (Pons
Ælie) on the east ; the second by Carlisle on the west ; and
the third or middle one, is that which cuts the wall at
right angles, about two miles to the north of Corbridge on its
way down to Scotland. Let us turn the hand on the dial plate
of time back seventeen hundred years, and in fancy gaze upon
Agricola and his small victorious band, after returning from
the line of the Grampian Hills, where he routed Galgacus
with his thirty thousand fierce Celts. It is possible he would

return by the middle way, crossing the line of fortifications extending between the Friths of Forth and Clyde at Castlecary, a few miles to the west of Falkirk. If this was so, it is very likely he would rest his weary soldiers at Corstopitum. There they would enjoy the luxury of the bath which was dear to every Roman citizen, and indulge in the exciting pleasures of the amphitheatre. What strange and exciting scenes must have been witnessed in Corstopitum and its neighbourhood, when proconsuls, propraetors, prefects, tribunes, centurions, and lieutenants, called optiones, were moving about on duty or pleasure, surrounded by dusky Moors and Numedians, olive-complexioned Hispanolians, Scythians from beyond the Danube, wild Thracians from the borders of the Euxine sea, Illyrians and Macedonians and natives from the islands made classic by the songs of the immortal Homer, Scandinavians from the boreal regions of the north of Europe, Dacians from the lands bordering the Carpathian mountains, Nomadic Sarmatians from the wild regions of central Europe, Germans, Gauls, and Britons. What a patchwork of humanity we have here, what a heterogenous mass of nationalities, and how different in breeds, manners, customs, and modes of speech. In the year 208, when Severus passed along the Adrian fortifications from Wallsend to Bowness, what a bustle there would be at Corstopitum, with couriers passing to and from the adjacent stations along the line. There is no trace now of the cemetery, the Corstopitum city of the dead,* of the gymnasium, or the amphitheatre, of the baths, or the villas, in which the patricians enjoyed the refined society of their friends, and ministered their hospitality with graceful courtesy. The Roman officer was frequently

---

* There seems now pretty clear evidence of the whereabouts of the Cemetery, which the writer had evidently not heard of, direct west from the station, on the west side of the Corburn, and about 150 yards north west from the mill, along the edge of the cliff, as it has fallen from time to time when being undermined by the force of the stream, immense quantities of human bones have been discovered, more especially within the last fifty or sixty years, in fact the falling away of the high ground seems to have first led to the discovery of the burying ground. Mr. Adam Harle states that when a youth he found in the field a little to the west of this place a human skull of immense size and wonderfully perfect, and that with a stick he frequently poked out of the cliff quantities of human bones of all kinds, in fact the ground appeared full of bones. About two years ago when the course of the brook was being altered apparently to its original channel, the cliff was sloped, when whole skeletons were found, and several Roman vencl stones were discovered. This undoubtedly was the Roman burying ground, which would appear to have extended westward, towards or near to Shoredean Brea.

a man of literary tastes, with a just appreciation of the
beautiful either in nature or art. I dare, say sir, the merits
of Virgil and Catullus have often been discussed in that field,
and that an acquaintance with the philosophers of the grove
has been the means of wiling away many a winter's evening,
which otherwise, would have been dull and monotonous. It
may be too, that while some of these gentlemen were poring
over the orations of Cicero, or endeavouring to square the
moral maxims of Seneca, with their notions of right and
wrong, others were making their offerings to the shrines of
their own ideal gods. The Romans (referring to their
governors) were too dignified to be intolerant; the consequence
was that their barbarian auxiliaries enjoyed full liberty in the
worship of their deities. Though camp life had its round of
military duties, and man's conduct was subject to civic rules,
the Romans knew well how to make both time and
circumstances subservient to their notions of pleasure. Many
a time the hills and glens on both sides of the valley must
have resounded with the howl of dogs, the sound of horns,
and the shouts of men, as they ranged the forest and
wild moors in the exciting pleasures of the chase, while hunting the boar, the antlered stag, or the savage wolf. Their
cusine I have no doubt, owed no little to their piscatorial
knowledge. The fish in the rivers had many amiable
enemies long before the age of Walton, and as the Romans
knew the value of both salmon and trout, there can be little
doubt, but that the Tyne and its tributaries have often
been flogged with both the zeal and patience of real lovers of
the sport by that people. Yes: the Romans understood
gastronomy, and had a fine appreciation of cookery in its
most scientific character, the men who could enjoy turkey
brains and dissolved pearls, knew how to make peace offerings to their stomachs. Many hundred years after the
Romans retired from Great Britain, the deer were in great
plenty in this district, both the Roman army, and its
tail of camp followers must have depended upon the
produce of the chase; hunting and fishing would therefore
be a necessity as well as a source of pleasure to them."
But all this has long since passed away, and its once
busy bustling multitudes have for centuries slept in the
solemn quiet of the grave, forcibly reminding us of the

uncertainty, as well as the unstability of all earthly things. Yet from the almost imperishable nature of their vast remains, we learn to a great extent their true history. Before referring further to the station, and particularising a few of the many interesting remains found there, we will describe as briefly as possible the line of the Watling Street, for a short distance south and north of the station. This great Roman highway as has been stated, was the middle road leading from London to Scotland ; when nearing Corbridge it crossed the present turnpike road to the south near Farnley Gate, and continued on the flat ground through the site of Mr. John Temperly's house, passing the front of Mr. Richard Carr's house, until it reached near the house occupied by Mr. Lawton, but in Mr. Little's field. It there from an angle (for the Romans made no curves in their roads) continued in a straight line close by the west end of the cemetery lodge,* to the bridge† entering the station at its south western angle, and took its departure from the north gate, continuing by a lane (which is the Roman road) in a straight line to the junction of the Sandhoe and Stagshawbank roads, (here at this junction the Roman road is clearly traceable for a considerable distance in the pasture field betwixt the roads and the Corburn,) thence proceeding northward nearly on the line of the Stagshawbank road (cutting the wall at right angles) to the next station Risingham. The Roman bridge as forming part of the Watling Street we next refer to. The length of the bridge cannot now be ascertained, nor even the number of pillars or openings, there is no evidence there were any arches. It is however evident at the time of its erection that

---

* In the field betwixt the railway and turnpike road the foundations yet remain, although the plough passes over them, yet in a dry summer if sown with corn it is plainly seen, being a week or nine days sooner ripe than the other part of the field.

† Another Roman road called the "Maiden Way" commenced at the south end of the bridge, and proceeded in a straight line direct south, passing near the east side of the old toll bar at Dilston, continuing further south for about three hundred yards, then at a right angle westward, nearing the Linnell Wood and onward through Hexhamshire, passing Alston on the north and still westward towards Penrith. When the "new road" was made in 1829, betwixt Corbridge bridge and Dilston, this ancient road was unexpectedly come upon and cut through, and was found to consist mostly of paving stones firmly bedded and united together ; the discovery attracted at the time considerable attention. "Besides the grand Roman way which proceeded from Dover in Kent, and crossed the Tyne here, there was another military road, which passed from this place south west through Dilston Park, over Hexham Fell to Old Town in Allendale, and meets with the Maiden Way at Whitley Castle." *Warburton's Map of Northumberland.*—MACKENZIE

it crossed the river at right angles, beginning on the south side, not at the edge of the river in its present bed, but some considerable distance into the plantation. We are not aware that there is any traditional account, or any written record of this once famous structure, except such as that obtained from the ruins as they existed within the writer's early recollections,[*] those remnants can perhaps hardly in themselves be called ruins, being complete as far as they existed, and were on the south side, consisting of the base of two or three pillars, with all the firm and massive stone work betwixt them as well as below, but more especially above them. This remnant when the river was low and clear showed a fine specimen of that substantial masonry so peculiar to the Romans. The base of the pillars thus standing might be three or four feet in height; from this base the pillars had risen. The base widened considerably towards the bottom and resembled so many steps, which consisted of three or four courses of stones, each course or layer projecting out beyond the higher something like the distance of a foot, the lowest course being firmly embedded in the solid masonry. One of these stones covers the mouth of the culvert, which is a little further down in the embankment at a place called the Gutter, this stone has a fine moulding running along the upper outside corner. The surface stones betwixt the base of each pillar had been firmly secured together with iron cramps sunk into the stones and covered with lead. The discovery and taking out this lead upwards of fifty years ago, afforded a rich harvest for a number of youths who were bathing there, one of them finding the lead loose, undoubtedly caused by the rusting away of the iron cramps, at once proceeded to take it out, but not in detached pieces, for it was found to run from stone to stone at right angles, and when taken out in large squares looked something like window frames. It is to be regretted that this fine remnant of Roman work should

---

[*] Mackenzie in the first edition of his *History of Northumberland*, when referring to this bridge has a foot note as follows:—
"The Romans were excellent architects, and by all descriptions given of their bridges in Britain, testified their geometrical knowledge; their arch was semicircular, their pillars multangular, with a sharp angle to the stream like the prow of a ship. The foundations of the piers were constructed of an horizontal arch made of stones in the form of a wedge, as appears by the remains here. In situations subject to rapid floods, a small arch was formed in the pier, to receive the water when it began to reach the bow of the arch."
—HUTCHINSON.

have been demolished as it was, upwards of forty years ago, by the orders of the then agent of the Greenwich Hospital Estates, and merely for the sake of obtaining the chiseled stones which were used for making culvert chimney tops, and other repairs on the estate ; the water-wheel case which was then being made at Dilston New Town Farm, was made from these stones. Some of the stones thus removed were of great weight, many of them being fluted, groved, and with fine mouldings ; a portion yet remains which could not be got at on account of the depth of the river, this portion adjoins the land. During the summer of 1880, we saw the extent of this remnant more distinctly than on any previous occasion, a good deal of what had previously been covered with gravel and mud was then seen ; the remains appeared to cover a surface of about one hundred square yards, the whole being quite level and appearing like a large floor newly laid with good-sized stone flags, lying in the same position as when laid by the Roman masons, having unmoved withstood the storms and floods of more than seventeen centuries. As before stated, the bridge had its commencement in the plantation, this is evident from the fact that the base of the southern pillar was partly in the land and certainly was not the breastwork, but a pillar ; and from the quantity of stones some distance into the plantation, not more than two or three feet below the surface, it is likely there may have been another pillar betwixt the one referred to and the breastwork of the bridge, if at any time the covering of these stones should be removed this would then be more correctly known. How far the bridge extended to the north side of the river is unknown. A few years ago the late William Coulson, then residing in Corbridge, (who first discoved the breastwork of the Roman bridge at the Chesters, North Tyne) by the permission and with the assistance of the late Mr. Cuthbert, of Beaufront, who kindly supplied the labour, endeavoured to find the northern abutment of this bridge, and who succeeded in finding some massive walling which had every appearance of being the approach to the bridge, and this is the more likely to be correct as the Watling Street is described as entering the station at its south western angle where this work was found and still remains as Mr. Coulson found it. In connection with the account of the bridge, and to make the position

of the Romans the more understandable, must be included an
account of the course of the river. The course of the
bed of the river has been very much altered since the
Romans left the country, both above and below the bridge,
above the bridge the river has been considerably further north
than at present, and evidently its course had been through
Mr. Ellerington's fields. On a plan made in 1779 a stream
flowing from the river is shown as branching in this direction,
commencing some distance west of the Devil's Water, and
again uniting with it at its junction with the Cor. Within
the writer's own recollection the river at its junction with the
Devil's Water, was further north to the extent of from 40 to
50 yards; some additional ground has been gained on the
north side, but the main result has been that of widening the
bed of the river. But it is the alterations below the bridge
that we more particularly refer to, and as having taken place
within the last 100 years. On the plan already referred to,
which is a plan of the township of Corbridge, that portion of
ground known as "the Green," called at the division the
West Green, and containing seven acres, extended as far west
as the plantation called Threepmook. The width of this field
at its east end from the fence adjoining the road to the south
side is shown as being 93 yards, at present it is only 33 yards,
so that at this point 60 yards of the West Green now forms
the bed of the river. This field which bounded on the river was
defended the whole length by a stone wall without doubt of
Roman construction.* The ground gradually narrowed
towards the west, and as is shown on the plan when within
about 150 yards of the Threepmook to have been only about

* As the station had bordered close to the river, the Romans, with their usual
foresight, had taken the precaution for the safety of their town and adjacent
ground, to erect a strong wall which would appear to have extended from their
bridge eastward for near 500 yards; as far as can be ascertained this protection
not only existed during the Roman occupation, but for centuries afterwards, in
fact it would appear to have existed, portions at least, until the close of the last
century. 50 or 60 ago the foundations and lower portions of this wall for a considerable distance were still there, and particularly noticed by youths while
bathing there. Some now living recollect well seeing those remains and describe
them as being of considerable length, in some parts only the foundations were
seen, in other places as if the wall had been thrown down; the thickness of the
wall would appear to have been upwards of three feet. About the time referred
to a quantity of the stones were removed and used for penning that portion of
the field bounding on the river to protect it from the destructive inroads which
the floods were making year after year; but this attempt was of short duration, even although assisted by Roman stones, for the impetuous Tyne soon
swept piles of stone and mason work before it. In the summer of 1880 portions
of the foundations were distinctly seen from the road side.

.25 or 30 yards in width. · From this point there is a slight
curve towards the south west which widens until the abut-
ments of the bridge had been reached ; within our own
recollection this field was regularly cultivated, having alternately crops of corn, potatoes, and turnips. The ground east
of the Green, as far as Corbridge bridge is shown on this plan
as waste ground, covered partly with brushwood and gravel.*
The river except in floods taking the south side and running
through the two southern arches, a portion of the plantation,
from the sandy hole as far as the Roman bridge, was at this
time mostly the bed of the river, which was much deeper than
it is now, and abounded with pike.† From the foregoing it
will be seen at once, that in the Roman period the river above
their bridge was much further to the north than at present,
and below the bridge much further to the south.

Roman remains in connexion with the station as has
already been hinted, have been found in abundance, consisting of altars, monumental and other inscribed stones, pottery,
deer's horns in abundance, also seals, signet rings, coins,
brooches, and such other articles as were usually found in
Roman stations, and have been disposed of to private parties,
and to public institutions. We notice a few of the most
remarkable and interesting. Two altars of great value to
antiquarians, were discovered in the church yard here ; both
altars having Greek inscriptions.‡ One is dedicated by
Diodora, the priestess of the Tyrian Hercules. This

---

* In the days of family and cottage spinning, and home weaving and bleaching, this gravel bed which adjoined the gardens was used as a bleaching
ground, and during a portion of the summer was generally, almost entirely
covered with linen webs.

† Pike were killed in considerable numbers by shooting them, and being also
caught by line and bait: during the summer of 1825, a great number were shot.
In that year more particularly, an attempt was made on a larger scale than
usual to protect the land on the south side near the junction of the Devil's
Water with the river, from being further carried away by incessant floods. A
number of men were employed during the whole summer in driving piles,
which yet remain now nearly half way into the river) and in walling, and penning, carting, &c., &c. The dinners of the workmen were carried to them every
day by boys, mostly the sons of those employed, who were usually detained
some hours watching for the fish rising to the surface of the water, two
generally rose together, when their backs were above the water the signal was
given two or three guns being in readiness, if near enough they were usually
killed and brought to land by a terrier or two trained for this purpose. The
writer, when a boy, has seen them caught by line and bait betwixt the base
of the pillars of the Roman bridge, which was a favourite place for pike fishers,
many being caught at this spot.

‡ Antiquarians are of opinion that the Greek element amongst the inhabitants of Corstopitum was probably strong.

altar Horsely esteemed one of the greatest curiosities in
Britain. In a letter he writes to Sir Roger Gale, Esq., dated
April 7th, 1729, we find the following rather amusing
incident :—"The last time I saw the altar erected by Diodora,
it was in the church yard at Corbridge. The church of
Durham had formed a design to remove it thither, but failed
in the attempt. I should be glad if they made a second
attempt with better success. Doctor Hunter told me pleasantly
he should threaten the people of Corbridge with a prosecution
from the spiritual court, for keeping a pagan altar in their
church yard."—This altar was understood to be in the
possession of the Duke of Northumberland; but Dr. Bruce
states it is not now among those preserved at Alnwick Castle.
The other altar is dedicated to Astarte, the Ashtaroth of the
Scriptures. Josephus tells us "that Hiram, king of Tyre,
and contemporary with Solomon, built two temples which he
dedicated to these deities. The Israelites in forsaking the
living God, not unfrequently betook themselves to the idolatry
of the Sidonians." This altar is in the collection at Netherby.
It will be interesting to refer to another altar, which is now
on the stairs of the entrance of the tower of the Castle,
Newcastle-upon-Tyne, this is always described as an elegantly
shaped altar. This is the description given by Horsely, who
first noticed it.—" The market cross stood upon an altar on
which there had been an inscription but is now defaced. On
both sides of the altar are the figures described below, they
were half covered under the ground or under the steps of the
cross, but the earth being removed they appeared at full
length, and are plainly two human figures; in one hand of
each nothing can be discovered. One of the figures seemed
to be in a posture of motion with a lyre or harp in his hand,
which made me suspect it might be Bacchus; and the other
holding a bow unstrung like Apollo; unless both may be
supposed to represent Apollo. There was a faint stroke went
up from one end of the bow, which possibly may have been
the string, or an arrow which Apollo held, together with the
bow." It is thus described by Dr. Bruce:—" The inscription
is defaced, but the carving on both sides remain: on the one
side is a soldier armed, the representation probably of war;
on the other is a warrior having laid aside his weapon, dragging an amphora of wine; a picture emblematic of peace."

Another description is as follows :—" It has an inscription which is now illegible ; on one side is a figure dragging something resembling an amphora. This altar formerly formed the base of the Market Cross at Corbridge, the ancient Corstopitum, the focus of it has been enlarged into a square hole six inches deep to admit the shaft, the altar is four feet four inches in height."

But what is considered the greatest curiosity that has been discovered here is a silver lanx or dish, called by the Corbridge people a silver table, shaped like a tea board and is in length nineteen inches and three-quarters, and its breadth is fifteen inches, and weighs nearly one hundred and fifty ounces. It was discovered under the following circumstances :—In the month of February, 1734, the daughter of a blacksmith named Cutter was gathering sticks on the north side of the river Tyne, in the vicinity of Corbridge, about two hundred yards below the bridge at a place where a small stream enters the river ; the girl noticed something peculiar projecting from the bank, her curiosity was excited, and it was not long before she found herself in possession of the treasure which she carried to her father. He perhaps anxious to know whether the object which had come into his possession was, as it seemed, really silver or some base imitation of it, detached the rim, which formed its stand, and offered it for sale to a well-known silversmith in Newcastle, Mr. Isaac Cookson.* Cutter obtained for the fragment the sum of £1 16s. Being no longer doubtful of the commercial value of his find, he quickly paid another visit to Mr. Cookson, and disposed of the dish for £31 10s. The dish was, however, shortly after claimed by His Grace the Duke of Somerset, as Lord of the Manor : after a great deal of litigation, it was ultimately given up to the Lord of the Manor, and is now at Alnwick Castle. It is described as being adorned with figures of Apollo, Vesta, Juno, Minerva, and Diana, each with their proper symbols, &c. The figures are in bass-relief, the minor parts having been executed with punches ; on the back are a few dotted letters which were probably the workman's signature. The work is neither of the best nor of the worst times. The figure of Vesta is extremely well executed—the posture free, the

---

* The stand has been replaced and the injuries effected by its removal, which were rudely done, repaired.

drapery soft and easy. Dr. Bruce remarks that Gale's conjecture as to its use is probably the correct one. "This is
big enough (he says) to contain the extra of a sheep or other
small victim which seems to me to be the likeliest employment
for it, and that it was one of those sacrificing utensils that
Vigil calls lances." There is an accurate cast of it in the
Newcastle Museum of Antiquities. Shortly after the silver
dish was discovered a silver cup was also found, the following
is the account and description given of it:—"This silver
vessel was found in the summer of 1736, on the west side of
the river Tyne, below the bridge at Corbridge, almost opposite
the place where the lanx was discovered." There is an account
of it in the minutes of The Society of Antiquaries of London,
which bears date October 28th, 1736, and is accompanied by
some illustrative sketches. The vessel weighed twenty ounces.
It was near four inches high and had a diameter of eight inches
and a quarter but has disappeared. We are told that "the
metal was in many parts corroded by the earth in which it
lay." This circumstance doubtless accounts for its disappear-
ance, unless it were carefully handled it would fall to pieces.
The following is the description given of a gold ring found on
January 3rd, 1810, and now at Alnwick Castle, which is
accompanied with a wood cut:—"The wood cut* represents
the outer face of a gold ring which was found by a man pulling
turnips in a field at Colchester. This curious circlet is now
in the cabinet of antique rings belonging to the Duke of
Northumberland. From the M.S. Catalogue of the collection,
prepared by Mr. Wray, the information here given is taken.
The hoop of the ring is formed of fifteen fluted facets, each
facet bears a letter with the exception of three, and these are
occupied with the leaf ornament. The latter word of the
inscription is a Grecian of no rare occurrence on objects of
Roman date, and is equivalent to............The whole legend
being expressive of the wish that long life might be the portion
of Almilida—it weighs seventy-five grains. The coins found
here have been numerous. Dr. Bruce relates in his *Roman
Wall:* "The Rev. John Walton, who about a century ago
was Vicar of Corbridge,† made a considerable collection of

* The face of the ring as shown on the drawing, is nearly three inches in
length, and five-sixteenths in width.
† Mr. Walton was appointed to Corbridge in 1719, and was Vicar for forty-
four years. His collection of Roman and other antiquities were sold by his

18

Roman coins, by purchasing such as were turned up in the neighbouring station of Corchester." The following circumstance is related concerning him: "A party of Jews having established in the neighbourhood (at Prior Manor) a Prussian Blue Manufactory, felt disposed to enter the market with the Vicar. Mr. Walton unwilling to compete with them by offering a larger price, had the fields, where the coins were found, strewed with imitations of genuine pieces; these were freely bought by the Jews, who, soon finding the trade a losing one, abandoned it altogether." The station, notwithstanding such systematic gleaning as has been carried on for ages, is not yet deprived of all its treasures, even now when the soil which covers the site is turned up, coins and other antiquities are found. It is supposed this was one of the first stations destroyed, but there seems to be no evidence given in support of this view; a considerable portion of the walls were standing in the middle of the last century. Hutchinson says: " The remains of the Pretorium are yet very conspicuous." Even now on the east side of the station several feet high of wall is beneath the soil. The reader may be disposed to ask what has become of the stones of all those buildings? Dr. Bruce partly answers this question when he states " The Church and the Village of Corbridge have arisen out of the ruins of the station." Several inscribed stones are in the houses of the village, one of which is thus described by Horsley: " In the fore wall of an old house in Corbridge, on the right hand as you enter the village from the east, is part of a Roman stone, not an altar, but an honorary monument with a curious inscription which belongs to one of the Emperors Antoninus, but to which is not certain.* The fine Roman stones in the crypt of Hexham Abbey Church are generally supposed to have been carried from this station. This was the opinion of Algernon, the late Duke of Northumberland. As there are several incised and carved Roman

executors to the Hon. and Rev. William Graham, and Lord Viscount Preston, of Wetherby.

* A correspondent to the *Hexham Courant* writing under the head of ' Corbridge Notes," gives the following translation of this inscription, and adds the remarks at the same time:—" To the most Mighty Emperor, Marcus Aurelius." Here in Corbridge we have a monument erected to one who was the ruler of the grandest of empires, and was one of the greatest and best of men that has ever lived, and that we, in Corbridge, may remember something of him, I may say that Marcus Aurelius was born in Rome, A.D. 121, and died A D. 180.

stones in the village not noticed in any record, it will **not**
be out of place to notice them here. In the north wall of **the**
house, now called Orchard Vale, adjoining the road, is **walled**
in, a Roman altar with an inscription, but now so defaced
that it cannot be read. In the west wall of the garden belonging this house, in the garden side, is fixed a pretty
Roman stone with an incised representation of a bow strung.
In the wall of a house in the Vicarage yard, walled in, is **an**
altar similar to that at Orchard Vale. In the same wall is
another stone with some curious symbols or figures on it; in
the same wall is a third stone, about two feet in height, with
a figure in bold relief, now much defaced, and would seem **to**
represent a Roman officer with a cloak around him. In the
Vicarage garden are several curious stones, some of them
monumental, others Roman, and some others of them
apparently of Saxon character. Another stone is in the
possession of Mr. John Walker, which shows two figures **in**
relief, apparently representing children in a reclining position;
the figures, although somewhat defaced, are yet distinctly
traceable. Another interesting stone is walled into the west
side of a brick house in the Market Place, belonging to Mr.
Thomas Harle. This stone is not entire, but what remains
shows well: in relief is the figure of an owl which was quite
perfect, until a short time ago, when a workman who was doing
some repairs to the outside of the house, defaced it by breaking off its head and one of its wings. The face of the stone
is divided by a pillar rising from a border at the bottom; on
one side are cut the letters "c" on the other side is a curve
as broad as the pillar, inside of which is perched **the**
owl. Those stones were found in the neighbourhood of the
Roman station. There is a stone in the inside of the Church
tower, nearly as high up as the clock, on which is the representation of a snake, coiled; an attempt was made some
time ago to get this stone removed, which was not accomplished,
but in the attempt the figure was much injured. There **is**
a somewhat curious small stone above the door-way of an
old house in the Middle Street, opposite the Black Bull
Public House, on which is represented the upper portion of
a human figure; antiquarians have been puzzled with it, **but**
the general opinion is that it is of Roman workmanship.
Mr. Greenwell has in his possession a fine revolving **Roman**

seal, set in an ornamental mounting, with the head and shoulders apparently of a warrior beautifully cut in a chalcedony; on the head is a helmet surmounted with a plume falling from the front loosely over the back of the helmet, on part of the left shoulder there is shown a covering of mail, on the other part of the shoulder is a shield. It has been in possession of the same family for two generations, and was found in the neighbourhood of Corchester. Mr. John Green, who for many years farmed the Hill Bank Farm, which is on the site of the station, when ploughing and turning over the soil found many Roman relics, and has in his possession a brooch, a little larger than half-a-crown, ornamented on the front, and is quite perfect, except the pin, which is broken off. He has also of the same material, a cloak pin slightly ornamented, which is perfect. Mr. Green possesses also several coins, both brass and silver, in a good state of preservation. A portion of a Roman stone, having a border and sunk panel, is fixed in the garden wall in the lane called Gos Croft Lane, near its junction with St. Helen's Lane, having no inscription, but has evidently been intended for one. A flat Roman stone covers the well at the junction of this lane with St. Helens, and has a fine moulding running along one edge. In the farm yard at Hill Bank, and in other places, are several substantial venel stones, which appear to have been used for sanitary purposes in connection with the station. Several jars, bottles, &c., have lately been found near the station. Mr. Hunter, of Dilston, has one, found there, in a fine state of preservation.

About 100 years ago, or as near as can be ascertained, when the family vault in Corbridge Church, belonging the Winships of Aydon, was opened to receive the remains of one of the family, a gold coin and a gold mourning ring were discovered deposited there, but none of the family had any knowledge when or by whom the articles were deposited. The ring is somewhat massive and is of 18-carat stamped gold, and, except the enamel, which is rather defaced, it is quite perfect but without any inscription. The gold coin is rather larger than a sovereign but remarkably thin, and has on one side the device of a man-of-war ship in full sail with the inscription in Latin, " Charles II., by the grace of God King of Great Britain, France, and Ireland;" on the other

side is the device of George and the dragon, but George is
represented as standing on the body of the dragon thrusting
his spear into its mouth, with the inscription " Glory to God
alone," both the device and lettering are remarkably well
executed. It is a fine coin, and was likely struck shortly
after the restoration, and probably to commemorate that
event. These are in the possession of Mrs. Winship.

Another old relic may here be referred to, although not of
Roman character, but equally interesting, as being associated
with the tragic events of the last unfortunate Earl of
Derwentwater, and that is the fine oak dining table from
Dilston Hall, removed at the dispersion of the family furniture
to the Hall Room of the Angel Inn, Corbridge, where it continued to stand until lately, when it was removed to Eastfield
House by its owner, Mr. John Walker, by whom it has been
completely renovated, and is a fine specimen of the substantial
oak furniture of that day.

Of the origin and founding of this ancient town we have no
reliable data. It is the opinion of Mr. MacLaughlan and
other writers that the Roman station was the site of an
ancient British town or stronghold.* But this idea does not
well agree with the tactics of that great General Agricola.
While he upheld the terror of the Roman arms and checked
all revolt, he adopted a milder policy. He taught the arts
of peace and commerce to the conquered race, and thus
many high-born Britons assumed the Roman toga, language,
and manners of life. To have taken forcible possession of
any of their towns, and thus driven them from their homes,
was not in keeping with the mild policy of Agricola. It is
however not too much to surmise, as has been already hinted,
for numerous British relics have been found in the neighbourhood, that Corbridge, so snugly situated, was at and during
the period of the Roman occupation, a British town, for the
Romans also taught them how to build substantial dwelling
houses. Betwixt the years (according to historians) 409 and
420 the Romans finally abandoned Britain. The Britons who
had lived in comparative peace, under Roman protection,
were in a wretched plight when that was withdrawn, the
Picts and Scots breaking through the unguarded walls, pillaged

---

* It has been estimated that at the time of the invasion of this country by
the Romans, there were no fewer than one million of Britons.

the northern country. As historians further inform us, being incessantly harassed by their northern foes, sought the assist- ance of foreigners called Angles and Saxons, who once having obtained a settlement in the land, seized the low-land territory and eventually drove them from the land of their birth and inheritance into the fastnesses of Cumberland and Wales ; as Corbridge is referred to in early Saxon history, the natural inference is that after expelling the British, the Saxons took possession of the town already built to their hands.

As Corbridge, as far as we can learn, is first referred to in connection with Christianity, it certainly will be in keeping with the subject to briefly notice its introduction into North- umberland, which would appear to have been first into this neighbourhood, not having a more fruitful field than this northern province. This is the account history gives, and the correctness of which we have no reason to doubt.* In the year 597 the Roman Monk Augustine, with forty other Monks, landed in Kent, they having been sent by Pope Gregory the Great to convert the heathen in this island. Ethelbert, King of Kent, received them graciously, assigned them a residence in the Isle of Thanet, and was afterwards baptized into the Christain faith. In 617 Edwin the Great became King, he was the first Christian and second King of Northum- berland. Having married the daughter of Ethelbert, was prevailed upon by the influence of Paulinus, a Bishop and a retinue of Christians to become a Christian. Having advised with his council, he and a great part of his nobility were baptized on Easter Sunday, 627. A few years afterwards in the reign of Oswald, a Christian King,† by the preaching of

---

* It is a pretty general opinion that there were many Christian soldiers in the Roman Army in Britain from an early period down to their departure, and that during the same period there is abundant evidence that several Christian churches were established in the land, but mostly in the south and western parts of the country.

† It will be fitting here to give a more particular account than is given in general history, of the great battle which took place betwixt Cadwalla and Oswald in the first year of Oswald's reign, and which resulted in the triumph of Christianity over Paganism. We quote from the Surtee's Society publica- tions. In this account there are some portions in Latin which we omit. The battle near Hexham in which Cadwalla was slain. This was the great battle of the Cumbrian Cadwalla, which saved the Christians in Bernicia from de- struction. It was won in A.D., 634. I have spoken elsewhere of the battle itself, and of the positions occupied by the contending parties, but a little may here be said of the places in which it began and ended. For several centuries there has been a controversy on these points. The scene of the fight is called by one writer Catseaul, and by another Cautseaul, an old word which is thus explained "pugmainfra inurum." Bede tells us that the fight began at

the Gospel of Christ by Adrian, a Christian Bishop, assisted
by the King himself. During the space of seven days, fifteen

a place called Hefenfelth, and that Cadwalla was killed at a place called
Denisesburn, now where Hefenfelt is, or Campus Caelestis as the historian
calls it. Bede says that it was a little to the north of the Roman wall, and
that the name Heavenfield was a presage of the victory which was to immor-
talize the ground. If the name existed before the fight, it points rather to a
bleak elevated position a "heaven-kissing hill." If it were subsequent to it,
the origin of the word is an obvious one. Leland tells us ....there is a
fame that Oswald won the battelle at the Halydene a two myles est from
S. Oswaldes asche, and that Halidew is it that Bede cunllith Havenfield,
and men thereabouts yet finde small wood crossies in the ground. The
name of Hali lew, of which I have early documentary evidence, is now lost,
but it may be identified with Hallington, which lies two or three miles to the
north cast of St. Oswalds. Amongst the charters now lost was one...............
Mr. Errington also told Smith, the learned editor of Bede, that Halidew and
Hallington were identical, acquiring the information from his own muniment
room. The place where Oswald set up his standard may be satisfactorily
made out. In a metrical life of the sainted King, which is quoted by Gibson
in his edition of Camdens Britannica, there occurs the following passage:—
................The account of the battle and the standard is given in the words
of Bede, but there is this variation .... Now there is only one Chapel or
Church dedicated to St. Oswald in the neighbourhood of Hexham, and that is
at a place about six miles from the town called St. Oswalds' a little to the
north of the wall, exactly in the position that Bede describes, and it is just
the place in which the King would choose to set up his standard. It seems
plain then that St. Oswalds is the place to which Bede refers, and I endorse
the view set forth in the Archaeologia ....Cadwalla however was killed
at Denisesburn, and the position of this stream has been entirely unknown.
People have endeavoured without just cause to place it in the immediate
vicinity of St. Oswalds, and for most part behind the Chapel. I have already
shown how unlikely that was from the character of the country. The following piece of direct evidence settles for ever this disputed point. This is in a
charter made between Thomas de Whittington and Archbishop Grey, in the
early part of the thirteenth century........... ....The original of this deed was
at York in the repository which has just been mentioned. There is a copy of
it in the roll of Archbishop Gray, giving the date.................Now the places
mentioned in this charter can easily be recognized. They lie across the Tyne,
eight or nine miles to the south cast of St. Oswalds, not far from Dilston and
the Devil's Water, and below the town of Hexham. Dilleswood still bears its
name and so does Devil's Water, and in the fork between Rowley Water and
Devil's Water, there is a place called the Steel. The name of Denisesburn is
lost, but it is almost certain from measurement, if from nothing else, that it
is identical with Rowley Water. There is a fame, as Leland tells us, that
Oswald won the battelle at Halydene, a too myles est from St Oswalde's
asche ; there is a place called Hallington in this direction mentioned, and it
was here probably that the battle was fully won. Cadwalla would thus be cut
off from his retreat, and the defeated Chieftain crossed somehow or other the
Roman wall and hastened towards the south, across the wild moor, with his
pursuers after him; over the heather he would go, down the green banks
below it, through the Tyne, and at a distance of eight or nine miles from the
battle field he was caught and killed at a little beck call Denisesburn, a tribu-
tary of the Rowley Water; he would be entangled in a net-work of woods and
streams when he was slain." In reference to the flight of Cadwalla described
as being over heather and moor, it appears more than likely that the wily
chieftain would choose the Watling Street in the first instance for the line of
his flight—his defeat being in the vicinity of that famous road—which would
thus enable him to hasten his flight; once on this road he would pass through
the opening of the Roman wall at Port Gate, which was on the Stagshawbank
road, would cross the Tyne by the Roman bridge or on its ruins. He would
then leave the Watling Street and take another Roman road called the
Maiden Way, which passed through Dilston Grounds, past the Linnels, through
Hexhamshire into Cumberland, which was evidently Cadwalla's object, but
being closely pressed by Oswald, he left the road to seek safety in the thicket
where he was caught and slain.

thousand received baptism and became Christians,* and in the year 650 the entire Saxon community, at least in this part of Northumberland, had embraced Christianity. All this seems to be confirmed shortly afterwards by the great undertakings of St. Wilfred, who founded the Church and Monastery of St. Andrew, at Hexham, the fifth stone church built in England. The splendour and sublimity of this building was considered the wonder of the age; and besides this, Wilfred founded several other churches in this neighbourhood. It is not until the following century that we have the following brief but comprehensive record : " That in the year 771, there was a Monastery at Corbridge." (See further account of the Monastery under the heading " Corbridge Church."

The following is from the publications of the *Surtees' Society:*—"In 795 there was another royal murder near Hexham. Ethelred, King of Northumbria,† was slain at Corbridge-on-the-Tyne, (another historian writes that Ethelred was slain at Cobre, April 18th, 794.) a place of great antiquity and repute. Although few traces of its grandeur are now remaining, it is probable, I think, the sovereign had a residence here in Saxon times: there was here also a Minster, which has already been mentioned, some remnants of this may perhaps exist in the present Parish Church. The death of Eaudulf, or Adulf, Duke of Bamburgh, is recorded by Ethelward, A.D. 912, the scene of Eadred's defeat is placed by the *Chronicon Pictorium* at Tyne Moor, hodie Corbridge Fell."

In 923 there was a battle at Corbridge between Ragnal the Dane and Prince Eabald, who was aided by Constantine of Scotland, the Norsemen were victorious and secured possession of the southern portion of Northumberland.‡ Christianity received no favour at the hands of

---

* A well not far from Haltwhistle called Arthur's well is said to be the place where all those were baptised.

† Ethelred the 16th King of Northumberland began to reign in 779, was expelled in 782, and was restored in 792 but only to reign seven years. In a discussion which continued for some time (in 1877) in the columns of the *Hexham Courant* on "tre origin of tithes," a correspondent, Mr. Isaac Hall, of Allendale, in a letter dated January 17th, has the following curious coincidence relating to the murder of another king :—"The same history, he writes, applies to tithes in England. In 795, Offa, king of Mercia, caused tithes in his own dominions to be due by right, which before were only free-will offerings, in return to the Pope for his pardon of the murder of Ethelbert, King of East Angles."

‡ Mr. Fairless notes in a private manuscript given to the writer, that before Bishop Tilrid died, this battle at Corbridge took place. Tilrid was Bishop of Lindisfarne, and died 928.

25

Ragnal, who had no regard for Bishops or Monks ; towns were burnt and Monasteries were sacked, their inmates often being destroyed with them. It is more than likely that Ragnal destroyed the Monastery at Corbridge, if not the town itself. To form some idea of the havoc caused by the ruthless Danes, (we quote from *Holinshred's History of the Kings of England* concerning them in the reign of the Conqueror.) "You must consider that by the invasion of the Danes the Churches and Monasteries throughout Northumberland were so wasted and ruined that a man could scarcely find a Church standing at this time in all the country, and as for those that remained, they were all covered with broom or thatch, and as for any Abbey or Monastery, there was not one left in all the country, neither did any man, for the space of two hundred years, take care for the building or repairing of anything in decay."* We have no allusion, either traditional or written, to any incident having taken place here resulting directly from the Norman conquest, therefore the records of this ancient town for a long period are scanty, but such reliable scraps as could be obtained, we continue to quote. The two following are exclusively in connection with the Church, but not the less interesting, whether as matters of church or general history :—From *Sidney Gibson's History of Tynemouth*— "The Priory (Tynemouth) also held the tithes of Corbridge, Ovingham, Wylam, Newburn, Elswick, Warkworth, Bothal, Amble, Rothbury, Wooler, Seton, Chollerton, and Dissington, and many of the Manors themselves became at a later period their property; also the principal part of these possessions was acquired by the Monastery from the gift of Earl Robert (*i.e.* before A.D. 1095) as appears by the under-mentioned charter of Henry 1. These, however, became greatly augmented in after years by the liberality of Kings and benevolence of faithful Christians. Henry I. confirmed to the Monks of Tynemouth all the tithes throughout Northumberland which Robert the Earl or his men had ever given to them." The following is a translation of the King's charter on this occasion :—"Henry, King of England, to Ralph, Bishop of Durham, and to all Baron's, health. Be it known that I have given, to God, and S. Mary, and S. Oswin

---

* *Holinshred's Chronicles* were first published in 1577 in two volumes, and again in three volumes in 1587.

and to the Abbott of S. Alband, and the Monks of ' Tine-mutha,' all their tithes in Northumberland, which Robert the Earl and his homages ever gave to them ; that is to say the tithes of Corebridge, and those of Ovingham, and of Wylam ; also those of Newburn, and those of Discington ; and of Calverdum, and Elswick : and also those of Bothal, and of Warkworth, and of Ambell ; and Roubyra, and of Walloure likewise. And seeing that I will and command it, let the above-said Abbot and Monks of Tinemutha, well and truly have, and in my place freely hold the same ; and let none upon pain of making forfeiture unto me take away anything from thence. Witness, Nigel de Albini at Branton." " Richard I. also confirmed the above charter, December 28th, 1189." From *Hutchinson's History.*—" Corbridge Vicarage.—This Church was formerly appropriated to Tyne-mouth and afterwards given in exchange to Carlisle, but for what, Leland in his *Itin*[*] does not inform us. King Henry I. gave the impropriation and advowson of the Churches of Warkworth, Corbridge, Whittingham, and Rothbury to his Chaplain, Richard de Aurea Valle, and after his death to the Canons of St. Mary in Carlisle, this was in 1128."

The following paragraph was given to the writer by the late Mr. Fairless, of Hexham :—" Colebruge, as Leland tells us, is the old name for Corbridge a village close to Hexham, this deed is prior to 1128, the year *Bishop Flambard died.*[†] Aluric

---

[*] Leland was an eminent English Antiquary, was chaplain to Henry VIII. By virtue of a royal commission, he searched various cathedrals and religious houses for curious records and remains of antiquity, died in 1552.

[†] Flambard stands very prominently in English History as being a Norman by birth, and came to this country with William the Conqueror, took holy orders, obtained several preferments, and in June 1099, was appointed to the See of Durham. He became Chief Justice or Prime Minister of Rufus, and was the chief instrument in the extortions (which knew no bounds) of that dissolute King. He was imprisoned in the tower of London by the new King Henry I., but managed to escape to Normandy, and was afterwards permitted to return and reinstated in the See of Durham. In 1121, he built Norham Castle, in Northumberland, as a defence against the inroads of the Scots, built or enlarged the Castle at Durham &c. As there is such a direct allusion to Bishop Flambard in connexion with this deed, it is probable, that as he had a hand in the arrangement of almost all public matters, that he was somehow interested in those charters also, possibly in framing them. We quote the following from a report which appeared in the newspaper a short time ago, headed :—More interesting discoveries in Durham Cathedral. " The excavations which have been going on in the old chapter house, have resulted within the last two or three days in the discovery of three massive gold episcopal rings. The particular bishops to whom they belonged have not yet been ascertained with any degree of certainty, but the authorities state that two of them were the property of Ralph B. Flambard, Philip de Pictavia, or Hugh Pudsey. The interesting relics were found in stone coffins, which were devoid of all remains, but amongst the debris was a quantity of

or Alfric, of Corbridge, is mentioned in two charters, they are grants to William, son of Aluric de Corbridge, of the lands which Richard, his brother, held in Dilstone, made by Henry Earl of Northumberland, and Henry I. (These deeds possess an unusual value never before printed.")

"In 1135, David, King of Scots, entered England and took Alnwick, Norham, and Newcastle; these, together with Bambrough, which he was not able to reduce, were the chief fortresses near the northern frontier of England. He had for a long time his head-quarters at Corbridge, this was before the Battle of the Standard.* Some state that his armies plundered the adjacent country, but this probably only refers to provisions, for it is affirmed that he respected the Monastery at Hexham and its privilege of sanctuary, and no maurading Scot intruded within the sacred precints; within the Sanctuary crosses which were around Hexham, everyone was safe. There is every reason to believe the same protection was given to Corbridge." In the reign of 6th King John, 1205, the manor of Corbridge was granted by the Crown to Robert, son of Rodger de Clavering, Baron of Warkworth, to hold with all its regalities in fee farm, by the annual service of £40, with the privilege of a weekly market and an annual fair on the eve-day and the day after the festival of St. John the Baptist. It had granted also the privilege of sending two members to Parliament,† which privilege was disused on account of the burthen of the member's expenses ; the names of two are recorded,‡ viz.: Adam Fitz Allan, and Hugh Fitz Hugh.

gold which extended from the head almost to the foot of the coffins, and supposed to be a portion of episcopal vestments."

* The Battle of the Standard specially referred to, took place at Northallerton, on August 22nd, 1138, where David was dreadfully defeated by the northern Barons, more than 12000 Scots lay dead on the field.

† The Parliamentary return of members, part I., 1213—1702, recently published' comprises the foregoing burgesses of Bamborough and Corbridge among the representatives of Northumberland and its boroughs, in the year referred to by Mackenzie. The Knights and Burgesses of 23 Edward 1295, were in number eight, viz.: County of Northumberland, Walterus de Cambou, Willielmus de Halton, Borough of Bamborough, Johannes de Greystands, Willielmus le Coroner Borough of Corbridge, Adam fil Alani, Hugo fil Hugonis, Borough of Newcastle-upon-Tyne, Hugo de Karliolo, Petrus le Graper.

‡ It is stated that at this time the expenses of each member was two-pence per day, which the constituency were required to bear; other constituencies besides Corbridge were unable to bear them, it was considered a great hardship to have to send men to Parliament. The following is a slip from the *Hexham Courant*, November 12th, and signed P.W.:—"In olden times the office of a member of Parliament, or rather a Knight of the Shire, or a deputy from a borough, was considered a very onerous thankless task. The

28

When King John on his expedition of vengeance into North-umberland visited the town of Corbridge, he was so impressed with the idea that it must have been a large and populous city, which could only have been ruined by an earthquake, or some sudden and terrible invasion, and that in either case the inhabitants would have been unable to remove their wealth, that his officers were ordered to make a diligent search for the treasures which were supposed to be buried in the ruins, but there is a tradition, without success.* In the reign of 6th King Edward I. 1278, the manor reverted to the Crown, and was afterwards granted by Edward III. to Henry de Percy, from whom it descended upon his successors the modern Dukes of Northumberland.

An extract from *Dobson's History of Hexham* may throw some light on the means of church building in those early times—referring to Hexham Abbey Church, he says : " The present noble Church was built during the Priorate of Bernard, early in the thirteenth century. It is supposed that Archbishop Gray, of York, contributed largely towards the expenses of the building. The Prior and Canon were themselves very wealthy, and doubtless maintained from year to year a regular staff of architects, masons, and other artisans as was the case at York." In general history we read : " In 1296 the Scots, under Sir William Wallace, burnt the town of Corbridge, plundered and burnt the Church at Hexham ; the Prior and Canons escaping with their lives, but were reduced to beggary."

Mr. Dobson gives a more particular account of this invasion, he says : " At the end of the thirteenth century, when Thomas de Fenwick was Prior, the prosperous career of the restored

---

sending of a burger to Parliament was just as distasteful to the towns as to the persons sent. The return of deputies to Parliament was a heavy tax indeed upon the boroughs; when by a statue of Richard II., they were obliged to allow each representative two shillings a-day, with all expenses incurred in going up and returning home. (Some time previous to this statue of Richard II., the members expenses were fixed at one shilling per day.) In the reign of Henry VI., eleven shillings a-day was the usual fee during their attendance in Parliament. It may be readily imagined that instead of dreading disfranchisement like modern boroughs, by a bribery commission enquiry, boroughs in those days were esteemed fortunate in being exempted from such a burdensome duty as that of electing a representative.

* "Thrice was King John a guest at the Priory at Hexham. In 1201, when he dug for hid treasures at Corbridge. Again in 1208, when on his way to Carlisle, and lastly in 1212, on his way to Durham, when England on his account was lying under the Pope's interdict."—(*Dobson's History of Hexham.*)

29

Monastery of Hexham was rudely interrupted by a destructive incursion of the Scots. On the 8th of April, 1296, the men of Galloway broke into Northumberland, plundering, burning, and slaying without regard to either age or sex. After destroying the Nunnery of Lambly and burning the Priory of Lanercost, they came to Hexham where they plundered and set fire to St. Andrew's Church, utterly destroying its nave, as well as the convential building which had been abandoned by the Canons. All the treasures, both of Church and Monastery, relics, gems, plate, charters, grants, title deeds, &c., were swept away. Among other cruelties the Scots burnt alive about two hundred boys within the Grammar School, of which they blocked up the doors." In the next item, which is from the *Records of Hexham*, we have a little insight into the social condition of the people: "In 1303 Archbishop Corbridge, who was a native of the village, was advised to send his contingent to serve in the wars, and to use every exertion to induce the tenants in Hexhamshire to serve." In 1306 Edward I. visited Corbridge according to Hodgson. Edward was testing records in the presence of several great officers of state at Lanchester on August 10th, at Corbridge August 14th, at Newbrough August 28th, 30th, and 31, Sept. 4th at Bradley, and in Marchia Scotiæ Sept. 6th and 7th, at Haltwhistle on the 11th, and at Thirlwell on the 20th of the same month, and at Lanercost on Oct. 4th, A.D. at which last house (the Priory) he continued all winter.

"Robert de Brus, who never missed an opportunity, entered Northumberland with a large army on the 15th of August, 1312. He burned Hexham and Corbridge, and taking up his quarters near the latter place, sent out his men in every direction to plunder and destroy. In the following year he occupied the same towns, and in 1315 there was another inroad in which the Bishopric of Durham chiefly suffered.

The following is an extract from the *Hexham Courant* :—

"Hexham in 1311.—On the 19th of June, 1311, as we read in *The Lives of the Archbishops of York*, William de Greenfield (1304—1315) successor of Thomas de Corbridge (1300—1304) entered in his register—'We have given to Master Peter de Insula four or five Bucks now fat in Cawood Park, and three Oaks there, and license to Sir John de Insula, or some one

in the name of the said Peter, to take and hunt the wild beasts within our liberty at Hexham.' It is stated in a foot-note that Peter de Insula was Canon of Bole and Sub-dean of York. He was probably born at Bywell, in Northumberland, and on that account Archbishop Corbridge, the native of an adjacent village, calls him 'Carissimu.' Insula was Archdeacon of Carlisle, Wells, Exeter, and Coventry, and Dean of Wells. He died in 1311. Sir John de Insula, his brother, was a Baron of the Exchequer and a great man."

In 1334 William de Kendal was Prior of Hexham. He was ordained Sub-dean of Corbridge by the Bishop of Carlisle.

1334 July 14 Daw Robert de Fergham of Corbridge Chaplain, Coll.

1343—4 Feb. 2nd Daw Robert de Fergham of Corbridge Chaplain, apparently re-appointed (Chaplain of St. Giles Hospital, Hexham.)*

1346 Oct. 17th was fought the batttle of the Red Hills, commonly called the Battle of Nevill's Cross, near Durham. David II., King of Scotland, assembled one of the most powerful armies which had ever crossed the border. He invaded England by the western marches. After burning the Abbey of Lanercost, the Scots pursued their usual route through Cumberland and Tynedale; they sacked the Priory of Hexham but spared the town, reserving it as a depôt for their plunder. The same orders were issued as to Darlington, Durham, and Corbridge. After crossing the Tyne and Derwent, David halted at Ebchester and then proceeded to Durham Moor, where he was met by the English Army in battle and defeated with great slaughter. David himself was wounded and made prisoner.

Having now gone over another important period in the history of this ancient town, viz. : from the Norman conquest, or rather from the reign of Henry I. to that of Edward III., extending over more than 250 years, during which time Corbridge sent its members to Parliament, had its weekly market, and it is probable had its four churches and would appear to have been at its height of prosperity at least in this

* This Hospital (the Spital) was founded by one of the early Archbishops of York for the reception of lepers. King John by a deed dated February 16th, 1200, allowed the lepers to be exempt from the payment of tolls in all they had to buy or sell. It is now the residence of J. J. Kirsop, Esq., bearing the name of the Spital. There are some fragments of old walls still preserved, and a figure carved in oak, supposed to commerate St. Giles.

era of its history. Its subsequent decline may have been caused, to a great extent at least, from the frequent rapacious and destructive inroads of the Scots, from Sir William Wallace downwards for generations. We now quote again from *Local Sketches* which gives the writer's own views of the frequent occurrences in those times. " The little town of Corbridge wears a sort of mediæval appearance. Its two old keeps or peels remind us of times when revenge was a virtue, and might constituted right. In those ' good old times' the Scotch and English borders, like as many rooks in spring, were continually harrying each others nests. In looking back from our present stand-point of civilization to the early ages in our national progress, we are apt to conclude that there was little enjoyment of what we consider the real comforts of life, but in this we forget, that in man there is a quality of adaptation by which he can enjoy life under what would appear to us the most adverse conditions. The fact is we can form a very inadequate notion of the delight our forefathers took in despoiling each other of their property, or even of their lives if necessary."

After those frequent destructive inroads of the Scots the town appears to have been only partially rebuilt, a great portion for ages suffered to lie in ruins; its weekly market having ceased to exist. Three churches appear never to have been restored, and several streets disappear from the page of history. The following short but comprehensive cullings from historians convey some idea of its condition for generations. Leland who visited Corbridge somewhere about 340 years ago, writes: "That the name of divers streets remained here, and he found great tokens of old foundations."

Another writer, of the name of Morden, who published a small *History of Northumberland*, from 150 to 200 years ago, states: " At this day there is nothing remarkable in this town but the Church and a little tower-house, inhabited by the Vicars of the place, yet there are so many remains of ancient buildings as prove it to have been a large and spacious town." In the era of its weekly Market, the Market-place had been supplied with a fine flow of water, most likely a continuous stream, (an essential to a business place of this nature) which had been conveyed in lead pipes from a spring in a field belonging to Mr. Ridley Carr, adjoining the east

end of the village.* So effectually had this supply of water
and its communication been lost sight of, that its very
existence seems to have been entirely forgotten and unknown,
until within the present century, when cuttings for drains
and other purposes discovered the fact, when various portions
of the lead pipe were found and taken out—the greater portion
of this pipe has now been taken out of the ground and the
line of the pipe distinctly traced from the fountain or spring
to its outlet in the Market-place. It is rather curious that
the same spring which supplied the old town with water, at
least 650 years ago, should only, within the last 30 years,
be utilised to supply the present town again. When for this
purpose the workmen were employed in cutting the ground,
for the reception of the new metal pipe, from the "low Pant"
to the spring or fountain, curiously enough—when commencing in the field—came upon the old lead pipe (till then
unknown to be there) which was followed direct to the spring
and was all taken out.† A description of this ancient pipe
and its line may be interesting to many readers of this book.
Its diameter inside is about two inches, made in lengths of
sheet lead of about two feet, imperfectly rounded and united
at the edges by a process called bunting; the lengths were
not all of the same thickness, and others of them wider at one
end than the other, and were all united together by the same
burning process, with a thick hoop or band of lead around

---

* The origin of the feeder of this large spring of water, has sometimes been
a subject of speculation, which the longest and severest drought has never
affected, and which nothing has been known to interfere with from its earliest
notice; and which will fill a three inch diameter pipe, and is quite sufficient if
properly utilized, to supply all the southern and western parts of the village.
Various theories have been put forth as to its whereabouts, but none of them
appear at all satisfactory. In the writer's view the only satisfactory solution
of the question is that the feeder is North Tyne, there takes the opening of a
rock, finds its way underneath Stagshawbank, continues on its subterranean
course underneath the lime stone quarries near Mr. Jamieson's brick works,
until it reaches the back of a rock in Mr. Carr's field and thus rises to the surface. When those quarries were worked many years back, the workmen and
others frequently listened to the dashing of a considerable run of water which
could at any time be heard at a great depth below the level of their workings.
This idea was first suggested to the writer when looking at the outlet or rising
of a similar stream in a field near Nunnick Mill, which has its feeder near
two miles further west in the Simonburn. We now quote from Mackenzie
and leave our readers to their own reflections.—"Below the waterfall opposite
to Tecket, the brook enters a subterranean cavity under a great rock. It
keeps its secret course for a mile and a half, (or more) and then rises in perpendicular bubbles in a field near Nunnick Mill, after supplying which with
its strong and clear stream (having first filled a dam which supplies the mill)
it falls into North Tyne."

† This pipe from which the silver had not been extracted was sold for a
considerable sum.

each joint, and of very rude workmanship. The writer has
a length which was taken out of the Middle Street. Mr. John
Walker, when lately making some improvements in front of
his house, came upon a considerable length which was taken
out, and he retains a fine specimen of it. Mr. John
Jemieson, Trinity Cottage, has perhaps the finest piece, which
consists of more than one length with a portion of a junction,
the junction or branch which is of great thickness and
curiously united with the main by thick straps of lead, a
considerable quantity of solder being used in the process of
jointing, this portion is evidently of rougher workmanship
than the other portions of the pipe.

The line of the pipe after leaving Mr. Carr's field is on the
north side of the Main Street, close by the front of the Low
Hall and Eastfield House, under Mr. Greenwell's and Mr.
Robson's houses on the north pavement in Middle Street,
except when nearing Mr. Atkin's house where it is underneath
it, when near the west end of the street it crosses over and
underneath the corner of Mr. McCall's shop and nearing the
south side of the Cross where its outlet probably was.

The line of this pipe since it was laid suggests a re-arrangement of the streets, both Main Street and Middle Street, (if
Middle Street existed at the time, which is doubtful) for some
of the houses which are on the line of the pipe have been
rebuilt on the site of very old houses which carries us back
for several centuries. The junction or branch of the pipe,
the only one found, was taken out in front of the Old Hall,
its line was direct across the street in the direction of the
lodge, which was built on the site of a very old house, and
when pulled down a few years ago to make room for the new
lodge, and other buildings now the property of H. S. Edwards,
Esq., a portion of a small window, in one stone, with two
shouldered openings was discovered, evidently of ecclesiastical
design. Other portions of ancient buildings have also been
found hereabouts which seems to rather confirm the traditions
that here has been a religious house, or as the tradition goes,
a Priory, and would indicate it to have been a place of
considerable importance, which was supplied with water from
this pipe, and this may probably be further supported from
the fact that the famous Roman table (as the Corbridge
people were wont to call it) was found within sixty yards of

c

this same place, and the Roman silver cup, also previously referred to, was found near here; and a Roman silver cup found rolling in the river, near Bywell, some few years afterwards, was supposed also to have come from this same place; all of which may have been preserved in this house and hidden in the earth to save them from some sudden plundering Scottish invasion, and from some cause, altogether lost sight of and forgotten.

When referring to the re-arrangement of the streets a reference may be made to the limited area of the present Church-yard, as pointing to great alterations which suggest a decreased population, requiring less room for interments. The street north of the Church, which bears the odd name of Scramble Gate,* had been a place of Christian interment. Human skeletons were found here in large numbers a few years ago at the time a drain was being made down the middle of the street. The bodies had always been laid with the head to the west; many of the skeletons being in a tolerable good state of preservation and would appear to have lain there for five or six centuries or longer. In making this drain, and from other drains and cuttings made by Mr. Jemieson, he ascertained the extent east and west of this ancient burial ground, the west line being parallel northward with the gable of the Church, and the east line being about fifty feet further to the east than the end of the chancel, but how far north the burial ground extended cannot be ascertained, as skeletons have from time to time been found on the sites of the dwelling houses and in the gardens beyond them; thus the ground once consecrated by the repository of the sacred dead, on which we cannot now say " tread softly," has for centuries been converted into a thoroughfare and covered with dwelling houses.

The many great tokens of old foundations and ruins of ancient buildings referred to by Leland, Morden, and others would seem to point to the three Churches apparently never rebuilt, as well as to the ruins of buildings being in their immediate locality. As traditional stories are circulated that there were six or seven Churches here at one time, although there is no evidence whatever to warrant such assertions,

---

* Scramble Gate takes its name from the ancient custom, still kept up here, of scrambling money for the populace to scramble for on the occasion of a wedding as the parties come out of church. This would then appear to have been a public way of entrance into the church.

that there were three other Churches besides the present one
there is no doubt, for of this we have indisputable evidence.
The three Churches referred to are now entirely obliterated.
Of the era of their origin, their period of existence, and their
overthrow, as far as we know, there is no written history.
What we do know is the fact that such Churches did exist, for
we have their distinct names, the sites on which they stood,
and scraps of unquestionable confirmatory support. The first
we notice was St. Helens, which stood on the north side
of the village in a field called Hall Walls, so named from
the old walls of the Church, now converted into garden
allotments; portions of the Church walls and the east end of
the chancel were standing at the beginning of the present
century. The writer has heard the late Mr. J. Fairless, of
Hexham, (who belonged to Corbridge) often relate that when
a boy, he was accustomed, with others, to play at hand-ball
against the wall of the chancel. The late Mr. Matthew
Greenwell, father of the present Mr. William Greenwell, often
referred amusingly to his exploits when a boy, in managing to
climb to the chancel windows, where there were several
pigeon's nests and carry off the young ones. It is many
years since all traces of it disappeared. The Church was
situated on the south side of the field, boundering on the two
eastern gardens called The Half Acres, the wall betwixt
those gardens and the allotment is built on the foundation of
a very thick wall, supposed to have been the foundation of the
southern wall of the Church ; on the north side of the allotment is a lane called St. Helens, no doubt derived from the
name of the Church.

Another Church dedicated to St. Mary stood a little to the
west of the Hill Bank Farm House, on the west side of the
lane leading from Colechester Road to Orchard Vale. The
materials served about 100 years ago to build the farm house
and out-buildings. The writer, when a boy, has heard old men
refer to seeing the walls standing in their day. In the south
end of the grainery there is a portion of a window of ecclesia-
tical design, thought to have belonged to the Church.

The third, called Trinity Church, stood a short distance to
the north-east of St. Mary's, its site has long since been converted into a garden and bears the name of Trinity. This is
the only one of those three Churches where evidence of inter-

ments have been found. Joseph Hall, who died a few years ago in his 100th year, told the writer that when a youth he cultivated this garden, and when doing so in deep digging, frequently came upon rows of chisselled stones, no doubt the foundations of the Church, which were always removed ; some years afterwards he found a rather large inscribed stone (at the time he was re-building his house in Princess Street) which he sent home with orders to build it into the wall of the new house, but when returning home in the evening, to his disappointment, he found the masons had used it for the foundations. Whether it was an English monumental or a Roman stone he could give no account. He further stated that numerous pieces of coffin furniture were dug up, but all broken, and all made of lead. About forty years ago as a hole was being dug for a gate post at the end of the lane adjoining Colchester Road and close to Trinity gardens, a large quantity of human bones were discovered, (including a great many skulls) not in the order of burial, but as if they had been deposited in cart loads ; most probably collected from this Church-yard when it had been made into a garden, at the same time, it is likely what coffin furnishings were then remaining would be secured ; the remnants referred to by Mr. Hall only remaining. Mr. William Robinson, who has just completed the erection of two houses on a portion of the east end of this garden, when digging for the foundations and carting away about three feet depth of soil, came upon a number of skeletons (upwards of twenty) all in the order of Christian burial and all of full-grown persons, some of large size, except one which was that of a child—and all quite perfect—on being examined not a single tooth in any of the heads was found wanting. They were all carefully removed and the soil carefully examined, in the hope, like King John, of finding "hidden treasure," but like that Monarch, were only disappointed. The only thing found worthy of notice was a somewhat large arrow or spear head,* which was amongst the bones of one of the skeletons. Near the bones was also found a buckle of the same metal. As to the period of those interments we can only conjecture, but from the perfect state in which the remains were found, and from what

---

* The writer has in his possession the arrow or spear head which is iron, and much rusted, the socket being mostly gone, but the arrow part entire.

inferential evidence we have, it may have been in the early
or middle part of the fourteenth century, as about this time
the neighbourhood becomes somewhat prominent. The Prior
Mannor would then be in existence, for in 1334 William de
Kendal was Prior of Hexham, and was ordained Sub-deacon
of Corbridge, by the Bishop of Carlisle; it is the opinion of
those who have thought over the matter that here was the
country or occasional residence of the Priors of Hexham, and
the house now occupied by Mr. Thomas Bell, which is a very
old one, is stated to have been the residence of the Priors,
and is called the "Prior's Manor House."* Trinity Church (if
not the other two Churches) was most likely standing at this
time† and used for Divine Service,—whether destroyed by
our northern foes or suffered to go to ruin from being disused
we have no record. The present would appear to have been
the Parish Church, and the only one repaired or restored and
used down to the present time.

For centuries the records of this interesting town, whether
written or traditional, are very scanty; supposed generally to
have been destroyed during the frequent destructions of the
town.‡ The following local and historical events are from

* Some one hundred years ago or more, a person of some means occupied
this house, was eccentric in his habits, and took to himself the title of "My
Lord Prior," and was known by that name.

† Trinity Garden still belongs to the Vicarage of Corbridge. The Chantry
or Chantrie, a farm house about half-a-mile to the north of Prior's Manor is
thought by some to have had some connection with Trinity Church. But as
Chantries were small Chapels, or side aisles, which pious and wealthy people
built in their respective Parish Churches, and were dedicated to their patron
Saints, and were liberally endowed with rents or lands for the Chantry Priests,
whose duty it was to pray daily at the altars erected therein, for the souls of
their founders and friends; it is therefore difficult to see what connection
there could be betwixt the two places; except the Chantry could have been a
kind of chapel of ease for the convenience of the Priest, or others living in that
neighbourhood.

‡ Previous to the "division," the freeholders of Corbridge were requested to
send their title deeds, and such documents as gave them the rights of their
freeholds to Mr. Donkin, of Sandhoe, one of the commissioners appointed to
adjudicate in the matter, so that each freeholder or shareholder might obtain
his fair proportion of land, but from neglect or oversight on the part of Mr.
Donkin, and the inconsideration and indifference on the part of the freeholders those deeds were never returned, but after the lapse of many years,
many of them were found scattered up and down the neighbourhood as
waste paper or parchment. We understand many of the documents were very
old, and might, had they been forthcoming, been interesting as historic records.
When the old establishment of the Donkin's, of Sandoe, was broken up about
25 years ago, a great number of old books, paper, and parchment documents,
considered by the party in charge to be of no value, were burned; it was
affirmed by those, who had some knowledge of the nature of their contents,
that many of them were the title deeds, yet remaining on the premises, belonging to the freeholders of Corbridge.

the writings of various authors and sources, as well as from
apparently well-founded tradition :—

There is a field about a quarter of a mile east of Corbridge
called Bloody Acres, or the field of blood,* in which there is
a traditional account of a great battle having been fought,
but at what period is uncertain, most probably an early one,
and may have been the site of the battle fought in 923 betwixt Ragnal the Dane and Prince Ealred of Northumberland,
who was aided by Constantine of Scotland, when the Dane
was victorious.

There is a traditional account of a plague having been here
at an early period. Mackenzie in his *History of Northumberland*, when referring to it, states : " The parishioners here also
purchased the sites of some old houses which stood against
the south wall of the Church-yard,† and this plot of ground
being consecrated, is used for sepulchral purposes. A
great quantity of earth and rubbish was at the same time
removed from behind the Church. The people employed in
this work dug up an immense number of human bones, which
attest the former populousness of the place. The inhabitants
however are persuaded that they are the remains of those who
died of the plague when it raged in the north. There is
a tradition that few survived its ravages, and that these were
preserved by leaving the town and encamping in a large open
field or common called the Leazes, a little to the northward.
When they ventured to return the streets were green with
grass. There is a well, about a quarter of a mile north from
Corbridge, called the Milk Well, which it is said took its name
from a milk market being held here, but when or under what
circumstances is not known. East from the village is an
eminence in a field called Gallow Hill, where it is said
criminals were executed. Another eminence, of higher
altitude, a little to the north-east of Corbridge is also named
Gallow Hill, where it is said criminals were also executed, and

---

* Until within the last one hundred years this field formed part of one great
common on which the battle would be fought; on this particular spot had
probably been the greatest slaughter.

† Those houses belonged to the Duke of Northumberland, and it is said
they were either sold at a nominal price or that the purchase money was
returned. They were built against the Pele Tower and extended westward as
far, if not farther than the present Church-yard gates, and were supposed to
have been as old as the tower, as the beams had rested upon projecting stones,
still visible, which would appear to have been built into the wall during the
erection of the tower.

a little further to the east of this hill is a field called Stob Cross, which it is thought derives its name from the tradition, that the worst class of criminals, after being executed, were there exposed on a gibbet the form of a cross.

An interesting article on Corbridge was published a short time ago in one of the Newcastle newspapers, from which we make two extracts: "In 1293 William Parson, of Corbridge, was taken for a burglary, convicted and died in prison." There is nothing remarkable in the burglary, but how such an occurrence at so early a date has been handed down is remarkable. The other extract is: "That an early writer on Northumberland was Thomas Kirke, of Corbridge, who in 1677 wrote an account of his journeyings in the north of England." No account that we are aware of is known in the village respecting this man.

Corbridge crops up curiously in connection with the suppression of the Monastery at Hexham. As that remarkable proceeding is so full of importance and interest, we may be pardoned for giving an authentic report of what actually took place. We quote from *Dobson's History of Hexham*: being a copy of a curious and stamped office document given by the late Jasper Gibson, Esq., of Hexham, to the Rev. John Hodgson, the author of the *History of Northumberland*, entitled "The misdemeanours of the Religious Persons of Hexham, in the County of Northumberland, 28th Sept. 38 Henry VIII."

"First, whereas Lionel Gray, Robert Collingwood, William Green, and James Rokeby, commissioners for the dissolution of the Monasteries aforesaid, the 28th of the month of September, in the year of our sovereign Lord King Henry the VIII, associate with their ordinary company, was riding towards the said Monastery of Hexham there to execute the King's most dread commandment of dissolution, being in their journey at Dilston three miles from the said Monastery, were credibly informed that the said religious persons had prepared them 'with gonnez and artilery mete for the warre' with people in the same house, and to defend and keep the same with force."—Assented.

That the said Lionel Gray and Robert Collingwood should, with a few persons, repair to the said Monastery as well to view and see the number of persons keeping the same house,

as to desire the Sub-Prior and convent of the same thankfully and obediently to receive the King's commissioners coming near hand to enter into their house with due entertainment according to the King's most dread commandment. The said Lionel and Robert accordingly did enter into the said town of Hexham riding towards the said Monastery, did see many persons assembled with bills, halberts, and other defensible weapons, ready standing in the street like men ready to defend a town of war, and in their passing by the street, the common bell of the town was "rongen," and straight after the sound of it, the great bell in the Monastery was "ronge," whereby the people forcibly assembled towards the Monastery where the said Lionel and Robert found the "yats" and doors fast shut ; and a Canon called the Master of Ovingham, belonging to the same house, being in harness, with a bow bent with arrows accompanied with divers other persons all standing on the leads and walls of the house and steeple. Which Master of Ovingham answered these words hereunder written :— We be twenty brethren in this house, and we shall die all, or that ye shall have this house. The said Lionel and Robert answered with request and said : 'Advise you well and speak with your brethren, and shew unto them this our request and declaration of the King's gracious writings, and then give us answer finally.' And so the same master departed into the house, after whose departure did come into the same place five or six of the Canons of the house, with divers other persons, like men-of-war in harness, with swords girt about them, having bows and arrows and other weapons, and stood upon the steeple-head and leads in defence of their house ; the said Lionel and Robert being without............The said master of Ovingham being in harness with the Sub-Prior being in his canons apparel, not long after did repair again to the said Lionel and Robert, bringing with them a writing under the King's broad seal, and said these words hereafter written, by the mouth of the said Prior : 'We do not doubt but ye bring with you the King's seal of authority for this house, albeit ye shall see the King's confirmation of our house under the great seal of King Henry VIII. God save his grace. We think it not the King's honour to give forth one seal contrary to another, and before any other of our lands, goods, or house be taken from us we shall all die, and that is our full

answer ; ' and so the said Lionel and Robert returned and
met the rest of the commissioners approaching near the town,
and so altogether reculed back to Corbridge where they lay
all that night." The sequel was Henry was so irritated
at the opposition to his will, which several of the Monasteries
but notably Hexham, which had encouraged others to resist
were displaying, issued a characteristic order to his Com-
mander-in-Chief, the Duke of Norfolk, to tie up, to the terrible
example of others, "the Monks and Canons of Sallye Hexham."
Six only of the twenty Canons of Hexham are supposed to
have been so "tied up," and tradition relates that Edward
Jay, the last Prior, was hanged at the gates of his own
Monastery.

1622. December 23rd died Sir Francis Radcliff, and was
buried at his desire at his Parish Church in Corbridge.

1644. January 15th the Scots army, destined for the assistance of Parliament, crossed the Tweed in the depth of a
severe winter, their whole force amounting to 18000 foot and
3000 horse experienced no serious opposition till they
arrived under the walls of Newcastle.............Early on
Monday morning Sir Marmaduke Langdale and Colonel
Fenwick sallied out of Newcastle and surprised and routed
two regiments of Scots horse quartered at Corbridge. This
does not appear to have been a serious defeat, for the next
day they quartered along the Tyne from Ovingham to Corbridge where three English regiments of horse faced them all
day, but drew off in the night, leaving behind them only a
Scots Major, "Agnew," Colonel Fenwick's prisoner, to preserve
Fenwick's house, near Heddon, from plunder. There is a
tradition that when the Scots were quartered here the church
was used as a stable for their horses, and that they were
fastened to the north wall of the nave.*

---

* The following petition shows the way and manner in which the Scottish
army were maintained when quartered in this district :—
"To the Right Worshippfull Commissioners to the high and Mighty Court
of Parliament. The humble petition of Henry Hinde, William Brown,
Anthony Hunter, Matthew Colestone, tenantes to Baron Ratcliffe, of Dilston,
for the whole hamlet of Neuton Hall, in the county of Northumberland, 1644.
Humbly Sheweth, that whereas some of us, have been a long time tenants
and inhabitants there, and farmed that land of him : And all of us conditioned
with him, that he was to undergoe (in his rent) all and all manner of cease-
mentes, the ceasements laid on the church only excepted : And now the rent
of the said land is demanded of us by Mr. Booteflower which we did not
expect should be required, neyther of the landlord nor any others, in regard
that at Candlemus last, our hay, corne, horses, sheepe and beastes, were

42

1745. When a party of the train bands under the command of Mr. Fenwick, of the Coat-yards, were guarding the pass at the bridge of Corbridge, they received intelligence that the rebels were advancing along the south side of Corbridge Fell. The bridge was immediately barricaded with carts and waggons filled with dung, and the train bands resolutely waited the result, but when day-light appeared, the supposed rebels proved to be a large drove of kyloes.

1757. April 15th, Mr. Green, a shop-keeper at Corbridge, whilst putting his gun in order inadvertently snapped it near a ten pound box of gunpowder, and a spark falling into the box, it immediately blew up with a tremendous explosion, by which he was much scorched and his clothes set on fire ; four other persons were much injured. The door being open the house was saved from destruction.

1761. March 9th, the terrible riot at Hexham took place, when fifty-two persons were killed and fifty wounded ; two belonging Corbridge were amongst the killed, viz.: Ralph Shotton and Thomas Richardson ; six more were wounded, viz.: Robert Pattinson, William Richley, Matthew Robson, John Smith, Robert Nicholson, Eleanor Young, and William Vickson Aydon.

1765. Feb. 6th, a market was held at Corbridge for corn, poultry, butter, &c. About three hundred persons attended when a proclamation was made for holding a market weekly on the Friday, pursuant to an old statue previously referred to. This market did not continue long, the reason why is not now known, probably being too near to Hexham. As the Hexham people had been displeased at its re-establishment, its short duration was thus satirically referred to. " Corbridge market began at half-past eleven and ended at thirty minutes to twelve."

1767. As some workmen were clearing away the earth and rubbish from a limestone quarry near Corbridge, at a depth

---

violently taken from us, by the Scottish army; the traine of Artillery lay in our poore steede five days and six nights, the which, our losses wee made partly to appear in our Seedells given in lately at Hexham, and the charge of continuall biltiting and ceasements both before that and ever since, soe that the whole rent (for some years to come) will not countervaile our great losses, and charge imposed uppon that land, and the which we are unable to pay, and to releeve our families, all which we leave to your pious consideration and humbly take our leaves.

The truth hereof we are ready to be deposed and wee have some officers hand to a note in parte hereof."—ARCHÆOLOGIA ÆLIANA.

of about 18 inches from the surface, they found four perfect skeletons. The bones were very fair and exactly in the form they had been in the body when living. They seemed to have been full grown persons as the teeth were white and complete in the jaws. The oldest people in the neighbourhood did not remember having heard any tradition or account of any person having been buried near this place.

1767. This year workmen commenced pulling down Dilston Hall, pursuant to orders from the governors of Greenwich Hospital.

1771. There was a great flood in the Tyne which swept away, in its furious progress, every bridge except Corbridge. The river was then swollen to such a wonderful height that many of the inhabitants of Corbridge washed their hands over the battlement. This was done at the south end of the bridge, the battlement, at that time, being much lower than at present.*

1776. This year an Act of Parliament was passed for the division and enclosure of certain open common fields, stinted pastures, and common moors or waste grounds within the manor and parish of Corbridge in Northumberland. In 1779 July 31st, the said division was completed.

1790. On the road called Diddridge, leading to the limestone quarries and about three hundred yards from its junction with Aydon turnpike road, as a man was driving his

---

* The following is the account given by the Rev. John Wesley in his remarkable journal of this great flood:—"1771, December 7th.—I read to-day a circumstantial account of the late inundations in the North of England, occasioned by a sudden and violent overflowing of three rivers—the Tees, the Wear, and the Tyne. All these have their rise within a few miles of each other, in a mountain at the head of Teesdale and Weardale, on which there was nothing more than a little mizzling rain, till the very hour when the rivers rose and poured down such an amazing quantity of water, as utterly astonished the people of Sunderland at the mouth of the Wear, overflowed all the lower parts of Newcastle-upon-Tyne, and filled the main street of Yarm-upon-the-Tees with water nine or ten feet deep. Such an overflowing of these rivers none ever saw before, nor have we an account of any such in history. Rain was not the cause of this, for there was next to none at the head of these rivers." What was the cause we may learn from a letter written at the time by a clergyman in Carlisle:—"Nothing is so surprising as what lately happened at Solway-moss, about ten miles north from Carlisle. About four hundred acres of this moss rose to such a height above the adjacent level, that at last it rolled forward like a torrent and continued its course above a mile, sweeping along with it houses and trees, and everything in its way. It divided itself into islands of different extent, from one to ten feet in thickness. It is remarkable that no river or brook runs either through or near the moss." "To what cause then can any thinking man impute this but an earthquake?" and the same doubtless it was, which about the same time wrought in the bowels of that great mountain, whence those rivers rise, and discharged from thence that astonishing quantity of water."

wain, drawn by horses and oxen along with several others to the kilns for lime, he was accidentally killed by being jammed betwixt two wains; a boulder limestone, built into the wall, marks the place where the accident occurred.

1793. August 14th, was executed at Morpeth, Margaret Dunn, who had been found guilty of stealing cash and wearing apparel from a house in Corbridge—asserted that she fell a victim to the crime of another woman—*Local Records*. The circumstances, which are somewhat remarkable, in connection with this affair are as follows :—This woman was servant or housekeeper to a man of the name of Summerbell who resided in a house in Watling Street; she formed an intimacy with some dragoons, quartered in the village at the time, who were shortly afterwards ordered to Newcastle. Dunn followed them : first robbing her master of his purse, which consisted of a stocking, which with its contents were fastened to the rigging tree of the roof of the house which she managed to get down* also the contents of the chest which consisted of wearing apparel, which was carried out of the house, the empty chest being found concealed amongst some bushes in the " town loaning." Dunn was followed to Newcastle, and when apprehended, the missing articles were found in her possession. As the money could not be sworn to, she was found guilty of having in her possession a shirt, which was sworn to, which had been made and given to Summerbell by his sweetheart, who died shortly afterwards, on which on the side-piece were his initials in needle-work, neatly done with threads of hair from a lock off her own head. It appears Summerbell never wore this shirt, but preserved it as a sacred treasure.

1807. As the miller's wife of Corbridge mill was sitting in the window she perceived something extraordinary in the mill race (the ancient brook Cor) and on giving the alarm, it was found to be a large shoal of the chub fish, called "dares" in the neighbourhood; the mill wheel stopped their progress, and in order to secure them, some bundles of straw were at once put into the brook at its junction with the river which allowed the flow of water, but prevented the return of the fish;

* A short time ago this house (the property of Mr. John Harle) was pulled down for the purpose of rebuilding; when the thatch was removed, the rigging tree being exposed, was inspected by several persons who had become familiar from village gossip with the occurrence.

a small net was soon procured when a large quantity was taken; many of the villagers hearing of the occurrence hastened to the spot, amongst whom the fish were freely distributed.

1808. October 5th, died near Corbridge, Mrs. Hodgson, aged 105 years.

1809. In the spring of this year as some workmen were levelling a piece of ground on an allotment at Aydon South Common, belonging to Mr. Bullman of Newcastle, they found an urn with the mouth downwards which would hold about four gallons, having a smaller one within it with the mouth also downwards, and which contained a quantity of small bones, which crumbled to pieces on being moved.

1822. May 19th, died at Corbridge, John Chambers, aged 100 years.

1822. March 28th, when Mr. Carr was ploughing in a field in front of Stagshaw House near Corbridge, he encountered a large flat stone, which on being removed, was found to cover the mouth of a cavern about four feet deep, three feet long, and two-and-a-half feet wide, cut in the solid rock. This rude tomb enclosed a small antique urn, composed of clay and sand uncovered, and coarsely ornamented; it contained a few ordinary-sized teeth in perfect preservation, the mouldering remains of a skull, a small heart-shaped amulet of grey slate stone, perforated for suspension; and a tongue-shaped piece of flint, probably an arrow head. There was no inscription on the stones, no coins were found, nor any means of ascertaining the date. A neighbouring farm house retains the name of "The Chantry," whether in any way connected with those remains did not appear.

1824. December 25th, the river Tyne was swollen to a great extent. The Carlisle mail (coach) which ought to have reached Newcastle at seven o'clock at night, did not arrive till half-past eleven on the following morning, as they were obliged to stop all night at Hexham, not deeming it safe to attempt to cross the bridge at Corbridge. The turnpike road approaching the bridge, for a distance of near half-a-mile, being flooded to a considerable depth with a strong current.[*]

* The writer well recollects seeing this flood, which continued at its height nearly the whole day, thus causing considerable damage. The ground betwixt the bridge and the railway, and the entire Eales being completely covered,

46

1826. May 13th, a man named Anthony Jackson, belonging Corbridge, was killed on the Stagshawbank turnpike road when returning from Stagshawbank fair. Deceased was seated on the end of a barrel, in a brewer's waggon, when some mischievous person passing struck the horses which caused them to run away. He was thrown out with great violence, and fell on his head, causing almost instant death. A stone fixed in the wall, on which is an inscription, now nearly effaced, marks the place of the accident.

1827. This year "the new road" was made from the end of Corbridge bridge to Dilston low town, the old road being circuitous and inconvenient.

1828. February 28th, died at Corbridge, Bartholomew Lumbly, alias "The Merchant," a man of some means and eccentric in his character ; to please himself and to entertain and please others, more especially visitors, he built on his own property in the Market Place, and on the west side of his dwelling-house (now the property of Mr. Thomas Harle), a very neat and tastefully designed square building with a battlement on all sides, which he appropriated to the exhibi-

---

west of the station road as far as the cemetery ground was also completely submerged ; the flood skirting the north side of this rising ground, and again spreading out covering all the haughs west as far as the Devil's Water. The only house then in the locality of the flood was Orchard House, near the railway station, in which the water was as high as the oven ; the occupants having to take refuge in the upper rooms. In *Richardson's Local Records* it is stated : "That altho' the mail coach dare not attempt to reach the bridge, 'The true Briton' did attempt and managed to reach it in safety, but the horses had to swim a considerable distance." This is certainly incorrect, as it was impossible for the horses to swim against a strong current and draw the coach, in fact, at no time was the water so deep as to require the horses to swim. We however well recollect witnessing what was considered a very hazardous undertaking.—Mr. Cuthbert Snowball, of Dilston High Town, had arranged to have a child baptised on that day, (being Christmas Day) after the morning service at church, the infant and those in charge were conveyed to Corbridge in a cart, but on the return journey, it was found that the water had risen to a great height, indeed to its highest pitch, but the driver, like a true Briton, being anxious that the friends should not be debarred from enjoying the Christmas Day as well as a Christening dinner, undeterred by the flood, dashed with his precious charge into the water and ultimately succeeded in reaching the opposite side in safety, although the spectators (some of whom are still living) feared that the cart would be overturned and its occupants find a watery grave. During the flood the trunk of a large oak tree was lodged on the gravel bed above the sandy hole, it lay there two or three years, being inspected by many persons ; we recollect it was rather decayed in the middle, and appeared to have been so when standing, as all the other part was quite sound and quite black ; it was nine or ten feet in diameter, and from twenty to thirty feet in length ; it was split up with mell and wedge, and then sawn into lengths by the workmen in the employ of Mr. Green, joiner and cabinet maker, Corbridge, and made into articles of furniture.

tion of a collection of curious and interesting articles, such as are common to museums ; a small garden was attached to it, extending down to the river, which was laid out with great taste and beauty, and was at the time one of the "lions" of Corbridge. After the death of Lumbly, and having no immediate relatives, those interested in the settlement of his affairs having little regard for his collection of curiosities, carted them to the river side where they were destroyed, including all those referred to by Mr. Wright, which certainly might have been preserved.

1829. October 13th, during the night there was a strong gale, accompanied by a heavy and long continued rain. The river Tyne was alarmingly swollen on the following morning, there had not being so high a flood since December 30th, 1815, though its effects were comparatively trifling, owing to its short continuance and rapid fall.* Orchard House at this time was occupied by a family of the name of Ellison, who foolishly kept open the back door of the house, when several articles of furniture, which were on the ground floor, were carrid out and lodged in the orchard amongst the branches of the trees.

1829. This year the southermost arch of the bridge was taken down, being considered unsafe, and a new one erected in its place.

1830. May 28th, died at Corbridge, William Surtees, who entered the army as a private soldier when only a youth, but his uniform good conduct and general intelligence was soon noticed by his superiors, by whom he was promoted to the office of Quarter-master in a new corps called the Rifle Brigade. He served under the Duke of Wellington in the Peninsular war ; on his retirement from the army he spent the remainder of his days in his native village. After his death a book was published, which was previously compiled by himself, in which is recorded in a plain and unvarnished way, the leading incidents of his life, including descriptions of the various battles at which he was present. In the Church at Corbridge, in the wall on the east side of the south transept,

* The floods in 1815, 1824, and 1829, would appear to have been the highest since the "great flood" in 1771, the highest being in 1815, that in 1829 being very little higher than in 1824.

is inserted in a black ground, a white marble slab, on which
is the following inscription :—

In Memory of William Surtees,
Quarter Master, Rifle Brigade,
Who died at Corbridge, his native village,
May 28th, 1830, aged 49 years.
Author of a work, entitled 25 years in the Rifle Brigade,
In which corps he was esteemed a brave soldier
And an honourable man,
But he looked beyond the grave,
And gave every assurance that he was a Christian.

1833. During this year the substantial embankment was
erected, by the late Mr. Thomas Harle, by the south side of
the plantation to prevent the incessant high floods from overflowing and injuring the crops on the Dilston haughs.

1863. This year gas was first introduced into the houses
and streets of the village.

1866. March 1st, died at Corbridge, Joseph Hall, and was
interred on the 3rd, on which day, had he survived, he would
have been 100 years old.

1849. This year the garden allotments, seventy-four in
number, situate on the north side of the village in a field
called " Hall Walls," the site of the ancient " St. Helen's
Church" was kindly granted by Algernon, Duke of Northumberland, to the use of the cottagers in the village for spade
cultivation, at a moderate rent charge.

1868. This year an eccentric lady of considerable ability,
calling herself " The Lady Amelia, Countess of Derwentwater,"
claiming to be the grand-daughter of John, the only son of
James, the unfortunate Earl of Derwentwater, and thereby
the only legitimate heir to the Greenwich Hospital Estates,
made her claim under the following romantic circumstances.
Emerging from Blaydon (where she had been for some
time residing) with a few faithful followers, took up her
abode in one of the rooms of the Old Castle at Dilston, her
friends waving a flag from one of the windows of the upper
rooms, thereby proclaiming that she was now in possession of
her ancestrial home. Mr. Grey, with as much courtesy as
the circumstances would admit, had her removed from the
Castle to the turnpike road, where she was lodged in a

tarpaulin house (sent her from Blaydon) for six weeks, during which time the whole neighbourhood was in a ferment, great numbers of persons daily visiting her. One verse from "A National Song," composed for the occasion and published at Blaydon, conveys a correct idea of the state of affairs :—

"At Dilston a countess sits by the road side,
All through the long night and all day,
And thousands have been from their homes far and wide,
Their tribute of pity to pay ;
For so lonely she sits, near her ancestor's home,
'Neath the folds of a tarpaulin shed ;
To think that a Stenart so strangely should roam,
With a pallet of straw for her bed !

Then stir up the nation its duty to own,
For a Radcliff we know her to be,
And her claims must be righted, her wrongs be made known,
In England the land of the free."

For several years afterwards, by the aid of her faithful retainers —hailing from the borders of the Derwent—she continued to annoy the officials of the Greenwich Hospital ; during the last few years of her life she resided in the neighbourhood of Consett ; in 1880 she ceased to give any further trouble, and was consigned to the quiet silence of the grave. The antecedents of this remarkable woman were never satisfactorily known.

1872. March 15th, the Corbridge Cemetery was opened for interments, the first being on March 25th, and from that date down to December 31st, 1880 there had been 281 interments during the same period a few widows and widowers had been interred in the Church-yard.

1871. October 9th, the remains of the Derwentwater family were removed from the vault of Dilston Chapel and were re-interred in a vault erected in the burying ground connected with the Catholic Chapel in Hexham, with the exception of the last Earl, whose remains were sent by rail to Thorndon, in Essex, to be re-interred in the family vault of Lord Petre. On October 13th, four days after, the Dilston estates were sold by auction to W. B. Beaumont, Esq., M.P. ; thus the last link which united the family ties to Dilston was rudely broken.

1877. As Mr. Robert Patterson, of Aydon, farmer, was ploughing in a field belonging to Mrs. Winship, to the north-

D

west of Shildon Lough,* on what is known as ancient land, and near an ancient well called "Elisha Well," he turned up a remarkable stone, which on examination would appear to be an ancient British battle axe ; it weighs five pounds, and is in shape like a hammer, having a hole through the middle for the purpose of fixing a shaft—one end being wedge-shaped, and the other rather flat like a hammer head—it is in the possession of Mrs. Winship. The late Mr. Dobson Winship, of Aydon, whose ancestors for centuries were owners of these lands, related how he had heard that from some cause or other, after a partial and temporary subsidence of the Lough, a canoe was found, but no further account of this discovery had reached him. It is probable that hereabouts was an early British settlement. About a third of a mile east of the Lough ground, and about the same distance south of the Roman wall, on an eminence called Camp Hill, are the remains of a Roman encampment. The last time the writer saw it, about 20 years ago, the western portion of the camp was still visible, its boundary and trenches were distinctly traceable. The eastern portion was under a state of cultivation.

1879. As some workmen were cutting a drain in a field on the north side of the village, a little to the south-west of the pottery, at a depth of about two feet from the surface,

---

* Hutchinson writes as follows :—"At the south side of the hill was formerly Shildon Lough, where a pleasure boat was kept and where large flocks of wild ducks resorted. A great quantity of rain fell about a century ago at the commencement of the harvest, when the Lough overflowed and burst like a deluge to the westward, sweeping away in its progress not only the crops but the fences. At Corbridge East Field the water turned into the Tyne, leaving immense numbers of pike in every standing pool, nor did the Lough ever after contain so many fish. When Shildon Common was improved the Lough was completely drained and is now converted into pasture ground." Our first recollection of seeing this much talked about Lough, was about the time Mackenzie wrote his history; it then contained a good deal of water, which we believe in a dry summer disappeared. The ground to the extent of several acres was covered with rushes and a strong rough kind of grass, which formed good breeding cover for peewits and curlews, great numbers of which, especially the former, were found here ; we do not recollect ever seeing any wild ducks, but the eggs of snipes, peewits, and curlews, were found in quantities. On nearing the Lough the curlews became alarmed and wheeled above our heads screaming at the presence of the intruders ; we well recollect our first visit to the Lough along with several companions, which was for the purpose of catching young peewits, which we succeeded in doing ; and then doing with them as our predecessors told us they did in their boyish days, run races with them in going home, the writer well recollects that his did not perform well, being too old, after running a few yards it took to flight, those of his companions were capital runners. This was not only the writer's first, but last visit to the Lough on this errand. Since that time the ground has been more effectually drained, and has been good pasture ground for many years.

they found a complete skeleton, apparently that of a full-grown man, eight teeth being in the head ; although perfect, it would appear to have lain there some hundreds of years.

1881. February 3rd, as Henry Whitfield, farmer, of Byers Hall, near Hartley Burn, a strong and powerfully made man, 27 years of age, six feet two inches in height, and weighing fifteen stone, was riding on a young and spirited horse, he attempted to ford the river Tyne, near Featherstone Castle, when it was considerably flooded, and was accidentally drowned, supposed by falling off his horse and being stunned or made insensible by the fall. Although £100 reward was offered for the recovery of his body, it was not found until March 17th, when it was discovered by two tramps lying in a pool about four feet deep near one of the pillars of Corbridge Bridge. Although a number of workmen were employed at the time in widening the bridge none of them discovered it. The reported circumstances under which the body was found are rather remarkable. One of the tramps of the name of James Dublin, residing in Hexham, who had only been out of gaol two days, affirmed that he dreamt two or three nights that he saw the body lying against a bridge. He had been the day previous looking at the railway bridge which crosses the Tyne above Hexham, and also at Hexham Bridge. On the morning in question he left Hexham in company with a man of the name of Frederick Clark, who was at the time travelling with a "grinding barrow," on coming to Corbridge Dublin told Clark about his dreams and how he had been seeking for Whitfield the day previous, but that he would find him at Corbridge Bridge ; arriving at the bridge betwixt eight and nine o'clock, he at once looked over, and his first sight was that of the body of Whitfield, one of his hands being above the water and his face uppermost and quite discernable. It was thought he must have lain there for a few days, having being brought down by the previous floods—previous to the morning of finding the body, the river had been higher and somewhat muddy, so that the body was not discernable until that morning—the following day the river had again risen and become muddy, and continued so for several days. The deceased, when found, was without his coat which had been pulled of, and was found entangled, a few days previously, near Warden Mill. The body was very little mutilated, the

features being quite distinct, and he had both his spurs on.

1881. February 9th, at night there was a great flood in the river Tyne, owing to the rapid melting of the snow on the high grounds on each side of both the Tynes; it had not been so high for 24 years, the entire Eales were flooded and was eighteen inches high on the kitchen floor of Orchard House, near the railway station. A portion of the Stanners and Stanners Road were carried away, and a good deal of damage done to the fields by lodging a considerable depth of sand, happily after it reached its height at midnight it rapidly began to fall, at which time it was running freely over the embankment above the bridge into the haughs, and in a short time must have covered them. The embankments at Widehaugh, and at the Thorns, and at Anic Grange were broken through and the low lands consequently were much flooded.

1881. April 30th, was completed the widening of the fine old bridge over the river Tyne at Corbridge, and to say the least, it is a remarkable specimen of design and workmanship. The bridge was erected in 1674, at which time the traffic was comparatively small, and was for the most part done by pack horses, which accounts at once for its narrowness. This, considering the great increase in traffic and the use of conveyances of so many descriptions, has for a long time caused great inconvenience and been the cause of many accidents, some of them of a fatal nature. Its widening had been for some time under the consideration of the county magistrates. In 1880, however, the work was decided on, the additional width to be three feet (eighteen inches on each side) and the old glent stones, which helped to add to the list of accidents, removed. Accordingly plans of the work were prepared and tenders invited; a number of estimates were received, differing in amount from a little over £700 to near £2000; ultimately the tender of Mr. William Wilson, of Upper Denton, (near Gilsland) was accepted, being somewhere near £940. The undertaking was begun in the first week in November, but owing to the unusually long and severe winter, was not finished until the time referred to. During this period the traffic, which is very considerable, was unavoidably interrupted, for as one side of each arch was done at a time little more than one-half of this narrow space was available for traffic. Although the work was proceeded with during the depth of

winter, when the dangers arising from long, dark nights were to be provided for, yet such were the judicious and excellent arrangements of the contractor, that throughout the entire work, neither crane nor scaffolding of any kind was used, and the whole was completed without the slightest accident to man or beast. The bridge on the top has a fine appearance, the old glent stones being removed, and instead of these a narrow curb stone runs along against the bottom of the parapet on each side. It was the set intention of the magistrates to interfere, as little as possible, with the character of the structure; in this they have shown sound judgment, for on viewing the bridge from below, the work appears an improvement rather than otherwise, for the corbels are so judiciously arranged that the whole has a castellated appearance. In connection with the widening of the bridge it was suggested, as a further improvement, to fill up the hollow betwixt the bridge and its approach from Corbridge, which was estimated to cost £80. A public meeting was held in the Drill Hall, Corbridge, to consider the matter, when a deputation was appointed to wait upon the magistrates assembled at the Quarter Sessions, to ascertain to what extent they would support the project. The magistrates finally agreed to bear one-half of the cost if the village would guarantee to bear the other half, which, on behalf of the village, was agreed to by the deputation. The amount was obtained by subscription in the village and neighbourhood.

A reference to some of the old social and domestic customs of our forefathers, which have long since ceased to exist, may prove interesting to many of our readers:—

The first to be noticed terminated at the division in 1779. Previous to the division, and for ages, every freeholder had his share in each of those large portions of land, then undivided, and had his milk-cow or cows, which were pastured during the summer months in the "stinted pastures," called Stagshawbank and the Leazes or Waddow Leazes. The Leazes contained 336a. 1r. 28p. Each night and morning the herd was collected together (by a man kept for the purpose) for the convenience of being milked; the place of gathering was at the lower end of the Leazes lane, at its junction with the Watling Street, about 200 yards of the road being covered with the cattle at those times. This portion of the

lane, from this long continued usage, is known by the name of "The Cow Lone or Loaning," every freeholder having his stint or stints according to the extent of his holdings, so that he or his tenant owned a cow or cows. Provision was of course made for the housing of the cattle during the winter months, so that almost every house had a barn and byer attached to it. The fare of our predecessors, as well as their dress, was plain and simple—milk, barley, and oatmeal being their staple articles of diet.—Butcher meat, except once-a-week, being then considered a luxury rather than a necessity, and was therefore comparatively little used, at least by the working men.

Another Common-field, called the "East Field," contained 347a. 0r. 36p. Each freeholder had his proportion in this field, which for the most part was cultivated by the respective occupants, no grazing being allowed till after the 30th day of September, when on the evening of that day, "the great bell" of the church was rung, giving notice that all crops not previously removed must be protected at the expense of the occupiers of the same, this usage also terminated at the division. In this same portion of Common-land was a well called "the Main Market Well,"* this is now enclosed in a garden belonging to Mr. Bullman. In ancient times the fair, now known as Stagshawbank midsummer fair, was held in this field, and probably had been so from the time it was granted by King John in 1205, until it was removed—first, for some years to the vicinity of Shaw-well, and afterwards to Stagshaw-bank, as is reported, for the convenience of the Scotch cattle dealers. The ancient Watling Street, along which they brought their cattle, being over Stagshawbank Common or Moor. There is a tradition that there was a great contention amongst the parties engaged in the management of the fair, which arose out of the new management of reckoning time,† some maintained that it should still te held as originally granted on the 23rd day of June, whilst others contended that it should be held on the 4th of July; the dispute is said to

---

* There is no tradition as to the origin of the name of this well, but probably it has arisen from its application in some way or other to the purposes of this great annual market or fair.

† September 2nd, 1752, the new style of reckoning time was adopted by Great Britain, by which the day immediately succeeding was called the 19th of that month.

have been very fierce, neither party being willing to give in, so that for some time the fair was held on both days; the elements however brought matters to a decision which reason failed to do. On the original day there was a terrific thunderstorm, the disputants being wherewithal superstitious, the present day, the 4th day of July was agreed on, and still retains the name of midsummer fair.

An ancient custom, which on account of its antiquity and peculiarities, deserves a more than ordinary description, called "The Full Plough." The last performances of the Corbridge "Plough" lingers only in the memory of a few of the oldest villagers, and which included the well-known sword dancing. In the *Newcastle Courant* of December 26th, 1879, appeared two articles on "sword dancing," in reply to an enquiry the previous week. Both writers considered this custom to be slowly dying out, and was chiefly executed by pitmen from the Tyne and Weir; they both refer to its origin, as amongst other quaint and curious customs, which marked the yule tide of our forefathers. Some consider it to be a relic of an ancient war dance, either of Saxon or Danish origin; others think the sword dance is the antic dance of Chorus Amatus of the Romans; others again think that it is a composition made up of the gleanings of several obsolete customs anciently followed in England and other countries. The sword dancer's song, with the music, which is given in one of the articles, is from the stores of the Antiquarian Society. Their proceedings are thus described:—"The performance was executed by parties of a dozen or more, each with a sword by his side and profusely decorated by particoloured ribbon, resorted to the towns to perform this play, accompanied by song and music. The 'fool' and the 'bessy' were two of the most conspicuous characters in the group, their part being by their antics and witticisms intended to provoke the laughter and stimulate the liberality of their audiences. The captain of the band, who usually wore a cocked hat and peacock's feathers in it by way of cockade, having formed his party into a circle, round which he walked, the 'bessy' opening the proceeding by singing the first verse; the captain following by introducing the various characters personified by singing the succeeding verses. The fiddler, who was one of the party, accompanied the song, in unison with

the voice, repeated the air at the end of each stanza, forming an interlude between the verses, during which the
characters, as introduced by the singer, made their bow,
walked round and joined the circle. The 'besssy' sings :—

> " Good gentlemen all, to our captain take heed,
> And hear what he's going for to sing,
> He's lived among music this forty long year,
> And drunk at the elegant spring."

The captain then proceeds :—

> " Six actors I have brought who were ne'er on a stage before,
> But they will do their best, and they can do no more,
> The first that I call in, he is a squire's son,
> He's like to lose his sweetheart, because he is too young ;
> Altho' he be too young, he has money for to rove,
> And he will freely spend it all, before he'll lose his love.
> The next that I call in, he is a tailor fine,
> What think you of his work ? he made this coat of mine ;
> So comes good master Snip, his best respects to pay,
> He joins us in our trip, to drive dull care away.
> The next that I call in, he is a soldier bold,
> He's come to poverty by the spending of his gold ;
> But though he all has spent, again he'll wield the plough,
> And sing right merrily as any of us now."

Two more verses are then sung representing the characters
next called in, and lastly he introduces himself and walks into
the circle ; after a little more ceremony the dance commences.
It is an ingenious performance, and the swords of the performers are placed in a variety of graceful positions, so as to
form stars, hearts, squares, circles, &c., and are so elaborate
that they require frequent rehearsals, a quick eye and a strict
adherence to time and tune ; towards the close each one
catches the point of his neighbour's sword and various movements take place in consequence, one of which consists in
joining or plaiting the swords into the form of an elegant
hexagon or rose in the centre of the ring, which rose is so firmly
made, that one of them holds it up above their heads without
undoing it. The dance closes with taking it to pieces, each
man laying hold of his own sword."

This account describes, for the greatest part, the performance of the Corbridge " full plough," which consisted of
twelve men of the village, generally young men, dressed much
the same as described and using the same song, but their
movements were regulated by a long cord called the " plough

cord.* When in marching order this cord was double, ten being inside, five having hold on each side, one in front, and one behind ; when thus marshalled they often ran at a rapid pace; whether the cord (the origin of which we have not been able to trace) was used in any other way to assist them in their movements we have not been able to learn. Their proceedings were always conducted during the mid-winter weeks, and their perambulations, which were generally in the districts north of the village, extended as far as Belsa, Capheaton, Swinburn, and the various other mansions in those neighbourhoods, including the villages and farm houses in all those localities. Their popularity may be gathered from the fact that one season the "plough" realized the sum of £70. Their proceedings, for the season, closed by a ball being held at one of the inns in the village, and was called the " plough night." This was the origin of those Christmas gatherings afterwards held for many years, and known by this name. It is now nearly seventy years since the last group of performers was broken up, and the last "plough" held. We well recollect three of those who survived the others, viz.: the squire's son, the captain, and the fiddler. It is many years now since all these men went to their final resting place.

Another old custom, and which still continues, deserves to be noticed only on account of its origin and not for its continuance, which has been in modern times often a moral nuisance rather than otherwise, we mean the " Coins foot gathering" of men and boys. Passing over the orthography of the coins or coignees, point to its position as a place where nearly all thoroughfares converge. The origin of this custom will be made the more understandable by a reference to the turnpike roads, or rather lanes, which were then in existence, and had been for ages previously. The only road or lane, for general use, from Hexham to Newcastle (which was also the

---

* Mackenzie in his *History of Northumberland*, on old customs, remarks:— " That in some parts of the country this pageant is called the ' fond' (*i.e.* the fool) plough, and sometimes the white plough, on account of those who composed it being dressed in their shirts without coat or waistcoat, upon which great numbers of ribbons, folded in roses, are loosely stitched." Hutchinson, who wrote his *History of Northumberland* more than 100 years ago, says: " Others in the same kind of gay attire draw about a plough called the ' stot' (*i.e.* the steer) plough, and when they receive the gift make the exclamation ' largess'! but if not requited at any house for their appearance, they draw the plough through the pavement, and raise the ground of the front in furrows. I have seen twenty men in the yoke of one plough."

58

Newcastle and Carlisle road) was on the north side of the
river from Hexham eastward, past Shordean Braes, Corbridge
Mill, through Corbridge, and on the line of the present road
to Newcastle, as far as the lane which leads to Peepee, this
lane being the original road, proceeded through Plain Tree
Banks, Ovington, Ovingham, Wylam, Newburn, and on to
Newcastle.* In the *Award Book* those portions of this road
at Shordean Braes and the east field are called ancient lanes,
a wide road not being required for ordinary purposes, such as
the conveyance of goods and articles of general merchandise,
what was then required being mostly conveyed to and fro on
horses, for those purposes, called pack horses, or by persons
on foot.† It was not until the rebellion in 1745 when it was
found impossible, for want of a good road, to get troops, but
more especially cannons, despatched quickly and conveniently
from Newcastle to Carlisle, that a good road was decided on.
Accordingly in June 1749 a survey was made from New-

* From the following extract in the *History of Newcastle*, published by
Brand in 1789, this would, at the time referred to, appear then to have been
the road to Newcastle:—' In the year 1297, the Scots renewed their former
hostilities by making an inroad into England, slaying the inhabitants of
Northumberland, and burning and laying waste the country. The inhabitants
with their wives, children, furniture, and cattle, fled to Newcastle-upon-Tyne;
whither also the enemy marched down the northern bank of the river. The
townsmen having made every necessary preparation for resistance, sallied
forth in order to fight them, upon which the Scots turned another way."
' When David II., King of Scots, in 1346, with his powerful army invaded Tynedale from the west, after making Corbridge, (as well as Hexham,) a depot for
his plunder, proceeded to Durham by this road as far as Scotswood, where he
crossed the Tyne, from which, there is a tradition the name of Scotswood is
derived; the river at this place bordered on a forest or wood, which was
probably used to assist them in crossing the river."
In 1745, General Wade's army which had been encamped on Newcastle
Town Moor, 20,000 strong, left for Carlisle to intercept the march of the Pretender, but the General hearing at Hexham that Carlisle was taken, ordered
the army back to Newcastle; the army would thus pass twice through
Corbridge by this ancient way.
Wright in his *History of Hexham* states: that as the Pretender found many
partisans from Hexham, "after 1715, General Wade encamped at Kingshaw
Green, at once to repress any efforts of the discontented, and superintend the
progress of the great military way from Newcastle to Carlisle." His army
would once more pass through Corbridge on this same narrow road and would
cross at the "old bridge," (which was about half-a-mile above the present
Hexham bridge) by which was reached the ancient road to Carlisle.

† Two miles east of Corbridge on the Newcastle road, which is on the line
of this ancient lane, or road, is a house known by the name of "Stoney Vage,"
derived from the custom of its having been a rest or halting place for the
"pack horses" trading betwixt Newcastle, and the western parts of the
country, hence the appellation stop or stay, the voyage or vage, viz. rest. It
is within the writer's early recollections, and some others yet living, of seeing
a strong powerfully made man passing through the village, carrying a heavy
load of goods from Carlisle to Newcastle; on his return journey, his load
generally consisted of articles of cut glass swung over his shoulder, weighing
several stones, but, poor fellow, he was soon worn out.

castle to Carlisle, under the authority of the government, for the projected military road between those places. The \ making of this road was begun near the Westgate, Newcastle, July 8th, 1751, and was finished before 1755 as the following extract from the *Journal* of the Rev. John Wesley will show:—"1755, May 21st, I preached at Nafferton, near Horsely, about 13 miles from Newcastle; we rode chiefly on the new western road, which lies on the old Roman Wall, some part of this is still to be seen, as are the remains of most of the towers, which were a mile distant from each other, quite from sea to sea. But where are the men of renown who built them, and once made the land tremble? Crumbled into dust, gone hence to be no more seen till the earth shall give up her dead." Mr. Wesley would travel on this road as far as Wall Houses. Some short time after the completion of this great road, a new road on the south side of the Tyne was made from Hexham to Corbridge, and thence by Aydon to a junction with this road, near Wall Houses, and thus called "the branch end." On the completion of this branch road, an enterprising man of the name of Johnson constructed a wain or waggon for the conveyance of goods betwixt Hexham and Newcastle by this road, the first conveyance it would appear of the kind for the purpose, used in this neighbourhood. The owner made two journies weekly, passing through Corbridge by the way of Coins.* It was his return journey from Newcastle which gave rise to this assemblage. It should however be borne in mind that at this period the great powers of commerce, of knowledge, and of civilization, in its true sense, had hardly begun to develop themselves, therefore every opportunity of obtaining information on the great or smaller affairs of the nation was resorted to; this was an opportunity the Corbridge people embraced of assembling together and waiting for Johnson's return to "hear the news."†

* The Coins was then much more convenient than it is now, not only for accomodating an assembly, but for general traffic, extending from the gable of the Angel Inn, to the gable of Mr. Forster's house on the opposite side, and continued the same width to Hill Street. The owners of the property on each side, about a century ago (when most people did just as they liked) narrowed the street, dividing the spoil betwixt them. The owner of the Angel Inn, for his share, getting the site of the chemist's shop and premises; the other the northern portion, on part of which stands the United Methodist Free Chapel.

† The arrangements of the people in those matters have been so altered by the irresistable march of progress, that a reference to them may with propriety be made, contrasting them as they then existed with those of the

60

Although this way of obtaining news has long since passed away, yet the assemblage still continues—and sometimes for hours together, in rain or fair weather alike—to discuss and settle local and national affairs, and has been significantly designated " the Coins foot Parliament." It has been suggested to the writer that he should notice another interesting periodical gathering at this place, but for a different purpose, and which continued from the beginning to the middle of the present century, which was the meeting together of reapers every morning during the time of harvest—for the two-fold purposes—of first obtaining an engagement for the day, and next that of " sticking together" so as to obtain a good wage, for they understood quite well that the farmer must have his corn cut at whatever cost. It should however be understood that at this time, as all the corn was then cut by hand, reapers were in great demand, particularly if it were an early harvest, at which seasons the " outside crops" were as early as the " inland." As every tradesman's, as well as every labouring man's sons and daughters grew up, with very few exceptions, learned to " shear," in an early harvest there was a general turn out as this was the time higher wages were to be obtained; general work in the village was laid in—weavers, tailors, shoemakers, joiners, blacksmiths, &c., were in the turn out—also many of their wives, and sons and daughters. The meeting took place at seven o'clock, numbering from 100 to 150 reapers, or sometimes more. The farmers from the outside farms brought long carts for conveying the

---

present time. About the close of the last and commencement of the present century, one newspaper was received once a week in the village by Mr. Winship, owner and occupier of the Angel Inn, who was accustomed to entertain the people assembled at the Coins, by reading aloud " the news of the week."

As late as from 1820 to 1824 or thereabouts, all the newspapers for Corbridge, Sandhoe, and neighbourhood, which did not number more than eight or nine weekly, were received every Friday morning, at the shop of Mr. Thomas Surtees, Water Row, (the then news agent) to be called for by the respective subscribers, or in some cases forwarded to them. About the same period all the letters for the same districts including Ministeracres, were brought every forenoon from Newcastle by the royal mail, drawn by four horses, and were all enclosed in a small bag, and left at the Angel Inn for delivery as best they could be. As the mail coach drew near the inn, the sound of the guard's horn was the signal for a large and sagacious dog to be in readiness to receive the bag, which was thrown by the guard from his box to the dog, who invariably caught it in its mouth, and carried it into the house ; many a time the writer has witnessed this performance. The number of newspapers in the year 1880 sold by Mr. Donnely, on an average were—weekly 260; daily 720—being a total of 980 every week. The increase in the number of letters, and other postal matters are quite in proportion to the increase in newspapers.

reapers there, bringing them home again in the same way. If a great number of carts was in, then was the time to hold out; sometimes the wage was not agreed on till near eight o'clock, when some one would bid threepence or sixpence a day more than had previously been offered, which was accepted as a general bargain; the carts were soon filled, and in a few minutes the ground was clear. Those employed as regular workers on the various farms in the neighbourhood, went with their respective employers, always with the understanding that they should receive the general wage.

In connection with the reaping, which was instituted by the God of Israel, was another ancient custom, that of gleaning.* This was quite a business, for their were many Ruths, as well as farmers. after the character of Boaz; † who, although they did not order the men to leave handfuls to be gathered, yet were kind enough to allow gleaning. The corn gleaned was of great benefit to many families, as greatly helping them to tide over the winter. In fact this was one inducement for several of the heads of families to go out to harvest, as some farmers only allowed gleaning to the children of the shearers. There were others, however, who allowed all to gather who entered the field, being quite aware of this fact, that if there were no young gleaners, by and bye there would be no reapers; the gatherers learning to shear during the dinner hours, and the reaper's ten and twelve o'clock rests. As the harvest was so important, both as regarded the "shearing and gleaning," it was always looked forward to with a great amount of interest; family gleanings averaging from three to ten bolls, or even more. It is quite clear to those who recollect those times that there was manifest much more forethought and thrift, by the labouring population generally than there is now, notwithstanding that the wages were much lower and money harder to earn—there was a greater amount of self-reliance—provision, if possible, being made for a "rainy day."

We naturally wind up these remarks on harvesting with a short account of the finish or "kern supper." The origin of this ancient and somewhat singular custom we will not enter into, but simply state that some think it is of Jewish, and others that it is of Pagan origin, which was celebrated in

* Leviticus xxiii, 22. Deuteronomy xxiv, 19—20—21.
† Ruth ii,———

different ways in different neighbourhoods ; we only refer to
it as it was observed in this locality. The "kern" was of
course on the last day of reaping, which was so arranged as
to be finished about four o'clock, and with the majority of
reapers, especially the younger portion, was looked forward
to as a day of special enjoyment. The custom on several
farms was to have a colour and a large dressed doll called the
"kern baby or harvest queen"* carried on the top of a pole;
the colour and image were carried to the field with the
reapers, sometimes accompanied by a fiddler, amidst great
rejoicing. If there was no fiddler, then the performance (for
such it was) was commenced by one of the light-hearted
females repeating the well understood signal "kern-a-kern
a hee-hoo:" after which there was a chorus of cheers and
tripping of feet until the field was reached.† Matters went on
thus merrily until near the finish when there was often a
struggle for the "last cut," after which a kind of song or ditty
was rehearsed, something like the following :

> "Our master kind has cut his corn,
> God bless the day that he was born,
> Many years yet may he live,
> Good crops of corn to cut and sheave."

As the closing part of the days' proceedings is so accurately
described by Mackenzie in his account of *Northumbrian
Customs*, we quote his remarks : "When the harvest is finished
the reapers and servants of the family are provided with a
plentiful feast, accompanied with mirth, dancing, and singing.
This is called the 'harvest home or feast of ingathering,' but
generally the 'mell supper, kern or churn supper.' On this
festive occasion there is much freedom and jollity, intermixed
with rustic masquerading, and playing uncommon tricks in
disguise. Sometime a person attired in the hide of an ox
personates the devil. This sport is probably the remains of
an opinion which anciently prevailed of an evil genus that
reigned on earth during the absence of the sun from our
hemisphere, and which was thus typified by a person appearing in a horrid disguise. Bourne supposes that the original

---

* The image is thought originally to have represented the Roman Ceres, the
god of plenty

† The first kern supper the writer recollects seeing with the colour flying,
&c., &c., when he was a boy some 58 or 59 years ago, was that of the then
Vicar, the Rev. G. Wilson, who cultivated his own land, and finished with
what is understood as a jovial kern supper.

of the harvest supper is Jewish, but the rejoicing after harvest
is of higher antiquity. That men of all nations where agri-
culture flourished should have expressed their joy on this
occasion, by some outward ceremonies, has its foundation in
the nature of things." After the introduction of reaping and
raking machines, a generation ago,* reaping and gleaning
naturally terminated.

Another custom which has existed for ages, but now
in a very unassuming manner, is the usage of declaring
and maintaining the rights of the lord of the manor,
which is done on the mornings of the two annual fairs held on
Stagshawbank, and called in Corbridge phraseology "riding
the fair." This consists in a procession on horseback, of the

---

* The reaping machine recalls a circumstance which took place before the
writer was born, but which he has often heard referred to by the old people.
At that time it was considered, if not an insane act, one at least dangerous to
the welfare of the labouring classes, but like the commencement of the
steam engine, it proved to be only the beginning of the greatest and most
important developement which has yet been made in agricultural machinery.
We refer to the reaping machine. Strange as it may appear from our present
stand-point, it is nevertheless true, that somewhere about 60 or 70 years ago a
reaping machine, (where it was made and who was its inventor was not known,
that was kept a secret, the maker not daring to try it in his own neighbourhood) was brought to Corbridge for a trial; the maker was allowed to have it
tested in a field of barley at the east end of the village, belonging to a
gentleman of the name of Hall. A great number of persons both young and
old, men and women, assembled to witness the performance; in fact, the
village was almost emptied of its inhabitants; there were also a considerable
number of persons from the adjoining farm places. It was a time of great
excitement; it appeared as if the future welfare or ruin of the labouring
people hung upon its failure or success. Mr. Edward Fairley who died in 1880,
and Mr. John Bowman, senior, still living, who is 86 years of age, were both
present on the occasion, and recollect a good deal in connection with the
effair, (which they related to the writer). The machine was drawn by two
horses, and they described it as having two broad flat knives fixed together in
the shape of a ʌ, and the form of the machine somewhat round and high,
and in appearance resembled a pike of hay. The horses during the trial
plunging before it amongst the standing corn, but it would not cut any, and
proved a complete failure; when this was known loud and repeated cheering
from the large assembly testified their joy at the result. It was well for the
man in charge (both Mr. Fairley and Mr. Bowman stated) that it did fail, for
the feeling was so strong against him, that had it succeeded, it was likely that
both the machine and its owner would have been roughly handled; the poor
fellow being aware of this, did not attempt to remedy its defects, but took his
departure as quickly as possible, leaving his machine behind, which was
allowed to rot away in the Angel Inn yard.
The great revolution which has since then taken place, both in public
opinion, and in the perfecting of reaping machines, may be estimated from
this fact alone.—That during the last thirty years, upwards of one thousand
reaping machines have been made and sent to all parts of the kingdom from
the celebrated machine works of Mr. Sinn, of Newton-on-Tyne, whose extensive works are within two miles of the spot where the first machine was so
unsuccessfully tried. The writer recollects well witnessing, in their early
and progressive days, a trial of several reaping machines, and with what
delight he noticed a machine from this establishment doing its work so comparatively easy and with almost perfect adaptation to its requirements.

64

Duke's officials first proceeding from the Angel Inn to the Market Cross, where the proclamation is read by the manor bailiff or his deputy, declaring and defining the rights and prerogatives of the lord of the manor. This procession, half a century ago or more, was considered a great treat to see, and always followed through the village by a number of youngsters and a few adults. In addition to the bailiff, were two sturdy yeomen, originally the Duke's constables; the embodyment of legal manorial authority, one carrying the ancient halbert, the other carrying the staff, each painted and gilded in an imposing form; also two pipers, one called the Duke's piper, well dressed and wearing the Duke's livery, the other known as the Duchess's piper, somewhat gaily and fantastically dressed and wearing the Scottish plaid; at the cross the procession was generally augmented by several of the Duke's tenants; on arriving at Stagshawbank they were joined by several more of the Duke's tenantry, all of whom proceeded to ride round the boundary of the fair, after which performance and again reading the proclamation, the company proceeded to the manorial tent where they were regaled with abundance of good things to eat and drink.* Of late years this custom has been shorn of its ancient grandeur and is now conducted in the plainest manner, having only one piper, and attracts very little attention.

In connection with midsummer fair we notice (with its associations) a once popular and general custom, and which extended over a radius of twenty miles or more in all directions, viz.: the custom of men and women in about equal proportions (each dressed in their Sunday clothes) assembling and meeting together there, almost, if not, in thousands. Friends met each other there who often had no other opportunity of doing so, but the great majority met there with no other object than that of having a day's enjoyment, which sometimes, like so many promised earthly pleasures, was reversed by unwelcome torrents of rain, making it a day of misery rather than one of pleasure,—these however were

---

* A court was held and now is (although now merely formal) on and during the fair, and in the proclamation is called the court of "Pie Powder," which according to Dr. Johnson, is "a court held in fairs for the redress of all disorders committed therein," and signifies from Pied-foot and Pouldre, dusty that for any misdemeanour the offenders could at once, with the dust on their feet, be taken before this court. The bailiff of this division of the manor constitutes the court.

exceptions. The attending of this fair was considered the
one great holiday in the whole year, and was generally made
a special condition in the agreement betwixt master and
servant.* For the information of those who were not born
thirty years ago, something like an outline as to how the
people held high carnival on that day may prove interesting,
although it is only those who have been there in the early part
of the present century who can form an adequate idea. It
should be understood the time referred to was long before
the days of railroads, and in many localities before ordinary
turnpike roads, and a little further back still, in many
neighbourhoods before the days of civilization in its true
sense had begun. Upwards of fifty years ago the old people
used to relate how, in their early days, young men from the
districts beyond Bellingham came in groups or clans for no
other purpose than to provoke a fight, which they never
failed to do; when the well understood battle cry of "tarset
and tarryburn, yet, yet, yet," resounded through the fair, then
dogs and human beings joined in a scene of wild confusion.
In the writer's earliest recollection this fair was in full swing;
happily those scenes of brutality had become things of the
past. This fair, which was one of business as well as
pleasure, was the largest held in England for one day! and
for business, people came to it from all parts of the United
Kingdom.‡ Besides horses, sheep, cattle, and swine, various

---

* There were no nine hours' movement, nor a one weeks' holiday, nor even a
half holiday in those good old times—twelve hours, and in many cases fourteen
was the labourer or workman's day—six full days in the week, with some exceptions of two hours on the Saturday, but these were special.

† Mackenzie who published his History in 1825, thus refers to it.—"On the
common called "Stagshawbank," two miles north west from Corbridge, and
three miles north east from Hexham, are held two of the largest fairs in
England; one on the fourth of July when upwards of 100,000 sheep are usually
shown, principally of the black-faced heath kind, which mostly come from
the south west of Scotland. There are also a great number of cattle, horses,
and swine, and various articles of merchandise." The other fair is held on
Whit-Saturday, and is one of business only.

‡ Mr. Raine in his memoirs of Mr. Hodgson, the historian, gives the following
account of their visit to Stagshawbank Fair:—"I met Hodgson at Newcastle,
from which place we started on the 4th of July, 1825, on our expedition. My
brother rode on a favourite pony; Hodgson and I sat side by side in his little
carriage, and a few miles to the west of Newcastle, I first became acquainted
with the Roman wall. The day was fine and my companion was in better
health than usual, and very communicative and amusing.

Upon reaching Stagshawbank, a large open track of ground not far from
Corbridge, inclining swiftly from the Roman wall to the Tyne, we found ourselves in the midst of a great annual fair held on this declivity, chiefly for
cattle, but in truth, for goods of all kinds—'things,' as an old inventory at
Durham has it, 'moveable or moving themselves.' At this place, which is a

E

articles of merchandise were offered for sale, consisting of
men's hats, boots and shoes, these articles generally filled
several stalls, the former being mostly from Hexham, and a
considerable quantity of the latter from Corbridge.* Jewellery
and hardware stalls were prominent; saddlery and farming
goods, such as hay rakes, forks, &c., were always plentiful;
and always a large supply of cooperage goods, such as tubs,
barrel churns, &c. Webs of cloth coarse and fine were shown
to advantage on the green carpet by the side of the pond.|
The far-famed gloves, known as the "Hexham Tans," suitable
for all purposes and for all classes, always formed noticeable
articles of sale. Care was always taken by some thoughtful
business man to make provision for the better part of man's
nature. A great variety of useful books were shown, suitable
for the most profound thinker as well as useful for the general
reader. On the south side of the Horse Fair, in the
distance you saw a strong-made man somewhat elevated, with
a crowd around him offering articles for sale; on approaching,

solitary field at a distance from any population, there are great well-known
periodical gatherings of buyers and sellers, from the whole north of England,
on the western or eastern coast; and the southern counties of Scotland, send
forth in abundance, their men and goods to buy, sell, or be sold. Here we
met Hodgson's eldest son, a lively and intelligent lad of thirteen, well mounted
on a stout Shetland pony, upon which he had ridden across the country from
Whelpington, in company with a friend, to see, for the first time in his life,
the humours of this far-famed fair, but upon which, upon an offer being
made to him by his father, he willingly turned his back and became our companion. Before our departure, however, we spent an hour in surveying this
scene of bustle and activity, which to myself and my brother, as well as to
the boy, was of a very unusual kind. In a large pasture upon the slope of a
hill, with a wide prospect extending down the valley of the Tyne as far as
Gateshead Fell, and in every other direction except to the north, having an
almost unlimited view of a spreading tract of country, there were gathered
together without the slightest attempt at the order which is of necessity
observed in markets and fairs held within the walls of a town—horses, sheep,
and cattle, and swine, and in short, everything which is bred or of use in
farming operations, with thousands of other things which it would be no
easy task to enumerate; and then there were people of all ages, from all
quarters, and in all kinds of costume, the Scotsman in his kilt and the
Yorkshireman in his smock frock, and every variety of booth or hut for
refreshment or dissipation."

* Boots and shoes were subject to an official inspection by two cordwainers,
annually appointed for this purpose at the court of the lord of the Manor,
held in Corbridge, and called "searchers and sealers of leather." If upon
inspection any of these goods were considered of inferior quality, they were
condemned as such, seized and brought to Corbridge; often to be laid aside as
lumber in the court room.

†From the Household book of expenses of Sir Francis Radcliffe, of
Dilston:—"1678. May. My Lady Radcliffe to buy cloath att Whitson faire at
Stagshaw, £10."

Articles of merchandise were sold alike at both fairs until the beginning of
the present century, when they continued for a time to be mostly sold at
midsummer fair, and for many years before their discontinuance, were sold
exclusively at the latter fair.

we observe that it is Mr. C———, from the once famous Dog
Bank, Newcastle, selling watches by auction, being for the
most part forfeited pledges, the auctioneer assuring the public
that each watch he offered was far superior to the one just
sold, as once belonging to some squire or gentleman whose
name was well known in the neighbourhood. This man
regularly attended the fair for many years and had his share
of business. Amidst all this whirl of busy life, the " little
busy bee " was not forgotten, for there was always a good
supply of " bee skeps," to meet the wants of those whose
tastes were after the sweetness of honey in the comb. In all
the articles named and others not named, the day being
favourable, a good trade was done, in fact this was almost the
only opportunity during the whole year that numbers of persons, especially from the outlying districts, had of obtaining
them.*

The stomach, that important part of humanity, was never
once overlooked or forgotten; for the supply of immediate
wants (outside the tents) there was an abundance. From a
long row of gingerbread and orange stalls could be heard
some dame crying out lustilily " boole up and buy a way,"
others were shouting at the top of their voice " London spice
twopence a package," while others displayed along the length
of their arm twenty-four squares of gingerbread offered at a
shilling the lot ; oranges, cherries, Barcelona nuts, &c., were
plentiful. The vendors of all those articles whose names were
many, each striving to make as good a day's work as possible,
used all their skill to attract the attention of the public to the
superior quality of their goods, " crack and try before you buy,"
with a measure half-filled with the bottom, was the ditty of
the nut mongers, making the fair with other clatter, often
mingled with the roar of Wombwell's lions, almost a Babel.
It is stated by one who took notes on these occasions, that
tons of gingerbread and ship loads of oranges were devoured
on that day. In addition to what was consumed in the fair,
immense quantities were carried home, for it was the custom
for almost every one to do so, carrying it in their pockets or
handkerchiefs (for there were no bags in those days), and this

* Some idea may be formed of the usual extent of business from the amount
of £10 being taken by one jewellery and fancy hardware stall from Hexham,
and a few years later, another stall in the same line from Corbridge, took
upwards of £30 when the popularity of the fair was on the decline.

was called "their fair." The usual kind of drink was ale of which a considerable quantity was used;* as this was long before the days of teetotalism, few had any scruple to take as much at least as to quench their thirst, in fact no other beverage was thought of or provided : notwithstanding this, the writer is persuaded, all things considered, there was less intemperance than at the present time amongst similar gatherings.

To the thoughtless and giddy, this fair held out many temptations, all the little gambling arts which were then in use were in full swing; two of the most notable in this class, we notice.—That well-known character, the famous showman of the North "Billy Purvis," a man of many parts, attended regularly for nearly a generation. He had a booth, inside of which it is said he performed wonderful sleight-of-hand tricks, without the aid of apparatus. From the stage outside his booth, could be heard at a considerable distance, his stentorian voice shouting "come this way and see wor show," which at once let you know the whereabouts of "Billy," who with his painted face and gaudy dress, with his witticisms, drollery and gestures, always attracted great attention ; poor Billy has long since ceased to walk on a broader stage than that of his booth, having laid down his load of life in Hartlepool, and his place knows him no more. Another well-known character, a queer little hunchback fellow, who was known by the cognomen of "wallop-a-way" attended equally with "Billy," his vocation always appeared to be a simple way of getting a few pence, and could hardly come within the range of gambling. He was a noisy little fellow ; shouting all day long "a penny a throw, a penny a throw, miss my pegs and hit my legs." He always had a good number of lookers on, and did a good share of business principally amongst the juveniles ; poor fellow, he has long since followed in the wake of "Billy," and his voice is heard no more. Many shows were there of different sorts, the most attractive being that of Wombwell's collection of wild beasts, &c. The writer well recollects when a youth his first look at this wonderful exhibition as being a grand sight, and recollects also a little incident which occurred at the time.

* There were tents from districts extending to twenty miles or more in all directions, to which all parties from those said localities resorted ; each tent being known by a large fly on which was the sign of the inn or public house the name of the owner, and the place it hailed from.

A woman who was walking too near the side of the cages, of which in an upper apartment were kept a number of monkeys was eyed by one of them, which quietly pushing his long leg through betwixt the bars of the cage, and with his paw unceremoniously pulled off the crown of her bonnet, to the no little dismay of the good lady. At one time there were besides Wombwell's, two other large collections, owned by persons of the names of "Pit Cock," and "Polito," these exhibitions invariably secured a large attendance. Now to return to Corbridge from which we have somewhat (we trust not uninterestingly) wandered. On the afternoon of that day it used to be said that Corbridge could be easily taken. For business, persons attended the fair in the forenoon and those for pleasure in the afternoon; those who had been doing business returning again in the afternoon, when few only were left, as the old and infirm, the sick, and mere children, and a few others whose home duties necessitated their remaining. The exodus homewards commenced about five o'clock, which increased to about seven, when it became general; by eight o'clock, the great proportion of pleasure seekers as well as those of business were wending their way home, which many of them could not reach before morning; such is a brief outline of the doings of the busy multitudes on that once great day, as Corbridge was the thoroughfare for nearly all who came from the south; we often, more than a generation ago, when looking at the crowds of people so eagerly rushing onward to the "Hill," were forcibly reminded of the lines written by Dr. Watts.

> "The busy tribes of flesh and blood,
>   With all their cares and fears,
> Are carried downward by the flood,
>   And lost in following years."

Near half-a-century ago the writer was personally acquainted with many from a distance, and with a great number of others by observation, who both for pleasure and business regularly attended this fair, and many of them for years afterwards. But as time rolled on their numbers gradually decreased, and of all those whom we knew or had any recollection of, about the time we refer to, only one to our knowledge attended the midsummer fair in 1879; the great proportion of them having

ended the journey of life, and not a few of those with whom we were well acquainted, had previously prepared for the life beyond.

Another ancient custom, and the last we notice, has also been swept away by the irresistible rush of social progress, viz.: " The Court Leet and Court Baron " of His Grace the Lord of the Manor, which was generally held at Easter. It must have been of considerable importance as a court of justice and equity at the time it was granted and long afterwards, and probably the only court of decision for such matters as was included within its limits, which was for the recovery of small debts, many such cases we have heard tried, several of them of an amusing nature. A school master of the name of Armstrong, a man in his day of some importance in the village, was the local bailiff of the court, whose business it was to summon jurymen, to serve summonses for cases of trial, and to see that the decisions of the court were executed. The court day at this time was a kind of holiday, being generally considered a day of some consequence ; the retinue of the court officials attracting a good deal of attention as they paraded the streets in their official capacity, to decide by their united wisdom such cases as their attention had been called to, which were generally matters of alleged encroachment, always taking care in a verdict of approval, to secure an acknowledgement to be paid to the Lord of the Manor. A part of the ordinary business of the court was to revise the list of freeholders, to appoint two searchers and sealers of leather, to appoint two constables who were duly sworn as such, and originally, to protect and defend the rights of the Lord of the Manor (and before the appointment by the government of rural police constables, were also sworn before the magistrates to serve as constables for the parish). After the formation of county courts for the recovery of debts the business was of the most formal kind, the most important part was that of being regaled with a sumptuous dinner, provided for the officials of the court and jurymen and a considerable number of freeholders and tenants of his Grace, who attended by invitation ; thirteen years ago this court became one of the things of the past.

71

DESCRIPTION OF THE VILLAGE.

BEFORE giving a description from our present stand-point, we quote first from Hutchinson, who visited Corbridge in about 1765 or 6. "Though the town makes a pretty appearance at the foot of the vale when you see it from Hexham, it disappoints the traveller greatly on his entrance to find it dirty and disagreeable."

Hodgson, who was here as late as 1830, gives the following account. "Corbridge, 6th May, 1830, the town (for such its antiquity demands that it be styled) is dirty, and in all the streets except that through which the Newcastle and Carlisle road passes, is filthy with middens and pigsties, with railing before them of split boards, &c. The population seem half fed; the women sallow and thin armed, the men flabby, pot bellied, and tender footed; but still the place bears the appearance of being ancient. Many of the houses, even in the back streets are large, and should be carefully examined for arms, &c." So far as relates to the streets this description is correct, but in reference to the appearance of the inhabitants, what Hodgson says, mostly refers to one family which we believe he happened to come in contact with, and which to our knowledge is greatly overdrawn; we are inclined to think he must have been in a bad humour when he penned these remarks.

The late John Jemieson was the first who really took any interest in the sanitary improvement and appearance of the village, being to a considerable extent invested with this power as "road man" for the township. He spared no trouble within his reach to improve the condition of the streets, and to have removed the pigsties, ash heaps, &c.; in doing so, he incurred the displeasure of not a few of the inhabitants, as invading their ancient privilege of doing as they liked.

The village as it exists at present is large and well built, delightfully situated in a beautiful valley on the north bank of the Tyne, on a gentle slope towards the south, with its gardens dipping into the river, and is sheltered from the chill blasts of the north by high hills; and on the south at the distance of half-a-mile, rises a hill of considerable altitude, the sides of which are studded with beautiful villa residences and ordinary dwelling houses; on the top of the hill is a beautiful little mansion and farm stead, lately erected by Joseph Temperley,

72

Esq., who for several years purchased from time to time considerable portions of land, part of which was under cultivation, other portions uncultivated being covered with whins and heather, which by his energy, skill, and liberal purse was soon brought into a high state of cultivation. From the top of this hill, in all directions is seen one of the most delightful prospects in this part of the country. A little to the south, peeping through amongst the trees, is the far-famed mansion "Ministeracres," the residence of the family of Silvertops; near it the more modest mansion "Healey," the summer residence of Robert Ormston, Esq., of Newcastle, and a little to the west, the straggling village of Slaley; from this elevated position could at one time be seen, the following parish churches and chapels of Ease, viz.: Whittonstall, Slaley, Warden, St. John Lee, St. Oswald's, Hexham, Corbridge, Halton, Newton Hall, Bywell, St. Andrews and St. Peter's, Ovingham, Ryton, and Newburn; recent plantations now prevent some of these from being seen. At the foot of the hill is the railway and station, betwixt which and the village is the lovely "Tyne," with a beautiful valley opening to the east presenting a wide extent and a great variety of undulating scenery; towards the west, is a fine prospect extending over many fertile haughs, giving a panoramic view of hill and dale, of wood and water, commanding at the same time a full view of the ancient market town of Hexham, with its venerable abbey church, rich in ecclesiastical antiquities; beyond Hexham is distinctly seen the site of the British encampment on Warden Hill. On the rising ground at no great distance is seen nestling amongst the trees, Beaufront Castle and the mansions of Sandoe and Stagshaw; about a quarter-of-a-mile behind the latter is the large common, on which are held the famous Stagshawbank Fairs; a little further to the east, stands out with its grey massive walls as if in bold defiance—the Border Fortress—Halton Castle, and near it, yet beautiful in antiquity, Aydon Castle; another interesting spot presents itself to view, the shattered ruins of Dilston Castle with its ancient domestic chapel: the last but not the least interesting object is the beautiful recently erected Corbridge cemetery, the last and quiet repository of its inhabitants. Descending from the top of the hill, and standing on Farnley Road or on the ridge of the hill, a little to the east of Shorncliff House, Corbridge has a delight-

ful and pleasant appearance, and can be there seen with the best effect; this is in a great degree owing to the num-\ ber of gardens it contains, and by which it is almost surrounded, a great proportion of the houses having gardens attached to them; the scenery is not a little enhanced by the appearance of the fine old bridge which spans the river. The village is also seen with good effect from a western stand-point.

The absence of all manufactories or anything causing injury to health, the situation of the village, its fine springs of water, its health-giving breezes, its pleasant walks, its nearness to the railway station, all contribute to make it a delightful and enticing resort for visitors in quest of recreation, enjoyment, or health. We now quote from Mackenzie's history, published in 1825: "Corbridge is about sixteen miles west of Newcastle and four miles east from Hexham. It is esteemed a peculiarly healthy place, and of late has been much frequented by persons out of health.* It is divided into eight streets, viz. : the Main Street through which runs the post road from Newcastle to Hexham ; Prince Street, upon the Harlow Hill Road ; Dunkirk Street, upon the ancient Watling Road : the Middle Street ; Hearn's Hill ; Scramble Gate ; the Water Row, and Back Row. These streets by the returns in 1821 comprised 230 houses, which were occupied by 1254 inhabitants, viz. : 613 males and 641 females.† Most of the inhabitants are mechanics, principally

---

* It appears from the bills of mortality, in 1822, that out of thirty-seven deaths, eighteen were from 60 to upwards of 100 years of age. In examining the register of burials for this year, we find that one died at the age of 99 and another at the age of 100 years.

† According to the Census of 1871 the population of the Parish was as follows :—

Corbridge Village...............	1123	and Township, including Village	1397
Dilston Township............	255	Halton Shields Township...	67
Thornbrough do.	85	Clarewood do. ...	53
Aydon do.	64	Whittington Great do. ...	209
Aydon Castle do.	34	Do. Little do. ...	22
Halton do.	39		
		Total in Parish	2225

The returns for 1881 show the population of the parish as follows :—Corbridge village, 1186; township, including village, 1593; which is an increase on the township, as compared with 1871, of 196; of this number 749 are males and 844 are females, inhabiting 337 houses.

The parish is curiously divided into what is called the civil and ecclesiastical districts; the civil parish comprises the townships of Corbridge, Dilston, Thornbrough, Aydon Castle, Aydon, and Little Whittington. The other four townships comprise the Chapelry of Halton; the whole designated the ecclesiastical parish, and containing, according to the present census, a population of 2363.

shoemakers; a considerable quantity of shoes being made here for the lead and coal miners, and the inhabitants of the adjacent country. Corbridge contains eight inns and public houses, also sixteen shops for the retailing of various articles. The market place is a spacious area, near the centre of which stood a cross, which was taken down about fifteen years ago. It is now in the possession of George Anderson, Esq., who has erected it in Nuns Field, near his ancient house in Newcastle.* A new handsome cross was erected in 1814 by the late Duke of Northumberland............Nearly the whole village is parcelled in small freeholds, varying in value from forty shillings to three or four hundred pounds per annum. The Duke of Northumberland, as Lord of the Manor, holds his Court annually. This place is greatly improved in its appearance and comfort within the last thirty years, as nearly one-fifth of the houses have been rebuilt or are entirely new buildings. But among the late improvements there are none of greater utility to the inhabitants than the erection of two pants, about seven years ago, one of which is situated in the Market Place, and was erected at considerable expense by the late Duke of Northumberland, as the water had to be conveyed in leaden pipes upwards of five hundred yards: the other is in the Main Street, and was erected at the expense of the inhabitants." Since Mackenzie's day the rapid march of progression has produced great and beneficial changes, both in the material and physical state of the village, as well as in the social condition of the people. A great number of thatched houses have been rebuilt, and several of them converted into substantial dwellings. A beautiful terrace now occupies the site of Dunkirk Street, and is named Dunkirk Terrace.† Another terrace has lately been erected by Mr. John Middlemas, builder, and called West End Terrace. There have also been erected several entirely new and handsome dwelling houses. The Wesleyan Methodists have in lieu of their old chapel in the Back Row, erected in Princess Street, a large and substantial chapel and school-room; the chapel which is in the gothic style of architecture, has an open roof

---

* Judging from the description of the cross, as given by Horsely when he saw it, it is not improbable that this was the original market cross.

† Dunkirk derives its name from a Presbyterian Chapel having once been there called "Dun-Kirk," the lower portion of the walls were taken down during the erection of the terrace.

and is well finished throughout, in which a splendid organ
has recently been erected. The Primitive Methodists have
also erected on the north side of the Market Place a neat and
comfortable chapel with a school-room attached to it. The
United Free Methodists have a chapel on Heron's Hill, not
attractive from the outside, but comfortable within. Special
attention having been given to the sanitary state of the village,
every street now having a main drain, into which branch
drains are introduced from nearly every dwelling. A great
improvement has also been made by the introduction of gas,
which now gives its cheerful light both in the streets and in
the greater proportion of the dwelling-houses and shops; in the
suburbs are several new and beautiful villa residences which
greatly enhance the appearance of the village and its surroundings. Since Mackenzie's account was published the number of
public-houses have been reduced from eight to six, and the
shops have increased from sixteen to twenty-six, several of
them having splendid fronts, in which are offered for sale
all the various articles of merchandise required for ornament,
comfort, or convenience. We have hinted that great changes
have also taken place in the social condition of the people,
we will now notice some of those in connection with the
industries of the village : The first we notice is that of spinning and weaving, at the time referred to (from fifty to sixty
years ago.) There were thirty pairs of looms which were
kept almost constantly at work, so that to produce the
necessary materials with which to supply the looms, nearly
in every cottage and dwelling house was a spinning wheel
with which the dame and her daughters were kept plying
their fingers, especially during the long winter months, spinning generally twelve cuts to the hank ; its was considered one
of the essentials of a good wife that she should be a good
spinner, qualified to provide for the use of the house and
family sufficient linen cloth. Now, spinners, spinning wheels,
nack reels, weaver's looms, and shuttles, have long since been
amongst the things that were, and the last of the long line
of famous Corbridge weavers, viz. : William Turnbull, a short
time ago, at an advanced age, threw the last shuttle
of life, and by the side of his wife now rests quietly in the
new cemetery ; nearly the same may be said of that
once flourising business specially referred to by Mackenzie

viz : shoe making ; there were several shops where from four to six or seven men, and from two to four apprentices, were kept constantly at work (averaging about fifty persons) like the weavers, they worked hard and long hours, so that a great number of shoes were made every year ; quantities were specially made for Shields' dealers and sold into ships, and were called "Shields' shoes"; a few of the masters attended the great periodical shoe fairs, held in the Bottle Bank, Gateshead, and at Stanhope, in Weardale, as well as Stagshawbank fair.* An amusing incident is related as having taken place betwixt the master of one of these establishments and the well-known George Silvertop, Esq. ; this man did the "foot engineering" for the household at Minsteracres, being so well pleased with the kindness of his employer, determined that as he deserved so he should have a higher title, viz. : that of Lord ; accordingly in making out his next account headed it "Lord George Silvertop, Esq.," when settling, Mr. Silvertop reminded this knight of the stool of his mistake, by saying, I'm not a Lord, Tommy ! but the good fellow could hear of nothing less, and vehemently exclaimed "you sall be a Lord, sir, you sall be a Lord," to the no little amusement of Mr. Silvertop. At the present time there are only, in the whole township, five men and one apprentice employed in this business. It may be mentioned in passing that the lime trade, which was a brisk and profitable business from fifty to one hundred years ago, gave employment to a considerable number of hands, supplying customers as far distant as the borders of the Derwent. The ruins of the numerous old lime kilns speak out louder than words, that this once valuable industry has long since ceased to be. Another remarkable and general kind of industry, or rather a compound of industry and hard practice, is not only now obsolete but unknown in practice, at least to the present generation, that of great numbers of persons walking from Corbridge to Newcastle (starting early in the morning) doing their business and walking home again the same day, except occasionally getting "a cast" in some gardener's cart returning from the market. An intimate acquaintance of the

* In addition to the number of shoe-making establishments, was a clog-making business, where generally three men were kept employed ; the owner regularly attended Hexham market, where a great number was sold mostly to persons from outside districts.

writer on his first visit to Newcastle, when a youth, walked there, was shown various sights in Newcastle, visited the museum and walked home again the same day. About the same time, Mrs. Stokoe, 64 years of age, walked to Newcastle to visit a sick friend and returned the same day. These are only instances of what was so often being done; the average rate of walking was four miles an hour. The contrast between then and now needs no comment.

The gardening business having been an important branch of the Corbridge industries is the last we refer to, as to its rise, prosperity, and decline. Its rise as to anything like importance commenced about the beginning of the present century; previous to this time the principal kind of fruit grown were plums, which were grown in abundance in the neighbourhood,* and were a regular article of merchandise, not only being sold at Newcastle, but in the outlying neighbourhoods. The late George Tweddell was accustomed to relate, how he had heard his father refer to one of his successful journeys to Newcastle market with plums, towards the close of the last century. The fruit was conveyed in panniers over the back of a horse. He as usual took the ancient road on the north bank of the Tyne, through Ovingham, Wylam, and Newburn, entering Newcastle by the Skinner Burn, proceeding along the Close to the Sandhill, where he was met by a fruit merchant who at once bought his plums for £5. From eighty to ninety years ago, regular orchards were formed for the growth of various kinds of apples, pears, gooseberries, &c.; the first planted as far as we can ascertain, was the crofts and hole orchards, shortly after, was planted others by the late father of the present John Bowman, senior, and also by the present John Bowman. Their example was followed by several others in the line, hence the number of orchards which exist in the neighbourhood, soon after being planted, became a profitable investment, an idea may be formed of the value of such fruit nurseries in favourable seasons, by the produce of one of the half-acre orchards, situate in the Back Row, at the time occupied by a man of the name of William Richley, which realized in one year or to use the modes of speech used

---

* The timber of the plum tree being plentiful, was used exclusively in the then extensive making of spinning wheels and mackreels, being of a fine nature easy to work, and taking a fine polish it was better suited for that purpose than any other kind of wood.

" cleared " upwards of £40. The cultivation of the ground
for garden produce was soon found to be equally profitable,
and its resources became fast developed, on many occasions
the value of the onion crop for that season, was considered
equal to the value of the land on which they were grown.
The famous Corbridge potatoes continued for many years a
remunerative business, and commanded the highest price in
Newcastle market. For a long time this business had its full
share of prosperity, but as the means of quick and easy conveyance of goods increased betwixt continental ports and the
south of England, as well as Scotland, it gradually began to
decline, and is now barely remunerative, no orchards having
been planted within the last thirty years.

While all those businesscss, and others besides, have
experienced great changes, have declined or become extinct,
other industries have sprung up, and give employment to a
great many persons. On the north side of the village are
two manufactories for making firebricks, retorts, sanitary
pipes, &c., each of which does an extensive business ; near
the railway station is another firebrick and retort manufactory,
which, it is said produces articles of most excellent quality,
and belonging the same enterprising firm is a public saw mill,
which also does a good business.

Amongst the beneficial institutions must be noticed the large
and commodious public schools, in which on an average 220
children daily receive the ordinary branches of education,
including scriptural instruction, and which are conducted by
a master, mistress, and pupil teachers; the girls at convenient
times are taught needlework by the mistress and four ladies
belonging the village, whose services are gratuitous.

From the reports of the Government Inspector, these
schools obtain a high standard for proficiency in the various
branches which are taught. The schools, master's house, and
grounds are freehold, are held on trust, and are under the
management, according to the provisions of the deed, of a
committee of seven persons, being subscribers annually of not
less than ten shillings each to the funds of the school, and
are appointed by the subscribers, except the Vicar who is an
exofficio member. The schools which were opened on October
10th, 1855, owe their origin to the late Rev. F. Gipps, by
whose unceasing exertions they were successfully completed,

and remain a graceful and lasting monument to his memory.

A library and news room has for some time been established in the village, in which are a good supply of interesting books, but this valuable institution has never received that support nor been patronised to the extent its importance demands.

The latest though not the least necessary and valuable improvement has been the providing for the parish a new burial ground, which is "beautiful for situation." A few extracts from a report which appeared in the *Hexham Courant* in connection with the consecration, briefly explains the whole matter.—" After a new burial ground was decided on, a serious question arose as to whether the new ground should be an extension of the present church yard, conveying all the powers of right to the vicar -as at present ; or that it should be a cemetery, giving equal rights to the nonconformists. Ultimately after a great deal of discussion, it was on the 16th of May, 1870, decided by a large majority that the new burial ground should be a cemetery, and in this decision the majority showed their sense of right, justice, and equality. The Burial Board was then appointed, which consisted of five members viz : the Vicar (Rev. F. Gipps), C. G. Grey, Esq., and Messrs. Robert Forster, Thomas Blandford, and Joseph Green : at the end of the first year Mr. Green retired, and Mr. Ellerington, Red House, was elected in his stead. Power was given to the board to obtain £1,500 to complete the whole, and the Board was happily successful in procuring the services of an architect, whose plans and judicious arrangements, have enabled them to keep their expenses within the estimated sum. The Cemetery is situate on the south side of the village and river, bordering on the turnpike road leading to Hexham, and about three hundred yards from the end of the bridge. A better site could not have been chosen ; it is also an improvement on the landscape, and a great ornament to the neighbourhood. The Board has erected two chapels, that to the right on entering the grounds being for the use of the Episcopalians, and to the left for the use of the Nonconformists ; each chapel provides seats for upwards of forty persons. The style of architecture adopted is Gothic of the early English period, simple lancet headed windows prevailing throughout, those to the gables being tripartite, the centre one being carried higher than the others. At the

junction of the vestry and chapel walls is a graceful looking spirelet, giving unity and character to the design, and forming a distinctive feature in the district. The interesting and impressive ceremony was commenced at one o'clock yesterday (March 15th, 1872), when the Bishop was received in his robes at the door of the Episcopal chapel by the members of the Burial Board present, Mr. C. G. Grey, Dilston, and Mr. Robert Forster, Corbridge. In the absence of the Vicar, chairman of the burial board, through indisposition, the vice-chairman, Mr. C. G. Grey, presented to the Bishop the petition for consecration, and his Lordship having given his assent to the prayer, a procession was formed, which traversed the ground set apart for Episcopalian interments in the following order: members of the Corbridge Burial Board, Mr. C. G. Grey, and Mr. Robert Forster, and Mr. Michael Thompson, Clerk to the Board, the Bishop, the Rev. John Cundill, Durham, Rev. H. C. Barker, Hexham, &c., &c.: on returning to the chapel, and after the legal documents had been signed, the Bishop delivered an interesting and impressive address, in which he stated "That our law gave power to set apart portions of ground to be for ever used as places of interment, and in the case of the Church of England, the law appointed the Bishop to be the legal agent in setting apart such portion of ground. This ground which they had just been round became consecrated, that is set apart for this good and holy purpose for ever, not by the psalm that was read in going round, nor by any religious service, but it was set apart for ever by the law, by his signature to the document they had heard read, the deed of consecration; from that day forth, he having signed the document as the legal officer to do so, that piece of ground was set apart for the interment of members of the Church of England, and no power, except the authority of parliament could apply any portion of that ground to any other purpose."

So judiciously have the Board discharged its duties since its formation that at the close of 1879 £400 of the borrowed capital had been paid off, and the rate which at first was three-half-pence in the pound, reduced one half.

Leaving the modern, we now direct our attention to the ancient and interesting objects in the village; the first is the Peel Tower, Mackenzie thus describes it: "At the north-

east corner of the Market Place is an old square tower which
was used as a prison. The entrance is at the east end by an
iron door, made of flat bars rivetted together; it is six feet
six inches high. There has been another inside door leading
into the dungeon, which is arched with hewn stone; it is
eight feet eight inches in height, and thirteen feet in breadth,
a slit-hole admits light on the south. Within the outer
door are stairs that lead to the first apartment, which has a
fire-place, and is lighted by three small windows, which have
been secured by upright iron bars. The upper apartment is
similarly constructed. The floor has rested upon projecting
stones, most of which are broken off. The height of the
tower is thirty-three feet, and the walls are four feet three
inches in thickness. The top, which seems to have been
covered with lead, has a battlement with four projecting
turrets at the corners. His Grace, the Duke of Northumberland. caused the dungeon, which was filled with filth, to be
cleaned out and a new door to be hung, in order that it might
be appropriated to its original purpose." Camden calls it "a
little turret built and inhabited by the Vicars." Camden's
conjecture is the right one, as to its originally being a prison,
Mackenzie is wrong. The late Mr. Fairless gives the following
account: "At Corbridge is a Pele Tower. It was originally
the residence of the Rector, as Elsdon is at present. It is
stated to have belonged to the Vicars of Corbridge, similar
to Embleton, Rothbury, and Elsdon,* and to have been built
about the year 1318, during the reign of Edward II., at the
time the manor belonged to Henry, first Lord Percy of
Alnwick." It is quite clear that it was originally intended to
answer two purposes, a place of residence for the Vicar, and
also a place of defence; its existence as it is at this day,
proves it to have been sufficient for these purposes. Tradition
states that the lower or arched story was used for the safe
keeping of the Vicar's cow.

Another extract we give from Mackenzie in reference to
the tower at Elsdon: "The rectory house stands at a small
distance from the church, and commands a fine prospect. It
is a very strong ancient tower, with a circular stair case at
one corner. Its lowest story is spanned with one large arch

---

* Thirty-seven such towers, Mr. Fairless stated, were built in Northumberland about the same time.

F

82

On its front is the Umfranville Arms, underneath which is a mutilated inscription in this form.........which Hutchinson reads.—Robertus, or Rogerus Dom de Rede, and which he imagines refers to Umfranville, lord of Prudhoe, who died about the year 1325."

There can be no doubt that the tower at Corbridge belongs to the church; but when and how it came into the possession of the Duke of Northumberland, does not appear to be known.

THE PARISH CHURCH.

This is by far the most interesting object we have here, connecting the far past with the present in the most sacred associations, like a chronological monument, uniting three vastly dissimilar periods, as the eighth, the thirteenth, and the nineteenth centuries, and certainly deserves special notice. It is dedicated to St. Andrew, and is generally supposed to have been founded by St. Wilfred, when he presided over the See of Hexham. That Prelate it would appear founded many churches, and is thought to have been the founder of that at Bywell dedicated to St. Andrew, who must have been a favourite Saint with Wilfred. Considering this to be true, as most probably it is, the Church or Monastery at Corbridge would be built either at the close of the seventh, or the very beginning of the eighth century, between the years 674 and 709; the earliest mention is very brief. "In 771 there was a Monastery at Corbridge." That at this time there was established a Monastery and worthy of historic notice, proves that it had previously existed, and thus carries us back to the period suggested. Digressing a little from the account of the structure, we notice, it is rather remarkable that in some of the Tyneside churches, such interesting official proceedings should have taken place. The Rev. A. Johnson, Vicar of Healey, some short time ago in a paper read at Bywell on churches, &c., from which we quote states "In the writings of Symeon, of Durham, we read that on the 11th of June, 803, Egbert the 12th Bishop of Lindisfarne, was consecrated at Bywell; Lindisfarne frequently suffered from the ravages of the Danes, one of the attacks was made about the time

we are speaking of, and brings Bywell into notice. They plundered everywhere, overthrew the altars and carried away all
the treasures of the church, some of the monks they slew,
some they carried away captive, and others afflicted and
abused they turned out naked ;" "Thus," says the historian,
"was the Church of Lindisfarne spoiled and stripped of its
ornaments, nevertheless, the Episcopal See still remained
there, and those monks who had escaped the cruelty of the
barbarians, remained for a long time after with the sacred
body of St. Cuthbert. In the 11th year after the plundering
of this church, Higbald having completed twenty-two years
in the episcopate, died on the 8th Kalends of June (i.e. May
25th) and Egbert was elected in his place, and consecrated by
Eanbald, Archbishop ; and Eanbert,* and Badulf, and other
bishops, who had assembled for his ordination at a place called
Bignell (Bywell), on the 3rd Ides of June (June 11th), being
the seventh year (803) of the reign of Eardulf the son of
Earnulf, who had succeeded to the throne on the death of
King Ethelred."† It will be seen at once what an agreement
there is with these quotations, and the following accounts
given in reference to what took place in Corbridge Monastery :
" In 786, in conjunction with Eanbald, Archbishop of York,
and Higbald of Lindisfarne, a prelate of the name of Aldulf,
was consecrated in the Minster of Corbridge which is close to
Hexham." It will be noticed that this ordination took place
seventeen years previous to that of Bywell, and that the same
Archbishop was present on both occasions, and Higbald would
then have been five years in his episcopacy at Lindisfarne.
A remarkable coin was found in this church, and which
deserves to be noticed as bearing upon the Saxon character of
the place, having likely lain there since the middle or latter
part of the ninth century, the period it would be in circulation.
About twenty-eight years ago when the chancel was undergoing considerable alterations and restorations, and
when the floor was being lowered, one of the workmen
found this coin and showed it to Mr. Fairless, who at
once pronounced it to be a Saxon coin, which he retained,
giving the finder a Roman coin instead. In one of the volumes
published by the Durham Society, the following account is

---

* Eanbert was Bishop of Hexham, 600—6.
† Ethelred was slain at Corbridge on the Tyne, in 795.

given of it: "Mr. Fairless has in his possession another remarkable coin which was found in the Church at Corbridge. On the obverse is a crowned head to the right, and the scripture (or writing) Barnred Re; on the reverse Moncered Eta. It was perhaps struck by Burgred, of Mercia, but Dr. Haig thinks it was minted for Buern, the Admiral of Osbert, King of Northumbria." From the same authority we give another quotation: "In the year 781, 2nd October, Tilbert was consecrated Bishop of Hexham, at a place now unknown, called Wolfswell; * according to Mackenzie, Tilbert was the eighth Bishop of Hexham." After these digressions we now proceed more particularly with our subject. As regards the size of the monastery and minster we have no information, whether of larger or smaller dimensions than the present church; but it was customary in the rebuilding of churches, from the earliest times, to build as much as possible on the old foundations. The Saxon Church was undoubtedly destroyed by the Danes after their victory in the battle fought at Corbridge, in 923. To such an extent did the Danes destroy the churches, religious houses, and monasteries in Northumberland and Durham, that until late years, the general opinion amongst antiquarians was, that scarcely any portion of mural Saxon work remained above ground; but recent and more careful examinations of the old churches have led to the pleasing and interesting discovery that many portions of undoubted Saxon remains still exist in several churches in both counties. As this subject is now become one so full of interest, we venture to quote from an excellent paper on Escomb Church, read by Mr. Longstaffe, of Gateshead, at the monthly meeting of the Newcastle Society of Antiquaries, on the evening of July 30th, 1879. "For the pre Norman period we have divers towers, a chancel at Jarrow, a remarkable west-end at Wearmouth of very early and superior workmanship, and a fine crypt at Hexham, composed of small ornamental Roman stones; but at Escomb we find a church, Saxon from end to end.........The lights at the west-end closely resemble those in Jarrow chancel, and

---

* In *Wright's History of Hexham* is the following account of this transaction: "In 781, Tilbert was consecrated Bishop of Hexham, at a place called Ulfeswelle (probably Haltwhistle) that is Wolfs-well. In the episcopacy of Tilbert, mention is made of Heghald, the praesul or abbot of the monastery, and both the bishop and the abbot are said to have been at Corabridge, at the consecration of Bishop Aldulf, by Eanbald, the Archbishop."

the chancel arch, tall in proportion, reminds one of that at
Bridgestock Church, and of the tower arch at Corbridge."
The same opinion was held concerning the monastery at
Corbridge as of other Saxon Churches,[*] that no vestige now
remained. The tower arch referred to by Mr. Longstaffe
was, until the restorations and repairs made to the church in
1867, so walled up and plastered over, and had been for ages,
that it was generally overlooked, or little attention was given
to what portions were seen. This arch which is now fully
exposed is tall in proportion, being sixteen feet high by eight
feet wide, and is evidently of Saxon origin, and an interesting
remnant of the monastery. One peculiarity in this arch, and
which is corroborative of this view, is, that the side walls are
built of large Roman stones, eight on each side, on the top of
which are capitals of much larger dimensions, projecting
on three sides with fine moulded facings,[†] and appear to
have been altogether one of the gateways of the adjoining
station. It is a noticeable feature in the building of Saxon
churches that the Roman style of architecture was not only
copied, but where convenient, Roman materials were freely
used. At Corbridge, in the Roman station, they found a large
quarry of hewn stones ready for use. The arch itself is a
half-circle composed of large hewn stones, not springing from
the capitals in the usual way, this does not appear to have
suited the architect's proportions of height, it therefore rises
from another Roman stone parallel with those underneath,

---

[*] It is remarkable and proved beyond dispute, that the early Saxon places of
worship were not called churches, as is shown from an inscription on a stone
placed over the entrance to the chancel in Jarrow Church. When this church
was altered and repaired in 1782, it was found built up in the north wall of
that edifice, and bears one of the most curious inscriptions now remaining
in England, which is the dedication of the Basilicae (not church) of St. Paul,
on the 9th of May, 685, in the 15th year of King Egfrid. According to a note in
Brand's History of Newcastle, on the Monastery of Jarrow, "the word
Basilicae of Gentile Rome, buildings where the magistrates held the courts
of justice were converted into churches on their conversion to Christianity,
and thus came the word Basilicae to signify a church."
" The early Christian Churches were constructed after the model of these
familiar buildings (Basilicas). The space under the testudo (or roof) became
the nave, the lateral galleries, or (porticus) became the side aisles and the
magistrate's tribunal the apse. There are several churches in Rome each still
named a Basilica, the oldest of which is that of S. Pietro, is said to have been
built by Constantine on the site of the circus of Nero. Throughout Italy also,
many of the principal churches retain in the name an evidence of the original
model after which they were built. The Roman Basilica is, in fact, the form
from which all Christian Church buildings arose."—*The Globe Encyclopædia.*
[†] The projections and facings are now much broken, until about forty years
ago the inside facings were entire, but were broken off to make room for the
back of the organ, which at first was fixed on a gallery against the wall.

built on the top of the capitals. Mr. R. J. Johnson, of Newcastle, who was entrusted with renovating and repairing the ancient Saxon Church at Escomb, in an able and carefully written paper read in the church on the 30th July, 1880, in the presence of members of the Architectural and Archæological Society, who met for the purpose of viewing the structure, remarks : " The noble chancel arch is most remarkable, it is taller and narrower in proportion than that at Corbridge, but has the same splendid breadth of voussoir (the arch stones) and massive impost " (the capitals already referred to.) Mr. Johnson further remarks in a private letter, "In both the arches at Escomb and Corbridge, the stones are of remarkable breadth, and give a fine character to the work." It is therefore clear that the entire west-end betwixt the columns, which support the nave arches is of the same date, built exclusively of Roman stones, and is of good workmanship. There was an idea held by antiquarians, that here was also a Norman Church, and that the principal doorway of the present church is of Norman workmanship and a remnant of that structure. The late Mr. Fairless describes it as "An elaborate Norman doorway," in further proof it is stated that similar doorways exist in the churches of Ifley, near Oxford, and of Broadway, near Weymouth, and which are both considered of Norman origin. In reference to Corbridge however, we fail to find any trace or evidence of the existence (save this doorway) of a Noman Church, in fact inferential evidence is to the contrary, for from the ravages of the Danes until near the close of the twelfth century very little was done in the North of England in the restoration or rebuilding of churches. In a correspondence the writer has had on this subject with Mr. Longstaffe, of Gateshead, that gentleman states : " I cannot see how the Corbridge doorway can be Norman ; it is some time since I saw it, during the alterations, but I believe that all the north country antiquarians who have studied early architecture agree as to its Saxon character." The question of the Norman Church at least, until further evidence is adduced to show to the contrary, may now be considered settled. The present structure is thus described by Mr. Fairless, who had carefully studied its architecture : "This fine old church is of the first pointed style of architecture, it consists of a nave, transepts, choir, and chancel ; the tower, containing three bells, rises from the

west-end of the nave and appears chiefly to have been built
of Roman stones." Another writer since the alterations thus
describes it : " The present church is supposed to stand on
the site of the original Saxon Monastery; it is cruciform,
consisting of a nave, two aisles, north and south transepts, a
chancel, and side chapel; the tower rises from the west-end
of the nave ; it may fairly be considered one of the largest
and finest parish churches in this part of the country," the
inside measure is 100 feet from the west-end of the nave
(exclusive of the baptistry) to the east-end of the chancel, and
88 feet betwixt the north and south ends of the transepts.
This church which had for ages been sadly mutilated, in
1867 was repaired and restored (except the chancel which had
been previously done) by the praiseworthy exertions of the
late Vicar, the Rev. F. Gipps, who collected the money himself, and personally superintended the work. The repairs and
restorations were carried out with great taste and judgment,
as far as the funds allowed. After these alterations and
renovations the original ground dimensions of the structure
would seem to have been nearly realized. An observable
feature from the outside of the church is the fact of the
chancel roof being higher than the nave, this is owing
to the former having been raised to its original pitch, when
the chancel was restored twenty-eight years ago, while
this has not yet been done to the roof of the nave.
The height of the clerestory and the mark of the gable
end can be distinctly seen on the outside of the tower, the
gable running up to a point above the clock dial. It has
been remarked by a recent writer " That if the roof were
raised to this pitch and the clerestory windows put in, which
would then be quite easy to do, the church would indeed be
a magnificent building," the writer trusts that some day this
will be done, as the church is in every way worthy of it.* The
only original portions of the outer walls now remaining would
appear to be the south wall of the chancel with its four

---

* Mr. Longstaffe, of Gateshead, the learned antiquarian, at a meeting of the
society of antiquarians, held in Newcastle, August 26th, 1880, when making
some remarks on the proposed renovation of Ponteland Church, expressed
his views as altogether opposed to high pitched roofs, and thus refers to that
church : " The proposal at Ponteland was to have a higher pitched roof, that
was such an achronism, and such an absurdity, that he really wished something could be done to prevent it."—*Newcastle Journal.*

pointed windows,* and its fine trefoil door-way, and that portion of the end wall underneath the triple lancet window; also that portion of the wall, underneath the windows, in the end of the south transept, and that portion of the west wall on the north side parallel with the tower, in which is a lancet window. The interior of the building may thus be described: The nave is separated from the aisles by three arches on each side, resting on octagonal pillars which support the roof—an open one of oak. The eastern arch on each side of the nave spans the transept, and rests on double columns which rise from the west end of the chancel. The transepts are not alike, the north transept having an aisle on the west side and contains two fine arches, which support the roof, resting on the same style of columns as the other arches; on the west side of the south transept is a fine arch which spans the south aisle of the nave.

The chancel is an interesting part of the church, being a fine specimen of early English architecture throughout. The arch between it and the nave is of rare form and beauty, having, (as Mr. Fairless was accustomed to point out,) a peculiarity about it seldom met with in Gothic architecture. This arch, instead as is usual, rising direct from the capitals of the main columns, springs from brackets, on which are two shafts, which rest upon the capitals of the pillars and rise to the full height of the nave roof and has a wonderful lofty and graceful appearance, which is best seen from the west-end of the nave, the appearance of which is also improved by a fine open roof.† The side chapel, in which the organ stands, is separated from the chancel by four arches resting on octagonal pillars. The west-end of this chapel is spanned by a graceful arch, which shows well from the north aisle of the nave. Inside the

---

* Since the writer first knew the church these windows have been mutilated. In the inside, just underneath the shoulder from which the arch rises, and attached to it, were two balls apparently about four inches in diameter, one on each side and which formed part of the shoulder stone, hanging like large drops, gave to the windows an artistic as well as an ornamental appearance; some years ago all these balls were broken off. Their place of attachment to the shoulder stone is still observable; by whom or by whose orders this injury was done we are not aware. Another mutilation has recently been made at the east end of the chancel. To allow the reredos to be fixed close to the wall, the fine moulding which runs along the wall just underneath the window, was rudely broken off and cut away, by whose authority or orders the workmen in charge of the job did it we don't know. This moulding had ornamented the structure for 600 years.

† The height of this fine arch from the floor of the nave to the highest inside point is 36 feet.

church, besides the structure, the objects worthy of notice
are first two piscinas which appear of the same date as the
church, one is in the south wall of the chancel, within the
communion rails, the other is in the end wall of the south
transept, and suggest that in early times an altar may have
been here.* In the side chapel are some remarkable arch
stones evidently the under course of a door-way, similar to
those of the under course in the principal door-way of the
church, cut on both sides as well as underneath, but much
deeper and bolder in the mouldings and other ornamental
work, and is undoubtedly of Saxon character, and like the
present door-way is of superior workmanship; these stones
were found built into a portion of the walls pulled down at
the restoration of the church. There are a few tomb stones
deserving attention. The entire church, like nearly all other
old churches, had been a complete sepulchre, every foot of
ground seems to have been a repository of the sacred dead.
The chancel had been the burying-place of the vicars and
other persons of note. It is generally thought that many of
the ancient lords of Dilston were interred within the edifice.
Several coffin-shaped monumental, as well as many other
ancient stones—besides the arch stones referred to—were
found in the walls which were taken down during the process
of restoration, several of which are in the side chapel; one
was taken out of the floor of the church (which is now
broken,) but all the parts are there; it has an inscription
running along the edge of the stone and a cross down the
middle, in relief, and is in memory of one of the lords of
Tynedale. In the opinion of the late Mr. Gipps, it is one of the
oldest monumental stones in the church. There is another
stone lying along side of this with an incised cross fleury.
Another fine stone, similar to this one, is standing in one of
the corners of the north transept; before the late restorations
this stone served for the head of a square window which was
in the south wall of the nave. Under the window of the north
transept is an ancient tomb, under an arch, bearing the

* "Piscinae are small stone or marble cups or basins placed in small
recesses in the wall on the right hand side of the altar, which have apertures
at the bottom connecting them with the earth, down which any thing that
has been consecrated by the priest is put after use, as for instance the water
in which he washes the tips of his fingers after handling the consecrated host."
—*Richley's History of Bishop Auckland.*

following Latin inscription:—"Hic yacet interris, Aliinci filius Hugo," which means something like the following:—Here lieth in the earth, Hugo, son of Aslini, and is thought by some to refer to the founder of the present church. In the floor adjoining this tomb are two coffin-shaped incised stones, now much defaced, on one of them can be traced a cross and a hatchet; there are several other stones of this class in the chancel, laid even with the floor, and are very entire, after having been trodden underfoot for ages; they have crosses in relief, and one in particular, of a rather remarkable nature. It is the opinion of an able writer that these are the most ancient funeral monuments found within our churches, and by able antiquarians are thought generally to belong to the thirteenth century; one more stone in the chancel should be noticed, which records the death of one of the vicars of the name of Henry Guy, who had been chaplain to King Charles II.* The Church contains some fine stained glass windows, particularly the east window, which is to the memory of the wife of John Grey, Esq., of Dilston; and a window in the south transept, put in by Mr. Lee, of Dilston, to the memory of his wife; also the end window of the south transept, to the memory of the late Rev. Frederick Gipps, Vicar. In the west wall of this transept is a monument consisting of a white marble slab, surmounted by a freestone border of Gothic design, beautifully carved, having a neatly carved figure on the lower portion, to the memory of Lionel Winship, of Aydon,—the last descendant of a long and honourable line of ancestors, who were large owners of property in the township of Aydon—all that is now left of this ancient family is vested in his estimable widow, now living in Corbridge.

---

* In the church yard there are no monumental inscriptions of particular interest. The two following epitaphs are somewhat quaint:—
"Here lies the body of John Nixon, who departed this life ye 29th of April, 1759, in the 57th year of his age.

Lament me not as you pass by,
As you are now so once was I,
As I am now so you must be,
Prepare for death and follow me."

"Here lies the body of Robt. Aldcroft, who died July 12th, 1791, aged 33 years. Jane, daughter of Robt. Aldcroft, who died November 7th, 1792, aged 7 years.

When God cuts short the thrid of life,
Then sudden death parts man and wife."

91

The baptistry is in the tower recess and has a fine modern florigated font, presented by a lady to the church; but it is to be regretted that the old font, supposed to have been as old as the church, should have been purposely broken to pieces.

The seats throughout the church are open benches, and are all free, with the exception of those in the chancel. The edifice is well lighted with gas, and warmed by hot air flues.

In the building of the church, Roman stones had been freely used throughout. The period of its erection can only be determined by the style of its architecture, which is generally admitted to be the first pointed style of English, which was introduced at the close of the twelfth century.* Hexham Church which is considered the finest specimen of early English in Britain, and is generally admitted to have been built at the close of the twelfth and the beginning of the thirteenth centuries inclusive, shows two, if not three variations in the style of architecture; the first or earliest portions show some lingering remnants of the Norman style. In judging of the time of the erection of this church, in addition to the character of its architecture, we must take into account the importance of the town; its more than probable large population, and the church accomodation required for the parish. In 1205, the privilege of a weekly market was granted, and also the holding of an annual fair, and shortly afterwards the privilege of sending two members to Parliament: we may therefore fairly reckon that from the beginning to the end of the thirteenth century, Corbridge would be in a flourishing condition, if not at the height of its prosperity. A large church would therefore be required to meet the wants of the population; all things considered we may suggest the middle or early part of the thirteenth century, during the reign of Henry III. 1216—72, as the period of its erection, and when completed, as far as we can now judge, with its high pitch roof, its clerestories and their windows, with its roof probably covered with lead, would

---

* This style was introduced after the Norman at the close of the twelfth century, and continued until the close of the reign of Edward I., 1272—1307. This style is distinguished by long narrow windows without mullions. The second period of Gothic architecture commenced at the very beginning of the fourteenth century, and continued till the close of that century. This style is characterised by the form of its large windows, the pointed arches being divided by mullions and the tracery thrown into graceful curves.

certainly have an imposing appearance from the outside,* with the inside no less beautiful. Of such a structure the inhabitants might well feel proud; but its elegance and beauty, however much admired, were of short duration, for at the close of the century in 1296, and again in 1311, the Scots burnt Hexham and Corbridge, directing always their first attacks on the churches and monasteries, first plundering them of their valuables. After the withdrawal of the Scots armies we can conceive the church as being almost a complete wreck, the roof, together with the internal fittings burned to the ground, great portions of the outer walls thrown down, the arches and columns only left to tell of its former grandeur, the walls evidently in a few years afterwards rebuilt and the church made fit for service, for in 1382, William de Glaston was appointed vicar; but there are traditional records that the church subsequently and more than once, was despoiled and burned by the Scots,† and had to be as often rebuilt, this

---

* Since writing the foregoing, we have met with a short account (in an annual called *Weardale Forest*) on Stanhope Church, from which we give the following extract, as showing the probable period of its erection and its style of architecture, and think there is a great similarity to the description we have given of Corbridge Church, except the slight difference as to the time of their respective erections. We have not seen Stanhope Church and cannot therefore give our view from observation, and it would almost seem the height of presumption, to dissent from the view of such a high authority as Canon Greenwell: if therefore, the Canon is right in his conjecture as to the period of the erection of Stanhope Church, we think we might be justified in fixing the erection of Corbridge Church at the beginning, instead of the middle or early part of the century. The reader, if conversant with early English Church architecture, will form his own opinion. "Stanhope Church," says the Rev. William (now Canon) Greenwell, at a meeting held at Stanhope, July 12th, 1866, "is one of the most perfect and interesting of the ecclesiastical structures of the middle ages remaining in the county, in one respect, indeed, unique, being the only one of the whole number which has retained intact its ancient high-pitched leaden roof. A careful survey brought the not very readily deciphered architectural history of the building to light, and unfolded the story of its gradually progressive growth and internal evidence. Then, it would appear that the church consisted originally of a chancel and nave of nearly equal length, the latter without aisles, and having its western gable surmounted by an open bell cot. The date of this, the first church of which there are visible remains, may be fixed at about 1200. Very shortly after its completion we find evidence of extensive alterations and enlargements having taken place, the south aisle and the tower differing not the least in point of style from the still existing original portion of the chancel, whereas the north-west and the south-west angles of the nave distinctly prove them to have been added unto the original structure. Their date cannot well be placed later than about 1210. The north aisle, with its arcade considerably slighter in proportion than that to the south, though following its general design, seems a little, though but a few years later, and may be dated 1225."

† Traces of the fires can be distinctly seen on several stones built into the walls, and on the stones of the principal doorway, and on those of the tower arch. Some affirm they can see marks of cannon shots on some of the stones, but this cannot be, for cannon was not known in those early troublesome times. There was a battle here on a small scale in 1644, betwixt the Scots

is not only shown by the kind of building, but the materials
used in the building of the walls, for the builders evidently
had no scruples about sacrilege* for numbers of tombstones
of an earlier period (already noticed) had been freely used,
many of them ruthlessly broken ; this must have been long
after its destruction by Bruce. The east side of the south
transept, with its mullion window, the walls taken down during
the restorations, with other portions yet remaining, and the
roof of the transepts, show a period not earlier than the beginning or middle of the fifteenth century, from about 1400 to
1460. From this time down to the modern period of
restoration as we learn from the churchwardens' books,
comparatively little alteration had taken place, a portion of
the side chapel being suffered to remain in ruins ; the original
triple lancet window in the end of the chancel, called in the
churchwardens' books lead windows, was taken out and replaced by a huge wooden one, some others shared the same
fate. The repairs, for the most part, consisted in repairing
the roof and in new roofing portions from time to time, until
the whole was done. After having briefly followed the structure through its various vicissitudes, the tower, a most important portion of the building, remains to be considered. It
is quite clear that the tower formed no part of the early Saxon
building (we have previously, we think satisfactorily, shown
that the entire west-end is pure Saxon work,) but it is built
against the west-end, without any kind of binding to unite the
two when the top of the gable was reached, the east side of
the tower had then been built upon it, which is quite traceable
on the outside, but the sharp pitch of the gable is more particularly seen in the inside. Various opinions have been given
as to its character, some have thought that the lower portion
of the tower is Saxon work, the higher of a later period, but
this view certainly cannot be reconciled with a close examination of the whole work, for if any portion of the tower proper
is of the Saxon period then the whole must be so, which is
the only satisfactory solution of the question ; that of its
having been built after the monastery does not at all affect its

---

who came to support the parliamentary forces, and the Royalists, but that fight
was mainly betwixt horse soldiers.

* In the side chapel is a fine small ornamental cross, with several other portions of carved stones, which also had been used in the building of the walls.

94

Saxon character, for this period, as far as relates to Corbridge, would extend over two centuries, as the monastery was erected at the beginning of the Saxon period.—The tower may have been added in the middle or towards its close.—It is a peculiarity in the walls, which are three feet in thickness, that Roman stones have been exclusively used throughout, both inside and outside, from the foundation to the top, and the workmanship is uniformly of the same kind, this can be best seen in the inside, but the gable portion appears to show an earlier period; on each corner of the second course of stones from the top, is a stone projecting north and south, apparently, when fixed, of about eight inches square, having carved on the ends a human face; although now mutilated by exposure to the elements, the leading features on some of them are still traceable; the top course of stones appear never to have been renewed, the action of the atmosphere, for several centuries, has caused many of them to look as though they had been beautifully carved, whilst others seem to have received an even rubbing at the hand of "father time" during the same period. In support of the views we have ventured to put forth, as to the Saxon character of the whole tower, we again quote from those high authorities we have referred to before, viz.: Mr. Johnson and Mr. Longstaffe. Mr. Johnson in the paper he read in Escomb Church remarks: "We have also such fragments (of Saxon work) as the towers of Bywell, Ovingham, and Corbridge,* whatever be their date." Mr. Longstaffe states in a letter to the writer: "The towers of Bywell, Ovingham, Whittingham, Norton, and Billingham, and possibly parts of other churches, are Saxon. The subject is very large and obscure, and as to relation of dates, I have hardly made up my mind and so cannot correspond upon it. One thing is clear, that early Saxon art is superior to later, but this is only 'history repeated.'" The openings in the belfry had originally been of the same style as those in the towers of Bywell and Ovingham Churches, but at a comparative late period had been altered into their present form, although at the time this was done, it was evidently intended as an improvement, it certainly is a mutilation of the

---

* The towers of Corbridge and Ovingham are both alike in measure, each being eighteen feet square. That of St. Andrews, Bywell, is three feet smaller.

original structure. Having disposed of the character of the tower, we now notice a few minor matters ; the first is the three bells which are of different sizes; their age and the time when they were first hung, can only be determined by the assistance of the churchwarden's books, in which we find, in 1678, the following entry : "For the great bell rope 00-05-00," traditionally this has been described as the "great bell" down to the present time, and has been more used than the others, being rung alone on special occasions.* In 1715 there are sundry items entered amounting to £5 9s. 1d. for brasses, gudgeons, staples, screwing, timber, &c., which evidently refers to a re-hanging of the bells with new material. An agreement for the bells had been made with some one the previous year which seems to refer to this work, for which "agreement" 3/6 is charged. The alterations in the belfry openings, without doubt, had been made when the three bells were first hung, with the idea of allowing the sound from enlarged openings to be more distinctly heard. In fact the altering and enlarging of these openings had also formed part of the plan for supporting the heavy beams on which the bells are hung ; it appears further, that at the same time, the present pitch roof had been added, and judging from the appearance of the whole work, aided by the entries in the churchwarden's books, the bells will have been tingling there for some four centuries or thereabouts. It is likely that previously there would be one bell, in accordance with the original idea in early Saxon times, of simply letting the people know when and where Divine Service was being held;† one of the present three traditionally called "the little bell" being cracked (possibly the original) was re-cast in 1729, and has on it, the name "John Walton, Vicar, 1729," which in the churchwarden's account cost £3.

The clock which is in the storey below the belfry has the following inscription upon its frame :—"This clock ordered 1767, by Elizer Birch, Esq., and Mr. Richard Brown, Church-

---

* In 1721 there is an entry in the churchwarden's books of 2/0 for laying the great bell tongue, and every few years are entries for new ropes for the bells; and every year, for ages, are two or three entries "for butter and oyle for the bells," which shows they were kept in good working order. It is questionable whether the churchwarden's books, for the last forty years, show entries amounting to 3/0 for either "butter or oyle for the bells."

† One of the first bells used in England, for religious purposes, is in Jarrow Church.

wardens, and finished in the wardenship of Bart. Winship, and John Morpeth." The following inscription is on a small dial on the clock :—" This clock was simplified and repaired by John Bolton, late of Chester-le-Street, but now of Durham, A.D. 1818. The Rev. George Wilson, Vicar; Messrs. John Atkin and Joseph Hall, Churchwardens." Until 1861, there was only one hand on each dial which showed the hours only, and which were of comparatively little use to the public, who were guided as to the time by its striking. At this time a subscription was made towards defraying the cost of two new hands on each dial, as well as the necessary alterations to complete the work, which was satisfactorily executed by Mr. Robt. Forster. We finish our account of the church by appending an extract from an able and beautiful written article which appeared in one of the local newspapers, by one of the members of the Tyneside Field Club on one of their visits in 1867, headed : "Hexham to Corbridge by Dipton Dene and Dilston." "After dinner (at the Angel Inn, Corbridge,) we saw one of the lions of Corbridge—the ancient church, now undergoing restorations. The remains of the Station Corstopitum, the first syllable of which survives in the modern name of the village, and of the Roman Bridge, we had not time to visit. Lion the third is the present bridge, notable as being the only one on the Tyne which the great flood in 1771 did not carry away, and which has now to be crossed in going to and from the station. Corbridge Church is exceedingly interesting. It is built of Roman stones, and the tower is of Saxon masonry ; it suffered greatly during the border raids, being oftimes partly destroyed, and then built up again in such a hurry that the original design had, before the restorations begun, well nigh vanished. When the blue bonnets came over the border the priest of Corbridge used to take refuge in a fine old Peel House still standing in the church yard. It is perhaps to its many mishaps that Corbridge Church owes its chief peculiarity, the fact that no two of the principal walls are at right angles with each other. During the process of the restorations, many interesting discoveries have been made. In the end wall of the north transept a tomb was found in excellent preservation, and on scraping the plaster from its west wall, the arches and pillars were discovered which had once formed the transept

aisle; these have been restored, and the new west wall of the transept is now being reared on the old foundations which still exist in the church yard. One other fact about the church, and I must bring my record of this most pleasant day's wanderings to a close. The lintel of one of the windows in the nave is actually formed of an ancient tomb stone, which, by the sharply incised scissors upon it, was evidently that of a woman,* the inference is plain—when their church was pulled down by the Scots, the good folks of Corbridge were not very particular as to where they got their materials, notions about sacrilege did not trouble them."

At the east-end of the village is a house called "The Low Hall," its antiquity appears to have been overlooked, but it certainly deserves more than ordinary attention. When Horsley visited Corbridge somewhere about 160 years ago, he describes it as an "Old House." At the east-end of this house is a small pele tower, which forms part of the building; the tower is three stories high, the lowest room being roofed with one strong large stone arch; the beams of the upper rooms have rested on stone corbels, its walls are of great thickness, particularly the north wall in which is a spiral stone stair case, which leads from the floor to the upper rooms and to the top of the roof, on which is a battlement; the east wall has two chimneys, proceeding from the middle and upper rooms, which indicate that it was built for a dwelling, but made strong for defence and security against an attack. Its arrangement and mason work, as well as the arrangement of the house and out buildings, much resemble the design and masonry of the massive tower and dwelling house "Halton Castle," and would appear to have been built about the same period. Who its original owner or occupiers were we have no knowledge. Its name "Low Hall" was given to it probably from its situation being at the east or low end of the town; "hall" would indicate that of a superior dwelling or manorial residence or something akin to that, and may have had some relation to the religious house or dwelling on the opposite side of the street, as previously referred to. In later times, some two or three hundred years ago, after the period of assaults from the Scots were no longer dreaded, it had been a residence

---

* This is the stone previously referred to, as now standing in the north transept.

G

of some importance, a new staircase had been added outside the tower on the north side, and covered in by a toothall, by which a more convenient entrance had been gained into the upper rooms; its remains show it to have been of a superior character. This house with certain lands, belonged to a gentleman of the name of Reginal Gibson, who in the rebellion of 1715 was favourable to the cause of the Pretender, and it is said, joined a portion of the rebels at Reedsmouth;* for this offence his property was confiscated, and afterwards sold. The authorities being wishful that Gibson should have his property again, arranged with a person of the name of Tweddell to purchase it on Gibson's behalf at a nominal price, but as the story goes, Tweddell finding he had secured a good bargain kept possession. The estate was sold in lots somewhere about forty years ago. The house, now with the fields and grounds attached to it, is in the possession of Mr. John Walker.

Reference has already been made to the Prior Manor House. There are several other old dwelling houses in the village, having been erected two, three, or even four centuries ago, but there is nothing known in connection with any of them deserving special notice, except that the Golden Lion Public House, and the houses adjoining, were built with the stones—taken from that portion of Dilston Hall erected by Sir Francis Radcliffe in 1618—when the hall was taken down and the stones sold in 1768. Also the front of the house in Main Street, belonging to Mr. Fell, which was built at the same time with the stones taken from the west front of the mansion, which portion was added to the building by the last unfortunate Earl. The Angel Inn is an old house and certainly by far the oldest Inn in the village, and has always been designated the "Head Inn." It was most likely the four Commissioners and their retinue lodged here, when on their unsuccessful mission to suppress the monastery at Hexham.

The bridge which crosses the Tyne is a remarkable structure, and contains seven wide arches with outlets at every pillar.

* The rebels as they are called met at "Green Rig." Reedsmouth may be four or five miles from Green Rig; the family of Charltons lived there at that time, who favoured the cause of the Pretender. Gibson was related by marriage to this family, and it is likely he had first gone to Reedsmouth to meet his friends, two of whom are named as being in the rebel army at Preston. It is not said whether Gibson was amongst the prisoners or whether he had followed them so far.

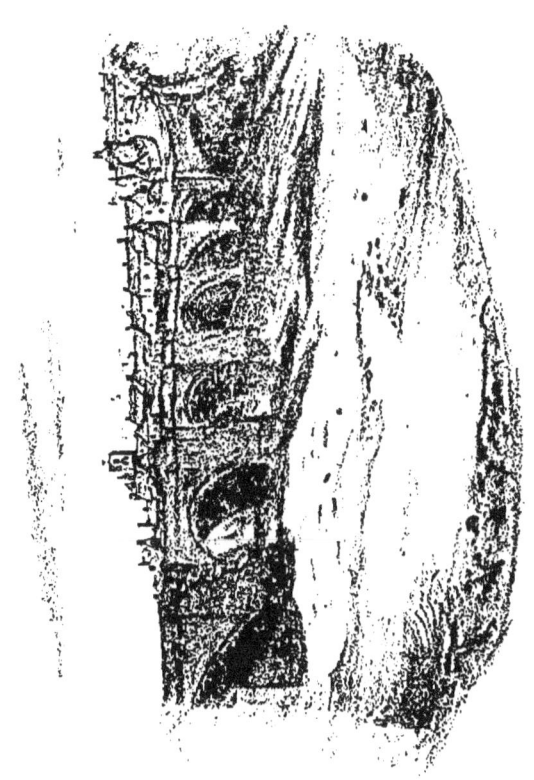

It was built in the year 1674 as appears from the date upon it. Few structures are stronger than this, as was evinced by the great flood in 1771, which swept away in its furious progress every bridge on the Tyne except this. Syke in his *Local Records*, when referring to the strength of this bridge, attributes its endurance to its being built on the foundations of the Roman Bridge; here he is in error, the Roman Bridge having been near half-a-mile further west; its stability arises from its firm and solid masonry from the foundations to the battlement. There is no written, and very little traditional account concerning its erection. There is a tradition that a man of the name of Johnson was the builder, and that during its erection one man had a penny a day more than the other workmen, his duty consisted in filling, as the work proceeded, every crevice and opening with hot running lime, so that the whole became almost one solid mass; this was clearly shown to have been so, when the south arch was taken down in 1829 for the purpose of rebuilding, as it was thought unsafe on account of a rent which was caused by the great flood in 1771, a stack of hay being forced by the torrent underneath it, causing it to rise in the middle, it was, however, even with this defect, found to be no easy matter to take down, being so firm that portions had to be thrown down by blasting.

About a quarter-of-a-mile below the bridge is an ancient ford across the river, approached on the north side by an ancient lane leading from the east-end of Main Street,* crossing the ford, the road proceeds south through the Stanners into an ancient loaning which has its junction with the turnpike road a little to the north of the railway station. This is called the ancient "Drift Road," and before the erection of the bridge formed the altered line of the Watling Street. The original road being by the Roman Bridge as previously described. When referring to the Drift Road, it may be stated for the information of those not acquainted with the

---

* A few years ago an agreement was made, betwixt the ratepayers of the township and H. S. Edwards, Esq., with the approval of the magistrates in their official capacity, whereby the portion of this ancient lane which approached the ford was granted to Mr. Edwards, in consideration of a new road to be made at his expense about fifty or sixty yards further to the east and leading to the said ford. The last time we heard of this being used, arose out of a dispute a man in charge of some cattle had with the toll gate keeper at Corbridge Bridge, who at once took the cattle by this ancient ford and road, and brought them again on to the Watling Street near the railway station.

" Drifts," that the origin of the name " Drift Road " arose from the fact that for ages the Watling Street was the great highway for the large herds, drifts, or droves of cattle which annually left the Highlands of Scotland for Smithfield Market, in London,* and came periodically in droves or drifts, sometimes extending a distance of two miles;† they were large cattle with horns of prodigious size, generally of fine shape and proportion, but sometimes of the most curious shape and form.‡ The driving of the herds was quite a business, and always when passing through Corbridge excited considerable attention ; they were always under the charge of one man, who was called the " topsman," and who had the advantage of a pony to ride on. To a given number of cattle was appointed one drover. The cattle were generally shod with flat plates of iron to preserve their feet during their long journey. A man often accompanied them for this purpose, and often, in his day, Clemison Lough, blacksmith, of Greenhead, and brother of Lough, the great sculptor, who was famous in this line of business, met them some miles before they reached Greenhead, and followed them some miles beyond, until every animal was well shod, and in good walking order, when he returned and was in readiness to meet the next drove : fierce looking animals they were, and certainly would be in their native pastures, but when passing through the village, were as docile as lambs, thousands passing through

* The Watling Street, as has been already noticed had its starting point behind Cheapside, in London, and was the middle Roman Road to Scotland, and used for general purposes, until other good and more convenient roads were made after the rebellion in 1745, as the following curious incident will show. A messenger was sent from London, on horseback, by this road, with money which he carried in saddle bags, for the payment of General Wade's army. On arriving at Corbridge, he lodged all night at the vicarage, being the guest of the Rev. John Walton, but on reaching head quarters he found, on examining the bags, that a considerable sum had been extracted, he at once wrote to Mr. Walton informing him what had occurred, stating that the bags had never been out of his possession during the entire journey from London to Newcastle, except at Corbridge ; the money was never recovered.

† A toll of so much per head, being demanded by the collectors appointed by the Lord of the Manor, for all cattle passing over this portion of the manor, was often the cause of much contention, sometimes arising from the delay occasioned by their being all counted as they passed through the toll gate at the bridge, and sometimes from the direct refusal to pay the toll, which if persisted in, a bullock was taken possession of as a hostage until it was paid; sometimes the drift would reach Riding Mill before the topsman made up his mind to pay the toll, when one of the drovers was sent back to pay the amount, and release the animal.

‡ It appears that a few years ago this remarkable breed of cattle had almost become extinct, but by the exertions of one large and enterprising breeder have again become numerous.

every year : seven or eight weeks were generally occupied in completing the journey.* A generation has passed away since the last drove walked through Corbridge. They are now conveyed by the "iron horse."

Corbridge Corn Mill. originally the Manor Mill, is built near to the south-west corner of the Roman station ; its water-wheel being driven by the core of the Romans. Being the mill for the use of the manor of Corbridge, it belonged to the Duke of Northumberland, who continued to hold it, until within a few years ago, when it was sold to the late William Cuthbert, Esq. According to a lease made and dated 1783, it was re-let to its then occupier, Robert Richley, together with the land attached to it, at the annual rental of £40. The term commencing from the feast of the annunciation of the blessed Virgin Mary next ensuing. The rent to be paid on this feast-day, and on the feast-day of St. Michael, the Arch-angel, next ensuing. It is stated that the family of Richleys, (of whom Henry Richley Butcher is a lineal descendant) were occupiers of this mill for three hundred years, and that the heads of the six last generations were respectively of the name of Robert. The mill portion of the building is now in ruins, but the house is still occupied.

The Cross, in the Market Place, when erected by the Duke of Northumberland, in 1810, was considered a handsome structure, its base is now sadly out of repair and presents a wretched appearance.

The ancient rights of the inhabitants of Corbridge will now be noticed. The first we refer to is the Plantation Walk, which is on the south side of the river, and extends betwixt the bridge at Corbridge and the bridge on the turnpike road at Dilston, a walk (as well as ground to ramble over) which the Corbridge people had enjoyed from time immemorial. It was thus described by Mr. Willis, Counsel, at the late assize trial, who had previously gone over it : " If my opinion is worth anything, extending over an experience of twenty-five years, I must say I never witnessed a finer walk than this." It might well be a matter for rejoicing, when the attempt to de-prive the people of their ancient right was nullified by the

---

* The drovers, six or seven weeks after passing through the village south-wards, returned by the same road, and were noticed to walk fast; the entire journey would be somewhere about 900 or 1000 miles.

decision of the Court of Assize, held in Newcastle in July, 1879, and the right thus secured to them for ever. There was due important development which arose out of the evidence of the plaintiff, and which should not be lost sight of, which is the fact, that the plantation ground never belonged to the Earl of Derwentwater, and that in 1779 it was waste ground, and called by the old people the Saughs, pronounced Sawes, "the Plantation" being a modern name. How the Commissioners of the Greenwich Hospital came to plant it is not satisfactorily known, for surely the Corbridge people had, at least, equal rights with the Commissioners; but one thing is certain, and which was rightly described by the learned Judge during the trial : "That the Corbridge people at the time when it was waste land used it freely, and had continued to do so down to the present."

Another pleasant walk not much used, owing probably to its not being known by visitors, is the Stanners Walk, set apart by an act of parliament, and described in the *Award Book* as follows : "And we do hereby also assign, set out, and appoint one other road four feet in breadth, and which, for distinction's sake, we shall call by the name of Farnley Foot Road, beginning at and leading from the south-end of the bridge, over the river Tyne at Corbridge, into that parcel of ground called the Stanners, and from thence along the same leading eastward into an allotment hereinafter awarded to the Duke of Northumberland, in Farnley, and from thence still leading eastward, to the east of the ancient inclosures, in the Isles, otherwise the Eales, and from thence turning south up Farnley Bank, and from thence further south through the Duke of Northumberland's allotment (hereinafter awarded) into Farnley Road, at a stile to be placed there by the Duke of Northumberland, or the owner or occupier of this allotment, opposite to the north-west corner of an allotment on Farnley, hereinafter awarded to the said Francis Tweddell." When we traversed this walk in April, 1881, we found the stile in the stone wall, which leads into Farnley Road, al right, but in Farnley Bank, where the road leads through a small gorge, it was obstructed by thorns and rubbish, and in crossing the railway, we found only one stile in the fence on the south side, on the other side a high gate had to be clambered over.

103

Another short but pleasant footpath, not generally known and therefore not much used, is thus described in the Award:—"And we do hereby also assign, set out and appoint a road or footway four feet in breadth, as the same is now used, and which for distinction's sake we shall call by the name of Leazes Public Foot Road: beginning at and leading from the north end of an ancient lane called Gos Croft Lane,* northwards through a parcel of ground hereinafter allotted to his Grace the Duke of Northumberland, and another parcel of ground hereinafter allotted to Bartholomew Winship, to an ancient stile in the said Leazes Road."

Another pleasant and interesting walk, extending about a mile and a half, is from the north-east end of the village to Aydon Castle, commencing on the turnpike road leading to Aydon, by an ancient lane proceeding northwards for about two hundred yards, and is called Wine or Wain House Lane.† The next portion of turnpike road is called Didridge, and was set off at the division as twenty-five feet in breadth from thence, by an ancient bridle road through the fields by the dene to the castle. The dene is a picturesque spot, with its streamlet rippling through amongst the trees, shrubs, and ferns. Above stands the castle, (hereinafter referred to) half a mile further on is Halton Castle, and a little further on still is the site of the Roman station Hunnan, a great portion of which is still visible and traceable in the pasture field on the south side of the military road; when returning, visitors can do so, either by the Leazes Lane, or by the Chantry Road, and Watling Street.

Another agreeable and refreshing walk is by the north side of the river, west from the village as far as Corbridge mill, then northwards by a continuation through the pasture on the township road, to its junction with Colchester road, then

* Gos Croft Lane evidently had its origin from its being the ancient lane leading to the Priors Manor House or dwelling. Gos would suggest primarily to have been God's, as this was property belonging to the church, and until lately, was Dean and Chapter land belonging to Carlisle. The house being snugly situated in a small enclosure or croft, would thus aptly be designated God's croft, in the same way as church yards are called God's acre.

† Wain House Lane is thought to be the original name, this being the old road to the ancient lime kilns, which were close by, and had been in use for centuries; wains being the name for such conveyance as were then used for leading lime. A house being here most likely for the use of the men employed at the quarries and lime kilns, and as a halting or resting place for oxen and horses, as well as the men employed in carrying away the lime, hence the name wain house lane.

proceeding to Corbridge. This walk skirts the south, the west, and north sides of the Roman station. About half way betwixt the mill and Corchester road on the west side of the Cor, is the site of the cemetery—the Roman city of the dead.

An ancient well, although at the present not approachable on account of recent obstructions, but which should not be forgotten, as possibly it may be required again for public use, and is described in the Award as follows :—"And we do hereby also assign, set out, and appoint a certain well or spring of water in Tinkler Bank, and within the allotment there, hereinafter awarded to the Vicar of Corbridge, and which, for distinction's sake, we shall call by the name of Tinkler Bank Well ; and we do hereby direct and award that the said spring or well shall for ever, hereafter, remain, be and continue open for the use of all and every the person and persons interested in the division hereby made, for the purpose of getting water thereout, and carrying the same away on foot only, at their freewills and pleasures ; and that the said Vicar, and his successors, shall make and for ever hereafter maintain a good and easy stile in that part of the fence of his allotment, adjoining Tinkler Bank Road aforesaid, and opposite to the said spring or well ; as is and shall be most convenient for the purpose of occupying and using the said spring or well."*

The last reference we make on this subject is to the Bridge End Watering Place, although used, its conditions are not generally known. We quote again from the Award : "And we do hereby also assign, set out, and appoint a part of the said common called the Stanners, (and formerly used as a way) as and for a passage to the river Tyne for a common watering place for cattle, and which for distinction's sake, we shall call by the name of Bridge End Watering Place, and as the same is now staked and set out by stakes and land marks, boundering on that part of the said Stanners, so mentioned to be sold to the said Edward Gray, and hereinafter awarded to

* There are many persons living in the village who recollect the particulars of this well, which was known by the name of the "priest's well," on account of its being in the field belonging to the Vicar. There were two troughs supplied by a fine feeder or flow of water. The occupiers of Orchard House (the only house at that time in the neighbourhood) got their water from this well, a foot path being along the foot of the field. The stile on Tinkler Bank Road referred to in the Award was wide and easy, with a good path to the well.

him on or towards the east, on Hexham turnpike road, and the said bridge over the river Tyne at Corbridge, on or towards the west, on the river Tyne on or towards the north, and on part of Dilston estate on or towards the south, and we do order, direct, and award that the said parcel of the Stanners shall for ever hereafter, remain be and continue open, as, and for a common watering place,* for the use of all and every the owners and occupiers, of messuages, mills, lands, tenements, and hereditaments, interested in the division hereby made, and all other persons whomsoever."

We now refer to the various charities bequeathed from time to time, to the poor of the parish. Mackenzie in his history gives the following account concerning them : " Madam Elizabeth Radcliffe, widow of Sir Edward Radcliffe, of Dilston, Bart., and mother of Francis, Earl of Derwentwater, by will in 1668, gave out of an annuity or rent charge of £20 per annum, which she then had of Mr. Francis Sutton, of Green-croft, £10 to the poor of this parish, to be distributed

---

* There is an idea that this watering place is also an outlet or way from the plantation above the bridge for the timber cut down there, and for other purposes. We have heard the Greenwich Hospital agent assert this to be so, but a reference to the facts, which it is proper here to make, will show this idea to be altogether false. At the time of the division in 1779, when this watering place was so particularly specified and awarded by the Commissioners, it is clearly shown that it was intended exclusively for a watering place, and ordered that it should be so for ever, and therefore could not be used for any other purpose; being bounded by the bridge on the west, and the Stanners on the east, and betwixt those boundaries formed a very deep portion of the river—long known by the name of Tom Cutter's hole. The river at that time, as has been previously described, except in floods, from the sandy hole, flowed on the south side of the gravel bed, by the side of the plantation, taking the two southern arches. The alteration in the course of the river, from the south to the north side, took place from fifty to forty-five years ago. It is necessary to state that when the award was made that portion of land, now known as the plantation, was set down in the plan as waste land, and called by the Corbridge people the Sawes or Saughs, otherwise Willows. Although the ground or land was called waste, the willows grown there were of considerable value, having been for generations used as a right by the people in the village for the roofs of thatch houses, as a kind of wicker-work betwixt the rafters, to which the first layer of thatch was secured, and when cut down in the proper season, were very durable. The willows in a thatch house, recently pulled down in the village, having stood for at least two hundred years, were found to be quite sound, so much so that the owner intended to use them for pea sticks. Not only were the willows used for the roofs of houses, but were used also when plastering the inside instead of laths. It will be clearly seen that the plantation (using the modern name) never belonged to the Derwentwater estates. When the Greenwich Hospital Commissioners assumed the authority to plant this public ground does not appear to be known, it was certainly some time after the division, and might be near the close of the last century. We think it however of importance that the authorities of the township of Corbridge should keep, maintain, and preserve this watering place intact, as well as all other walks, roads, wells, &c., secured to them and the public by act of parliament, or by the right of ancient usuage.

annually on St. Lucie's day (St. Luke's), or thereabouts. Mrs. Ursula Mountney left twenty shillings per annum for the same use. Madam Ann Radcliff, of Dilston, sister to Francis, Earl of Derwentwater, in 1699, gave to the poor of this parish to bind apprentices, the annual produce of £338 6s. 8d. Mrs. Ann Swinburne, of Dilston, by will in 1702, bequeathed a sum of money to the poor of this parish, to be distributed at Dilston upon St. Thomas' day before Christmas. Her executor, Matthew Gill, left for this and other purposes £269 4s. 1d. In 1742, Gill Brown made a payment of £5 to the poor, but denied at the same time, and still denies, that it had any respect to the charity left by Ann Swinburne, since which time no payment has been made. It does not appear that any certain sum was left for the payment of this charity, but it is supposed out of the above £269 4s. 1d., £100 or perhaps more was intended to pay the £6 per annum, but the interest falling from 6 to 5 per cent., William Brown paid only £5 for his two or three last payments, pleading as supposed, that the sum left would not produce more (Returns of Char. Don., 1787—8). The Rev. Robert Troutbeck, Vicar of this parish, by will declared and published 12th May, 1706, gave to the poor of this parish, and the chapelry of Halton, a certain messuage and lands in Corbridge, which cost him £100, the annual rent to be distributed to them by one of the name of Troutbeck, or by the Minister or Churchwardens for the time being. (We have not ascertained the present annual produce of this charity, but are assured that eating a good dinner forms part of the business of the trustees.) Hannah Brown, and Mary Robson, in the year 1804, bequeathed £100, the interest of which is to be distributed among twenty indigent people residing in Corbridge, by the Vicar of that place for the time being, and two gentlemen of the name of Brown, so long as such can be found. The acting trustee, Mr. John Brown, purchased a house and part of a garden on Hearon Hill with the above sum, and enrolled the charity in chancery. In reference to the before-named charities, it may be stated that the charity left by the Rev. Robert Troutbeck now produces the annual sum of £23 4s., which, with the twenty shillings left by Mrs. Ursula Mountney is distributed at the same time as one sum. The charity left by Madam Ann Radcliffe, now realizes the fixed sum of £30 per annum, viz., £10 for the

binding of apprentices, and £20 for the poor; this sum is paid out of Nafferton Farm.

Mrs. Rogers about the year 1833, bequeathed a sum of money, the interest of which is annually disposed of to the poor of this parish, in oatmeal; this bequest is in the hands of the Charity Commissioners, and realizes the sum annually of £5 13s. 2d., these charities are dispensed by the Vicar, Churchwardens, and Overseers, for the time being.

It has been suggested that in this book a reference should be made to the old family names of those belonging the village and neighbourhood. It seemed at first a rather difficult matter to collect such authentic information as to make the subject sufficiently correct and interesting; but just at this juncture, an old Churchwarden's account and minute book was kindly placed at the service of the writer by the Rev. Mr. Hodgson, and another by Mr. Blandford, Churchwarden; with the assistance of these curious books, the matter seemed now comparatively easy.

We first give a list of the Vicars from the year of our Lord 1128, with two intervals which we extract from *Hutchinson's History of Northumberland*, together with the names of those since Hutchinson's time :—

Richard de Aure Valle	1128.	Jeremone Nelson	1674.
William de Glaston	1322.	Robert Troutbeck	1685.
John de Cotesford	1356.	Henry Guy	1706.
John de Brownfield	1370.	Thomas Todd	1709.
Thomas de Ormsheved	1379.	Charles Whittendale	1718.
John de Brygg	1409.	John Walton	1719.
Thomas Ormesby	1412.	Robert Wardle	1765.
......Daker	1501.	Thomas Wilson	1773.
Anthony Musgrave	1528.	George Wilson	1785.
Phr. Richard Marshall	1544.	Henry Gipps	1829.
John Dobson	1588.	Frederick Gipps	1853.
Richard Lambert	1614.	George C. Hodgson	1874.
John Fenwick	1665.		

In the Churchwardens' books we have the names of the Churchwardens from the year 1676, from which we make selections down to the beginning of the present century, of such names as appear to have some near or even distant relation to, or connection with families now existing, as the most authentic way of complying with the wishes of several friends.

as also of many others who we are sure will be interested in the subject. From the time the extracts begin until 1767 there were four Churchwardens for the parish, viz.: two for Corbridge, one for Diiston, and one for Aydon and the other outlying townships. Rather than give one single name we prefer to quote all for the year referred to.

July 14th, 1676.

1676.—Thomas Hoaron, John Readhead, Christo Ridley, Matthew Armstrong.

1677.—Edward Hudspith, Michaell Spain, Will Lee, John Hoaron.

1679.—Sir Francis Radcliff, Will Carnaby, Michael Dyber, Reginal Langlands.

1681.—Will Greenwell, George Downe, Will Milburne, Robert Joplin.

1682.—John Hutchesson, Thos. Tailor, Will Fawset, Will Milburne.

1684.—Lionel Romsby, Will Rugolly, Sir Francis Ratcliff, Will Lee.

1685.—Sir Francis Radcliff, John Greenwell, Ralph Readhead, Henry Angus.

1686.—Sir Francis Radcliff, John Cooke, Matthew Browne, Edward Elliott.

1687.—Sir Franciss Ratcliff, Bart., Rodger Younger, Richard Simson, Cuthbert Nicholson.

1689.—Francis, Earl of Derwentwater, Mr. Symonds Meldon, Michael Spain, John Henderson.

1690.—The Earl of Derwentwater, Lionel Winship, Hubell Hudspith, John Langlands.

1691.—Bartw. Lumbly, John Doning, Ralph Davidson, Willm. Milburne.

1693.—Thos. Nicholson, Richard Gibson, John Burdas, Will Milburne.

1697.—Michael Spain, William Smith, John Lawson, Henry Forster.

1699.—Edward Green, Cuthbert Joplin, William Richley, Matthew Browne.

1701.—Cuthbert Nicholson, Thomas Gyles, Lionel Winship, James Brown.

1702.—John Greenwell, Ralph Reedhead, Richard Brown, Wm. Lee

109

1703.—John Lumbly, Abraham Fawcitt, Phillip Aydoun, John Davison.

1704.—William Fawsett, John Burdess, Char. Laidler, John Lawson

1705.—John Heppell, Mr. Nicholas Greenwell, Thos. Giles, Richard Linton.

1708.—James Brown, Mr. Wm. Weldon, Matthew Greenwell, John Usher

1711.—Edward Browell, Lyonel Winship, junr., Thos. Nicholson, Mich. Bell.

1715.—Michael Linton, Wm. Dodd, Robert Forster, John Noble

1719.—Reginal Gibson, Walter Nixon, John Laidley, John Bowman.

1720.—Mr. Thomas Reed, Matth. Thompson, William Fawsett, Robt. Hall.

1721.—Lyonel Winship, John Lumbly, Abraham Fawsett, Robert Whitfield.

1724. Wm. Noble, Geo. Lee, John Dening, John Thompson.

1727.—John Bates, Robert Hoggert, John Webber, Edward Gyles.

1729.—Robert Forster, Thomas Robson, Joseph Forster, Matt. Thompson.

1735.—Thos. Fawsett, John Bowman, Joth. Richley, Ed. Giles.

1737.—Wm. Noble, Jno. Lumbly, John Bates, Michael Brown.

1740.—Mr. Winship, Richd. Gibson, Whitfield Green, David Brown.

THE FOLLOWING REPRESENT CORBRIDGE ONLY:—

1743.—George Gibson, Matthew Greenwell.

1744.—Thos. Fawcitt, jun., John Bowman.

1746.—John Forster, Barth. Lumbly.

1752.—Ra. Redhead, Thos. Lumbly.

1754.—Thos. Fawcitt, George Rowell.

1761.—John Walker, Joseph Fairless.

THE FOLLOWING REPRESENT THE PARISH:—

1766.—Eliezer Birch, Esq., Mr. Rich. Brown.

1773.—John Noble, Matthew Greenwell.

1774.—Josh. Walker, Wm. Greenwell.

1776.—Robert Forster, John Spite.

110

1778.—Lionel Winship, John Brown.   \
1780.—Thos. Richley, St. Gibson.
1786.—B. Winship, George Simpson.
1790.—Jos. Walker, Wm. Lethard.
1791.—John Richley, William Bowman.
1792.—Rich. Carnaby Charlton, St. Gibson.
1793.—Thos. Surtees, Wm. Greenwell.
1795.—Michael Brown, Robert Forster.
1800.—John Walker, William Ridley.
1802.—Wm. Ridley, Bartho. Lumbly.
1803.—Jno. Reweastle, Wm. Richley.
1808.—Stephen Gibson, William Fairley.
1809.—John Simpson, Robert Forster.
1811.—James Hall, N. B. Reed.
1819.—James Manchester, Robert Anderson.

It will be seen by the perusal of these extracts, that several family names have ceased to exist in Corbridge, their descendants being resident in other localities, and even in other countries; in reference to a few others whose names are not only extinct, but all knowledge of the families are lost in that great storehouse of forgotten things, (many names we have not quoted are in this class.) As all these names are a short but easily understood history in themselves, there are only a few which require a passing notice, and little more than ordinary attention. It will have been observed that Sir Francis Radcliff was five times churchwarden for Dilston when he was a baronet, and twice after he was created earl. In 1676, is the name of John Readhead, churchwarden, and in 1685 is Ralph Readhead; their lineal descendants are still living in Corbridge, of the name of Ralph. The descendants of several other old families are yet resident in the village. The two names more particularly referred to are those of Birch and Greenwell. Eliezer Birch, Esq., (by which title he is designated) was not a native of Corbridge, but took up his residence here about the middle of the last century. Where he came from, or his antecedents, were never satisfactorily known. There was an opinion, held by a few, that he was a refugee from Ireland; others held different views of his whereabouts; one thing was certain respecting him,—he was a gentleman, both in purse and character. He first built for himself a substantial

house to live in, which is now occupied by Mr. Walton and
Miss Snowball; he erected Princess Street Well at his own
cost, and suggested the utility of a clock in the tower of the
church, which was erected by subscription, himself by agreement subscribing one-half of the cost. During the time he
was churchwarden in 1766, the workhouse was erected, no
doubt through his energy; the original plan was to have it
covered with thatch, but his views were too advanced to agree
to a thatch roof, he therefore proposed to pay the difference
betwixt the cost of thatch and slate roofing, which according
to the accounts in the churchwarden's books was £82. It
was thought he contemplated making further improvements
in the village, but death put an end to all his earthly plans,
for he died in July, 1767, at the comparatively early age of
forty-seven. A small stone resting against the church-yard
wall, on the west side of the pele tower, records his death.
The other name, that of Greenwell, is unquestionably by far the
oldest name now existing in Corbridge and neighbourhood.

We quote from an article which appeared in the *Weekly
Chronicle*, some three years ago, on family names, and when
referring to this family, the writer remarks, that "this
venerable house traditionally is of Norman origin, and is
second in antiquity to none now existing in the palatinate of
Durham." The writer particularly traces the family from the
conquest downwards, and states, that "a few centuries ago,
distinct branches of this family were founded at Broomshields
and Ford, in the parish of Lanchester, and at Corbridge, in
Northumberland, and are afterwards referred to as the Greenwells of Broomshields, and the Greenwells of Greenwell Ford,
and the Greenwells of Corbridge." The article describes
this branch of the family as becoming settled at Corbridge
and Aydon, late in the sixteenth century, and gives several
names, as William Greenwell, John Greenwell, Captain
Whitfield Greenwell, Nicholas Greenwell, and Dr. Greenwell.
With the assistance of the churchwardens' books, we can
clearly, for the last two centuries, trace the line of this
family, which, at the close of the seventeenth century, is
divided into two branches; in 1681 we find Wm. Greenwell,
churchwarden, and in 1685 John Greenwell, churchwarden.
William and John Greenwell appear to have been brothers,
and what seems quite probable, might be grandsons of the

famous Will Greenwell, the sturdy yeoman of Corbridge, who stands out so prominently in connection with the battle at Aydon Castle. From John Greenwell descended Mr. Nicholas Greenwell, Ralph Greenwell, Captain Whitfield Greenwell, and Dr. Greenwell, who for some time resided in the house now occupied by Mr. Spraggon, and who was the last survivor of that branch of the family in Corbridge. From William Greenwell in a clear and distinct line, alternately, Matthew and William Greenwell, descended the late Matthew Greenwell, whose only son, William, now living in Corbridge, is the lineal descendant of this honourable and ancient family. During the two past centuries this family, in the transaction of parish business, stands out more prominent than any other.

Amongst the curious items in the church books is one as follows: "1743, a call to let ye flagging of ye church 0s. 4d." This once useful village official " Town Crier " (we have not his name) had his successors, and amongst those of the last generation should be mentioned John Robson, *alias* John the Bellman, the first town crier we recollect hearing. John was the descendant of an old family now extinct in Corbridge. He was a soldier in his early years, having taken the bounty and enlisted in the Northumberland Militia. He was stationed at various places in England, and also in Ireland, where he took his wife, Peggy. After having completed his period of service in the army, he settled in his native village, following his trade of shoe and slipper making, in which he was greatly assisted by his wife. In addition to his ordinary calling, he added that of " Town Crier," which at that time was very remunerative, the " calls " being frequent and often two on the same round. The price of a call had risen in John's day, like many other things, from fourpence to sixpence each. John had a fine clear voice which could be heard at a good distance, and in addition was furnished with what made his movements and appearance attractive, viz.: a beautifully polished and good sized bell, a splendid light drab cloth overcoat reaching nearly to his heels, beautifully trimmed, and equally as good a hat with a gold band about it, all made to represent the Duke's livery; these were given to him by a gentleman of the name of Lumbly, *alias* Bartie the merchant (who was remarkable for his loyalty to the powers that be,) but on condition that every time he went round the village with his

" ting-a-ring " he should wear them, and at the end of each call, should touch the brim of his hat and shout " God save the King and the Lord of the Manor." Scores of times as he began to move to his next halting place, have we seen and heard him do this : first, placing the bell on the bend of his left arm, leaving his right hand free to do the usual homage to the brim of his hat, but after many years of this performance the tongue of poor Robson's own bell ceased to move, and he followed in the wake of his predecessors. Other bellmen since Robson's day have succeeded each other, and in their turn have passed the corner of life, but the mantle of Robson's loyalty fell on none of these, perhaps no loyal merchant offered them a fine drab coat, and a gold banded hat. The village is now without the services of this once indispensable functionary, but so gradually adapted are social arrangements to existing circumstances, that the business of the village moves on as smoothly as if no such official had ever existed. Robson had a son who was blind, but who possessed other remarkable faculties which deserve to be noticed. He was known in the village and neighbourhood as Blind Harry. When about two years of age, he entirely lost his sight through small pox. As he grew up, his powers of hearing, feeling, and recognition were such, that when he reached manhood, he was acquainted with nearly every person in the village, and could enter every house without any apparent difficulty in finding the door. Not only had he a good knowledge of Corbridge, but became almost as familiar with Hexham, and was accustomed to go there from time to time, sometimes accompanied by a little sister, to dispose of their goods (home-made slippers). We well recollect our first visit to Hexham when a boy, and our first sight of the tower of the Abbey Church, which was under the care and guidance of Harry. For many years he was groom for Dr. Lowrey, who kept two horses, and well did Harry perform his duty. It certainly appeared somewhat strange, to hear him in a dark night going into the stable, to dress and feed the horses without the aid of a light, or it might be to saddle them for his master's use ; but after several years in this service, Harry began to drink and frequent the public house, and as an inevitable result began to neglect his business, the doctor bore with him for a season, which was of no avail, and in the

π

end he lost his situation, and ultimately removed from the village. One instance of his powers of recognition may be given; a few years afterwards, as he was passing through the town, and nearing a group of four or five persons, who all remained silent, except one who spoke to him, he instantly knew him by his voice, and joining the company, soon made out, without speaking, the others except one, whom he seemed to have a little difficulty in recognizing, but after a little groping about his person, said, "it is Michael," and so it was. He could recognize any person by their voice after an absence of twenty years, if he had been previously acquainted with them. As a means of obtaining a living, he hawked pottery ware about the country, in company with a woman who it is stated became his wife, having a donkey and cart to assist them in carrying their wares. The goods were purchased at Newcastle. It was on one of these occasions that one of the most ludicrous incidents in Harry's life occurred, somehow or other he was alone with his donkey and cart and lost the friend of Baalim, but was determined not to lose his cart ; he therefore performed the extraordinary feat, of actually dragging the cart from Newcastle to Hexham, where he then resided, always keeping the middle of the turnpike road. At that time the road was in a miserable condition with mud, so that when passing through Corbridge he was covered from head to foot. In addition to his other remarkable faculties, he was extremely sensitive in the tread of his foot, by this he appeared to be guided in his journeys, seldom missing the right way, and when approaching danger was always cautious as if he appeared to see it; we only recollect seeing him fall on one occasion, which was caused by a low obstruction in the street, but we are not aware he was ever known to run or walk against a wall or house, or any great obstruction which was directly before him : at these times he at once appeared conscious of danger, and as carefully avoided it ; neither are we aware, although he lived beyond his threescore years, that any accident befel him during the wanderings of his chequered life. He was accustomed to come to Corbridge to receive the dole at Christmas, to which as a parishoner he was duly entitled, which he did until near the close of his life. It is now some years since Harry, having filled the measure of his days, crossed the dark stream.

115

Before bringing this book to a close, the writer has been specially requested to give a few pages of extracts from the minutes and accounts in the churchwardens' books referred to, extending from 1676 to 1800. The historian of Bishop Auckland, Mr. Matthew Richley, remarks, " some may think it beneath the historian to record apparent trifles, but these records not only really constitute and reflect the provincial manners and customs of our forefathers, but also the natural or physicial state of the country during that period." These records form a considerable item in the history of Corbridge, we therefore quote them freely.

For a century-and-a-half (as appears by the churchwardens' books), the business of the church and parish was managed by a little parliament, consisting of the vicar, churchwardens, and " four and twenty." The following extracts will show the order of business. The first schedule of names is headed, " The four and twenty of Corbridge Parish," there is no date to this entry, the page containing the date, with several others having been cut out of the book, but as far as we can make out would be not later than 1693 ; in this schedule of names is Henry Collyson, gentleman, who was at the time the owner of Aydon Castle. Henry would appear to be the last of the family who possessed the Aydon Castle estate, having been ruined by becoming bond for a friend.*

The next entry is dated A.D. 1710, July y⁰ 11th.

"At a meeting of y⁰ Vicar, Churchwardens, and as many of y⁰ 24 as could be convened," then follows the names of twenty who were present. The business of that meeting was " to appoint twelve of that number to form a vestry, to meet upon urgent occasions of y⁰ Parish."

" May 20th, 1730. Ordered by y⁰ Vicars, Churchwardens, and four and twenty in pursuance of public notice given for that purpose, y' fourpence a pound be levied immediately in y⁰ parish of Corbridge for newcasting y⁰ Bell (the little Bell) and y⁰ ordinary expenses of y⁰ parish for y⁰ current year."

---

* There are three entries on the first page of the churchwarden's books which should have been entered in the Register Book of Deaths, &c., which are as follows : "Edward Ratcheson, buried Nov. ye 5th, 1698. Thomas, son of Joseph Bell, buried Nov. ye 15th, 1698, and the Lord Henry Collison, gentleman.'
Amongst the names of the killers of wild animals we find " Mr. Colleson, in Aydon Castle, one fox head, November the 23rd day, 1691."
'" Mr. Colleson, in Aydon Castle, one fox head, July 14th day, 1695."

116

Then follows the name of the Vicar, and the names of nine others present, each in their own handwriting.

" March 26th, 1744. Agreed at the said meeting of four and twenty, that there be four meetings yearly, namely : Monday after Easter day, Monday after Midsummer day, Monday after Michaelmas day, and Monday after Christmas day ; and that the Vicar, any of the Churchwardens, or any of the four and twenty that do not appear on the said days, shall pay for every such default the sum of one shilling to the overseers of the poor then in being, to the use of the poor of the said parish, witness our hands." Then follows the names of the Vicar, Churchwardens, and thirteen others, amongst these names is "Shafto Downes" well written, this name appears often afterwards amongst these officials as " Mr. Downes."

" March 13th, 1763, at a meeting of the four and twenty according to public notice, for that purpose, ordered that two farthings a pound be laid on and collected according to the real value in the Parish of Corbridge for the expenses and repairs of the Church." Then follow six names.

" At a meeting of the Vestry, June 22nd, 1789, it was agreed that any of the four and twenty leaving the parish, and not occupying any property in it, should be disqualified from voting upon any Parish business whatever, until again elected according to the established custom of the place;" then follow twelve names.

This Parliament continued, in form at least, until 1831, after which time it appears to have been finally dissolved.

As schedules of the names of the four and twenty may be interesting to some of our readers, we give them for four years as taken from the books :—

1693.

Willm. Carnaby, Esq.	Mr. Thos. Hoaron
Will Greenwell	James Langlands
Will Winship	Henry Collison, gentln.
John Hoaron	Robert Hudspith, senior
Christopher Fawset	Charles Armstrong
Mr. Alexr. Hoaron	Simond Weldon
Will Lee	Lionel Winship
Chris. Ridley	John Cooke, junior
John Lumbly	Will Carnaby
Ralph Readhead	Will Rishelley

117

John Hutshesson   Richard Linton

Will Smith   George Hoaron

1710.

Thomas Heron, senr.   Paul Hudspith

Lionel Winship, senr.   Wm. Hudspith

Thomas Heron, junr.   John Greenwell

Matthew Brown   John Lumbly

Ried. Carnaby   Abraham Fawsett

Lionel Winship, junr.   Robert Spane

Wm. Fawsett   Ralph Readhead

Barthw. Lumbly   John Denning

Mattw. Greenwell   Michl. Usher   Reginal Gibson

1727.

Mr. Aynsley   Mr. Douglas

Mr. Reed   Ralph Redhead

Reg. Gibson   Wm. Hudspeth

Richd. Carnaby   Lionel Winship

John Greenwell   Abm. Fawcet

Mat. Thompson   Wm. Fawcet

Ed. Winship   Ed. Giles

Mat. Brown   John Lumbly

John Denning   Wm. Laidler

John Usher   Wm. Noble

Mr. Weldon   Mich. Davidson

John Bates   Robt. Hoggart

1789.

Mr. Michael Brown   Mr. Reginal Gibson

Mr. John Snowball   Mr. Edward Bell

Mr. Bartholomew Lumbly   Mr. John Rewcastle

Mr. John Reed   Mr. John Richley

Mr. John Bowman   Mr. William Thompson

Mr. George Gibson   Mr. George Bates

Mr. Lionel Winship   Mr. Richd. Carnaby Charlton

Mr. William Winship   Mr. John Smith

Mr. James Hall   Mr. John Brown

Mr. Bartholomew Winship   Mr. William Greenwel

Mr. William Heppell   Mr. Paul Brown

Mr. Joseph Walker   Mr. John Nicholson

From these Books we learn the progressive value of rateable property in the Township and Parish, the following extracts will suffice to show it :—

	£	s.	d.
1677, Memorandum, Corbridge Church Sess is at 1 penny pᵣ pound	01	05	00
Dilston is at 1 penny pᵣ pound	00	16	04
The out-Quarter is at a penny pᵣ pound ...	01	00	10
Soe yᵗ yᵉ Sess of yᵉ whole parish is at 1 penny pᵣ pound...	03	02	2

For the year 1712—

	£	s.	d.
Dilston Sess at 1d. pᵣ pound is	,,	16	04
Corbridge Sess at 1d. pᵣ pound is	01	05	00
* Thornbrough out-qᵣ at 1d. per pound is...	01	00	10

It will be seen that during a period of thirty-five years no alteration was made in the rateable value of the parish, being for Corbridge, £300; for Dilston, £196; for the out-quarters or Townships, £250.

"September 11, 1754, at a meeting of the four and twenty, Ordered that one penny a pound be laid on and collected according to the real yearly value in the Parish of Corbridge, for the expenses and repairs of the Church." On a blank leaf is a rider to this ordering, which is as follows :—

Real value of the Land of Corbridge Parish—

		£				£	s.	d.
1754	... ...	3031	1					
Rectory	...	311	0					
Vicarage	...	70	0					
		381	0	Corbridge	...	5	6	0
				Aydon ...	...	3	15	8
For Church Sess	2650	1	Dilston ...	...	1	19	6
	†at 1d. pᵣ pound is...	...	...	11	1	2
	at 2d. pᵣ pound	...	...	22	2	4
	at 3d. a pound	...	...	33	3	6

The rateable value of the Township of Corbridge being £1272 0s. 0d.

---

* Sometimes the townships, including Aydon, Thornbrough, Aydon Castle, and Little Whittington, are called—the out-quarter—the outlying districts—Thornbrough, Aydon, &c.

† It must not be inferred that the rate during all these intervening years was uniformly the same; it was laid on so as to meet the expenses incurred, and was sometimes 3d., 4d., and as high as 8d. in the pound; one year it was "two farthings" in the pound.

ON MILITIA ACCOUNT. £ s. d.

1793, April 25th. For an assessment on the
inhabitants of the parish of Corbridge, at
one penny in the pound 15 7 2
The amount rated upon being 3644 7 6

July 5th. For Cash received of the Chapel
Wardens of Halton, being equivalent to one
penny in the pound for the whole parish 5 5 0
The amount rated on being 1260 0 0

1797. For an assessment at 2d. in the pound
collected from the inhabitants of the
Township of Corbridge 15 15 0
The rateable value being 1890 0 0

In 1880 the rateable value in the Township
of Corbridge was 13105 10 0

The value of labour, wages, goods, &c., will now be
noticed.

RINGING WAGES.

	£	s.	d.
1676. For Ringing 1s. 0d. 1677. For Ringing Gunpowder Plot		1	0
1729. Paid to Chas. Armstrong (Sexon) for Ringing 29th May		1	0
To Wm. Robson, (Beadle) same time		1	0
1754. For four days ringing to Sexton and Bedle		8	0
1755-6. Oct. 22nd. Ringing King's Coronation		2	0
,, Gunpowder Treason		2	0
,, Duke's Victory at Culloden		2	0
,, King's accession ...		2	0
,, King Charles' Restoration		2	0
1760. 22nd June. Prince Ferdinand's Victory over the French		2	0

OTHER WAGES, &c.

| 1678. For Two labourers' Wages for the Church, 2 days (each) ... ... | | 2 | 8 |
| Two labourers a day ... . | | 1 | 6 |

	£	s.	d.
1707. To Bartho Lumbly for ½ a day's (Mason) work	0		8
1740. Richard Potts' Salary as Sexton ...		10	0
Wm. Robson's as Beadle		5	0
A pair of Shoes for Wm. Robson as Beadle		3	6
To Wm. Lumbly 3 days mending ye Church Roof		4	0
To John Brown 3 days		4	0
To Barth. Lumbly 1 day		0	8
To Michael Lumbly 1 day		0	8
To Wm. Lumbly 3 days putting in a stone window		4	0
1743. A Labourer seven days at ye Church		4	8
1749. To Thomas Nicholson for 4½ days making the Gates, Checks, painting and setting them up		6	0
To 5½ deals for Church gates		8	3
Oak wood for the cheeks		3	6
Oyle and Paint for gates and cheeks		1	6
To John Forster for Bands, Crooks, Staples, Bolts, and Nails		7	0
Do. for a Spade Shatt and Shoulders, and mending the great Lock		1	6

In a list of entries for repairing the Church roof is the following :—

	£	s.	d.
Do. drink for the workmen, being a bad day		0	6
1763. To Beadle's Salary 5s. 0d., and a pair of shoes 4s. 6d.		9	6
1767. By paid Thomas Cutter for a Borer, Hanging ye Bell Tounges, a Bolt for Ch. yard gate, a Weathercock, &c.	1	19	10
Beadle's Salary		9	6

We must give two extracts for work of another kind :—

" I agree with ye Gentlemen of ye Vestry, to wash and mend ye Church Linen, but they must find Cloth, Thread, and Buttons when wanted. To wind-up ye Clock, to enter ye Church Wardens' accounts, and what transactions of ye Vestry are necessary in ye Parish Book. I will write ye presentments and a copy of ye Register, and a Schedule to collect ye Sess

by, for y° Sum of 30 Shillings a year, witness my hand
this 20th of April, 1767, Jacob Smith."

"I agree with the Gentlemen of the Vestry, to wind-up the
Church Clock, enter the Churchwardens' accounts, presentments, and a copy of the Register, a schedule to collect the
Church Cess by, and what things are necessary about the
Parish Books, for the consideration of Twenty Shillings a
year. As witness my hand, this 27th day of August, 1774,
William Ridley." (William Ridley who was a beautiful writer
and appears to have been a good business man, was a schoolmaster.)

The following curious extract will show that the vestry,
when necessary, could exercise its powers of discipline.

"At a Select Vestry, held in the vestry room this 3rd
of August, 1766, pursuant to notice given. Present: Reg.
Gibson, Barthw. Winship, Rich. Haswell, Thos. Fawcitt,
John Bowman, George Gibson, Ed. Bell, John Morpeth,
Matt. Greenwell, W. Laidler, Rd. Brown, Jn. Noble, and
Eliezer Birch.

It is the unanimous opinion of the persons present that
the parish has a right to a sermon on one part, and prayers
on the other part of every Sunday as usual.

And it is also the unanimous opinion of the persons present,
that Mr. Martindale, the Curate of Corbridge, supplying St.
Andrew, Bywell, every third Sunday, hath a great tendency
to encourage idleness, and a disregard of the observance of
that day in the Parish; and it is the desire of the vestry, that
Mr. Brown, and Eliezer Birch, Churchwardens Elect, and
Reg. Gibson, Rd. Haswell, and Bar. Winship, do take the first
convenient opportunity to represent the same to the Vicar."
(Robert Wardle, Vicar.)

From this time to the end of the century, the usual items
for the repairs and expenses of the church, &c., regularly
appear; but there are two special items entered for a long
period in every year's account, but which have long since
terminated. The first is the cost of writing presentments,
which were documents written by the churchwardens (or
rather by some person employed by them), bearing their
signatures and presented to the Bishop of the Diocese, giving
a report of all those who refused to attend church to hear
Divine Service, or who refused to pay "Church Sess," or for

any other breach of the church regulations over which the
Bishop claimed jurisdiction.* The last entry on this head is
as follows: "1767 By p^d. J. Smith writing a schedule, presentments. a copy of ye Register; entering these accounts each
4s. 0d.

After this date the cost of writing them was included in the
agreement made with Jacob Smith and his successors.

Two of these early and curious documents were published
by Mr. Wm. Lee, of Haydon Bridge, in the *Hexham Courant*
a short time ago, which we here insert. "1681. May 9th,
the Churchwardens of Corbridge presented Sir Francis Radcliff, the Lady Elizabeth Radcliff, Mr. Franciss Radcliff,
Madam Dorothy Massey Radcliff, Madam Anne Ratcliff,
Madam Barbara Radcliff, Mr. Richard Hailes, Thomas Bradley, Esq., Mrs. Katherine Fenwick, Dorothy Elliott, and
Bridget, the wife of Thomas Gibson, as popish recusants; and
on October 25th, Richard Cook, of Dilston, gardener, and
Bridget Logan, wife of Patric Logan, gardener, were presented
as Papists, and not for coming to Church to hear Divine
Service. "1682, May 17th, the Churchwardens of Corbridge
presented Mr. Edward Radcliffe, and Mr. Thomas Radcliffe,
among many others, for papists, and for refusing to pay
assessments for the Church, and for the maintainance of a
bastard child found at Dilston."

The following order of presentment was made at a vestry
meeting held on October 23rd, 1748. The only one par-
ticularised in the Churchwarden's books:—

"Whereas James Thompson, of Dilston, within the parish
of Corbridge: Abraham Bunting of the same, Jno. Mitford for
the same, Matthew Thompson of the same, Wm. Hogart of
the same. Thos. Brown of the same, Wm. Stokeld of ye same,
John Stokeld of the same, Paul Brown of ye same, Wm.
Hepple of the same, Michael Brown of the same, have refused
to pay their respective sess for their several lands, in Dilston
aforesaid, for ye year 1747. We the major part of the four
and twenty of and for the Parish of Corbridge, do hereby
order that a presentment shall be made, at the next visitation,
against the said several persons, for the non-payment of there

---

* To what extent the Bishop's power extended in those times, whether in
reference to the compulsory payment of rates, or to the discipline he could
exercise upon refractory members, we have not been able exactly to make out.

said sess, or against the said James Thompson for all, or such part of the said cess, as shall appear to be paid him by yᵉ Tenants of Dilston aforesaid." Then follow 18 names.

The other items referred to are premiums paid out of the Church cess, for the heads of wild animals, and the heads of birds, called "gledes."* The following extract will explain :— "Stephin Armstrong in the birks for killing of two foxes in Dilston Fell and bringing their heads† to our church door, May the 30th day, 1678." In addition to the usual yearly entries, there is a consecutive list of the names of all those who have presented heads at the vestry from 1676 until 1724, with the day of the month and the year in which they were presented, covering several pages closely written.‡

A few miscellaneous extracts, and a copy of the accounts for the year 1676, and a few extracts from the old registers, will bring the *History of Corbridge* to a close.

1677. Tho. Heron for two Gledes' heads ...		0	6
1678. For three passengers		1	6
For sending about the Parish about the Prayer day, Nov. 13th		1	0

---

* The glede or common kite is a distinguished species of British hawk, and most destructive in farm yards, carrying off fowls, ducks, &c., and is a great enemy to young grouse and black game; hares are sometimes carried by the kite to its nest. In this neighbourhood the kite has for a long time been extinct.

† The premium paid for a fox's head for a long period never exceeded one shilling. It is however, now estimated, that every fox's head shown (not at the church door, but by Mr. Cornish as killed by the Tynedale hounds) cost over £100, which simply proves "progression repeated," that foxes like most all other things have risen in value, from one shilling to £100 or upwards.

‡ In several places the writing is so defaced that it cannot be made out, and portions of several leaves are torn off, but the following numbers which certainly do not show the whole, are what we have been able to decipher during the period referred to :—
Foxes' heads, 367; Fulmarts', 653; Brocks', 119; Wild Cats', 141; Otters', 27; Gledes', 153.—Total, 1460.
In a Monthly Journal of Natural History called *The Zoologist*, published in London, there is an interesting article (in the May number for 1881) referring to the number of wild animals of this neighbourhood. The following is the heading of the article :—
"Some ancient records relating to the wild animals of Northumberland. Communicated by T. H. Nelson (Bishop Auckland). The following extracts, for which I am indebted to Mr. Robert Forster, who is engaged upon a History of Corbridge-on-Tyne, are taken from the Churchwardens' books of that parish, and relate to the heads of wild animals, which for two centuries were paid for out of the Churchwardens' 'cess.' These notes are interesting as showing the former abundance of several of the species named, compared with the present day, when in many parts of England, most of them are very rare, or altogether extinct."

	s.	d.
For the great Bell Rope	5	0
For the Act of burying in Wollen*	2	6
1679. For passengers, two nights and a day, 1s. 4d., for another passenger, 6d.	1	10
1680. To a distressed woman	1	0

" These are to certifye any whome it may concern y^t ye bearer hereof Matthew Armstrong, in the Parish of Corbridge, and County of Northumberland, yeoman, is a soldier in my Company in the King's first Regiment of foot guards, under the command of his Grace, Henry Duke of Grafton." The signature of the certifier cannot be deciphered.

1690. John Still, of the Linnell Wood, 5 fox heads, June 5th	5	0
1692. To Abraham Fawset, fox heads	2	0
1698. Joseph Gibson, 2 fox heads, slain in Thornbrough Wood	2	0
1702. Michael Stoker, 1 otter head	0	4
1707. For a Spade	2	6
Wm. Brown, 4 wild Cats' and 11 Gledes' heads	3	4
John Hoggart, in Dilston, for Foxes', Fulmarts' and Brocks' heads†	4	8
Wm. Bell, 12 Fulmarts' and 1 wild Cats' heads‡	4	4

* This refers to a copy of an act passed in the reign of Charles II. The following is an extract from this singular act:—" Whereas an act made in the eighteenth year of His Majesty's reign, that now is intituled an act for burying in wollen only, and was intended for lessening the importation of linen from beyond the seas, and the encouragement of the wollen and paper manufactories of this kingdom. (As the provisions of this act were evaded, the following, being more stringent were passed.)—" And it is hereby enacted by the authority aforesaid. That from and after the first day of August, 1678, no corpse of any person or persons, shall be buried in any shirt, shift, sheet, or shroud, or any thing whatsoever is made or mingled with flax, hemp, silk, hair, gold, or silver, or any stuff or thing other than what is made of sheep's wool only; or to be put in any coffin lined or faced with any sort of cloth or stuff, or any other thing whatsoever, that is made of any material but sheep's wool only, upon pain of the forfeiture of five pounds of lawful money of England, to be recovered and divided as is hereafter in this act expressed and directed."

† Hoggart was the warrener or gamekeeper at Dilston. The following extracts are from the Dilston household book of expenses:—

Feby. 25th, 1682. Claudius Carr, for a ferret delivered to John Hoggert for the warren, Dilston, 5s.

June, 1686. Four Chists for the Young Pheasants, and one Chist for Hogort's firits, and other work £1 0s. 4d.

November, 1686. John Hoggart, Warrener, his half-year's Wages due at Mart £5.

The rabbit warren covered the entire of Widehaugh, which, after the breaking up of the house at Dilston, was let to a succession of tennants until the beginning of the present century, when the warren was broken up and the ground put into a state of cultivation, and is now occupied by Mr. Stobbs.

‡ The wild cat appears to have been of quite a different specie from the domestic cat; the last seen in this neighbourhood was killed in Aydon Castle

	s.	d.
1707. In March of Dipton House presented ...	0	3
1709. For our charges at the Bishop's Court ...	6	6
1709. For the Bell ropes...	6	6
1709. For Butter for the Bells, 2d. ; for Bread for yᵉ Sacrament, 2d. ; to J. Armstrong for 2 days' ringing, 2s.	2	4
For a Coffin for Ann Smith	4	0
1711. Wants of Abr. Fawcitt for the haugh close	0	2½
Wants of Wm. Smith for Reginal Gibson's House	0	3
Tackets and Hemp for the Bell Leathers... ...	0	1
1713. Ralph Bell, of Lamb Shield, 1 Fox slaine at Linolds	1	0
1714. Edward Winship for a Wild Cat's head	0	4
1714. ¼ a pound of butter for the Bells	0	2¾
1715. A pint of Oyle and a bottle	0	6
1715. Spent about the Parish business, 1s. ; to passengers, 1s., is...	2	0
Nov. 5. For Ringing, 3s. ; and butter for the Bells, 2½d.	3	2½
For one Gill of Oyle for the Bells	0	2¼
To Thomas Forster for 4 Glede's heads	0	8
To Mr. Errington's men for 1 Fox head and a Brock* killed in Farnley	1	4
For going to Matfen about the Parish business	1	0
1716. For the Church-yard hedge repairing ...	0	9
1717. Paid 3 passengers	1	0
1721. To Esq. Fenwick's man for 2 Fox heads	2	0
1721. Pᵈ for the Book for yᵉ fast abᵗ the plague in France	3	6
For Powder and Shot for killing the Jackdaws	0	3½
1721. The Court fees at Whitsuntide Court at Morpeth	8	6
Our own charges at the two Courts at Morpeth†	10	0

Dene, somewhere about the year 1822, by the then Stagshaw gamekeeper, and is described as being of a sandy grey colour, and very much larger than the common cat.

* The only "Brock" the writer recollects seeing alive, was caught in Aydon Castle Dene, by the Gamekeeper to William Crawhall, Esq., when that gentleman resided at Stagshaw. It was kept in a cage made on purpose for it, but after being in captivity several months appeared as wild and restless as at the first ; it was considered a fine specimen of its kind.

† Court charges are singular as well as extraordinary, there are charges for occasionally attending the court at Corbridge ; but regularly in each year accounts for attending the Bishop's Court, the courts at Morpeth, and at

	s.	d.
John Dodd, Esq. Fenwick's man, one Fox head Jan. 21	1	0
1722. Ralph Greenwell for killing the Jackdaws 3 years	3	0
1722. For muster money	1	6
1724. May 11th, permission given to Lord Derwentwater to enlarge his pew on the north side of the Church		
1727. Expenses going twice to Newcastle and once to Capheaton	3	4
1728. For Bell ropes	5	10
For mending the Church Spade	0	2
Trinity Sunday for bread and wine	4	10½
Christmas day for three white loaves	0	3
1730. For wood taken away by some of Ld. Derwentwater's tenants	12	0
1741. Thongs for letting down corpses	1	6
1741. 3 Fox heads by Mr. Fenwick's huntsman*	3	0
1743. Two Fulmarts' heads to Saml. Jamieson (this is the last entry for heads)	0	8
1744. A Bottle of Wine broke	1	6
1745. Mending the Steeple ladder	0	4
1747. For cleaning the church for the Bishop's coming	1	0
1748. For a Swill	0	3
Spent bargaining with workmen	1	0
1749. June 26. To Charles Armstrong for fetching leather to hang the Bell tounges ...	0	3
1750. To Sexton for Cleaning yᵉ Church pʳ year	10	0
1754. Beadle's Salary, 5s. 4d.; do. Shoes, 4s.	9	4
1756. John Richley's new House not tenanted	0	1½

Newcastle; and are named as the Court at Easter, the Spring Court, the Midsummer Court, the Michaelmas, and Martinmas Courts. The charges are named as "My own and our own charges," "Court Fees, and Riding Charges." It appears that the churchwardens were accustomed to attend the courts as well as the vicar, in one entry there are riding charges for three churchwardens. Query:—What was the nature of their business?

* About this time a huntsman belonging to Mr. Fenwick was drowned (possibly this same man) when crossing the Tyne during one of their hunts. His body was afterwards found on the coast of Holland, and was known by his name being on his horn, which was fastened to a leathern belt about his waist; it is stated that at the time he was dressed in a green velvet coat; although the report is well authenticated and known, and is said to be in some of our local records, we have not yet been able to find it.

127

This year an arrangement was made to establish a Work-house, and to rent a house for the purpose; one of the stipulations was, "to take the benefit of their work and labour for the better maintainance and relief of such persons as shall be chargeable to our said Township."

1759. Oyle for the Bells	...	...	...	...	...	0	4½
1760. 8 days' washing spots of Pews		...	...			4	0
1762. A Bell Wheel...	...	...	...	...	...	12	0
3 Gallons of Wine at 5s. 8d. per Gallon	...	...				17	0
1766. Paid Wm. Armstrong for a pair of Stocks* 1						1	0

1767. By p⁴ Thos. Richley for work done at
laying yᵉ floor in yᵉ Steeple, altering yᵉ ladder,
making and painting yᵉ weather Boards in yᵉ
Steeple, and finding some stuff 3 11 5½
By paid at hoisting yᵉ great ladder   2   0

"Jan yᵉ 29th, 1767. At a public meeting of the four and twenty, pursuant to public notice given yᵉ Sunday before for yᵗ purpose (13 being present) ordered yᵗ the Churchwardens and Overseers of the Poor of Corbridge agree with John Ions, of Haltwhistle, to keep yᵉ Poor house at Corbridge, according to yᵉ afore written contract, and yᵗ thomas Lumbly is to pay only 5s. next year for yᵉ poor Land. Ordered yᵗ proposals be taken in for building and repairing yᵉ poor House at Corbridge according to yᵉ plan, and delivered in sealed up to yᵉ Rev. Mr. Martindale before yᵉ 5th of Feb. next. Witness our hands.".............

"At a meeting of the four and twenty this 9th day of Feb., 1767, by adjournment from thursday last, to take in proposals for building yᵉ poor house (12 being present.) Sundry proposals were given in, Cuth. Snowball being £109 17s. 5d. was yᵉ lowest, an agreement was entered into with him accordingly."†

---

* These stocks, which were made to hold three persons at once, were kept in the church, and brought ont every Sunday and set against the churchyard wall in the Market Place. We recollect in our boyhood often seeing them, and also examining their construction, but never saw any one in them, per-haps their very appearance was a terror to evil doers.

† This house was at the north end of Dunkirk Terrace, and considering the extent of the building, viewed from our present stand-point of estimate, appears exceedingly low. It formed a square, having a paved court yard in the centre; was two stories in height, built of stone and covered with grey slates, and was a house of considerable importance, was not only large enough to accommodate all the poor in the parish, but also many from other parishes and townships After the present "Poor Law Union Act" came into operation, and the workhouse at Hexham was erected, it being no longer required for its

128

Feb. 9th. (same day) at a public meeting the afore-named contract was executed with John Ions. This agreement being of such a remarkable nature, is our apology for publishing a copy of it in full. The framers of the conditions of this contract had evidently been alive to the dangerous and mischievous properties of spirituous liquors, possibly they may have had before them the name first given to this spirit by the celebrated Arabian Alchemist, who designated it "Al-Goul," (the evil spirit.) There are not two opinions, but for the use of intoxicating drinks, there would be no need from time to time for the enlarging of Hexham or other workhouses. "At a public meeting of y⁰ inhabitants of y⁰ Township of Corbridge, in y⁰ County of Northumberland, for y' purpose respectively, assembled upon usual notice thereof first given ; It is contracted by and with y⁰ consent of y⁰ said inhabitants so assembled as aforesaid, and also with y" consent of Ra. Soulsby, Esq., one of his Majesty's Justices of y" Peace, for y⁰ s⁴ County, dwelling near y⁰ Township of Corbridge aforesaid. Between Rich⁴ Brown and Eliezer Birch, Churchwardens, and John Bowman and George Walton, Overseers, of y⁰ Poor of y⁰ Township of Corbridge, of y⁰ one part, and John Ions of y⁰ Parish of Haltwhistle, in y⁰ County of North⁴ Weaver, on y" other part, That y⁰ s⁴ John Ions shall and will for y" space of one whole year, to commence from y" 15th day of May next, at his own proper cost and charges in y⁰ House called y⁰ Poor house in Corbridge aforesaid, and for which He is to pay no rent during the time of this Contract, provided He maintain y" windows whole, and at y⁰ expiration thereof, deliver up peaceable possession of y" same in good condition (necessary wear and tear excepted): Find, provide, and allow unto all such poor people as shall be lawfully entitled to relief and maintainance from y" township of Corbridge aforesaid, and shall be brought to him by y" Churchwardens and Overseers of y⁰ poor aforesaid, or any of them, or any of their successors for the time being, sufficient meat, drink, Firing, Washing, Lodging, Employment, and other things necessary for their keeping and maintainance, and that he will at his own expence, mend, keep-

---

original purpose was let into tenements, and afterwards sold for the benefit of the poor of the Township of Corbridge, to Mr. John Oliver, of Durham, who built upon its site the two northern beautiful dwelling houses.

clean, and manage to y° best ·advantage, as well y° cloaths of y° poor people aforesaid, as also y° Bedding, which may bȯ provided for them, and shall be accountable for y° same, as also of their other small effects which they may have in y° poor house aforesaid, to the Churchwardens and overseers of y° poor of Corbridge aforesaid, or their Successors for y° time being, and that he will not during the term of this contract, agree with any other Person for y° maintainance of any poor people whatsoever, such only excepted as shall be allowed of under y° hand writing of y° Churchwardens and overseers of y° poor of Corbridge aforesaid, or their Successors for y° time being. And that in consideration thereof, the said Church-wardens and overseers of y° poor and their Successors, shall pay or cause to be paid to y° said John Ions, the Sum of nine pounds, and also y° further Sum of Sixteen pence-a-week, at four quarterly payments, for and during y° time every poor person brought in by them for maintainance does continue in y° poor house aforesaid ; and further y° Churchwardens and overseers of y° poor of Corbridge aforesaid, and their Succes-sors for y° time being shall provide necessary Cloaths for their poor, which for men and Boys shall be a wide Horse-man's Coat, a Waist Coat with Sleves, and a pair of Breeches made of Cloth of y° mixture of White and Black wool of their natural colour, with flat white metal Buttons, one cap, one pair of Stockings knit of y° same material, two Shirts and one pair of Clogs; and for y° women and Girls, one Gown lined in y° body and Sleeves, and one petticoat made of Stuff, the warp of linnen and wool dyed ash colour for y° weft, one white under flannel petticoat, one apron of y° same sort as y° Gown dyed blue, two white linnen Caps, two Shifts, two Handkirchiefs for y° neck, one pair of knit Stockings, y° same as for y° men, and one pair of Clogs, together with Bed and Bedding. And in case any of y° poor people prove so un-governable and refractory y° there should be a necessity to have them committed to y° house of correction, it shall be done at y° expence of y° township of Corbridge aforesaid, and further the Churchwardens and overseers of y° poor aforesaid shall, in case of Death, bury their own poor. The said John Ions to have moreover and take unto himself y° Benefit of y° said poor people's work, Labour, and Service during the said term, provided he maintain good order, and give his attendance

J

to what is y⁰ proper business of y⁰ house, and prevent y⁰ sell
ing and using (except in y⁰ way of medicine) any Spirituous
Liquors in y⁰ house aforesaid, and cause a large Roman P
with y⁰ first letter of y⁰ place whereof such poor person is an
inhabitant, of blue Cloth to be placed and continue upon y⁰
Shoulder of y⁰ right Sleeve of y⁰ uppermost garment, in an
open and visible manner. And it is hereby agreed between
y⁰ parties aforesaid, that if y⁰ Churchwardens and overseers
of y⁰ poor of Corbridge or their Successors for y⁰ time being,
shall agree with y⁰ Churchwardens and Overseers for y⁰ poor
of any other township or parish, to take their poor into y⁰
house aforesaid, and signify y⁰ same in writing under their
hands to y⁰ said John Ions, in such case the said John Ions
shall take into y⁰ house aforesaid such poor people as shall be
brought him, and are entitled to maintainance from such
township or parish with whome such agreement is made, subject to y⁰ forms and conditions which y⁰ Township of Corbridge
is by this contract (the nine pounds a year only excepted,)
and further it is agreed between y⁰ parties aforesaid, that the
Minister, Churchwardens, and Overseers of y⁰ poor of Corbridge and their successors for the time being, shall have y⁰
liberty at all reasonable times to go into y⁰ house to see that
all things are rightly conducted. In witness whereof the
parties have hereunto set their hands, this 9th day of
February, 1767."

The ordinary charges for providing and washing the Church
linen, as well as the usual items of cost for provision, for the
Sacraments, appear in every year's accounts, also particulars
"for y⁰ necessary expenses and repairs of y⁰ Church" continue,
but present nothing striking. We, however, continue a few
further extracts from the general orderings and agreements of
the vestry :—

"1771.—June 16th. At a meeting of the four and twenty,
it is ordered that the Overseers of the poor pay nothing to
Thomas Usher as long as he receives three shillings a week
out of John Richley's club."

"1775.—March 19th. It is agreed this day that Alexʳ
Manners, of Corbridge, be paid the sum of one pound ten
shillings by the Overseers of the poor of this Township, for,
and to assist him in buying a Galloway at this time by us, &c."

131

"1779.—July 28th. At a meeting of the vestry held this day, in pursuance of notice given, it was agreed that John Brown, of Tinkler Bank House, be paid one shilling per week by the Overseers of the poor of the Township of Corbridge."

"June 9th, 1789. At a meeting of the vestry which was called on Sunday. the 7th of June inst., there appeared James Hall, Churchwarden; William Smith, Churchwarden; Bartholomew Lumbly, and the Rev. George Wilson, Vicar; and it was the opinion of Bartholomew Lumbly, that the number was not sufficient to do parish business. The intention for which the vestry was called was frustrated."

There are particulars of militia accounts extending from 1781 to 1812, we give two extracts :—

"May 28th, 1781. At a meeting of the vestry this day, pursuant to public notice given for the purpose on Sunday last, it is ordered that one penny in the pound be laid on and collected throughout the parish of Corbridge, for paying the bounties due to men that have been balloted to serve in the militia by us.—Joseph Walker, Rich⁴ Brown, Reg¹ Gibson, George Gibson, John Richley. Tho⁵ Richley."

"To cash collected again according to Mr. Henn's certificate at 2s. 6d. per man."

			£	s.	d.
1808, Sep. 29*—Corbridge	Township	...	10	8	0
Aydon Castle	,,	...	0	2	0
Great Whittington	,,	...	1	16	0
Halton	,,	...	0	18	0
Oct. 13th—Dilston	,,	...	2	2	0
17th—Aydon	,,	...	1	12	0
Little Whittington	,,	...	0	2	0
Nov. 17th—Halton Shields	.,	...	0	10	0
Clarewood	,,	...	0	16	0
Thornbrough	,,	...	0	14	0
			18	18	0
William Ridley. 6d. in the Pound on £18 18s. for his trouble			0	9	6
			18	8	6

* We extract the following from Mackenzie:—" The people of Corbridge, during the war with the military despot of the continent, displayed their

132

" Briefs," which are things of the past and are somewhat interesting, form a considerable portion of the accounts, and extend over a great number of years. We give a few extracts :—" Briefs, 1676, then collected towards the re-building of the Church of Newent, in the County of Glossestor, one shilling and ninepence."

March 30th. 1690. Collected in the Parish Church of Corbridge, for a fire in East Smithfield, in the County of Middlesex, and suburbs of London, the sum of four shillings and elevenpence farthing."

		s.	d.
1738. June 10th. St. Mary's Church of Gateshead, collected	... ...	2	1
1744. Eynsford, fire July 23rd, and collected	...	1	9
Buckerell, fire July 31st, and collected	...	1	6¾

The next rather curious extract shows that in those days, of sometimes fancied innocency, there were persons who at one stroke, showed that they not only had no scruple about sacrilege, but no conscience as to keeping the fourth and eighth commandments :—

" 1744. Marthill, Woodhall, Storm, lost when the vestry lock was broken open, by the 24th, when the Clerk was at Halton on Sunday afternoon Service."

There are accounts of sundry bonds of indemnity extending over many years, we give the following extracts : " Bond of indemnity against Mary Baron's Child, 22nd March, 1749."

attachment to the independence of their country, by raising a company of volunteers, which has lately joined the local militia of the country." They were required a month in every year to assemble at Alnwick for drill, at the close of this service they arranged mostly in a body to start early for home the following morning, taking the roads across the country, and arriving about six or seven in the evening. We never recollect when hearing them relate their adventures at Alnwick, and their journey home, complaining of being weary or tired with their days' journey, which would be from forty to fifty miles ; three of the last of these "Loyal Men," in their declining years, resided within a few yards of each other in the Market Place, Corbridge, from whence they all took their last march, received their last drill, and went to meet their comrades on the other side, each of them having considerably passed the appointed time of three score years and ten—one of them, Thomas Fairless, was the drummer. We have often heard him relate, jocosely, how on one occasion, when in the discharge of his disciplinary duty, he had to flog an unfortunate comrade, who had stolen a shilling, how he whirled the "cat-o-nine-tails" round his head as if to gather force for the infliction of a severe stroke, when in fact it was only a feint, for at the same time, striking lightly ; but the drum-major standing at his back and discerning his movements at once struck the poor drummer a severe blow, reminding him that he must do his duty, this so affected his brother, (the late Joseph Fairless, of Hexham,) that he fainted, fell down, and had to be carried out of the ranks.

133

" The acknowledgemont of the Churchwarden and Inhabitants of Birkley that Margt. Urwin belongs them, dated yᵉ 11
Aug., 1758."

" Will Watson's affidavit of his settlement 6th April, 1765."

Robert Smith,   } Ann Bently,   } 1st Feb., 1768.
Francis Armstroug, } Indemnity,   }

The distribution of "communion or oblation alms" are also
carefully noted down, the following extracts will show the
proportions at the time :—

	Easter, 1749.		Midsummer, 1749.		Sept., 1749.	
	s.	d.	s.	d.	s.	d.
Esther Carr	0	6	0	4½	0	3
John Brown, Mercht. ...	1	0	0	6½	0	3
Ann Ramsay, agd., sick...	0	6	0	4½	0	3

The distribution of the Dole or Charity left by the Rev.
Robert Troutbeck, in 1706, is very carefully recorded from
year to year. The amount of the Charity in 1752, was £6 ;
in 1782, £10 ; in 1809, £20 ; and in 1880, £23 4s.

The following is an exact copy of the year's accounts for
1676 :—

CHURCHWARDENS.

" Thomas Hoaron, John Readhead, Christo. Ridley, Matthew
Armstrong, rec. Church Sess in all £3 1s. 6d. for the year
1676.

DISBURSEMENTS.

	£	s.	d.
Disburst. at Newcastle for court fees ...	00	08	00
For our own Charges	00	12	00
For a lock for the Church Chest	00	00	06
For Paper	00	00	02
To Thomas Horan, one fox head, two fulmarts' heads	00	01	08
To Matt. Armstrong for washing Church linen	00	04	00
For Fetching a Chest	00	00	08
For Parchment and copyinge of yᵉ Red-chester	00	01	00
For Ringing	00	01	00
John Taylor for a Brocke head	00	00	04

	£	s.	d.
Bartholomew Lumbly, and Matt. Brown for mending yᵉ Church Gate	00	01	00 \
For writing of presentments	00	01	00
To Charles Cutter for accounts*	00	08	00
For a great lock	00	10	00
Thomas Carr	00	03	00
For wine and bread for communion at Christmas, and for bringing them ...	00	03	00
Cuthbert Robson for two fox heads ...	00	02	00
John Cooke for a brocke head	00	00	04

BAPTISMS, MARRIAGES, AND BURYELLS.

THE Vicar, the Rev. G. C. Hodgson, having again favoured us with an inspecction of the oldest parish register book (commencing with the year 1654) of Buryals, Baptisms, and Marriages, and kindly allowed us to extract from these curious and interesting records; we have therefore done so freely, as these Parish Registers show the antiquity not only of the names of many of our suburbs, which modern inovation has not been able to destroy, but the names of families still existing (and of many of which we have no recollection). All the old family names in Dilston have long ago became extinct, and also all those in Aydon; several still exist in Corbridge and in Great Whittington, and possibly in other places in the parish. Mr. Richley in his interesting

* The descendants of Charles Cutter continued until the beginning of the present century, when the last in the line, a female, married a man named Thomas Chambers, their only child, a son, died when a youth, thus one of the oldest families in the village became extinct; there are some incidents in connection with the family which induces us to refer to them. They appear to have been smiths by trade, and their accounts for repairs in connection with the church often appear. They seem to have been good workmen. The present vane on the church tower, which is made of iron, with brass bushes, was made by them in 1767. The family held a freehold in the village, and at the "division" they got their proportion of land on Corbridge south common, which consisted of a small close boundering on the north, on "Dilston High Lane." The female branches are said to have been somewhat haughty in their manners, and rather peculiar in their dress; one of them was accustomed so often to visit this close, and walk the lane with such an air of dignity, that by way of derision it was designated "Lady Cutter's Lonning," and is now best known by that name. The name of that portion of the river immediately below the southern arch of the bridge is known as "Tom Cutter's Hole," and is understood to be derived from the circumstance of one of the family of the name of Tom, having got possession of some goods in an unlawful way, to prevent detection threw them into this place, which was at that time very deep, and was the course or bed of the river; and it has retained this odd name ever since. It was a little girl belonging the family of the name of Cutter, a blacksmith, who found the silver table, referred to in the former part of this work.

History of Bishop Auckland, and who has largely extracted
from the old parish registers, prefaces them by stating,
"That the introduction of parochial registers into England
was in consequence of the injunction of Thomas Lord Crom-
well, which according to Hollingshed, were set forth in September, 1588 (30 Henry VIII.), but not much attended to
until the reign of Queen Elizabeth, who issued injunctions
concerning them in the first, seventh, and thirty-ninth years
of her reign. Many of these old registers are most beautiful
specimens of penmanship, and go far to prove that the parish
clerks (who were usually registrars in those early times when
learning was possessed by few) must have been selected from
the most highly-educated inhabitants of the parish. In a fly-
leaf of the second volume of those of St. Andrew's we find
the following entry :—

Memorandum.—"That Joseph Lax off the Deanery, in the
Parish of Andrew Auckland, was chosen Parish Registrar, by
consent off the Parish, and sworn according to the said Act of
Parliament, the 4th day of January, 1653. Francis Wren."

In the book from which the following are extracted, and
which extends over fifty years, are some good specimens of
penmanship, and it is observable that the same person has for
twelve years consecutively, and in the most orderly and beautiful manner entered all the registers ; both before and after
this period they appear to have been entered irregularly and
by many different persons, although some of the entries are
well written, yet for the most part the writing is of an inferior
kind, and in many instances the ink having been bad they are
illegible. The Baptisms begin with 1654, and the Marriages
and Buryalls in 1657. We give them in order, the Baptisms
first, the Marriages next, and lastly the Buryells.

BAPTISMS, 1654.

Ralph, son to William Greenwell, of Corbridge, baptised
July 28th, Anno 1654.

Dorothy, daughter of Elizabeth Armstrong in Corbridge,
she was baptised fifth day of Desember, 1654, (sureties)
Cudbert Hudspeth, and Ann Heron, and Isabell Fasset, all
in Corbridge.

Baptisms in ye year of grace, 1657.

Elizabeth, the daughter of Athear Johnson, in Halton, she was baptised the 28 day of February, 1657, her sureties, John Robson in the Carhouses, Susana Hunter in Ryell, Mary Bell in Halton Shealdes.

Barberee, the daughter of Ruth Harle Hudspeth, she was baptised on the 6 day of Desember, 1657, her sureties were Thomas Fawsyte and Barbere Wilson, and Mabell Greenwell.

William, the son of Charles Sharpe, in Dyllson, he was baptised the 21 day of February, Anno. D.D., 1657, his sureties were William Lee in Woo, and John Cousson in Hexham, Elisabeth Dawson in Woo.

John, the son of Anton Hall, in Corbridge, he was baptised the 8 day of February, Anno D.D., 1657, his sureties were Thomas Kirsop in Corbridge, William Hall in Thornbrough, and Mary Readhead in Corbridge.

Elisabith, the doughter of George Bell, in Letell Whutton-ton, she was baptised the 18 day of Aprill, 1657, her sureties, John Wuilkinson in Ryell, Mary Langlands in Great Whuttonton, John Langlands in Great Whuttenton.

Elinor, the daughter of Arthur Pigg, in the Linellwood, she was baptised 80 day of January, 1658, her sureties were John Nixon in Stifort.

Henry, the son of Thomas Forster, in Halton, he was baptised the sixt day of February, 1658, his sureties were Henry Robinson, Great Whittington, and Pollin Joplin in Clarewood, Ann Gibson in Great Whittington.

Ralph Lee, somte of Henry Rowell, in Corbridge, he was baptized the 13 day of June, 1658, his sureties were William Carnaby, Ralph Winship in Aydon Hall, and Jybell Hudspeth in Corbridge. (Aydon Hall was the name of the residence of the ancient family of the Winships of Aydon, a small part of the Old Hall is enclosed in the present modern residence.)

Elizabeth, the daughter of Robert Hudspeth, in Corbridge, was baptised uppon Satturday, the 16th of May, the aforesaid year (1659) her sureties were Robert Hudspeth in the Hole, Dame Hudspeth, wife to Gawen Hudspeth, and Dame Hudspeth, daughter to William Hudspeth.

137

Peter, son to Alexander Wilkinson, of Great Whittington, baptised y⁰ 12th of October, 1662.

Ann, daughter to Anthony Hall, of Corbridge, baptised February 1st, 1662.

Ann, daughter to George Bell, of Little Whittington, baptised Feb. 15th, Anno Domini 1662.

Barbary, daughter to Richard Dunn, of y⁰ Carhouses, baptised Feb. 2, Annoy Domi. 1662.

Agnes, daughter to John Morray, of Great Whittington, bapᵗ the 9th of Aprill, 1663.

Thomas, son to John Couper, of Great Whittington, baptised the 16th day of August, in y⁰ yeare of Oʳ Lord, 1663.

Isabell, daughter to John Richley, of Corbridge Mill, baptised 16th of August, in y⁰ yeare 1663.

Margery, daughter of Alexander Heron, of Corbridge, was born and baptised the first day of October, 1663.

Jane, daughter to John Martindale, of Corbridge, baptised October y⁰ 4th, Anno Domi 1663.

Edward, son to John Nixon, of Corbridge, baptised the 11th day of Novembʳ, Anno Doni. 1663.

Ann Errington, daughter to Francis Eerrington, of Halton Sheeles, bapᵗ March the 10th, Anno., 1664.

Michael, son to Matthew Greenwell, of Corbridge, bapᵗ October 9th, Anno. 1664.

Thomas, son to Alexander Wilkinson, of Great Whittington, bapᵗ November 3rd, 1664.

James, son to John Barron, of Dilston, baptized September the third, Anno Doni. 1665.

Thomas, son to Robert Gibson, of Great Whittington, baptised December the 3rd, Anno Domini 1671.

Ralph, son to Mr. Ralph Carnaby, of Halton, baptised March y⁰ 7th, Anno Domi. 1672. (The Carnaby's were ancient possessors of Halton and Aydon Castle, on a mantlepiece in one of the rooms in Aydon Castle the arms of the Carnabys are carved.)

Paul, the son of Henry Forster, in Corbridge, bapᵈ August the 17th, 1676.

Ecistor, the daughter to Thomas Carr, in Corbridge, baptised the 9 day of Aprill, Anno Domi. 1686.

Mabell, daughter to John Greenwell, in Corbridge, baptised the 6 day of January, 1686.

138

John, son to Will Carnaby, in Corbridge, bap. April the 28\ day, 1686.

John, son to Ralph Readhead, in Corbridge, baptised Feb. the 12 day, 1685.

Charles Armstrong, baptised July 17th day, 1683.

Elener, the daughter of Matt. Brown, baptised August 5th day, 1683.

Isbell, daughter to Mr. Henry Colleson, in Aydon Castle, bapt. August the 2 day, 1696.

Henry, the son of Edward Winship, baptised September the 27 day, 1691.

Ann, the daughter to Bartholomew Lumbly, baptised December the 4 day, 1692.

Mary, the daughter of William Pearson, in Corbridge, baptised January the 14th day, 1693.

John, the son of William Snowball, in Thornbrough, baptised September the 9 day, 1694.

William and Edward, the sons to William Robson, in Di'ston, baptised March the first day, 1695.

Henry, son to George Angus, in Thornbrough, baptised May the 6th day, 1697.

Margaret, daughter to George Blake, Schoolmaster, in Corbridge, baptised May yᵉ 29th day, 1697.

Sarah, daughter of Robt. Angus, in Corbridge, baptised April 20th, 1701.

John, son of George Gray, in Corbridge, baptised May 14th, 1704.

Thos., yᵉ son of Robt. Foster, in Corbridge, bapt. November yᵉ 28th, 1704.

Eliz. and Dorothy, daughters of Mic. Robson, in Little Whittington, bapt. Feb. 19th, 1704.

George, the son of Thos. Jopling, in Corbridge, bapt. March yᵉ 15th, 1704.

Edw., son of Willm. Ramsay, in Corbridge, bapt. March 31, 1705.

Michael, son of Matthew Brown, in Dylston, bapt. Oct. 26th, 1704.

Margaret, the daughter of Jo. Jordan, in Corbridge, bapt. Jany. yᵉ 18th, 1704.

Matthew, son of John Armstrong, in Corbridge, baptised June 8th, 1705.

139

Marriages in ye year of grace, 1657.

Anton Hall, in Corbridge, and Caterm Sarnebe, in Corbridge, they were marite the 26 day of January, Anno 1.6.5.7.

John Ramshe, in Halton, and Isabell Browne, in Halton Sheals, they were marit the 8 day of June, Anno Dom. 1.6.5.7.

Wilvam Gibson, in Dyllston, in the parish of Corbridge, to Jane, the daughter of Janet Hippell, in the Parish of Harbourne, they were married the 16 day of November, Domi. 1.6.5.7.

Martin Lee, in Corbridge, to Elsabeith Haste, in Broumhaugh, in the Parish of Biwell, they were maried the eight day of Desember, 1.6.5.7.

Thomas Todd, farmer, in Hexham, to An Reid, in Adou, they were maried the seventeenth day of Desember, Anno Doi. 1.6.5.7.

John Hall, in Dilston Park House, and Bello Stobbart, in Dilston, in the Parish of Corbridge, they were marite the 15 day of February, 1.6.5.8.

Robert Vickerson, in Halton, and Mary Bell in Halton Shealles, they were marite the 4 day of Maye, Anno 1.6.5.8.

Wilvam Hall, in Corbridge, and Caterron Atkinson, in Corbridge, they were marite the 29 day of Maye, 1.6.5.8.

Thomas Younger, in Yorgal, in the Parish of Sant Jonle, and Isbell Conke, in Clarewood, in the Parish of Corbridge, they were marite the 16 day of November, 1.6.5.8.

Matthew Carr, of Slale, and Jane Stobbert, of Dilston, they were married the 14 day of February, 1659.

Robert Hudspeth, of yᵉ Hole, in Corbridge, and Isabel Hudspeth, of the same town, were marryed the last day of June, in the yeare of our Lord 1659.

Ralph Hinedauge, and Ann Rutor, both in the Parish of Corbridge, were married 16 day of November, 1659.

William Wigam, in Aydon Castle, and Barbara Davidson, in the White House, they were married the 16 day of November, 1659.

Entered in another part of the book for 1659, the following are written by another hand :—

140

Jhone Reedhead, and Jane Trumble, in Aydon Castle, were married the 24th day of May, 1659.

Henry Robinson, in Great Whittington, and Mary Reedhead, in Corbridge, were married the 2nd day of June, the foresaid yeare (1659.)

Cuthbert Robson, and Margaret Hudspeth, in Corbridge, were married the 28th of June, the foresaid yeare (1659.)

Matthew Willson, in Allendale, and Margaret Reed, in Clarewood, were married the 28th of June, the foresaid yeare (1659.)

Christopher Hudspeth, in Brumly, and Rebecca Robson, in the Carr Houses, were married the 28th of June, 1659.

John Lawrie and Isabell Sharpe, both of Corbridge, were married the first day of November, 1662.

Bartholomew Gibson and Agnes Carnaby, both of Corbridge, were married the twentieth day of Januaire, 1662.

James Langlands, of Great Whittington, and Jane Prudhoe, of Welton, marryed the 17th day of March, 1663.

James Baits, of this Towne, and Jane Liddell, of ye same Towne, marryed the 11th day of June, Annoye Domi. 1663.

John Robson, of the Carrhouses, and Margaret Wilson, of Clarewood, marryed May 5th, Anno 1654.

John Cooke, of Aydon, and Mary Winship, of ye same Towne, marryed June ye second, Anno 1664.

Michael Leethatt, schoolemaster, and Elizabeth Younger, both of Corbridge, marryed June 16th, Anno Domi. 1664.

Matthew Cowen and Eliner Forster, both of Corbridge, marryed April the 18th, Anno 1665.

William Hudspeth, of Corbridge, and Elizabeth Frewd, of Halton, marryed July the 23rd, Anno 1667.

Matthew Cutter, of Corbridge, and Margery Greenwell of the same Towne, marryed January 19th, Anno Domi. 1668.

Franciss Swinburne, of Dilston, and Ann Blenkinsopp of ye same Towne, marryed the 28th day of January, Anno Domi. 1668.

Edward Green and Elizabeth Burdass, of Styford, marryed Aprill ye 28th, Anno Domini 1670.

Robert Mowbray, of Western Dukesfield, and Elizabeth Sharpe, of Dilston, marryed May ye 7th, Anno Domini 1670.

John Hoggart, of Dilston, and Elizabeth Wilkinson, of Styford, marryed by a lawless Priest at Newcastle, July ye 20th, Anno Domini 1671.

Richard Barron, of Great Whittington, and Margery Ratchester, of y^e same Towne, marryed by a lawless Priest, June 18th, Anno Domino 1672.

William Richelly, of Corbridge, and Elizabeth Hudspeth, of ye same, marryed May ye 21, Anno 1672.

John Watson, of this Towne, and Isabel Robson, of Linnels, marryed June 10th, Anno 1673.

Bartho. Lumbly, of Corbridge, and June Usher, of Broomhaf, maryed ye 12th of Nov., 1674.

Michael Spain and Mary Linton, in Corbridge, marryed the 25th day, 1676.

Fargus Jordan and An Wolden, both in Corbridge, were marryed August the 26th day, 1680. (The family of Jordans were masons, and were employed by Sir Francis Radcliffe to work at Dilston; in the book of household expenses kept by the house-steward, are entries for wages paid to this family at 8d. per day.)

Will Fawset and Isabel Hudspeth, both in Corbridge, were married April the 20th, 1681.

Matthew Browne and Jane Hudspeth, in Corbridge, were married November the 30th day, 1682.

Edward Wilkinson and Eliner Fawset, both in Corbridge, were marryed May the twenty-second day of May, 1684.

Will Radchester, in Great Whittington, in the Parish of Corbridge, and Elizabeth Hudspeth, in Brumhaugh, in the Parish of Biwell Andrew, were married May the first day, 1684.

Edward Winship, in Aydon, and Ann Hudspeth, in the Prior Mains of Corbridge, were marryed December the 6th day, 1688.

Robert Barnes and Ellener Hall, both in Corbridge, were married July the 23 day, 1689.

William Wright, in Bishop Aklnein, in the County of Durham, and Margaret Shepherd, in Dilston Hall, were marryed June the 18th day, 1689.

Henry Rowell and Sarah Lumbly, were marryed June the 19th day, 1690.

John Lee, of Little Whittington, and Mary Younger, in Aydon Castle, were marryed Aprill the 29, 1690.

William Lighton and Isabell Urwin, both in Great Whittington, were marryed January the 13, 1691.

142

William Pearson, in Hexham, on the one part, and Margaret Story, in this towne and Parish, on the other part, marryed Aprill 23 day, 1691.

Joseph Gibson, in Styford, and Margaret Hutchinson, in Thornbrough, marryed May the 8 day, 1693.

George Hopper, in Styford, and Jane Hudspeth, in Corbridge, marryed April the 30th day, 1696.

Peter Nicholson and Elizabeth Hudspeth, in Corbridge, marryed June the 2 day, 1696.

George Blake, Schoolmaster, and Anne Ridley, in Adonn, marryed February the 2 day, 1696.

Matthew Greenwell and Elizabeth Hudspeth, both in Corbridge, marryed June the 13 day, 1698.

Robert Forster and Anne Lumbley, both in Corbridge, marryed January 26th, 1700.

John Errington and Isabell Hudspeth, both in Corbridge, marryed January the 6th, 1701.

John Browne and Anne Henderson, both in Corbridge, marryed January the 8th, 1701.

John Laidler and Elizabeth Straight, marryed with a Lycens, December 14th, 1702.

Ralph Preacher and Anne Hudspeth, both in Corbridge, marryed June 1st, 1703.

Lyonel Colpits and Alice Hudspeth, marryed August 15th, 1703.

Matthew Glendinning and Mary Hudspeth, marryed December y° 11, 1703.

William Greenwell and Jane Sinton, both in Corbridge, marryed June 6th, 1704.

Burialls in ye year of grace, 1657.

Henry Tate, his soulle, prase the Lord, he dyed and was burried the 30 day of November, in the yeare of this our Lord God 1657.

William, the sonne of John Green, in Dyllston, he dyed and was beuryed the 13 day of Jeneuary, Ano. 1657, in the Parish Chueurch in Corbridge.

Elizabeth, the daghter of John Hutchenson, who dyed and was beuryed the 15 day of Jeneauary, 1657.

143

Isbell Greenwell, widow in Corbridge, she died and was beuryed the 20 day of Febreuary, Anno Do. 1657.

John Squeire, in Dilston Mill, he died and was beuryed the 19 day of Febreuary, 1657.

Cateren Hudspith, widow in Corbridge, she dyed and was beuryed the 21 day of March, Anno D. 1658

Ann. the dagter of James Langlands, in Corbridge, she dyed and was buryed the 23 of Apareill, Anno 1658.

Charles Fenwick, in Corbridge, he died and was beuryed the 25 day of Apareill, Anno Domi. 1658.

John Smith, in Corbridge, he dyed and was buryed the 7 day of June, Anno Domi. 1658.

John, the son of Jemi Robinson, in Corbridge, hee died and was buried the second of August, 1658.

Thomas, the son of Robert Hudspeth, hee died and was buried the fourth day of August, 1658.

Matthew, the sonne of Matthew Greenwell, he died and was buried the second of August, 1658.

(Having previously referred to the family of the " Greenwell's," and when doing so ventured to suggest that Wm. Greenwell referred to in 1681, and John Greenwell in 1685, might have been grandsons of the famous " Will Greenwell," yeoman of Corbridge ; here again we notice that it has been suggested that Matthew, (the father,) above-mentioned, may have been a son, if not a brother of the famous " Will," for the period of the exploit which brings out this yeoman so prominently, would be in the year 1644. " William " and " Matthew " have continued throughout all their generations, down to the present time as family names.)

Thomas, the son of Robert Hudspeth, hee died and was buried the fourth day of August, 1658.

Isbell Younger, in Portgate, she died and was buried the 15 day of November, 1658.

Barbre, the daughter of Thomas Fawset, she died and was buried the 15 day of November, 1659.

(The family of Fawsett's, as far as we can make out, is one of the next oldest to Greenwell's and Hudspeth's, and whose descendants still continue in the village, bearing this family name.)

Edward Reedhead, departed this life the 29th of May, Anno 1659, being the sonne of Cuthbert Reedhead.

144

(What we have said relating to the family of the Fawset's, may be exactly repeated in reference to the family of Redd-heads.)

Elizabeth Dinnen, departed this life and was buried the 2nd of June, the forsaid yeare (1659).

Thomas Hymers, in Dilston, departed this life and was buried the 25th day of July, 1659.

(It will be noticed by those who are acquainted with bible history what a resemblance there is betwixt the wording of these entries and those recording the burials of the Kings of Judah. In the following entries the expressions " he or she died " is dropped and burials only mentioned. The sureties in baptisms from this time are also discontinued, and the whole entries afterwards much simplified.)

Robert, son to Thomas Golightly, of Corbridge, was buried the 27th day of Sep., Anno 1662.

William, son to Martin Swinburne, of Dilston, was buried the first day of October, Anno 1662.

Ann, daughter to Robert Hudspeth, of yᵉ Hole, in Corbridge, buryed yᵉ 10th of Jan., 1662.

Barbara, daughter to Robert Hudspeth, of yᵉ Hole, in Corbridge, buried Jany. 16th, 1662.

James Jobling, of the Carrhouses, buried November 21st, Anno 1663.

Elizabeth, wife to Matthew Cowen yᵉ younger, of Corbridge, buried January the 5th, Anno Domi. 1663.

Richard Pearson, of Dilston, buryed the 28th of March, Anno 1663.

Edward Stokoe, of Corbridge, son to William Stokoe, of Birkley, buryed Feb. 20th, 1663.

Sir Edward Radcliffe, of Dilston, Baronet, buryed December the eighteenth, in the yeare of our Lord, 1663.

John, son to William Gibson, of Great Whittington, buryed July the 12th, 1664.

Mrs. Susanna Forster, late wife to Mr. Ralph Forster, of Halton, buried May the 8th, Anno 1665.

Elizabeth Carnaby, of yᵉ White House, widdow, buryed January yᵉ 5th, 1667.

William Robinson, of Corbridge, Weaver, buryed July the 8th, Anno Domi. 1668.

145

The Lady Elizabeth Radcliffe, of Dilston, widdow, buryed December the 19th, 1668.

Isabel Swinburne, of Dilston, widdow, buryed December the 31st, Anno Domini 1668.

Mr. John Radcliffe, of Corbridge, buryed Novemb. 22nd, Anno Domini 1669.

Edward Reed, of Clarewood, buryed December yᵉ 8th, Anno Domi. 1669.

John Cutter, of Corbridge, buryed April the second, Anno 1670.

Matthew Greenwell, of Corbridge, buryed February yᵉ 27th, Anno 1670.

Richard Mills and Matthew Rotherford, both drowned together in yᵉ River Tyne, and buryed June 28th, Anno Domi. 1672.

Thomas Forster, of Great Whittington, buryed July yᵉ 24th, 1672.

Mr. John Fenwick, of Corbridge, Minister, buryed March yᵉ 28th. Anno Domi. 1674. (Mr. Fenwick, we presume, was a Presbyterian Minister, and officiated in the chapel called Dun Kirk, on the site of which is now erected the terrace which bears that name.)

Elizabeth, the wife of Henry Winship, in Aydon, buryed the 19th day of Sep., 1675.

Ralph, son to Fransis Hudspeth, buryed May yᵉ thirteenth day, 1677.

Sampson Hudspeth, in Corbridge, Pryer Mains, buryed October the 24th day, 1677.

Easter, the daughter of Ralph Hudspeth, buryed February the 28th day, 1678.

John Cooke, in Aydon, buryed January seventh day, 1679.

John, son of John Hogget, in Dilston, buryed September the 28 day, 1679.

Margaret Hudspeth, in Corbridge, widdow, buryed March yᵉ 17th day, 1679.

Jane, the daughter of John Hudspeth, in Corbridge, burryed August the 8th day, 1679.

Alis, the daughter of Ralph Hudspeth, in Corbridge, buryed April yᵉ 3rd day,—80.

John, son to John Hudspeth, buryed December the 19th day, 1680.

146

Sampson Hudspeth, in Corbridge, buried April the eight day, 1681.

Robert Hudspeth, in the Hole, in Corbridge, buryed August the 1st day, 1681.

Robert Hudspeth, in Corbridge, in the Hole. the younger, buryed September the 2nd day, 1681.

John Hudspeth, in the Hole, in Corbridge, buryed September the 11th day, 1681.

Edward Hudspeth, in Corbridge, buryed September the 20th day, 1681.

Tho. Hudspeth, in the Hole, in Corbridge, buryed September the 20th day, 1681.

(From the above extracts it will be noticed that in the different branches of this family, from 1677 to 1681, there had been thirteen burials.)

John Cooke, of the White House, buryed December the 28 day. 1689.

Alexander Hearon, Gent^m in Corbridge, dyed May the 24th, and was buryed May the 26th day, 1689, in this Parish Church of Corbridge.

Alexander, the son of Alexander Hearon, in Corbridge, was buryed February the 9th day, 1690.

(Alexander Hearon is here described as a gentleman, and for being such was, we presume, buried in the church; this family has long since become extinct, and as far as we can trace were an ancient family, and appear early in the church records, and were possessors of a considerable amount of property in the village. The house now occupied by Mr. Robert Atkin, Draper, Herons Hill, was their mansion or residence. Tradition states that from the name of this family Herons Hill was derived. It is thought they were a branch of the Herons of Chipchase, the name is differently spelled, sometimes Hearon, and sometimes Heron, and Herron; branches of this family resided at Dilston, and Aydon.)

Elizabeth Carnaby, of ye White House, widdow, buryed Jany. y^r 5th, Anno. 1667.

Lancelot, son of John Carnaby, in Corbridge, buryed March 14th, 1674. (The Carnabys of Corbridge, claimed to be the descendants of the ancient family of the Carnabys of Halton. They are also referred to as the Carnabys of Aydon and White House, and probably all the families in the White

147

House, Aydon and Corbridge, were branches of this once powerful family of Halton.)

John Hall, in Corbridge, buryed May the 25 day, 1694.

Frances, the wife of Nicholas Greenwell, in Corbridge, buryed November the 9th day, 1694.

Elizabeth, daughter to Mr. Henry Colleson, in Aydon Castle, buryed January the 5th day, 1695.

Elinor, the wife of John Fairlamb, in Corbridge, buryed June 27 day, 1696.

Ouswald, the son to Henry Colleson, in Aydon Castle, buryed April 10th day, 1698. (Henry Colleson was the owner of Aydon Castle.)

John Apulbry, Exciseman in Corbridge, buryed Desember the 19th day, 1696.

Abraham, son to Abraham Fawsett, in Corbridge, buryed May the 26th, 1697.

Mr. Mitford, Papist Priest in Dilston, buryed May 26th, 1697.*

James Young, in Whitesmorks, in the parish of Hexham, buryed July 23rd day, 1697.

William Patterson, in ye Boat-house, buryed January 21st day, 1698.

Mrs. Jackson, in Dilstonne, buryed March 20th day, 1698.

Robert Wanless, in the Linnell Wood, buryed December the 28th day, 1698.

Anne, wife of John Richley, in Corbridge Mill, buryed October 27th day, 1699.

Jane, wife of Henry Grey, in the Old Lynells, buryed October the 30th day, 1699. (So named from this place being the old or ancient line-mark which separated the parishes of Corbridge, Slaley and Hexham.)

William, son to John Greenwell, in Corbridge, buryed November 2, 1700.

Anne, daughter of Robt. Angus, in Corbridge, buryed April 27th, 1701.

Mary, wife of John Cooke, in the Whitehouse, buryed August 20, 1702.

---

* A legacy of £10 a year was left by Madam Ann Radcliffe, sister to Francis Earl of Derwentwater, in 1699, for the maintainance of a priest at Corbridge. We recollect a priest in receipt of this legacy fifty years ago, coming once a fortnight from Swinburne, and doing service in a private house in Herons Hill, occupied by a person of the name of Snowball. This legacy which was paid out of Nafferton Farm, has lately been redeemed.

148

Francis Radcliffe, Esq., buryed in Dilston Chapel, Sep. 16th, 1704.

Anne Swinbune, widdow, in Dilston, buryed 10th Decmʳ 1703. (Mrs. Anne Swinburne, of Dilston, by will dated 1702, bequeathed a sum of money to the poor of the parish to be distributed annually, at Dilston, on St. Thomas' Day; but either through the carelessness of her executor or his mis-application of the money, it has long been lost. It seems that the descendants of this lady, who were relations to the Radcliffs, resided at Dilston, as appears by two letters sent to Lady Swinburne, one by the Earl just after his marriage, in which he calls her "cousin," and the other sent her by the Countess on the same subject (their marriage) and whom she expects shortly to see.)

William Thompson, in Corbridge, buryed Oct. 5th, 1704.

Elizabeth Milner, a poor woman, buryed Oct. 11th, 1704.

John Ellitt, in Dipton house, buryed April 19, 1705.

There are probably the names of fifty individuals and families, which we have not quoted, who had continued for a long time in the village and neighbourhood, concerning whose history little is now known: amongst them, somewhat prominent, are the names of Dixon, Couper, Pigg, Gyles, Spaine, Langlands, Reed, Lawson, Lighton, Liddell, Linton, Simpson, Lowry, Armestrong, Carr, Jopling, Usher, Aken-head, Errington, Laidler, &c., &c.

A few brief references to these extracts and our book is brought to a close; the first is to the family of Hudspeth, whose descendants are still resident in the village. It is rather a curious coincidence that three out of the four oldest existing families in the village should be named in the first entries 227 years ago, viz.: Greenwell, Fawset, and Huds-peth. It is said the Hudspeths of Corbridge, are mentioned in the *Black Books of Hexham*, (these books are, for the most part, a history of the Priory) they appear to have consisted of at least three numerous families mentioned as living in the Hole, (now Orchard Vale) Pryor Maynes, and Cor-bridge. We have noticed that within four years there were thirteen burials out of this family, and a few years later, and within about the same period, nearly as many marriages, but mostly on the female side. Their employment was that of lime burning, which continued for a long period, in fact

until the decay of the lime trade. Entries appeared in the house steward's book, of the expenses of Dilston Hall, in the time of Sir Francis, (afterwards Earl) of sums having been paid for lime to the Hudspeths of Corbridge ; and in their own private account books (preserved until lately) were entries for lime sold to the Earls of Dilston. Some of the old names are yet retained in this remarkable family.

It may be interesting to some readers to have some idea of the population in the Township and Parish of Corbridge two hundred years ago, or upwards, from the proportionate number of burials at that time. We therefore give the number of burials, to which we add the number of baptisms, for five consecutive years, viz.: from 1671 to 1675. In the Township of Corbridge the number of burials, as entered in the register, are 83 ; in all the other Townships of the Parish, 57 ;—total 140. Baptisms in the Township of Corbridge, 73 ; in all the other Townships, 54 ;—total 127. Adon, Aidon, now Aydon, evidently had a much larger population than at present, and was the residence of several respectable families, all of whom, so far as relates to Aydon, are extinct ; the same may be said relative to Dilston. In reviewing these solemn and interesting memorials of generations long since passed away, and now that little is known of many who stood out so prominently, both from their social position and the part they took in public affairs, one is forcibly reminded, not only of the fact that one generation passeth away after another, and that we also must die, but of the application of that scripture which so beautifully pourtrays the remarkable and forgotten character of Joseph and his brethren, as is thus briefly recorded in the 1st chapter of Exodus : "And Joseph died, and all his brethren, and all they of that generation ; " and also that "There arose up a new king over Egypt, which knew not Joseph." The same order of men and things having gone on much in the same way throughout all ages, the present generation shall surely in their turn also pass away, and in the future become forgotten and unknown as so many of our predecessors are to-day. Well will it be with all those whose imperishable record is on high, and whose names are "written in the Lamb's Book of Life."

(Extracts from other ancient records are given in the Appendix.)

DILSTON HALL.

HAVING been specially requested, with the *History of Corbridge*, to give the leading features and incidents in connection with Dilston Hall, keeping within reasonable limits we proceed to do so; passing over the derivation of the name Dilston, as given by Mackenzie, the correctness of which is questionable; for evidently Devilstone is a perversion or corruption of Devylstonne. In the earliest records we are aware of, and previously referred to in the *History of Corbridge*, are two deeds or charters made in the reign of Henry I., in which Corbridge and Dilston are mentioned, although the date of these charters is not given, yet they would appear to have been made in the early part of that king's reign, (1100—1135,) carrying us back nearly eight hundred years; these charters are important documents. They are grants to William, son of Aluric de Corbridge, of the lands which Richard, his brother, held in Dilston, made by Henry, Earl of Northumberland and Henry I. This family point pretty clearly to the origin of the family of Devylstounes, for this name, as soon as the charters were given, was assumed by them, and William became Lord Devylstoune, or Lord of the Barony of Devylstoune. It is quite possible this family were Normans, brought over by William the conqueror, to whom he gave all these broad lands, and for the time being settled in Corbridge and Dilston, but apparently without any legal right to the estates, until the deeds or charters made by Henry I. which gave them an indisputable title.* This

---

* Mr. Sidney Gibson is of opinion that this family "were probably descendants of those Norman Lords, amongst whom the Conqueror so liberally parcelled out the broad lands of England, but whose history is lost," at all events, he remarks, "they were a family whose name was derived from Devylstoune." As we have stated, it is probable they were not the descendants but the persons placed there by the Conqueror, and the inference we draw is, that as soon as they received legal title to the estates, by the charters of Henry I., they adopted the name or title of Devylstonne, the name most probably of the previous Saxon owners, or may have been the name incorporated ɪ the deed or charters.

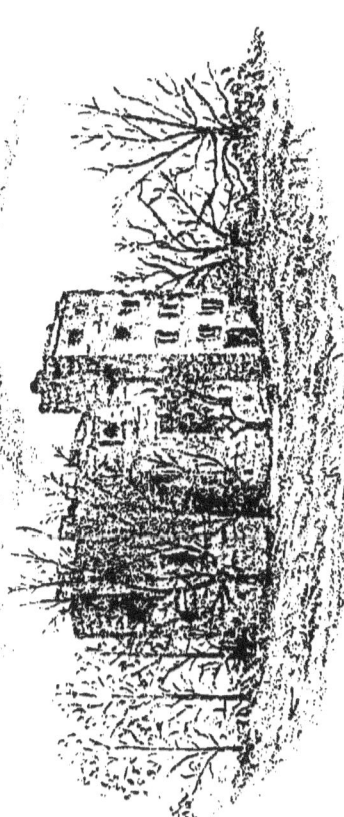

family after a few generations, was succeeded by the powerful family of the Lords of Tynedale, who in their turn were succeeded by the family of Claxtons, who not only succeeded to the Barony of Devylstonne, but to other estates of the Tynedales. This family after a while passed away, and was succeeded by the renowned family of Radcliffs. Sir Edward, son and heir of Sir Thomas Radcliffe, of the Derwentwater Estates, Cumberland, married (before 1494) Anne, only daughter and heir of John and Johanna Cartington, (lady of Cartington, Dilston, &c.) Sir Edward was succeeded by his eldest son and heir, Sir Cuthbert, who departed this life July 20th, 1545; and was succeeded by Sir George Radcliffe, his son and heir, who died May 31st, 1588; who was succeeded by his son and heir Sir Francis, the inheritor of the Radcliffe estates, in Northumberland and Cumberland, he married Isabel, daughter of Sir Ralph Grey, of Chillingham; Sir Francis enlarged the mansion house at Dilston in 1621, he died on the 23rd December, 1622, and was interred at Corbridge, in his parish church. He was succeeded in his lordships and possessions by his son and heir Sir Edward, who died in December, 1663, and was interred in the family vault at Dilston; his widow five years afterwards was also interred there. The latter part of Sir Edward's life was embittered by the outrages he endured; his estates were absolutely forfeited to the "commonwealth" for treason. In a proceeding at law, Sir Edward produced ancient deeds, records, and evidences of title, some of which were as early as the reign of King John. Sir Edward was succeeded by his son and heir Sir Francis Radcliffe, afterwards created Earl of Derwentwater, Baron Tynedale, and Viscount Radcliffe and Langley, who died 1697, and was interred in the family vault at Dilston. He was succeeded by his son and heir Edward, second earl. From the accounts written of Sir Francis, (father of Edward) he seems to have been a man of ambition, and kept up his paternal honours and estates in a princely style. Mr. J. Fisher, of Crosthwaite, Cumberland, wrote a short history of the Radcliffe family, from which we select a few extracts. He says—" Sir Francis Radcliffe wished to revive in his person, the earldom of Sussex which became extinct in 1641, by the death of his kinsman, Sir Edward Radcliffe, without issue. At that time he proposed

to marry his eldest son Edward, to the lady Charlotte, daughter of King Charles II, and Duchess of Cleveland, but it did not take place. Still bent upon an alliance with the royal house of Stuart, we find that Edward, his son, was married to Lady Mary Tudor, the youngest natural daughter of Charles II., who was at the time of her marriage in the fourteenth year of her age. In the month following this event (1688,) Sir Francis was created Earl of Derwentwater, Baron Tynedale, and Viscount Radcliffe and Langley. Perhaps there is not to be found in the page of history a more notable instance of the vanity of human wishes than that of Sir Francis Radcliffe to have his house ennobled. This ambition of his led to the ruin and extinction of one of the noblest families in Britain. The marriage of Edward, his son, with the Lady Mary Tudor, youngest daughter of Charles II., does not seem to have been a happy one. What sensible man could have expected more than a mere chance of happiness from such a match, the bride being only in her fourteenth year at the time of the marriage? There were four children by this marriage, the most notable being James the unfortunate third and last Earl, and Charles who survived his brother for thirty years, and then followed him to the scaffold, on a sentence passed in 1716......I have stated that the marriage of Edward Radcliffe the second Earl, with the youngest daughter of Charles II., was not a happy one; they entered into a deed of separation dated February 6th, 1700, and five years later, death finally parted them. It has been stated that she lived with Colonel Howard, of Levens Hall, near Milnthorpe, in the life-time of her husband. In the year after her husband's death she married Colonel Howard, who died during the following year, and two years later she married for the third time, James Rooke, Esq., whom she also survived, and outlived the dynasty of the Stuarts, for she died in Paris, November 5th, 1726, in the fifty-fourth year of her age. Edward died 20th April, 1705, and was interred in the family vault underneath the chapel, at Dilston, and was succeeded by his son and heir, James third Earl, and last possessor of the transient Earldom of Derwentwater. James Radcliffe, the third and last Earl, was born in London, June 28th, 1689; he was a year older than the eldest son of James II. Early in childhood he was taken to Paris for his education, where he lived

with his kinsman " The Young Pretender " (as he was then
and still is called,) on terms of intimate friendship, a friendship which existed as long as they lived. The young Earl
would be eleven years of age when his father and mother
separated. He seems to have lived in France principally
during his minority. It was during this time that he
formed an attachment to the charming daughter of Sir
John and Lady Webb. She had been placed in the convent
of Ursuline Nuns, at Paris, for her education, and their
acquaintance began in the spring-time of their lives.
Great were the rejoicings on his estates in Northumberland
and Cumberland, when in 1710, he came over to England to
visit them. Lord Derwentwater, it is said, " did what every
sensible man does "—he married. On the 10th of July, 1712,
he took to wife Anna Maria, daughter of Sir John Webb, of
Dorset, Baronet. Those who have written of his character
speak of him in the highest terms. They say : " He was
formed by nature to be generally beloved—he seemed to live
for others, and the poor, the widow, and the orphan rejoiced
in his bounty. He continually did offices of kindness and
good neighbourhood to everybody as opportunity offered.
He kept a house of noble entertainment, which few in that
country could do, and none came up to." He had just completed his 23rd year when he married. It was part of the
marriage contract that Sir John Webb should find the residence and table for the noble pair for two years, during
which time the new house, which the Earl had resolved to
build, at Dilston, was in course of erection.*

Early in the autumn of 1714 the happy pair took up their
residence at Dilston, making their tenantry happy by their
liberality, surrounded by social enjoyments, and the en-
dearments of domestic affection, and dispensing their princely
hospitality. This period of the Earl's life seems to have been
as happy as ever fell to the lot of man. The brief space of
five years elapsed between the first coming to his ancestral
estates (the last two only spent at Dilston) and the time of
his leaving them never to return. Late in August, 1715, the
Earl of Mar and other Scottish noblemen concerted a rising
in favour of the exiled prince—Lord Carnwath and Lord

---

* This evidently refers to the west front, which was added to the mansion
by the Earl, but it is stated was never finished.

154

Kenmure assisted. On the 16th of August the prince was proclaimed James VIII. in Scotland. The Earl's religion, his affections, and sympathies were all on the side of the exiled heir of the royal house of Stuart. His influence in the North of England alarmed the ministry of George I. A warrant for the apprehension of the Earl and his brother Charles was issued by the Government, hoping by making this move, to prevent the exercise of the Earl's influence against the house of Hanover. The Earl got notice of this and withdrew himself from Dilston Hall, and it is said, took refuge in the house of a humble cottager. He remained in concealment through the latter part of August, the whole of September, and the beginning of October,* during which period the gentry of the county meditated a rising to maintain the right of James III. to the throne.—Many arrests were made. Early in October the Earl's neighbours and friends were said to be ready to appear in arms. He was at this time in the 26th year of his age, and his brother Charles was four years younger. Early in the morning on the 6th of October, 1715, the domestic levy mustered in the court-yard at Dilston.

The following is the account Mackenzie gives of this rising:† "Movements indicating a meditated insurrection against the Hanoverian succession, being observed in various parts, the Ministry resolved to secure the persons of those who were known to be disaffected. Accordingly messengers were despatched to apprehend the Earl of Derwentwater and Thomas Forster, Esq., M.P. Having timely information of this circumstance, the Earl retired from his seat at Dilston,

---

* It is quite probable the tradition is correct, that the Earl and his brother Charles were concealed for some time in Beaufront Castle.—See article on Beaufront Castle.

† The day before he rose, Lord Derwentwater went to the old mansion of the Chief of Beaufront, Mr. Errington, to sound him, and if possible, induce him to join. Mr. Errington led the Earl in conversation to the top of the hill, commanding a view of Dilston Hall and its fine demesne, and besought him to pause, before he left his princely property for ever. The Earl pensively and mournfully replied that it was now too late. If the influence of his charming Countess decided, she paid dearly for it.

It has always been asserted by tradition, that on stealthily revisiting Dilston Hall, his lady reproached him, for continuing to hide his head in hovels from the light of day, when the gentry were in arms for the cause of their rightful Sovereign, and throwing down her fan before her lord, told him to take it and give his sword to her. There is no written evidence however, that such a domestic scene ever occurred, and the manner in which he wrote and spoke of her to the end of his career seems to contradict the story.

and Mr. Forster, after wandering to several places, came
to the house of Mr. Fenwick, of Bywell, where he narrowly
escaped being apprehended. The case being now
desperate, several Northumberland gentlemen resolved immediately to appear in arms. Pursuant to this resolution a
meeting was held the next morning, October 6th, at a place
called Green Rig. Mr. Forster, with about twenty gentlemen,
met at the rendezvous, and then rode to the top of a hill called
the Waterfalls,* from whence they might discover any that
came either to join or oppose them. They quickly discovered
the Earl of Derwentwater, who came that morning from his
seat at Dilston, with his spirited brother Charles, some friends
and his servants, mounted on his coach horses, and all very
well armed. In coming from Dilston Hall they all drew their
swords as they marched along Corbridge. They halted at the
seat of Mr. Errington (Beaufront Castle), where several other
gentlemen according to appointment came to Lord Derwentwater. When they had joined Mr. Forster and his company
there were in all about sixty horse, mostly gentlemen and
their attendants. After a short consultation they marched to
Plainfield, near the Coquet, where they were joined by others,
and then proceeded to Rothbury. Next morning, the 7th of
October, they marched to Warkworth. On Sunday morning
Mr. Forster sent Mr. Buxton, their Chaplain, to Mr. Ion, the
minister of the parish, with orders for him " to pray for the
Pretender as King"......which Mr. Ion declined ; Mr. Buxton
took possession of the church, read prayers, and preached.
Here, Mr. Forster in disguise, and by sound of trumpet proclaimed Charles Stuart, as King of Great Britain, &c., with
all the formality that the circumstances would admit ; on the
10th they marched to Morpeth, having been joined at Felton
bridge by seventy Scotch gentlemen from the Borders. They
had been considerably increased before, in their march from
Warkworth to Alnwick and other places, so that on their entering Morpeth they were 300 strong, all horse, for they would
entertain no foot. Mr. Forster being a Protestant was, from
policy, appointed general. He marched forward with an inten-

---

* The "Green Rig" is a piece of waste land adjoining the Watling Street
on the east side, about two or three miles south from Ridsdale. " The Waterfalls " is a farm house, about half-a-mile further east, from which a good view
can be obtained in all directions ; to the south along the Watling Street nearly
as far as Stagshawbank.

tion of surprising Newcastle, but finding the gates shut, he
turned westward to Hexham where he was reinforced by
another party of Scotch horsemen. Here he halted three days,
collecting arms and horses to mount the volunteers who flocked
from all quarters. The night before his departure Prince
Charles was proclaimed in the Market Place. Mr. Forster then
marched to Rothbury where he was met by another Scotch
nobleman in arms : the whole army then marched to Wooler,
on their way to Kelso, to join the Highlanders and others
according to arrangement; after a great deal of dissatisfaction
amongst themselves, the whole army marched to Langholm
intending to attack Dumfries, the key of the west, but this
idea was abandoned and they again entered England,
marched to Brampton, and thence to Penrith—where 12000
men were met to oppose them, but fled on the appearance of
General Forster and his followers, leaving several horses and
arms on the field; next day General Forster marched to
Kendal, and on the 9th of November entered Lancashire
where he seized six pieces of cannon. At Preston a regiment
of Militia and a regiment of Dragoons fled on his approach.
Here he was reinforced and resolved the next day to leave
Preston and enter Manchester, and then proceed to Liverpool;
but alas ! his infatuated career was at an end, for he was
informed that General Willis with four regiments of Dragoons
and one of foot were in sight. Preparations for their defence
were at once made—avenues were barricaded, men were posted
in the streets and bye-lanes, and such houses as were most
proper for galling their enemies. General Forster formed
four main barriers and arranged his forces for their defence,
&c. General Willis attacked all the four barriers at once,
but at every one his troops were repulsed with considerable
slaughter. Notwithstanding this success, the courage of
General Forster's little army failed on receiving intelligence
of the arrival of General Carpenter with his three regiments
of Dragoons. An offer was at once made to capitulate, which
was insisted on by General Willis, should be done uncon-
ditionally, which was agreed to. The Earl of Derwentwater
and Brigadier Mackintosh were delivered as hostages. The
rest is soon told—the next morning the King's troops entered
the town, seized the noblemen and gentlemen, secured the
Highlanders, who were drawn up in the Market Place, and

immediately shot all the half-pay officers. The number of English taken was 463, including 75 noblemen and gentlemen, mostly Northumbrians,* and the Scots amounted to 1005, among whom were 143 nobleman, officers, and gentlemen. The Earl of Derwentwater, with other prisoners of consequence, upwards of 200 in number, were sent to London and conveyed to their respective prisons in a most insulting manner. The Parliament met on the 9th of January, and the Commons immediately began business by expelling Mr. Forster, who was member for Northumberland, and impeaching the Earl of Derwentwater. On the 20th the Earl was brought from the tower to the bar of the house of Peers, when he delivered a written answer to the articles of impeachment, and on the 9th of February, he received sentence from the Lord Chancellor Cowper, High Steward on that occasion.

Great solicitations were made with the Courts and with the members of both Houses of Parliament in behalf of the Earl. The House seemed rather inclined to mercy, but it was finally agreed to leave the matter to his majesty, who did not think proper either to reprieve or pardon the Earl of Derwentwater. The same evening (the 23rd of February,) orders were despatched for executing the Earl of Derwentwater, and Nithsdale, and the Lord Kenmure, the next morning. During the few last hours of the life of the Earl, he wrote several letters to his friends, one in particular to the Countess, in which he gave full particulars of all that he observed; and that letter is still preserved in the family of Lord Petre, whose ancestor married Anna Maria, the Earl's only daughter. He also wrote a paper which he read from the scaffold. He was attended during the last few days of his life by the Rev. George Pippard, (a Roman Catholic Priest). Like all thoughtful men, he felt that it is a solemn thing to die—to pass that bourne whence no traveller returns. He therefore addressed himself to make the best preparation he could during the short time he had to live. The Earl is said to have sent for an undertaker of funerals, and expressed

* Amongst the Northumbrians, in addition to Charles Radcliffe, Esq., are the names of Thomas Errington, Esq., of Beaufront; Joseph Redshaw, Esq., of Durham Fields, near Hexham; Philip Hodgson, of Sandaw, Esq.; Robert Shaftoe, of Bavington, Esq.; Mr. Edward Swinburn, of Capheaton; Doctor Charlton, and Mr. William Charlton, sons of Mr. William Charlton, of Reedsmouth, &c., &c.

a wish to be buried at Dilston. He wished to have a silver plate placed upon his coffin, bearing an inscription to the effect that he died a sacrifice to his lawful sovereign. But the undertaker did not dare to comply with Lord Derwentwater's desire, and was accordingly dispensed with. No hearse was provided for the morrow, when the last sad scene was to be enacted. It was a murky morning, that 24th February, 1716, when the troops gathered round the scaffold which had been erected. It is said he walked majestically to the place of execution. It was noticed that paleness for a few moments overspread his features as he ascended the steps and mounted the scaffold, which, with the fatal block, were draped with black cloth, he came in sight of a crowd which numbered many thousands of people. He soon regained his composure, and his behaviour was resolute and sedate. He was attired in a complete suit of black velvet. He wore a broad brimmed beaver hat, turned up at one side and attached with loop and button to the low round crown, adorned with a black drooping plume. Below this black hat, the light flaxen curls of a flowing wig, worn according to the fashion of the day, fell upon his shoulders. He wore long black worsted hose, black leather shoes high over the instep, with high heels and silver buckles ; such was the Earl's attire. The young nobleman was again offered his life, (as he had been before) if he would conform to the established church and the house of Hanover, but he answered that " these terms would be too dear a purchase." Having taken off his coat and wig, a strife arose (says a narrator) about his wig between the keeper of the tower and the executioner, and a similar contest about his velvet clothes. He repeated previously the 51st Psalm, and again offered up prayer. Seeing that the Sheriff did not interfere, when the executioner took off his clothes, though the keeper made his complaint that they had been given to him by his lordship, he whispered to his chaplain to beg the Countess to be in no concern about his burial, for he did not care what they did with his corpse. Finding on the block a rough place that might hurt his neck, he bade the executioner make it smooth, which was done ; and his presence of mind and coolness astonished the spectators. The following short dialogue ensued—Lord Derwentwater— " I forgive all concerned in my execution." Executioner—

159

"I ask your lordship's forgiveness" Lord Derwentwater.—
"With all my heart I forgive all my enemies, I forgive the
most malicious of them, and I do forgive you." The Earl
then presented two half broad pieces to the executioner, and
told him he would receive an additional present from the
gentlemen who held his hat and wig. He told the executioner
not to strike till he had made a short prayer and pronounced
the name of Jesus loudly three times. His prayer was "Dear
Jesus be merciful to me." The third time he repeated it with
a loud voice, and in an instant his head was severed from
his body. A spectator said "It is impossible to
describe the consternation that appeared in the faces of all
that were there." As the head rolled on the scaffold
it was picked up by a faithful servant of the Earl's, who
was in attendance and who folded it in his handkerchief.
Lord Derwentwater's last request in the tower, was that his
body might be interred with his ancestors at Dilston; this
was refused, the Government fearing another rising in the
north. From the scaffold, the body wrapped in black cloth
was conveyed in a hired coach to the tower, where it would
have been buried if the Earl's friends had not contrived to
obtain possession of his remains by leave or stratagem (a mock-
funeral.) The head which was received by his trusty servant,
after being wrapped in a red velvet cloth, was borne away by
the friends of the Earl. The following morning by three
o'clock the body was conveyed from the tower in a hearse, to
the surgery of Mr. Medcalf, where the head and body were embalmed, and thence to the house of Mr. King, an undertaker.
The outer cover of the coffin was of crimson velvet, studded
with gilt nails, and bore a gilt plate thus inscribed : "The
Right Hon. James, late Earl of Derwentwater, died Feb.
24th, 1715—6, aged 27 years. The remains were taken
from London to Dagenham Park, near Romford, a house
which was rented by the Countess for a time, both before and
after his death. They rested some days in a private chapel
of that house, and his friends contrived to carry out his wish.
The carriage carrying the remains was driven by a servant
named Dun,* travelling by night and resting by day to

---

* As far as we are able to learn, Dun was the servant who took up the head
of the Earl when it was severed from the body, and folded it in a clean handkerchief; and who after seeing his charge safely deposited in the family vault
at Dilston, took up his residence at Nafferton, here we believe he lived to the

escape observation. And so his remains were borne to their last resting place in the Dilston Chapel, where in life he had often knelt,—a fit place for their enduring repose.

In the accounts which have been written concerning the death of the Earl, allusion has generally been made to the aurora borealis which appeared so remarkably vivid on the night of his execution, and it was said the streamers continued to be seen until the remains reached Dilston. The red streamers of the north are recorded to have been seen, for the first time in this part of England, on the night of the fatal 24th of February, 1716, and are designated "Lord Derwentwater's lights." When a similar phenomenon occurred on the 18th of October, 1848, the crimson streamers which rose and spread from the horizon, in the form of an expanded fan, the people said that nothing like this display of aurora borealis had been seen since the appearance of "Lord Derwentwater's lights."

Dilston Chapel has been referred to as the last resting place for the remains of the Earl, and mentioned as a "fit place for their enduring repose." But the vandalism of the fallen humanity of some men, and the changes brought about by the whirl of time and circumstances, have shown this to be otherwise. So far as we know his remains remained undisturbed until the early part of the present century, when they were rudely and mischievously dealt with. Mackenzie gives the following account of this transaction: "From accident or design the coffin of the Earl was broken open, a few years ago, and the body found, after the lapse of near a century, in a high state of preservation. It was easily recognized by the suture round the neck, by the openness of the countenance, and the regularity of the features. The teeth were perfect." But Mr. Surtees (in his *History of Durham*) says that "several of them (the teeth) were drawn by a blacksmith and sold for 2s. 6d. a-piece, a short time after the vault was closed." *

end of his life, having in his possession the handkerchief, which was never washed, but remained stained with blood as it was when the head was unfolded. That handkerchief he treasured as a sacred relic, and it was often shown to his friends. The writer in his early years has often heard the old chroniclers in the village refer somewhat minutely to all these transactions of Dun's.

* Mrs. Grey, in her *History of Dilston Hall*, quoting in a foot note from the *Tyne Mercury Newspaper*, says this took place in 1805, but adds, Surtees in his *History of Durham* says 1807.

161

" In 1784, when the father of the present Lord Howard, of Corby Castle, visited this touching spot, the vault was open and he saw the coffin of the last Lord of Derwentwater uninjured, either by sacrilegious hands or decay. Its covering of crimson velvet, its brass inscription plate and gilt ornaments looked quite new and fresh, and it had not then been opened. But in 1805 a deputation of the Greenwich Hospital Commissioners, accompanied by Mr. Byer, their Secretary, when visiting Dilston on their official tour of inspection, conceived a curiosity to inspect the remains of the murdered Earl...... .... Their curiosity gratified, the disturbers of the tomb had not the decency to cause it to be again closed ; they absolutely suffered - the remains of the noble victim to be left exposed to vulgar gaze, and a miscreant blacksmith dared to draw several of the teeth, &c." This account is in some respects incorrect, we believe the following to be a more correct version of the whole affair. (We may state, however, that we believe the vault was, after this, twice opened before the time referred to by Mrs. Grey, and on the first of these occasions the remains were interfered with.)

At this time two of the Commissioners of the Greenwich Hospital were on a tour in the North of England, and having a doubt as to whether, after all, the body of the Earl was at Dilston, the vault was ordered to be opened ; a person of the name of Wilson, a glazier and plumber in Corbridge, was engaged to open the inner or lead coffin, which was done by cutting out a piece of the lid extending over the face and neck ; when the Earl was seen as described, orders were given to have the coffin repaired and properly soldered, and the vault immediately made secure. A few days afterwards, an account of the opening of the vault, coffin, &c., appeared in one of the Newcastle newspapers, *The Tyne Mercury*, we believe, when some persons afterwards taking advantage of this information, forged a letter purporting to come from the receivers of the Greenwich Hospital at Newcastle, giving them authority for some purpose or other, to have the vault and coffin re-opened, they came to Dilston in a conveyance and presented the letter to a person of the name of Stokoe, who had charge of the place ; having accomplished their object, they left without any instructions for the closing of the vault or coffin,

L

the consequence was, that for several days the vault was visited by numbers of persons. A blacksmith of the name of Rutter, who only died a few years ago, was the man who drew the teeth, and others drew out of the outer coffin several gilt-headed nails ; the teeth were quickly sold for two shillings and sixpence each, one of which was shown in Mr. Lumbly's Museum at Corbridge, but it was soon found out that more teeth were sold than the Earl had in his head. As soon as this scandal reached the ears of the authorities in Newcastle, the coffin and vault were ordered immediately to be closed and made secure. At the time referred to by Mrs. Grey, as having been opened by Mr. Grey, the coffins were not interfered with, nor afterwards as far as we know, until their final removal from Dilston ; when the remains of the Earl reached Thorndon, and before being re-interred, to make surety doubly sure, the friends of the Earl had his coffin opened, when the remains of the unfortunate Earl were found to be there.

It was attempted by the Government to forfeit the estates to the crown immediately after the Earl's death, but on the case being heard in Westminster Hall, the settlement he made before his marriage was held to be valid ; the trustees entered into possession, and the Dowager Countess and her family retained the property. The Countess went to Hatherhope, thence to the house of her parents at Canford Manor ; after which she took up her residence at Louvaine, in France, where she died on the 30th of August, 1723, at the early age of thirty, having survived her husband only seven years. She was ere long followed from the world by her only son the Honourable John Radcliffe, who died on the 31st December, 1731, aged nineteen years. There are conflicting accounts about his death ; one is that he died in France, another that he died in London, and another that he secretly left this country and took up his residence in Austria, where he died at a good old age. That he died in France would appear to be the most probable.

There is no account of the young nobleman ever having been at Dilston, and the Countess appears never to have returned. There is, however, a tradition that several waggon loads of furniture were removed from the mansion, but there is no certainty as to their destination, probably to the house of her parents during her residence with them, if not to the house

at Hatherhope. It is quite certain, however, that the establishment at Dilston was maintained, by servants at least, until
the death of the young lord; such is the traditional account
supported by written evidence. In a letter to the Countess,
written by Thos. Errington of Capheaton (who was land
steward for the countess), and dated April the 5th, 1722,
after referring to some legal matters, says: "I doubt not but
Mr. Busby (Mr. Busby was the house steward at Dilston)
has acquainted your Ladyship that there is one Mr. Hallsall,
a monke, come to live with him at Dilston Hall, * there's no
doubt of it but it was Mr. Busby's desire to have one there,
which is a very good thing for the people thereaboutes. Mr.
Aynsley of Hexham, would buy some hollys and ewes at
Dilston if your Ladyship will sell any; and Mr. Sanderson of
Heely, would buy some firrs. I told them I could say
nothing in that affaire, but should acquaint your Ladyshipe
with it; all this famally are well, and gives their humble
services to your Ladyshipe and famally.

I am, your Ladyship's most obedient Servant,

THOS. ERRINGTON."

There are two entries in the churchwardens' books at Corbridge, referring to the Lord Derwentwater; one dated 1730,
the other 1724, we quote the latter. "1724, May 11th, at a
vestry meeting of the four and twenty, permission was given
to Lord Derwentwater to enlarge his pew on the north side of
the Church." The inference is plain, that although there was
service in the Chapel at Dilston, yet the inmates of the hall
attended service in Corbridge Church, and that the existing
pew was too small for their accommodation.

It was after the death of the Earl's only son that the
Government seized upon the estates and kept possession of
them ever afterwards. Before proceeding further, we extract
from the steward's account or household book which extends
from Martinmas 1681, to Pentecost 1682, in which we find
a large number of entries, illustrative of the life, habits, and
domestic economy of the Baronet's family. His domestic
establishment seems to have numbered thirty-three servants
at wages hardly exceeding in the whole £60 a year. The
following copy of entries will show their proportions :—Nov.

---

* It is likely Mr. Busby occupied a part of the mansion.

164

15th, Philip Horseman (the cook) in full for his half-yeare's wages ended at Martinmas, £5. 17th, Tom Brown, (herd) his Martinmas wages, £1 15s., more for his own charges coming and going to Tynehead, 1s., and 2s. more which he agreed with a man to help him to drive the sheep from Tyne-head to Dilston and for going back. Ralphe Thompson, his half-yeare wages due and ended at Martinmas, £1 2s. 6d. Jan. 12th, William Weare for helping to brew when we had no other brewer to assist Mrs. Jackson, 5s. 8d., at 4d. a day, and 2s. 6d. for five days' helpeing to make a lodge in the garden, in all 8s. 2d. 26th, Mabel Addison (kitchen maid) one halfe-year's wages entered at Martinmas, £1. Feb. 1st, Matthew Gill (the butler) his halfe-yeare's wages ended 20th Jany., £2 10s. 22nd, Margaret Lambert (chamber maid) in full for 15 week's service, she going away now sick, 11s. 6d. 25th, Thomas Redshaw (husbandman) his halfe-yeare's wages due 4th Feby., £2. March 2nd, Beely Barron, under maid in Ladye's chamber, one halfe-yeare's wages ended at Martinmas last, 15s. May 14th, Mark Stokoe. which he paid by Sir Francis his order to Ralph Hudspeth of Corbridge, in part of payment for winning 100 foother of lyme stones won at Corbridge, 12s. June 1st, Mrs. Anne Jackson (the brewer) one yeare's wages due at May day, £3, &c., &c.; (although the brewer had only £3 a year, yet the office was no sinecure, for in about nine months 975 bushels of malt were supplied to Dilston Hall, for which £137 10s. was paid, and a new brewing vessel was erected in 1681.)* We give some further extracts : "My Lady Radcliffe' and her daughter Mary received a yearly allowance of £200 for clothes. Mr. Franciss Radcliffe and his sisters Katharine and Elizabeth received each an allowance of £40 a year. Among payments to players and musicians we find a gift of 10s. to an old man named Howard, "an organist, and who tuned the virginals at Dilston," and

---

* The brew house was not taken down until about the year 1835, a short time previous to which the brewing vessel was removed; we recollect seeing it as fixed in the brew house, and was somewhat surprised at its large dimensions. About the same time, the window frames of the mansion, as well as the front door, which had been stowed away in the cellars of the castle or tower, were taken out and utilised ; the window frames which were very massive were used for making stiles on the various footpaths on the estate, and around Dilston and neighbourhood ; they served this purpose for many years. The brewing vessel was made of the best oak and used by Mr. Green of Corbridge, in the manufacture of several articles of furniture.

came thither with **Dr. Nairne** to sell a pair of organs.
Madam Catherine, by order of Sir Francis, gave £1 to Mr.
Palmer, the organist of Newcastle, and Jerry Kinleyside
received 14s. for his Christmas wages for piping, by
order of Sir Francis. The players who came from about
Stella and Blaydon to Dilston, and there played the play
called "Musadores," received by the Baronet's order one
pound. A poet that came out of Scotland, had given him
by Madam Catherine in charity, by the like order, about
candlemas, five shillings. There is a sum of £22 19s. 8d. to
Lancelot Algood, for the expensive luxury of legal proceedings. He was engaged at this time in a law-suit with the
tenants of Derwentwater, respecting the Town Cass, a suit
which lasted from 1684 till 1691, in which he was defeated.
The tenants although successful, had upwards of £100 to pay,
and the land in question was worth only, at that day, £20."*

1686, December. Mr. Miller, his bill from 29 Nov. till
Dec. 6, for thrashing corne, mending the highways between
Corbridge and Dilston ; and the Wreight's makeing 4 stone
carts, and 1 stone sledd, all at Dilston, £1 7s. 3d.

Mr. Roger Garstall, in full for all sorts of wine, and all
other accounts whatsoever, from the beginning of the world,
£36 0s. 7½d.

Mrs. Winship having kindly allowed a copy to be taken of
the original document, which is in the hand-writing of Sir
Francis, afterwards created Earl, bearing his own seal and
signature. No apology is required for inserting it entire, we

---

* The household accounts which had been carefully preserved for a great
number of years had been well and orderly kept, each year's records being all
tied together. All those documents, with many others, remained in the possession of the Greenwich Hospital Commissioners and the Lords of the
Admirality until the Dilston estates were sold, then arose a question as to
their disposal ; it appears they formed no part of Mr. Beaumont's purchase,
and as we understand is alleged, there not being room in the office at Haydon
Bridge for their keeping, it was decided to burn them. The great bulk of
them were stored away, in a room fitted up for the purpose, in a dwelling-
house adjoining the chapel-yard at Dilston; a part of them were sent to
London, but the other part which was considerable, consisted of the household
accounts, account books, the family correspondence, plans, award books, &c.,
&c.; they were brought out into the yard and put together into a large heap,
which continued to burn for some days, and all consumed, except some small
portions which were saved from the flames by the onlookers, and preserved
as relics from Dilston Hall. It is a matter of deep regret, by many living in
the village (who have a lingering love for Dilston and its associations), that
these interesting and ancient records should have been thus ruthlessly destroyed.

only regret that expence prevents us from giving a fac-simile of the hand-writing ; we preserve the original spelling.

COPY.

" June th nynth day, one thousand six hundred seventy six. To all christian people to whome this present writing shall come, know yee that I, Sr Francis Radclyffe, of Dilston, Bar^t doe acknowledge and confessesse my selfe fully sattisfied, contented, and paid the sum of thirty shillings lawfull money of England, for, and in consideration of a peel. of ground lying at the south west corner of a place called the Long Maynes, belonging to Thornbrough, and sould unto Lyonel Winship, of Aydon, by me S^{ir} Francis Radclife, Bar^t contayning about thirty-nyne yards in length, and twelve yards in breadth, which will be about four hundred and eighty square yards, which is the tenth part of an acre all but four yeards ; wherefore, I the said Sr. Francis Radclyffe, doe acknowledge my selfe fully satisfied, and paid the said sum of thirty shillings for the above said premisses. In witness thereof, I have sett my hand and seale, the day and yeare above sd. Test,

RICHARD HAYLES,*   F. RADCLYFFE."
JOHN COOKE.

After the death of the young lord, it does not appear that, for some time at least, any one had charge of the mansion or its contents ; nor does there seem to have been a sale of the household goods ; in fact, there was no one in authority to sell. The heir being dead ; the next heir, Charles, being disqualified, the goods were probably considered public property, and everyone seems to have helped themselves, possibly the servants may have had to do with their disposal ; we may be wrong in our conjecture, but this is the only way we can account for the numerous articles of furniture, furnishings, ornaments, kitchen utensils, &c., &c., portions of which were in almost every house in Dilston, Corbridge, and neighbourhood, including many in Hexham, and whether of great or of little value in themselves, were all treasured as relics belonging the Earl of Derwentwater ; a few of them are yet in the neighbourhood. We recollect many years ago being shown two or more standing or case clocks, which were brought from Dilston Hall, but they are not now in the

---

* Richard Hayles sometimes spelled Hailes, was the house steward.

neighbourhood. The late Mr. Fairless of Hexham, had in his possession a small mahogany chest of drawers, which he used to show as formerly belonging to the Earl of Derwentwater. The late Mr. John Surtess of Corbridge, had the spice box from the still room or kitchen, made of mahogany and used for keeping the different kinds of spices. The late Mr. George Tweddell had a beautiful copper coffee pot, also brought from Dilston; we believe it is in the possession of his niece Mrs. Tweddell. Miss Charlton, Corbridge, has a painting on glass of the head and shoulders of the Earl, it belonged her uncle the late Mr. Joseph Dodd, it was brought from Dilston Hall in the original frame, which is carved and had been silvered or gilded; Mr. Dodd was often asked to dispose of it, but he never would. A beautiful large carved oak picture frame was for a long time in the Angel Inn, Corbridge; after the picture had got destroyed it was taken into the garret and there put away as lumber; a few years ago it was taken possession of, and foolishly cut for the purpose of making it into a smaller frame; Mr. Adam Harle has a piece of it, which is a fine specimen of carving. But the most valuable relic hereabouts is the family dining table now in the possession of Mr. Walker, and which has been previously referred to. The late Mr. Bearpark of Hexham, had in his possession a great number of interesting and valuable Derwentwater relics, we are not aware how they were disposed of after his death.

The house itself appears to have been viewed in the same light (viz., as public property) for it was soon all occupied, and we have heard the old people say that it was at one time occupied by sixteen or eighteen families, * but it appears they

* Dilston village, in the time of the Earl, consisted of one street, which continued east and west, and adjoined the out-houses of the mansion on the east side, having a row of houses on each side of the village green, or what the old people who lived at Dilston almost a century ago called the " Town Genete," in the middle of which was a draw well, which was not altogether filled up until many years after Mr. Grey went to reside there; the writer has seen it many times; the courses of the walling stones as far as they could be seen showed good masonry. The slight hollow in the pasture field for some distance from the mansion was the Town Geneto; the foundations of many of the cottages and houses, particularly on the north side, have not been removed, many of the ruins being buried beneath the grass. One of the Swinburnes, a clock maker lived here; we recollect many years ago, falling in with a clock of this man's make, with his name and residence engraven on the dial, and also the date; unfortunately when we broke up the dial we did not preserve the date, but as near as we recollect it might be betwixt 1740 and 1750. An eight days' clock made by this person is in possession of a family at present living in Gateshead.

paid no rent, and this was asserted at Dilston to be one of the reasons for pulling the mansion down "to get quit of the rookery" as the occupants were called; the mansion was never repaired, but suffered to go to ruin, indeed its ruin seems to have been the object of the Commmissioners, for eventually it was ordered to be pulled down. We now proceed to give a description of Dilston Hall, the domestic Chapel, Grounds, &c.

We first give Hutchinson's description of the hall before it was taken down. "After we passed the Tyne by a fine bridge of seven arches, Dilston next attracted our notice; the Mansion House is now in ruins, its situation is fine, on the brink of a steep hill clothed with verdure, descending to the banks of the Devil's Water. The approach we made was romantic: the rivulet at its conflux with the Tyne flows out of a deep dell forming a grand natural cascade; after we passed a bridge of a single arch, which leads to the mansion, through this arch a mill is seen, over which are lofty and impending cliffs, the whole embowered by trees extending their branches from each side of the dell, and spreading out a leafy canopy at least one hundred feet in height, shadowing the lower objects with a solemn gloom..........We approached the mansion now consisting of desolate and ragged ruins; the hollow halls, hanging stairs, and painted chambers present a sad memorial of the fate of their last unhappy Lord."*

Mr. John Wesley in his *Journal* thus describes it: "April 19th, 1751, leaving Hindly Hill, Allendale, early in the morning, we scaled the snowy mountains and rode by the once

* There was another, a small mansion, which we have not seen noticed by historians, called "Radcliffe Hill," and was situate upon a piece of rising ground in a field on the east side of, and adjoining the road leading from the pasture field to the high town, and about seventy yards from the gateway which divides the road from the field; it appears from the scraps of information we have obtained, to have been from an early date the residence of branches of the Radcliffe family, and it is not unlikely but this house may have been the residence of Lady Swinburne, cousin of the last Earl, or Lady Mary who died in 1724, and was the last interred in the family vault. The late Mr. Cuthbert Snowball, who farmed the High Town farm when he was a young man, had it as a kind of storehouse for the use of the farm. We have heard Mr. Snowball describe the building as having a high-pitch thatch roof, but beautifully finished inside like a gentleman's mansion, and before it was taken down they held the dance, in connection with their churn supper, in one of the rooms (we think it was the drawing room;) after it was pulled down and the materials removed, the site was cultivated, and occasionally when turning up the soil coins have been found, if we recollect right, both gold and silver. Adjoining this house there were some cottages, probably for the accommodation of servants; about seventy years ago the whole of the buildings were removed.

delightful seat of the late Lord Derwentwater, now neglected, desolate, and swiftly running to ruin."

We now quote from Sidney Gibson's, Esq., *History of Dilston*: "Amongst the many places in Northumberland it would be difficult to find a spot more interesting in its memories, and more charming in its features of natural beauty than the sylvan and secluded domain of Dilston, which was antiently the inheritance of the Lords of Tynedale, afterwards the seat of a branch of the once powerful family of Radcliffs, and memorable as the house of James Radcliff, third and last Earl of Derwentwater, whose life and possessions were forfeited in 1716, in the attempt to restore the royal line of Stuart to the throne, and whose memory is affectionately cherished in Northumberland. The hall or mansion, which was about a mile south-west from Corbridge, stood upon an eminence of commanding height forming a cliff, round a considerable portion of which, the river, called Devil's Water, flows swiftly to the Tyne. The grey shattered ruins of the old Castle or Keepe is now all that is left of the residences of the Radcliff's in Northumberland." It appears that shortly before the death of Sir Francis Radcliff (who died on the 23rd of December, 1622, and was interred at Corbridge in his Parish Church) the Mansion House at Dilston was enlarged ; the hall or mansion thus enlarged,* formed three sides of an oblong square, inclosing a court yard paved with dark veined lime-stone, in diamond-shaped slabs, and entered by a large arch gateway which is still standing, on which the initials F.R. and I.R.,† and the date 1616, are still visible : the longest range of buildings occupied the northern side. In the centre was a large entrance hall,‡ which was built of stone, and

---

* There are articles of agreement for these works, made betwixt Sir Edward and the contractor, dated the 2nd of January, 1621, the contractor whose name was Johnson, of Little Longton, duly fulfilled his contract, and received for his services £205, one condition being, that "the new portion of the house wherein Sir Francis dwelt to be three stories in height, &c." The mansion when thus completed comprised twenty "hearths;" the range of buildings on the northern side extended about 120 feet, besides about 30 feet more, added afterwards by the last Earl.

† Mrs. Grey states, that these initials are those of Sir Francis Radcliffe and James Radcliffe ; this is an error so far as the letters J. R. are concerned, they are the initials of Isabel, the wife of Sir Francis Radcliffe (who made some improvements to the mansion), and daughter of Sir Ralph Grey of Chillingham, the head of one of the most illustrious of the Northumbrian families.

‡ The writer, when a youth, knew an intelligent old man of the name of George Lishman, who belonged to Dilston, and who was accustomed to relate how when he was a youth he played at hand-ball inside what he called the

approached from the paved court yard by a few steps. (The writer has seen quite distinctly the formation of these steps, the foundations of which had not been removed.) The court yard was bounded on its western side by the old tower or castle, which still remains; and against the western front of that structure, a range of buildings comprising several rooms was added by Lord Derwentwater, but these rooms were never finished in the interior. Mr. Fairless, of Hexham, preserves a fragment of carved work that came from Dilston Hall, and probably ornamented the panels of one of these rooms. The western façade presented in the upper story a range of nine windows, which commanded a fine view of the vale of Hexham. This front was raised on a sort of terrace or embankment, above a formal garden, extending further westward, and to the edge of the river cliff,* which is a precipitous declivity of a hundred feet. The intended state apartments were on this façade of the building. There was a large hall entered from the garden, with a drawing room, and dining room, on the northern side, and other rooms on the southern side. The princely possessions of the gallant Derwentwater were no sooner under the control of the Commissioners, than measures were taken to obliterate as far as possible, all things that could serve to remind the people of their loss. The hall was destined to be demolished; its materials were valued,† and the deer were to be sold.‡

Marble Hall: he often gave a description of the mansion as it was at that time, and as far as we can recollect, was similar to that given by Hutchinson, who visited Dilston about that time. Before the hall was taken down, a drawing of it was ordered to be made, as appears by the account accompanying the drawing, which is as follows: "Drawn on the spot by Thos. Oliver of Hexham, in Northumberland, and published according to Act of Parliament, July 17, 1766." The hall was taken down in 1767.

* We recollect just after Mr. Grey came to reside at Dilston, one very dry summer, in company with Mrs. Grey, distinctly tracing on the withered grass the principal walks in this garden, one was direct from the front door westward to the edge of the cliff, which was cut in the middle by another running north and south; where they intersected each other there was the appearance of having been a fountain. Near to the cliff were remnants, still allowed to grow, of the original rose bushes.

† In 1740, the materials of the house were valued at £751; the bell and the clock were given to the church of St. Augustine, at Alderstone, the donation dating 25th August, 1769.

‡ There were two deer parks at Dilston, one known as the old and the other as the new, the former was for the keeping of the common or small deer, the latter for red deer. The old park included the whole of Dilston Park Farm; the boundary wall on the north side, extended from Dilston Mill to the park troughs, and now forms the south wall of the present turnpike road to Hexham; a considerable portion of the original wall still exists, and is almost

171

After the hall had been dismantled and its contents and enrichments dispersed, the walls were demolished piece-meal for building purposes, and at length in 1765, the Commissioners ordered that the house be entirely taken down and the remaining materials sold. Ten years after it was directed that the grounds surrounding the house should be levelled, but what remained of the old castle preserved (the nursery was in these rooms) and that some trees be planted round the chapel..........The chapel, the scene of the domestic worship of the family, the vault beneath which is the place of the interment of several of its members, stands to the north of the hall. This little domestic chapel still stands amid the sheltering trees and the adjacent ruins of the old castle.'' Adjoining the chapel yard is a dwelling house said to be the residence of the residing priest.

entire from Widehaugh House to the park troughs; in this portion was the park keeper's house, being about ninety yards east of the troughs; the north front is in a line with the wall and reduced to the same height, the coins and doorway of which can be distinctly seen from the road. It is reported that when the title deeds of the estate were conveyed from the mansion they were for a time concealed in this house.

The Red Deer Park, as far as we can learn (for we have no historical account), was probably made during the life-time of the first earl, if not by Sir Edward after he enlarged the hall in 1621—2, and was on the south side of the mansion, the northern wall bounding for some distance on the road which led past the mansion, and was entered by a noble gateway. When this park was made, the north wall at about the middle, cut through the ancient Roman Road then in use (originally leading from the Roman Bridge over the Tyne into Cumberland), and which continued some 150 or 200 yards south into the intended new park, and then at nearly a right-angle took to the west; so much of this ancient road as was in the plan of the new park was diverted and bounded westward on the park wall, passing close by the chapel and the arch gateway which led to the mansion. This park extended eastward as far as the road which leads to Dilston high town. The wall on the west side of this road being the original wall, but now lowered on the west side, the boundary wall of the park was nearly in a line with the west side of Mr. Grey's house, a portion of which yet remains, and which formed nearly a square, the shortest side being the south, this wall yet remains; inside of the western portion of the north wall, were planted a double row of chesnut trees, intended to ornament the front of the mansion; several of these noble trees yet remain. Sidney Gibson, Esq., in his *History of Dilston*, states "these trees formed a carriage drive about a mile in length," but his informant was in error, for these trees never extended further east than those now standing, nor were they planted for any other purpose than that referred to. Until Mr. Grey came to reside at Dilston, a great portion of the north wall was standing ten or eleven feet high, apparently its original height, but the public road leading from Corbridge to Slaley and Hexhamshire, being again diverted, to meet the alterations made by Mr. Grey, this wall was at first lowered, and ultimately (on the north side) altogether removed. The fine gateway into the park about twelve feet in height, which was some little distance west of the chapel, was removed further south and made the west gateway into Mr. Grey's house, but in its re-erection it was lowered to its present height; it is noticeable that its style of architecture is the same as the gateway on the approach to St. Peter's Church, at Bywell. Another similar gateway is on the carriage road, near the front door of Halton Castle. The writer has a sketch of the grounds which he made in his early years, and which shows the grounds in the

172

During the residence of John Grey, Esq., at Dilston, as
well as that of his son, Charles, who succeeded his father
during a period of upwards of forty years, great alterations
were made, the grounds, &c., being greatly beautified by new
walks, lawns, shrubs, &c., not only visitors but the public
generally were allowed (by permission which was never
refused) to roam at their pleasure over the charming grounds,
and inspect the ruins of the castle, as well as the domestic
chapel. The estate has now, by purchase, become the property
of W. B. Beaumont, Esq., M.P.; notwithstanding this change
we have pleasure in stating that persons desirous of visiting
the grounds, castle, and chapel (when the family is not
residing at Dilston,) can do so by obtaining leave from Mr.
Balden, the resident agent.

We now give a short account of the little chapel, which
we have not yet seen described. This interesting domestic
place of worship, is an oblong square with a tower at the
west-end, entered by a door from the outside, the top of which
is reached by a stone spiral staircase, and in a recess on the
top of the tower the bell was hung. The roof of the tower as
well as the roof of the chapel was covered with lead, but owing
to the frequent depredations of thieves carrying away portions
of it, about thirty years ago it was altogether removed and
the present grey slate cover put on. The inside of the
chapel is thirty-two feet long, by fifteen feet wide, eighteen

neighbourhood of the mansion as they were before any alterations were made
by Mr. Grey, and much about the same as they were left at the breaking up
of the establishment after the death of the Earl's son, John, in 1730; in this
sketch he finds at the gateway this note, "large gateway into the park standing in 1830." Within the park and adjoining the chesnut trees on the east
was an orchard. Mr. Grey, in making the new turnpike road cut through this
orchard; one of the apple trees was allowed to grow (although fallen) during
the residence of Mr. Grey, and is yet there. As the writer does not refer to
this subject elsewhere, he here remarks that the servants' apartments were in
the east range or side of the mansion, east of this range of buildings was a yard
or open space, bounded by all the out-houses of the establishment, which consisted of a range of buildings extending from the brow of the hill on the north,
to the turnpike road on the south; in these were the clock and bell tower, and
adjoining them again on the east, was the village elsewhere referred to. The
carriage way from the front door of the hall was through the existing archway, then north along the open space before named, down the bank north of
the mansion (on the top of which was an archway) over the narrow bridge,
and by a sharp turn northward on to the mill road. The mill-race was
originally carried over the stream below the bridge. This bridge is seven feet
betwixt the parapets, and has a span of forty-five feet. In the stewards' book
of expenses there are entries of "£19 lent to, and £6 and £10 paid to Mr. George
Jordan and Mr. John Whitfield, for building the new stone bridge over against
the Roe Park wall," whether this is the bridge referred to we cannot say, but
judging from its present appearance it would seem to be of an earlier date.

feet high, and is entered by a door at the south-west corner. There are three windows in the north side, one in the south side, and one in the east-end, all of the same design, and seem to indicate the style which prevailed during the whole of the fifteenth century, having square heads with deep moulding, being divided by two mullions into three openings with pointed tops or arches, and having originally being protected by wire grating on the outside, remnants of which yet remain; the windows are not of uniform size, the east one being very much larger than any of the others.

The furnishings of the chapel consist of a desk, a few pews, and a seat secured along the whole length of the south wall, which, judging from the appearance of the timber and the nature of the mouldings and panels, must have been there in the time of the Earls. The vault is at the east-end of the chapel beneath the desk and pews, and approached from the inside by a flight of stone steps, the entrance to which is covered by large stone flags. The period of its erection is uncertain: we have heard some mention the time of the Reformation as the probable period, but others think at an earlier date: its general character would suggest the middle or close of the fifteenth century, or as soon probably as the Radcliffes became possessors of the estates. In the outside of the east wall is fixed the figure of a human being, which was found amongst some of the ruins of the out-buildings near the mansion upwards of fifty years ago, and was placed there to save it from injury or from getting lost. Recently there has been discoverd, cut on stone in the east gable, above the window on the outside, a fine coat of arms (which has been covered with ivy for generations) in a good state of preservation, being surrounded by a deep moulding, the outside size being two feet eight inches, by two feet five inches: the whole work shows a beautiful and elaborate specimen of design and carving in deep relief. Although it is likely the vault which was evidently made at the time of the erection of the chapel, was intended to be the family burying place, yet we have no account of any interment having taken place until that of Sir Edward, who died in December, 1663, being then in the seventy-fifth year of his age, and was buryed in the family vault of the chapel at Dilston, as was his widow five years afterwards; neither of these coffins, however, were

found in the vault, but it is probable as the vault has a soft floor, they may have been interred below the surface as other members of the family may have been before them. It is the opinion of those who have examined the vault that interments had at an early date been made underneath the surface. We now give the particulars of the coffins found in the vault, previous to their being enclosed in wooden coffins, which were covered with black cloth, preparatory to their final removal from Dilston. The coffins were all of lead without any outer coffin, except that of the last Earl's. The inscriptions are as follows :—

" F.R. Com, Dar, 21st April, 1696, aged 72 " (First Earl).

" Edward Earl of Derwentwater, died 20th April, 1705, in the 50th year of his age " (2nd Earl).

" The Right Hon. James, late Earl of Derwentwater, died Feb. 24th, 1715—6, aged 27 years " (3rd Earl).

B.R. 24 August, 1696.

F.R. 28 Sep., 1704, aged 48.

Lady Mary Radcliffe, daughter of Francis Earl of Derwentwater, died 3 March, 1724, in the 59th year of her age.

In addition to the coffins, in the vault were found two square leaden boxes about twelve or fourteen inches square, one of them had handles, the lead on one side of this was much corroded, and a liquid was noticed to ooze through a pore ; at the request of the brother of Lord Petre, who was present during the proceedings, this box was opened, and was found to contain a thick fluid of a dark brown colour ; this box was evidently much older than the other, and was thought might have contained vitals of the first Earl ; the other box was not opened but appeared to be in the same condition as when first placed there, undoubtedly containing the vitals of another of the family, both boxes were enclosed in wood and covered with black cloth, and taken with the other remains to Hexham, to be re-interred there.

The late Mrs. John Grey in her account of Dilston Hall, " drawn up for Mr. Wm. Howitt," and given to that gentleman on his visit to Dilston, and published amongst his " visits to remarkable places " (and which created a great amount of interest at the time), after referring to the previous opening of the vault, states : " Three years ago (as near as we can make out, for we were made acquainted with all the circum-

stances at the time, would be about the year 1838), in consequence of the accidental loosening of some of the stones, Mr.
Grey was induced again to open and inspect the vault. On
this occasion no one was permitted to enter but the members
of our own family, one of whom made the accompanying plan
of the coffins as they are situated in the vault, the decorations,
and the inscriptions they bear. They are all of lead; the
outer coffins having now decayed, with the exception of that
of the last Earl, of which the sides, nails, and gilt ornaments
are in tolerable preservation. The Earl's coffin was not re-
opened, but a square leaden box, which before appears
to have been overlooked was discovered, nearly buried
in dust below the coffin, in which, on part of the lid being
opened, the heart, &c., were found to have been deposited.
It was removed to a safer position, and the entrance to
the cemetery again sealed." We believe the vault was not
again opened until the formal removal of the coffins. As far
as we have been able to learn this box was not then found.
Mrs. Grey states it was removed to a safer position, but as
the stench arising from the contents was not only offensive,
but injurious, common prudence would suggest to the workmen employed (although it might not be known to either
Mr. or Mrs. Grey) to simply bury the box and its contents in the "earthy floor" of the vault, "in which (Mrs.
Grey judiciously remarks) bodies at one time must have been
deposited, the *debris*, bearing clearly the marks of human
mould." The question has been asked whose heart was this,
certainly not that of the Earl, for it is stated "The embalm-
ing of the body of the Earl rendered it necessary to remove
the heart, which was placed in a casket and removed to Angiers,
in France. Here it was in the care of a body of English Nuns.
It afterwards was removed to the chapel of the Augustine
Nuns at Paris; here it remained until during the turmoil of
the French revolution, it was taken from the niche in the
wall, in which it rested, and was buried in a neighbouring
cemetery." The late Countess in her pedigree of the
Radcliffe family says: "That it was the heart of John, fourth
Earl, who died at Frankfort-on-Maine, in his 86th year, and
whose heart was placed in an urn and brought to Devilstone,
where it was laid in the family vault." (this would be about
the year 1799.) The Countess complained that this urn had

been tampered with. The state in which the heart was found would seem to agree with her account, but there is no tradition or account that the vault was at that time opened, and the box being hermetically sealed, would preserve the contents, and might have been there for a much longer period. There is a tradition that the heart and viscera of Charles, the brother of the Earl, who was executed on Tower Hill, on the 8th of December, 1745, thirty years after his first sentence, was brought to Dilston and deposited in the vault. In a *History of Dilston*, the able writer referring to this "casket," says : "It may have been secretly deposited where it was found. There is great reason to believe that the frame to which this now motionless relic once gave animation, was that of Charles Radcliffe, whose heart, tradition declares, to have been taken by two servants of Lord Newburgh, to Dilston." It is now generally thought that the other two boxes, urns, or caskets, may have contained the heart and viscera of the first and second Earls.

As everything pertaining to the Earl is yet read with interest, we subjoin a few particulars relating to the re-coffin-ing of his remains, &c. The account given of the disposal of the Earl after his head and body were borne from the scaffold, is that they were embalmed, and then given to one King, an undertaker, who enclosed the remains in an outer or wooden coffin, covered with crimson velvet and studded with gilt nails, and bore a gilt plate having the inscription previously referred to, and was privately buried in the family vault at Dilston, where they remained until October 9th, 1874, when they were removed to Thorndon, in Essex, and re-interred in the family vault of Lord Petre. The undertakers when examining the coffin found it exactly as described ; the inscription plate which had been very thin was much corroded and illegible ; the velvet which had the appearance of black was quite rotten, and at the least touch gave way. It had been profusely studded with gilt nails, many of them after having been enclosed in the damp vault 158 years were fine specimens of gilding, being as beautiful as when first put in. An order it appears was given as soon as all the remains were removed to burn the original coffin which was made of elm wood, although the bottom and top were a good deal decayed yet the sides were quite sound ; but the person in charge managed to evade

the order, when the coffin was cut into portions, and given to
different parties belonging the neighbourhood ; some portions
were made into small cabinets and boxes, and others into
picture frames, &c.; the writer is in possession of a frame
made out of it. The nails which were numerous fell into
many hands, but several persons in attempting to improve
their appearance destroyed the gilding.

We now conclude our history of Dilston—" Melancholy
Dilston " as it is called by Hodgson the historian—with the
following pathetic and expressive verses, which were given to
the writer by a lady, upwards of forty years ago ; they were,
we believe, taken from a printed copy, but never having
seen them in any history we have met with, is our apology
for inserting them :—

> " Hail ! ruin'd towers of Dilston Hall,
>   Now mouldering in decay ;
> For ever fled thy glories all,
>   Thy chiefs have passed away.
>
> Hail ! ruin'd pile of brighter years,
>   A wreck of ages past ;
> A monument of blood and tears,
>   Now crumbling in the dust.
>
> Thy ancient splendours, feudal fame,
>   In dark oblivion sleep ;
> Thy ivied fragments, but a name,
>   The minstrel loves to weep.
>
> Young Derwentwater's lovely seat,
>   Where many a baron bold,
> And warlike knight of yore did meet,
>   And deeds of valour told.
>
> And many a high, and lofty dame,
>   And beauteous maid I ween,
> In thee have nursed a tender flame,
>   And sigh'd and wept unseen.
>
> Thy Chieftain's lands and wide domains,
>   Exulting strangers share ;
> His fall was thine, and what remains
>   The grave alone can share.
>
> No storied urn, no marbled dome,
>   Proclaims the sacred trust ;
> No highly sculptur'd clarion'd tomb
>   Contains his early dust.

178

Within the chapel's lowly walls,
　Whence evening vespers rose ;
Beneath, where death's dank vapour falls,
　His ashes do repose.

Say, was it well, his young heart's blood
　To drain with reckless hand,
Since for maternal ties he stood,
　And nature's choicest hand ?

Ah ! no, me thinks rash was the deed,
　And ill-advised the blow ;
Too oft the vanquish'd hero's meed
　Is steep'd in crimson'd woe.

E'en those who kingly powers uphold,
　Still plead the right divine,
Whose fathers bled and fought of old
　Against the ancient line.

O man ! how inconsistent pride,
　And selfish passions sway ;
How dark impetuous the tide,
　Thy reason bears away.

Adieu ! thou ravag'd time-worn pile,
　Thy star of glory's set ;
No more on thee shall fortune smile,
　Or chieftain feel regret.

Shades of the mighty and the brave,
　Pure souls to honour strung,
No more your crested banners wave,
　Your deeds of daring sung.

High on the breeze your fleeting forms,
　Around are heard to wail ;
Mid nature's sighs, and sweeping storms
　Your gossamer shadows sail."

As an appendage to what we have already written, it will
be interesting to refer to discoveries which have recently been
made when making alterations in the grounds adjoining the
old castle, it having been decided to remove the mound
west of the castle, for the two-fold purpose of beautifying the
landscape, and of showing to greater advantage the base and
lower portions of the castle. We may here first repeat, that
against the western side of the castle a range of buildings was
erected by the last Earl, which then became the western front
of the mansion. " This front," says Sidney Gibson, " was
raised on a sort of terrace or embankment, above a formal
garden ; " on this terrace we recollect seeing the sill of the

front doorway remaining, and in its original position, near to
the brow of the embankment. No other idea appears to have
been entertained, but that the terrace was specially made to
meet the arrangements for the new building. The excavations, however, soon showed this view to have been incorrect,
and revealed a surprising mass of ruins, consisting of remarkable walls, chambers, culverts, venel and corbel stones, &c.,
&c., which showed what would appear to have been first an
outer wall, forty-eight feet west from the castle, and in extent
ninety feet north and south, reaching on the north to near
the brow of the hill, and being six feet in thickness; also,
another wall running parallel with this one, of the same thickness, seventeen feet from the castle, and eight feet in height;
betwixt this inner wall and the castle were rooms or chambers,
fine ashler work and even plastering were found in some of
them; the rooms had been arched over and lighted by windows in the wall referred to, which had been protected by
iron bars which had been rudely pulled from the sills; these
rooms were entered by a flight of steps close to the walls of
the castle; some of the cross walls which extended from the
middle one to the castle and divided the rooms were four feet
in thickness. The whole of the walls were of the most solid
and massive nature, and were so firmly cemented together,
that it was found impossible to take them down in the ordinary
way, therefore blasting was resorted to. The whole of the
walls and ruins were evidently of the same period, and from
their massive proportions, their extreme solidity, the peculiar
nature of the stones, mortar, &c., &c., seem to point to a
period long anterior to the time of the Radcliffes, and to the
erection of the present castle, which appears to have been
built upon the ruins of a remarkable stronghold or fortress,
probably erected by the Lords of Devylstounes, as soon as
they got possession of the estates, by virtue of the deed or
charter made by Henry I. If so, they may have been assisted
in the work by that remarkable man, Bishop Flambard, who
himself was a Norman by birth, and who from the allusion to
him, had evidently to do with the framing of the Dilston
charters; he was a man of almost all work, and built in 1121
the great fortress of Norham-on-the Tweed, as a defence
against the inroads of the Scots. Of course these remarks
are only conjectural, yet arising out of the evidence before

us; but there are two things about which there can be no mistake—that these massive remains were built at an early period, and by some one. It is thought by some persons who saw them that they might be of the Roman period, but we failed to find the least trace of Roman work of any kind. We had the pleasure in the first week of April of examining what yet remained of these walls, ruins, &c., and through the courtesy of Mr. Balden who was present and kindly pointed out their leading features, we are enabled the more correctly to give the above brief account. In reference to the present tower or castle we have not previously said anything, the period of its erection is uncertain, judging from its character it may have been built in the reign of Edward II. (1307—1327). Modern work has been largely introduced, most likely first on the south, north, and east sides by Sir Edward, when he so greatly enlarged the mansion in 1621—2, and afterwards it is stated by the first Earl, and lastly on the west side by the last Earl, when he added the western range of rooms.

Dilston, with its vast domains, from the period of the Devylstounes, continued to descend from heir to heir, until after the death of Lord Derwentwater (as John, the son of the last Earl was designated), when they were taken possession of by the Government, and eventually on the 13th day of October, 1874, the Dilston Estates were sold by auction, at Newcastle-on-Tyne, to W. B. Beaumont, Esq., M.P., for the sum of £132,000, or thereabouts, which together with the timber on the estate, taken at a valuation, and other incidental expenses, raised the cost of the purchase to upwards of £200,000.

With the following extract from Wright's *History of Hexham*, we take our leave of Dilston :—

"The limestone beneath Dilston Bridge teems with the dubious remains of a former state of nature, so interesting to the geologist. Petrified rushes, fossile vermes, vegetable impressions, and varieties of fossil shells are very frequent; and a collection of occasional discoveries without scientific research or arrangement, preserved by Mr. Lumbly of Corbridge, shews a variety and a selection that must interest and amuse the mineralogist."

181

NUNSBROUGH.

HUTCHINSON after leaving Dilston visited Nunsbrough, which seems to have had special charms for that great historian, as it has more or less for all those who visit this charming spot. We give his description entire.

"From Dilston," says Hutchinson, "we made a short ride on the banks of the Devil's Water, where there are many fine sylvan scenes; we gained the western eminence above Nunsbrough, where lays the most picturesque, though confined landscape, the whole county of Northumberland exhibits. We ascended to the brink of the precipice, near two hundred feet high, from whence we looked down upon a sequestered vale almost insulated by the brook, consisting of a fine level plot of corn land of about eight acres, in the exact form of a horse shoe; the brook passing over a rugged rocky bottom, under the shadow of lofty hills, in various broken streams, was seen on each hand foaming from fall to fall, which gave a beautiful contrast to the deep hue of the groves. From the brook, the hills to the left rise precipitous, clothed with a fine hanging wood then glowing with a full sunshine; to the right the steeps laying from the sun, and in the deep shade, were broken and scattered over in wild irregularity with brushwood, and here and there a knotty tree presenting itself impending from the precipice; in front a fine eminence of brown rock lifted its rugged brow and clothed the circle, dividing the waters with a promontory a few yards wide. In the clefts and on the little levels of the rock some shrubs grew; on its crown stood ripened corn margined with hedge row trees, through which a cottage was discovered, and by its foot a winding road which soon escaped the eye in intercepting woods; the rays of light fell happily upon the cliffs and brightened their colouring. To the right and left the more distant brook showed itself in deep and rocky dells embowered by lofty oaks. To the right hand, the hill which surmounts the wood is topped with a plain of grass ground, on whose brink stands a farm stead, accessible by a narrow path winding up the steep, from whence the woods make a beautiful curviture; the distant back ground is composed of heath lands. On the left, woodlands were on the circus, winding on the mazy channel of the brook, here and there intercepted by

heathy eminences; the back ground very distant and tinged with a misty azure. To grace the little enchanted vale, reapers were busy with the harvest. In some parts the furrows looked like waving gold, in others they were embossed with upset sheaves. This is the finest natural theatre I ever saw. The circle is geometrically just ; the plain would have suited those exhibitions of which we read with an anxious curiosity, in the history of the ancients, they would have given it life, taken away the rusticity, and made it noble. When we descended to the vale below it appeared only to want some of the sacred rites to improve its solemnity and compound the idea of hallowedness with greatness. One possessed of a true taste for natural beauties is apt to be wound up to a pitch of enthusiastic rapture at such scenes as these, where every subject that can compose a rural prospect, are thus fortunately adjusted and disposed. It is not possible for me to write with temperance on such a subject."

Wright, in his *History of Hexham*, says : " Nunsbrough, which, although far from deserving the elevated encomium of Mr. Hutchinson, is still a very curious and interesting scene, possessing beauty enough to repay the travel of the most fastidious visitor."

AYDON CASTLE.

AYDON CASTLE—we again quote from Hutchinson—it should however be borne in mind that this description was written upwards of a century ago. " We approached Aydon Castle, about one and a half miles distant from Corbridge, now greatly in decay. The situation is formidable, and from the solemnity of its ruins, is at this time strikingly august. It is placed on the west side of a deep gill on the bank of a precipice, at the foot of which runs a little brook. By the traces remaining of this edifice it appears to have been of considerable extent and strength, encompassed by an outward wall, of pentagonal form, in which loop holes remain. One thing remarkable here is a stable with an arched roof of stone without any wood in its structure, the mangers being formed of stone troughs. It seems constructed for the preservation of cattle at the time of assault. The precipice at the east side of the castle is famous for 'Jack's Leap,' an exploit, the cause of which is lost

in the distance; some affirm it to have been a lover's leap; others again, and which appears the most likely, that in the time of assault when the beseiged were likely, without help, to be captured or slain, this being the only point unguarded by the enemy, that a man called 'Jack,' proposed to seek succour and to make this his place of exit,* which was agreed to, and that he succeeded in obtaining such help as enabled the defenders to obtain a complete victory." Tradition states that at this time the main force of the enemy was encamped along the top of the cliff in front of the castle. Mackenzie, in his history, gives the following account of this transaction :—"A correspondent, the late Mr. Lionel Winship, junr., of Aydon, says : That Sir Robert Clavering, during the civil wars,† surprised a party of Scots here, whom he attacked with such irresistible bravery that numbers were precipitated from this lofty rock, and only one person, named 'Jack' escaped death." Tradition also states that a sturdy yeoman, of Corbridge, called 'Will Greenwell,' in this battle worsted a Scotch officer who fled from the field, throwing money over his shoulder to stop the keen pursuit of his enemy, but all was in vain for Greenwell cleft him down with his sword. The late Dr. Greenwell of Corbridge was a descendant of this warlike yeoman." Since Hutchinson's visit, a great change has been effected both in the castle and its surroundings, for shortly after it came into the possession of the present owner, (Sir Edward Blackett, Bart.) the whole was put into a complete state of repair and is yet so preserved; it is admitted to be one of the most entire structures of the kind in this part of the country. The castle is protected by a high outer wall, as well as an inner wall, at the north-east corner of the outer wall, but in the inside, is the prison, which appears to have escaped the notice of historians, it is in a good state of preservation, and is used at present by the occupier for the

---

* This precipice must then have been very much more formidable than it is now, for since we first knew it a considerable portion of the perpendicular cliff has slipped from its original position into the bottom of the gill.

† The civil wars here alluded to were those which preceded the common-wealth, betwixt the King and the Parliament. In 1644 two regiments of Scots' horse were quartered at Corbridge, but were surprised and defeated by Sir Marmaduke Langdale and Colonel Fenwick, who had sallied out from Newcastle. As mention is made of Sir Robert Clavering as being also in command of the King's forces at Newcastle, it is presumable that at the same time another portion of the Scots' army were encamped at Aydon Castle, and were defeated by a detachment which also sallied out from Newcastle under the command of Sir Robert Clavering, and which is here referred to.

storing of agricultural implements. It is stated the chapel was built against the west-end of the castle and in a line with the front, but no part of it now remains. The arms of the Carnaby family (former owners of the castle and estate) are finely cut on a stone mantel-piece, in one of the upper rooms of the castle. In the kitchen, above the fire place, are several curious faces carved in stone. The following account of this structure is given by a local writer, and was published a short time ago in the *Newcastle Weekly Chronicle*: " Aydon Castle, a very picturesque and remarkable building, is now occupied as a farm-house. It was part of the ancient barony of the Baliols, from whom it passed to the family of Aydon. Their male line failing during the reign of Edward I. (1272—1307), that prince gave Emma, the heiress of the family, in marriage, to Peter de Vallibus. The castle afterwards passed to the families of Raymes, Carnaby, and Collison. It is now the property of Sir Edward Blackett of Matfen. Aydon Castle was probably built by Peter de Vallibus in 1280—1300.* The edifice is of great importance as illustrating the domestic architecture of that period. Being rather a fortified house than a castle, it was known as Aydon Halle in the thirteenth and fourteenth centuries. The building is surrounded by an outward wall pierced with arrow holes and enclosing three court yards, two large and one smaller. A shallow ditch surrounds the wall on three sides, on the fourth it is guarded by a deep ravine. The building was originally entered from the innermost court by a covered outer staircase. Over one of the chimney-pieces the arms of the Carnabys are carved. A window looking on the garden is decorated between its two lights with a curious head of our Saviour, on the side towards the ravine there is a remarkable round turret. The arched stables have been carefully fitted for defence. When the writer last paid a visit to Aydon, he was shown a rock below the castle called ' Jack's Leap,' from the only survivor of a party of Scots who was surprised here by Sir Robert Clavering, and who escaped by a jump when his companions were precipitated from a cliff. A Scottish officer who was pursued by Green-well, a yeoman of Corbridge, fled, throwing money over his

---

* When David II. King of Scotland on his way to Durham in 1346, moved down to Corbridge, the Scots assaulted Aydon Castle, in the neighbourhood, which was given up on condition that the inmates were allowed to depart with their lives.

shoulder in the hope of stopping his pursuers, but he was caught and killed. In the northern transept of Hexham Abbey Church, is a recumbent figure with clasped hands and with legs and arms cuirassed, the sword sheathed, and the shield charged with the arms of the Aydons. I may remark that a descendant of the famous Greenwell referred to above is still living in Corbridge."

HALTON CASTLE.

HALTON CASTLE stands about half-a-mile north from Aydon Castle, and consists at present of the tower or castle and dwelling-house. The tower, which also forms part of the dwelling, is a strong oblong structure 30 feet by 22½, having four turrets, one being at each corner; the remains of a much larger building may be seen on the north side of the tower. The castle and adjacent buildings have been put into a complete state of repair by their owner, Sir Edward Blackett.* In the interior of the tower is some massive stone work, including winding stair-cases, &c.; there are also in that portion of the building known as the dwelling-house, some massive oak beams resting on stone corbels, and some fine specimens of oak joisting of that period.

The period of its erection is uncertain, but probably about the same time, if not a little earlier than that of Aydon Castle. It was the seat and manor of John de Halton, in the reign of King Henry III. (1216—1272), and part of the reign of King Edward I., and of his son, William de Halton of Denun, (17 King, Edward I.) and first High Sheriff of Northumberland, (25 of the same reign,) on whose death it descended to the family of Carnaby, who possessed the whole manor for many generations.

HALTON CHAPEL.

STANDING close by the castle is a small building, held by the Vicar of Corbridge, used as a chapel of case to the parish church. This erection is about 250 years old, but of no particular style of interest. The interior, which was in a most deplorable condition, was restored a few years

---

* Mr. Wright, in his *History of Hexham*, when referring to Halton Tower, states that it is on the site of the Roman Station, Hunnum; here he is in error, the site of the Roman Station which is still visible, being about a quarter-of-a-mile further to the north.

ago by the exertions of the Vicar and the liberality of
John Straker, Esq., of Stagshaw, and Sir Edward Blackett,
Bart. Service is held here every Sunday afternoon. In the
chapel yard is a Roman altar, but the inscription is now
illegible. A portion of the communion service was recently
discovered by the Vicar at a farm-house in Great Whittington,
used for the purpose of feeding fowls, having on it the inscription finely engraven, Halton Chapel, 1697.

BEAUFRONT CASTLE.

BEAUFRONT CASTLE being in the neighbourhood, is deserving
of notice. Mackenzie describes it as follows : " Beaufront
stands in a commanding, yet sheltered situation, the ground
rising gently from the Tyne. This elegant mansion, viewed
either from Hexham or Corbridge, has a noble appearance
from the great length of the fronts and the number of windows. The gardens are extensive, and it was stated, in the
objections to the Newcastle Canal Bill that the present owner
had expended more than £20,000 in improving the gardens,
fruit walls, hot house, plantation, and walks.......It is now
the seat and manor of John Errington, Esq., called by the
country people " The Chief of Beaufront." This gentleman
having made "the grand tour," has preserved his court dresses,
comprising the costumes of all the European nations, which
are shown to persons desirous of seeing them. He is at once
remarkable for his eccentricities, his hospitality, and his
charitable disposition. Wright, in his *History of Hexham*,
after describing Beaufront as an elegant mansion, and long
the seat of the Errington family, then refers to Dilston,
which he says, "stands as conspicuously on the opposite side
of the Tyne, and it is said that the inhabitants of the two
halls were wont to inform each other of any important news
by the use of a speaking trumpet." Both these writers refer
to a previous mansion which existed until about fifty years
ago, when it was pulled down by the then owner, Wm.
Cuthbert, Esq., and the present beautiful castle erected upon
its site. The old hall or castle was surrounded by a battlement. on which were several effigies cut in stone, most of
them representing warriors in the posture of self defence,
wielding such arms as were then in use ; a few of which have

been preserved and are to be seen on the walls, on the north side of the castle. In the old hall, on the first landing of the front staircase was a place of concealment, which was kindly shown to us; one of the boards on the landing had been taken out and two wooden staples firmly fixed on to the under side, which was secured by its inmates, who were let down this opening by two wooden bolts ; when we saw it the board was much worn, having evidently been often shown to visitors. Our informant told us that one of the Erringtons and one of the Radcliffes, either the Earl or his brother Charles had been concealed here.

SANDOE.

SANDOE adjoins Beaufront on the east. It was the seat and property of Henry Errington. Esq., a younger brother of Mr. Errington, of Beaufront. Sandoe House, so well-known in this neighbourhood as the seat of the late lamented Sir Rowland Stanley Errington, Bart., the representative of one of the oldest families in the county, whose forefathers were " Lords of Langleydale." The hall, which was built by the late Sir Rowland, is described by the author of *Local Sketches* as "a quaint, queer looking building, in which the Elizabethan style of architecture prevails. Though the house has little to recommend it in its character as a gentleman's mansion, the situation is really a charming one, whilst the landscape beneath its front, is one of unrivalled beauty. The lawns, terraces, and fancy flower-plots are all laid out with exquisite taste, and both the rear of the hall and the village are embowered with arborescent plants..........As a hamlet, Sandoe in our time was a congerie of rude cottages, but Sir Rowland, by waving the magic wand of progress over it, has transformed the old village with its open green into a pretty sylvan retreat, where flowers and evergreens form both ornament and shade to the dwellings. The people have also lost much of their primitive rusticity of character, and, like the village, they are much improved, both in manners, habits, and personal appearance."

STAGSHAW CLOSE HOUSE.

STAGSHAW CLOSE HOUSE is delightfully situated on the east of Sandoe, and is the seat of John Straker, Esq., by whom the elegant mansion has lately been erected, and the pleasure

grounds not only greatly improved in appearance, but considerably extended; amongst other attractions on the grounds is a fernery, in which are a great variety of rare and costly ferns, so arranged as to cluster amongst rugged rocks, down which a small stream is made to dash, until it reaches a bason at the bottom, in which are several gold fish. This mansion is approached from the ancient Watling Street by a beautiful avenue of very tall trees, the only one in this part of the country.

At the east end of the common, on which Stagshawbank fair is held, are the kennels where a large and famous pack of hounds is kept, the owner having borrowed the classic name "Tynedale," they are named "The Tynedale Foxhounds." On Whit-Monday last, in company with a portion of the Tyneside Naturalist Field Club, we had, through the usual courtesy of Mr. Cornish, the huntsman, the pleasure of seeing through the establishment. The hounds, of course, and "beauties" they are, were the chief attraction. Mr. Cornish also showed us a tame fox which was kept in a small enclosure, it is a fine noble animal, with which the party, especially the ladies, were greatly delighted; it is rather remarkable that the hounds never attempt to interfere with it in its ramblings about the place. Mr. Cornish has also on the grounds a beautiful greenhouse, a rockery, gardens, and a fish pond, in which a number of trout were disporting themselves. After this visit the company made their way back to Corbridge by the ancient Watling Street. The fine avenue of trees which leads from the Watling Street to the mansion of Mr. Straker was particularly noticed; the uniform growth of the trees and their great height were greatly admired; one of the party, who had travelled a great deal through England, stated that he thought there was nothing of the kind to be seen equal to it, at least in the north of England.

On the east of Corbridge is Styford Hall, the residence of C. B. Grey, Esq., with its pleasant grounds, gardens, &c. Newton Hall, the residence of Colonel Joicey, possesses extensive pleasure grounds and beautiful gardens, containing many specimens of rare flowers and plants, an observatory, &c. Bywell, with its castle, hall, and churches are all interesting places, but beyond our limits to describe.

APPENDIX

HISTORY OF CORBRIDGE.

———◄·⦂·✳·⦂·►———

THIS Appendix consists mostly of extracts from ancient records contained in the several volumes of the "Archæologia Æliana," kindly lent to the writer by John Walker, Esq. In these interesting and valuable books are a great many records in connection with the Dilston family, mostly during the lives of Sir Edward Radcliffe and Sir Francis, afterwards created Earl; these records are copious extracts or copies from the household books, ancient documents, and special and general correspondence; we only regret that want of space compels us to confine ourselves to what more particularly refers to Corbridge and Corbridge Parish.

"Christopher Dennyson charged wth. the murder of John Hudspeth, Sonne of Thomas Hudspith of Corbrigg, w^thin this county, yeom', & removed from his ma^ties. gaole att Westchester, by virtue of his ma^ties. writt directed to the Sheriffe of the said county, dated the ij Julij an° quarto R's Caroli nunc Anglie, &c., for wth. fact he fledd thither.

Edward Dennyson charged wth. the said murder and removed from his ma^ties. gaole att Carlyle, there kept for his ma^ties. County of Cumberland, into wch. county he fledd and there was appr'hended, removed hither by virtue of his ma^ties. writt, dated vt sup^r.—Calendar of the Prisoners confined in the High Castle, in Newcastle-upon-Tyne, at the assizes for Northumberland, in the year 1628. Vol. I.

From a list of the Freeholders of Northumberland in the year 1628. Vol. II.

TYNEDALE WARDE.

Sir Edward Radcliff, barouett
Ralph Carnaby of Halton, Esq.
Henry Errington of Beaufront, Esq.
Ralph Grinwell of Corbrigg, gent.

Lyonell Winshopp of Aydon, yeom.
John Ridley of the same, gent.
Thomas Errington, of Sandoe, gent.

FREEHOLDERS in 1638—9.

Ralph Carnaby of Halton, Esq.
Henry Errington of Befrout, Esq.
Ralph Greenewell of Corbridge, gent.
Thomas Hudspeth de id^{un.} gent.

John Errington, of Whitting-ton, gent.
Xpofer Chester de Aydon, gent.
John Ridley of the same, gent.
Henry Winshopp of Aydon, gent.

Musters for Northumberland in 1538, Vol. IV.

CORBRIGE.

Roger Heron
Sampson Baxter
Gylbert Hudspethe
George Hudspethe
Edward Robson
Gylbert Hudspethe
Edmund Stobart
Thomas Jaeson
Rolland Stobert
Edmund Greiffe
Edwerd Greiffe
Robert Paysse
Thomas Fawsid

Thomas Spurstan
Richard Spurstan
Georg Spurstan
John Tempyll
Thomas Stokey
Vidua Trolop
Wyllm Milburn
John Watson
Wyllm Spurstan
Edwerd Hudspeth
Edmund Hudspeth
Willm Clerk
Thomas Thompson

Able with horse and harness

John Rankyn
Robert Yonger
Cuthbert Bron
Thomas Stobert
Thomas Spark
Henry Robson
Lawrence Tempyll

Thomas Dnenyng
Lawrence Bron
John Bron
Wyllm Watson
Thomas Eryngton
Nicholes Gildert
Thomas Story

Wyllm Davidson

Thomas Patyson

John Spurstan

Edmund Dennyng

Thomas Fogart

Hugo Huffton

Matho Bron

Robert Castell

Neither with horse nor harness

HALTON.

Gilbt Carnaby

Anthone Carnaby

Synvon Elyngton

Ambrose Swyneborn

Gilbt Elyngton

Priest.—Ric Watson Clark

Ruyan Stocoll

Robt. Enyngton

Thomas Ogle

Raynord Forster

Sir Edward Dent

Thoms Marshall

Willm Carnaby

Able with horse and harnes

George Talyore

John Pattenson

Rygnd Morton

Ric Wil'be

Willm Fetherstonhaugh

Bryan Walker

Lewes Ogle, bailif of Hexh.

John Stocoll

John Shaw

Rolend Redshaw, his ser-

vants able with horse

and harness

CLAREWOOD.

Robert Carnabye

Robert Rutter

Henry Johnson

Ric Farle

Able with hors and harnes

Robert Reid

Robert Males

Lawrence Truble

Wyllm Collyngwood

Martyn Reid

John Herrison

Barty don

Neither hors nor harnes

DILSTON.

John Cartyngton

Georg Dennyng

John Stobert

Lawrence Burdux

Robert Heron

John Burdux

Rolland Castell

John Temple

Rolland Burdux

Edmund Burdux

Gestre Eward

Robert Burdux

Archebald Smyth

Gilbert Hudspethe

192

Robert Tempill
Edmund Gibson
George Burks
Robert Scharpe
John Dennythe
Thomas Ayre
Gilbert Spark
Edmund Stobert
George Turner
Henry Yonger
Robert Wod
Gilbert Burdex
Edwerd Potts
John Sharp
Cuthbart Cartyngton
John Castells

George Gray
John Rodem
Thomas Lee
Edwerde Moyo
Edwerde Ainsley
Relland Spoyr
Willm Jackson
Cuthbert Tully
John Smythe
John Hyms
Willm Archer
Christofer Spoyr
John Robson
Thomas More
Lauret Bluyt

Able with hors and harnes

HADEN (AYDON).

Edwerd Chester
Matho Spurston
Gilbert Richardson
Robert Cooper
Robert Nicholson
John Pays
Edward Kell
John Wilson
Willm Pays

Edwerd Kell
John Wilson
Willm Pays
Edwerd Vschew
Thomas Kell
Edwerd Willie
Andre Gryn
Robert Whit

Neither horse nor harnes

Richard Troble
Willm Horner
Peter Lauson
Thomas Heslope
George Lauson

Cuthbert Carre
Thomas Ladlay
William Cooke
Henry Chekyn

Able men with horse lakking harness

Thomas Dobson
Edwerd Chekyn
Willm Farle
Archebald Born

Edward Ladlay
Christofer Burn
Willm Burn

Neither hors nor harnes

193

From Pipe Rolls (with remarks) during the three first years of King Edward I. (A.D. 1272, etc.)

And to the same £30 in Corbrigg, for which Robert, the son of Roger answers belows. (That is Robert accounts for that sum in another part of the Roll...)

Robert Fitz Roger for 10s. for £30 of rents for the Sergeantry of Corbrigg, and 35s. for the same for the last year.

Isabella, who was the wife (that is the widow) of Roger Fitz John, £33 6s. 8d., for the remainder of the farm of Corebridge for the 45th year.

Robert, the son of Roger, renders an account of £30 for the farm of Corbridge, so contained in Roll 32; and for £10 for increase rent for the same vill; and for £80; and he owes £10 for oblations.

And of three marks and an half from Thomas de Dilston.

And of half-a-mark from William de Tindale to have a writ.

PROOF OF AGE OF WILLIAM CARNABY.

Inquisition, 13 Henry IV. (1412.) Proof of age of William, son and heir of William de Carnaby, deceased, taken at Corbrigg. Witnesses depose that the said William was 21 years old on Thursday before Easter last; that he was baptised in Halton Church. John de Hole recollects the day because he bought an horse of Wm., father of the said William, and saw him baptised in the Church. Richard Craweester because he was in the Church, and in riding home his horse fell and hurt him badly. Nicholas Turpyn because he was in the Church, and in going home met divers huntsmen chasing a fox out of his wood. John Strother, because on that day he was with his neighbours hunting a hare, and met the woman carrying the said William to Church to be baptised. Thos. Hasilbrigg says the same. John Belasis says the same; and among the said women was Catherine, his niece, who told him that Isabel, mother of the said William, was in great danger of death. Nicholas Heron, because he met Thomas Ormesby, Vicar of the Church of Corbrigg, who told him that he had baptised the said William. William Carr and William Lawson, because they were the godfathers. John Hoggesson,

N

because in going home from Corbrigg, he met the said William being carried to Halton Church to be baptised. William Richardson, because going to Corbrigg to an arbitration, between William Raa and Nicholas Skelby, he met William Car, who told him he was one of the godfathers.

LOCAL MUNIMENTS, VOL. I., NEW SERIES.

John, son of Richard de Talyour, of Naustedis, conveys to Hugh, son of Richard de le Syde, of Corbrigs, chaplain, residing in Bywell, all his lands and tenements, in the vill and field of Bywell which he had by gift of his father, Richard de Talyour. Sunday, the feast of St. George, 1340.

Margaret, daughter and coheiress of Robert de Redeware, in her maidenhood and lawful power, conveys to Laurence de Duresme, of Newcastle-upon-Tyne, a moiety of a tenement in the town of Corbridge, in vico Sanctæ Mariæ, (the charter is endorsed "our Lady gat.") which in breadth lies between the land of Robert de Merington on the west, and the high way which leads to Tyne Bridge on the east,* and in length from the said vicus Sanctæ Mariæ unto the Tyne, viz.: that moiety which lies nearest the sun. (propinquins soli.) Witness, John de Fennewyk, now Sheriff of Northumberland, William de Tyndale, Lord Develeston, John de Hoga, &c., Corbridge. 13 Jan. 16 Edw. II. (1323.) Seal—pointed oval, a star of eight points, & Margareti Redwar.

John Lawson and John de Tyrwhyt, of Corbrigg, convey to Sir Peter Blonk and Sir Adam de Corbrigg, chaplains, a burgage in Corbrigg, in vico Sanctæ Mariæ, between a burgage of John Fayt on the east and a burgage of John de Merington on the west. Corbrigg, 20 Jan., 1370. Seals—1 oval Tabernacle Work. Under the virgin and child a standing figure, probably John the Baptist. On the dexter side, St. Catherine with her wheel; on the sinister, St. Margaret? 2 Circular within tracery a shield of arms, a chevron between three

---

* The bridge here referred to must have existed some hundreds of years before the erection of the present structure. A previous bridge had been there, but whether the one here referred to is uncertain, for the tops of piles forming the outside of the lower portion of two pillars, are seen in the bed of the river in a line with the middle of the two northern arches, but a few yards further down; they were first pointed out to the writer, several years ago, by Mr John Jemieson, who was engaged in doing some repairs to the foundations of the pillars of the bridge at a time when the river was low and clear; they have been noticed several times since.

martlets.............The arms are still worn by the Lawsons, of Brough Hall, near Catterick, and the seal is interesting for its demonstration of the origin of the name. The conflicting visitation pedigrees of the family do not reach to the date of the charter. John Lawson, coroner, no doubt the same person, witnesses a Whittonstall charter in company with John de Corbrigg, son of the forester of Corbridge in 1366.

John Fayt, conveys to John de Penereth, a tenement in Corbryg, at the head of a new street between a tenement of Penereth on the east and a tenement of Fayt on the west, and containing in length 4 perches 5 ells, and in breadth 3 perches; in exchange for which Penereth conveys a tenement there lying between tenements of Fayt, and of the same dimensions as the tenement conveyed by Fayt. Witnesses, William Hog, John Calvehyde, &c. Corbryg, Sunday before feast of St. Cuthbert, in March, 1375. Seal of arms in chief— a cross crosslet between two mascles in base, three saltires, 2 and 1.

Thomas Squire, (Armiger) of Corbrige, and Emma, his wife, convey to Richard Reynauld, of Newcastle-upon-Tyne, clerk, a messuage in Corbridge in the Market Place, lying in breadth between the messuage of Hugh fitz Simon and a messuage formerly of Hugh fitz Astelm, and in length from the highway unto a stone wall formerly the said Hugh Fitz Astelms. Corbridge in Easter-week, 1316, 9 Edw. II.

William de Herle, quitclaims to John fitz John de Corbrigg all his right in a messuage in Corbrigge, in the street of the Fisher's Market, which the same John had by feoffment of Agnes, formerly wife of Hugh fitz Asselm de Corbrigge, Blanchland Abby, Wednesday after the feast of the Holy Trinity, 8 Edw. III. (1335.)

John le Glover, of Carlisle, and Angnes his wife, convey by indenture to Angnes Ferchane, of Corbrige, a tenement in le Market-gate in Corbrige, as it lies between the place of the Hospital of Stanistar and a tenement of the said Angnes Ferchane, one head abutting on the King's highway and the other head upon the cemetry of St. Andrew's. To hold of the chief lord of the fee. Rent 3s. reserved. Witnesses, Adam fitz Alan, now steward of Sir Henry de Perci, John de Tirwyte, &c. Seal—(only one, and therefore probably Agnes Ferchames) circular, a lion rampant.

196

20 Nov., 1591. Michaoll Dood and Issable Dood, of Slealie, in Bywell Lordship, and within the countie of Northumberland, yeoman, convey to George Hurde, of Corbridge, yeoman, all their estate in one burgage in Corbridge, and in a street there called Prein Street, between a burgage of Cuthbert Baxter on the south, and a common water gait, called Gormire, on the north, with 3½ acres of land within the fields and territories of Corbridge, whereof an acre lieth in the east feald of Corbridge on the east side (of) the common between the land of Thomas Errington on the east, and the said common on the west; one other acre in the Loweryding between the Lord's demaine on the east and one acre and a half on a place in the said fealds, called the Laymes, beyond the Barne. To be holden according to custom of the manor and fee. (This deed was found blowing about the streets of Corbridge in 1856, and is thought to be one of those previously referred to, as having been deposited with the Donkins, of Sandoe, and afterwards picked up as old or waste parchment; about the same time a portion of another deed was found in a similar way belonging to the Fawcitts, of Corbridge.)

VOL. 2, N.S. FAIT FAMILY, S.D.

John Musgrave, son and heir of Robert Musgrave, his late father, and of Agnes his mother, to Sir Adam de Corbryk, Chaplain, and John Fayt, burgess of Newcastle. Release of a rent of 8s. 6d. due to him in the town of Corbridge out of a tenement in Smethingate, between Fayt's tenement on the east, and a tenement, formerly John Forster's, on the west.

1352. Thomas Fayt of Corbrig, to Thomas Cissor and Agnes his wife, daughter of the said Thomas Fayt. Conveyance of a tenement in Corbrig in the Smithygat, between a tenement of Sir Hugh de Roghsyd, Chaplain, and a tenement of Sir Gilbert de Mynsteracres, perpetual Vicar of Bywell.

1372. John Fait and Agnes his wife, and William Fait and Matilda his wife, to Adam de Corbrigg and Peter Blonk, Chaplain, fine of 28 messuages and 30 acres in Corbrigge.

1382. Thomas de Musgrave, burgess of the town of Newcastle-upon-Tyne, to John Fayte of Corbrigge, Sir Peter de Blonk and Sir Adam de Corbrigg, Chaplains. Conveyance of

three messuages and two acres in the town and territory of Corbrigg. One messuage lies in Market Place, between a messuage of William de Blenk howe on the N., and a messuage of William de Duxfield on the S.; another lies in the same street on the East side, between a common spout on the W., and a messuage formerly Alan de Felton's on the E.; the third messuage is at Corwell, between a messuage of John de Ebchester, Chaplain, on the N., and a common vennel leading to the Tyne on the S. Of the two acres, one is called Lymekilnes : the other lies at Briggepolles, between Thomas Baxter's land on the N., and land formerly William Fayt's on the S. At Corbrigg, Thursday, 18 April, 1395.

1406. Adam Prest of Corbrigg, to Sir John Fayt, Vicar of Symondburn, son of the late Sir William Fayt and Matilda. Conveyance of all lands, &c., in the town and fields of Corbrig, which he had by gift of William Fayt and Matilda his wife (R).

1491. John Lonesdale of Durham, Carbure and attorney of Nicholas Ingilwood, appoints Richard Lewynn, Robert Sylby, and John Blunt, his attorneys, to receive Selsin in his (Lonesdale's) name, of 28 messuages and 30 acres in Corbridge, which Lonsdale recovered in the name of Ingilwode, in the court held at Corbridge, 31 May, 22 Edw. IV. (1482.) At Durham, 10 Oct.

MISCELLANEOUS CONVEYANCES.

Walter, son of Hugh, the Butcher, of Corbridge, to Hugh, called Whinnvylle, of Corbrigge. Conveyance of a toft there on the south side of the cemetery of " Blessed Andrew" of Corbrigge, between a toft of Andrew Kinbel on the E., and the shop, formerly of John Del Corner on the W. Rent 3s. 2d. Witnesses, William de Tyndale, Alan fitz Richard, Hugh fitz Asceline, Adam de Routhsyde, Ralph de Wywell, Alan de Erington, Thomas, called Prest (Priest), the clerk, and others (temp Edw. I., 1272—1307).

Thomas, son of Hugh, the Butcher, to Michael Smith of Corbrigge, and Alice his wife. Conveyance of a toft in Corbrigge, between the messuage of Richard, called Prest, on the south, and the messuage of Blessed Mary,* which Sir

---

* It is probable the reference to the "Blessed Mary" here, and to "The Lady" elsewhere, alludes to St. Mary's Church; as the reference to the "Blessed Andrew" evidently refers to St. Andrew's Church.

198

Thomas, the Chaplain of Midegate, holds on the north; yielding to the Abbot and convent of Blanchland 18d. per annum. Witnesses, Robert de Barton, and the Witnesses to the last Charter.

1316. Isabella, daughter of the late Nicholas Stone of Corbridge, to Reynauld of Newcastle-upon-Tyne. Release of a messuage in Corbridge, in the Market Place.

(1296). Margaret, late wife of Gilbert Ferure of Corbryg, to Agatha, late wife of William de Herford. Conveyance of her part of the shops on the east side of the Cemetry of " Blessed Andrew " of Corbryg, which belong to her in the name of Dower, by the death of William de Karleton, formerly her husband ; yielding 6s. rent for life. Witnesses, William de Tyndale, Robert de Barton, John de Horseley, Richard Prest, Alan de Erinton.

(Cir 1316). Hugh de Blunvill, to William de Lundon and Agnes his wife. Conveyance of his shop, beside the Church of St. Andrew, of Corbridge ; yielding 3s. Rent(R).

1316. Symon Kymbelle of Corbrig, to William de London, Merchant. Release of 2s. Rent which he used to receive out of the shop, dated at Newcastle—R.

1328. Henry de Delntham, to Thomas, called Gray, of Corbrygg. Lease for five years, from Michaelmas, 1328, of all the lands and tenements in Corbrygg, which he previously held of the said Henry (no rent reserved) Gray shall do the services to the chief Lords of the fee, and keep up the house where Richard de Gateshened dwells. Delntham shall pay to Gray a mark of silver at the end of the term, and on pay- ment and not till then, may re-enter. After the term, until payment, Gray shall continue in possession as tenant from year to year.

1330. Hugh Somervile and Helota his wife, to Thomas, called Gray, of Corbrygg. Conveyance of all their land in Corbrygg on the north side of the way which leads from Stagschawe to Aynewyke, between the land of Gray on either side. At Corbrygg, Sunday before the feast of St. Cuthbert, in September 4, Edw. III.

1329. John fitz Alice de Corbrig, to Matilda, daughter of John, his son, conveyance of a toft in Corbrig, in Prenestrete, between a toft formerly Hugh fitz Asceline, and a messuage of Alan Chyori. At Corbrige, Thursday after the feast of St.

199

Barnabas. Endorsed "The tenement which Alan Cherry formerly held of John Jonson."

1322. Christina, called Feynane, of Corbrigg, to Thomas. called Prest, of Corbrigg. Release of a parcel of land in Corbrigg, which the said Thomas lately held in fee of Thomas the husband of the said Christina, and of 2s. rent issuing thereof. Witness, Sir William de Glaston, Vicar of Corbrigg, &c. Dated at Newcastle.

1324. John de Porta, of Corbrige, to Laurence de Durham, burgess of the town of Newcastle-upon-Tyne. Conveyance of a parcel of land in the town of Corbrigg, in a street called the Hydmarket. Witnesses, Sir Gilbert de Boroughdon, Sheriff of Northumberland, &c. 19 June.

1356. Emma, daughter of the late William Sawer, of Corbrigg, to John de Cotesford, perpetual Vicar of Corbrig. Conveyance of half an acre in the field of Corbrigg, viz.: in Colchester.

1334. John fitz Thomas de Wotton—To John fitz John de Corebriggs. Release of a messuage in Corbrigg in the street of the Fisher's Market, which the same John (fitz John) had by feoffment of Agnes, late wife of Hugh fitz Asseline, of Corebrigg. Dated in the Abby of Blanchland, Tuesday after the feast of the Holy Trinity.

THE RECTORIE OF CORBRIDGE: FROM THE PARLIAMENTARY SURVEYS.

All that the Rectory or Parsonage of Corbridge within the County of Northumberland, with all houses and barnes, edifices, oblacions, tithes of corn and sheaves, and all appurtenances, profits, and commodities, belonginge to the said Parsonage of Corbridge, except, and always reserved, the tithes and sheaves of Dilston, in the holdinge of Roger Gray, of Chillingham, Esq.; and also the mansion house with the tithes thereof, and the appurtenances thereunto belonginge in the houldinge of Thomas Hudspeth, and the temporall lands and tenements and theire appurtenances thereunto belonginge now in the holding of severall tenants: that is to say, the tithe of corne and sheaves of corne, and graine comeing, growing, ariseinge; and yearlye and every yeare reneweinge within the towneships, fields, and closes of the severall townes, villages, and hamlets of Corbrige. Halton, Aden, Castell, the towne

of Aden, Greate Whittington, Little Whittington, Halton,
Sheilds, Carrhouses, Clarewood, and Linnells, together with
all oblations, profitts, and commodities, with all and singular
the appurtenances to the aforesaid Rectory or Parsonage of
Corbridge (except before excepted), whatsoever belonginge.
All which aforesayde Rectory or Parsonage of Corbridge, with
all and singulare the appurtenances thereunto belonginge or
appertayneinge, are now in the possession of Cuthbert Heron,
of Chipchase, in the County of Northumberland, Esq., or
his assignes, and are worth upon improvement per annum
£200......The lessee to repair the Chauncell of the Church of
Corbridge with all necessary reparacion, and alsoe all the
houses, barnes, and edifices belonginge to the premisses att
his or their chardge and soe to leave them sufficiently
repayred at the end of the lease. There were to come of the
lease the third of June, 1649, twelve years.

The Dilston, *alias* Devilston Parte of the Rectory of Corbridge were at this time in the possession of Ursula Radcliffe,
daughter of Sir Edward Radcliffe, "and are worth per annum
£27."

THE VICARAGE OF CORBRIDGE: FROM A SURVEY OF THE MANOR
OF CORBRIDGE, &c., MADE IN THE MONTH OF JULY, 1650.

All that Vicarridge howse, a fowlde, garth, two little
ruinous out-houses, a garden, a dovecote, and a grasse garthe,
abutting uppon Prince Streete on the east, and Thomas Smithe
ground on the west, conteyninge one acre, worth per annum
£1 10s.

Certaine parcells of arrable ground lyinge dispersed in the
towne feilds of Corbridge, intermixt with other lands, and
conteyne, by estimacion, six acres' worth per annum 18s.

The tithe woole and lambes worth per annum £10.

The tithe hay worth per annum £5 10s.

Prescription money payde for haye and other tythes worth
per annum £6.

The tithes of piggs, geese, hens, calfes, mortuaries, oblacions, and other Church dues worth per annum £6 10s.

Summe, £30 8s.

" The present incumbent of Corbridge is Stephen Ander-
ton, a preachinge minister."

201

PRUDHOE CASTLE.

" The castle at Prudhou was built or largely refashioned by Odinel de Umframvill, in the reign of Henry II." (1154—1189.) A complaining Monk of Tynemouth, quoted by Leland in his............ calls him............ and says that he compelled his neighbours, and principally the husbandmen of St. Oswin...............He ordered an irreverenced King's Satellite in Corebrigin Civitate" (Corbridge) to invade their possessions in Wilum, near the Castle, and compel them to come.........Odinell first appears on the pipe roll in 1165."

In the great roll* for the seventh of King John (1206) relating to revenues paid to the King in Northumberland (the originals of which are in the Tower of London) these interesting records are printed without being translated, the original consisting, it would appear, of a mixture of Latin, Old English, &c., &c., and is therefore difficult to make out, but we are able to decipher the names of two persons in Corbridge, but the amount paid and other particulars we cannot arrive at. The name of one is Rob. fit Rogir.........de Corbrig......... The name of the other Etipi Robto in Corbrig XX iJ Ii. The name of Tindal several times appears, of Unframvill and of several others which we think belong this neighbourhood.

Having previously omitted to notice an ancient well in the village, we now refer to it. This well is in the garden occupied by Mr. Spraggon and is called St. Andrew's Well, on account, we presume, of its nearness to St. Andrew's Church, and its antiquity. The site of this well was formerly open or common ground, and supplied for ages the inhabitants of the western part of the town ; we have heard the old people, more than fifty years ago, refer to the time when the owner of the adjoining ground attempted to enclose the well and common ground, but the inhabitants opposing him, a compromise was made by which he agreed to leave a door-way in

---

* The revenues of the Kings of England in former times were collected by the Sheriffs of the different counties and annually accounted for at the Exchequer, before an officer called the Clerk of the Pipe. The accounts themselves were kept on long skins of parchment sometimes written on both sides, and the whole number of them for one year sewed together at the head and rolled in one bundle, from which they obtained the name of the great roll, which was otherwise called the pipe roll, from the form of the roll itself, which is put together like a pipe.—Cowell..............JOHN HODGSON.

the boundary wall, whereby the people could obtain water without let or hinderance ; this door-way still exists in the garden wall boundering on the road called the Well Bank, the outlet of the water being through the wall on the side next the river ; by and bye this door was closed, and for a time the people were compelled to go round the corner of the garden wall to obtain water, but this being inconvenient, they persisted in having their rights, when the owner of the garden arranged to allow the water to flow through the wall boundering on the Well Bank Road, a little below the door-way referred to ; at present it is enclosed by a high wall approached by a flight of steps. The water, in addition to its constant coolness, is said to contain remarkable properties.

Without commenting on these interesting extracts, we simply call the attention of our readers to the fact that they clearly show the importance of the town in the thirteenth and fourteenth centuries.

NOTE.—Since writing the *History of Dilston* we have been informed that after the Government obtained possession of the Earl's vast estates, that there was a sale at Dilston of the household furniture, &c., but it is quite certain that a considerable quantity of the household effects were dispersed in the way we have referred to on page 166.

www.ingramcontent.com/pod-product-compliance
Lightning Source LLC
Chambersburg PA
CBHW021342110726
47900CB00005B/1572